VANISHING
IN THE HAIGHT

Also By Max Tomlinson

The Colleen Hayes Series
Tie Die

The Sendero Series
Sendero
Who Sings to the Dead

The Agency Series
The Cain File
The Darknet File

Standalone
Lethal Dispatch

VANISHING IN THE HAIGHT

A COLLEEN HAYES MYSTERY

MAX TOMLINSON

OCEANVIEW PUBLISHING
SARASOTA, FLORIDA

ISBN 978-1-60809-394-6

Cover Design by Christian Fuenfhausen

Published in the United States of America by Oceanview Publishing

Sarasota, Florida

www.oceanviewpub.com

10 9 8 7 6 5 4 3 2

PRINTED IN THE UNITED STATES OF AMERICA

To my wife, Kate, who has read more than her share of rough drafts.

VANISHING
IN THE HAIGHT

PROLOGUE

SAN FRANCISCO, 1967—THE SUMMER OF LOVE
HAIGHT-ASHBURY.

The street signs on the corner slipped into late-night fog, blurring as the young woman swiped long dark hair out of her face and blinked to focus. She looked around, more than a little disoriented. She couldn't remember leaving the apartment. The tiny pink barrel-shaped pill she'd ingested a few hours ago had reached a new peak. Dropping acid was beginning to feel like one of the biggest mistakes she had ever made. Her scalp prickled with apprehension.

What was she doing out here?

Making a phone call. That was it. Make peace with her parents. Talk to her little sister. Alex needed her. She couldn't let her make the mistakes she had made.

It was time to go home.

The dime grew slippery in her hand.

Haight Street was empty, veiled in mist that wanted to be rain. She was underdressed, wearing only a short Afghan coat, a thin tie-dye top, miniskirt, and white go-go boots. San Francisco summers could be so cold.

The street signs curled at the edges. Her head began to spin. Her insides bubbled as she fought nausea from the clouds of smoke that had been hanging in the room where she shared a mattress with whoever crashed there that night. The stinging reek of unwashed bodies. Sour milk. Music too loud—turning to noise.

All she wanted now was to go back. Where it felt safer.

But first, she'd make that phone call. There was a pay phone at the end of Haight, where Golden Gate Park loomed in the shadows.

She pressed on. The sidewalk seemed to move underneath her, rocking from side to side.

Then two shimmering lights blinded her. She froze as fuzzy headlights approached. Were they making sounds? So many noises whooshed in and out of her ears. Distant guitars. She found herself falling forward. She caught her footing, regained her balance.

The car crawled toward her. A streetlight blazed off its green hood. It had started to rain. Dazzling beads of moisture on the hood grew larger, blending with the guitars, and she could taste the notes, like drops of water, cool and metallic, even as they blinded her.

When would this acid wear off?

Phone call. She would make her call, get back to the crash pad.

The sleek car floated over to the curb, taillights leaving a choppy streak in the air. The interior glowed, a single occupant lit by dashboard lights. The doors throbbed with drumbeats. An electric window whirred down. The music gushed out. Pounding drums. Pulsating keyboards.

She bent down, the sounds drawing her in.

A young man in a dark zip-up sweatshirt was hunched over the steering wheel. He wore a black watch cap pulled down tight on his head. She saw black-framed glasses on a thin face hollowed by angular cheekbones. His hands clutched the wheel. She saw a dirty nail. She wasn't sure what to make of him.

"You okay?" he mumbled, staring through thick lenses. His big pupils reminded her of a fish. "You're all over the place."

He was just checking up on her. Seeing that she was all right.

"Jefferson Airplane," she said, hanging on the music.

"Oh, right," he said. "Eight-track."

"Eight *what*?"

"*Eight-track* tape player." He stroked the car's dash as if it were skin. "Top of the line, this baby."

His car *was* like a spaceship.

"Is it . . . a Mustang?" she said, her voice echoing in her head.

"Falcon," he said. "Ford Falcon."

"Far out Falcon," she said.

"Yeah." He pushed his glasses up and toothed a grin. "Get in." He patted the passenger seat. "Check. It. Out."

She thought about it. It *was* raining.

But there had been stories.

"No," she said, then added: "No *thanks*."

"Oh, come *on*," he said. "You've seen me around."

"I have?"

"Your name is Margaret."

"Hey! How did you know that?"

He laughed, holding the wheel. "You're so ripped. Get in, Margaret. It's freezing. It's wet. It's not safe."

"What's your name?"

"Gary," he said.

"Gary." She didn't think she knew any Garys.

"You're out of your head. I could see that a mile away. I'll drive you home."

"Phone call," she said.

He blinked through his glasses. "*What* phone call?"

"I need to make a phone call."

"Okay, got it." He nodded to the beat. "There's a pay phone, end of Haight. By the park."

"I know." She did know that. She was glad to know something.

"I'll run you down there," he said. "Then take you home."

The song ended, the woman's brooding voice fading with a crescendo of guitars. Like the rush of waves on distant shores.

"Come on . . ." His voice became nasal.

Then the music kicked in again, a new track. A bass guitar, echoing and lonely, sounding Middle Eastern. Military drums. Electric guitar, ribbons of steel spinning up into the sky. The woman singing in a haunted voice. About dropping acid. Just like Margaret had done.

"I love that song," she heard herself say.

"Who doesn't?" he said. "Get in. I just got this car. Doesn't even have plates yet. You can be the first."

"The first *what*?"

He stared at her, his eyes hard and seemingly vacant at the same time. "My first passenger. I'll drive you down to the phone booth, you make your call, then I take you home."

She thought about that, and the song she liked, about the very same trip she was on.

"You're getting wet," he said.

"Why not?" she said, opening the door, the music spilling out in clouds. She climbed into the cockpit.

He reached over her, pushed the lock down on her door. The sharp stink of sweat from under his armpit shook her senses awake. She sat back, trembling. She turned, saw his eyes slitted.

"You have no idea who I am—do you?" he said. "Who I *really* am?"

Her heart thumped with anxiety.

She reached for the door handle. "I think I'll walk . . ."

"No, you won't," he said calmly. He snatched her wrist with his left hand, held it like a vise. "He never even told you about me, did he?" He bent her arm back. It hurt.

"He *who*?" she gasped. She tried to raise her right arm, but he twisted her wrist further, pushing her down into her seat.

She noticed something in his other hand. A handkerchief.

He grinned, the tip of his tongue showing, sending shivers down her back.

He held up the cloth. It smelled of some sweet chemical.

"My father," he said.

CHAPTER 1

It started to rain for the second time that day as Colleen Hayes parked the Torino in front of the derelict paint plant in Hunter's Point. She secured the steering wheel with a Club, got out, locked the car as well. In the distance the silhouette of Candlestick Park cut the wet night sky, its outline broken by a cyclone fence topped with razor wire that surrounded three sides of H&M Paint. Industrial waterfront protected the remaining border. On her patrols Colleen scanned the dirty water lapping the rubble and trash along the shore and looked for evidence of trespassing. Guarding this old plant was the only work she could come by, and she was glad to have it. Moreover, she could sleep on a cot upstairs in a windowless storage room behind the abandoned supervisor's office, heat up a can of soup on a hot plate, and save on an apartment, which she could not afford. They wanted two hundred dollars a month for a shoebox in this city, where everybody and his brother seemed to be headed, crowding the discos and bathhouses.

She selected another key, this one from the plant ring, and let herself in through a gate, where she crossed the weed-infested asphalt yard in front of the plant, full of pallets of undelivered paint in corroding cans, a dead forklift rusting out in the open, heaps of junk that could not be salvaged. Anything of value had been torn out long ago and sold to fend off creditors.

She took the external stairwell up to the office, her boots clipping the metal stairs.

Inside, on the top floor, a breathy view of the rain-soaked Bay Bridge and Oakland twinkled as Colleen pulled off her leather jacket and threw it over the back of the old roller chair behind a green metal desk. This was technically her office now, as no one else had used it since the plant closed. The single desk lamp pointed down at a dusty desk blotter with a four-year-old calendar. Moonlight filtered in through tall industrial windows, casting a pall of shadows across posters of paint products no longer for sale. Forgotten ledgers were stacked high on a sideboard.

After a decade in prison, pressed in with so many others, living in this empty dark factory was practically what the doctor ordered. Rats? So what? Cold? That's why they invented blankets. Dangerous? Try Denver Women's Correctional Facility on a bad night, with a full coven in heat. H&M Paint was close to heaven by comparison.

In the back room she brushed a strand of damp chestnut hair out of her face and was just about to make tea when the office buzzer rang like an electric saw, loud enough to be heard anywhere in the voluminous plant. Someone at the front gate.

Probably more punks, playing games.

Back out in the office, Colleen hit the intercom button on the wall. "Security," she said.

There was a pause. Out on the bay, the silhouette of a container ship crept under the bridge.

"*Ms.* Hayes?" a thin voice said in apparent confusion. The voice of a young man. But he sounded official.

"Who is this?" She didn't need trouble. She had three years' worth of parole left.

"Christian Newell—representing Mr. Edward Copeland. I was hoping to have a word with you. I *am* sorry about the late hour, but I've been trying to locate you and only just managed to accomplish that."

She didn't think people actually talked the way Christian Newell did.

"Are you a lawyer?"

"I am."

"Are you here to serve me papers?"

"No."

"Because if you say you're not, and then you are, it won't fly in court."

"Nothing like that at all, Ms. Hayes. I want to discuss a business opportunity—contracting your firm."

Her firm. Of one. It sounded like work. And that's what she needed more of.

"Come on up," she said, pressing the buzzer to release the front gate. "The outdoor stairwell, to your right. Watch your step—it's slippery in the rain. I'll turn the outside light on." She picked up the length of pipe she kept by the desk just in case.

Moments later, quick footsteps trotted up the metal stairs. A small fuzzy figure appeared in the reinforced glass window of the office door, the shadow of an umbrella over his head. She could see the outline of a bow tie. He wasn't a threat. She was bigger than he was. She set her length of pipe down against the doorframe and let him in.

Christian Newell shook out his umbrella, wiped his feet, even though the office was well past deserving that kind of attention. He entered the large room carrying a flat leather satchel with buckles on it.

"*You're* the night watchman?" he asked.

She took his coat and umbrella. *"Person*, I guess you'd say—now that it's no longer 1955. Hayes Confidential provides plant security."

He gave Colleen a polite but scrutinizing look she'd seen often enough. He saw a woman of medium height, not unattractive, but harder than most, her muscles built up by prison and time in the weight room. No fat. A face that didn't smile often. "I guess I didn't expect to find you . . . working as a guard yourself."

"I'm a little short-handed right now," she said, hanging up his coat and umbrella. "Filling in." She was the only person on a payroll—a payroll still waiting on its first payment.

"I see," he said.

They sat down either side of her desk.

Christian Newell had short dark hair combed over in a restrained business cut that made him look fifteen although he was probably in his late twenties. His skin was soft and pale. His eyes were deep and cautious, with long lashes. If he'd ever been anywhere near a woman other than his mother, Colleen would have been surprised. He removed a business card from a little gold case and placed it squarely down in front of her in the dust on the desk blotter.

Colleen read the card upside down without picking it up. She sat back in her creaky chair. A blast of rain scattered against one of the tall windows. She did the button of her denim shirt up against the chill. "I'm still new to San Francisco so forgive me if I don't know much about Edward Copeland."

"How much *do* you know about him, Ms. Hayes?"

"I've got a sneaking suspicion he's not destitute."

"Mr. Copeland is a former industrialist," he said, looking around the office. "Quite successful in his day. Perhaps he could have saved this place. But he's retired now."

"So why does he need me? I handle plant security."

"A private matter," Christian Newell said. "A family matter."

Colleen squinted. "So again—why *me*?"

Christian steepled his fingers. "Before we proceed, I'll need you to sign a non-disclosure. Regardless of whether you take the assignment or not." Christian picked up his satchel, opened it, extracted two sheets of paper, both heavyweight bond, and laid them out. They were duplicates, obviously one for her, one for him. Christian Newell's name was already signed and dated in fountain pen on both copies.

Colleen picked up a copy, read it over. She wasn't supposed to talk about anything they discussed. She set it back down.

"If I take this assignment, I'm going to have to talk to somebody about it at some point."

"The agreement is really just a formality."

"How many formalities have turned into legal nightmares?"

Christian divulged what might have been a smile. "It must be a hindrance to have a prison record and be trying to start a security consulting business."

He knew about her record, too.

"It does help keep me in a lower tax bracket," she said.

"Mr. Copeland still has numerous business connections. He can be quite helpful when he chooses to be. He could make a call and possibly hasten your license application."

She eyed Christian. "How much *do* you know about me?"

Christian Newell cleared his throat. "July 1967, you killed your husband, whom you suspected of molesting your daughter. Your daughter, Pamela, was eight years old at the time."

Something she thought about several times a day. "It was a little more than a suspicion."

"The court was not lenient, regardless. You served nine out of fourteen years for manslaughter. You were released from Denver

Women's Correctional Facility last year, came to California looking for Pamela, who had turned eighteen, and had taken up with a motorcycle gang. Things did not go well."

"Well, you seem to know plenty about me," she said. "And yet, my past isn't stopping you from wanting to hire me. So imagine my next question."

"Mr. Copeland thinks your past could actually be an asset in this case."

If her past was an asset, the work wasn't benign. But she needed money. She had enough to live on for the rest of her life if she died Friday. Early Friday.

"It wouldn't be worth suing me anyway." Colleen selected a ballpoint pen from a San Francisco Giants cup. She attempted a loop on the blotter, found the pen dry, picked another. She signed both copies of the non-disclosure and pushed one toward him. Christian Newell picked up the document, examined it, slipped it into his satchel, set the briefcase down by his side.

Colleen raised her eyebrows.

Christian Newell said, "Mr. Copeland has two daughters. One of them is still alive."

"I gather this visit is about the one who isn't."

Christian Newell pulled something from his breast pocket. It was a black-and-white high school yearbook photograph of a pretty young woman with pale white skin and long dark hair. Dramatic bangs cut across her forehead to reveal mischievous arched brows and lively dark eyes. She wore a low-cut gown and a diamond pendant necklace. An impish smile was ready to break out any minute.

"Margaret Copeland was brutally murdered eleven years ago," Christian Newell said, "in San Francisco."

"During the Summer of Love." Colleen took the photo, held it by the edges. This young woman was gone. She thought of her own daughter, ensconced in some commune in Northern California now, unwilling to talk to her own mother. Certainly not dead, but Colleen often worried what might become of her.

"She looks so young," she said wistfully.

"Just turned eighteen when she was found in Golden Gate Park. Beaten. Raped. Drugged. A dry-cleaning bag over her head. The only other thing she was wearing were a pair of white go-go boots. The coyotes had already started on her by the time a man walking his dog found her."

"It's quite an image." Colleen set the photograph down. "I'm sorry."

"Margaret was the problem child of the family. In 1967, she took off from home and got mixed up with the wrong crowd."

"She wasn't the only one." Again, Colleen thought of her daughter, Pamela. And she thought of Pamela's friend, Eva—she never learned the girl's real name—who Colleen found murdered by the bikers Pamela hung out with.

So many casualties. Some still breathing.

"Indeed," Christian Newell said. "The newspapers loved it. 'Wild child daughter of wealthy industrialist meets a drug-addled death in the Haight.' At the time, the Zodiac Killer was on the loose. Eventually, the San Francisco Police Department assumed Margaret was another of his victims."

"Assumed."

"No connection to the Zodiac was ever made. Margaret's case was never solved."

"Even with Mr. Copeland's money and influence."

Christian Newell nodded. "Even then."

"And what makes you think that a night watchperson, only recently settled in San Francisco, with no PI license, can solve an eleven-year-old cold case?"

"Lieutenant Daniel Moran."

That took her by surprise. Lieutenant Dan Moran, Santa Cruz Homicide. They'd had a rocky relationship last year when Colleen had come to California from Colorado, fresh out of prison. She'd helped Moran solve the murder of Pamela's friend Eva—inadvertently. She had broken some rules. She was lucky not to be back in prison. "How does Lieutenant Moran know Mr. Copeland?"

"Mr. Copeland makes it a point to know people who are good at what they do. Lieutenant Moran was approached but cannot take the case. He is . . . ah . . . retired."

Probably back on the bottle, Colleen thought.

"But Lieutenant Moran speaks very highly of you, Ms. Hayes. Since you helped solve a missing girl case in Santa Cruz—a case not unlike Margaret's."

"Did he mention that the girl in question still doesn't have a name? Except that the bikers who killed her called her Eva? She's lucky she didn't have a county burial and her ashes tossed out to sea."

"Because you put up the funds for a headstone. Found a church on the outskirts of town to take her remains."

Colleen gulped back salty bile. She had visited Eva's grave only yesterday. Placed white carnations in the green metal cemetery vase and spiked it into the damp ground below the headstone. She had separated the flowers out, straightened the arrangement. Then she had stood up, pulling her hair out of her face as a cold Pacific wind gusted through the churchyard, bringing ocean fog across the grave. Sorrow, mixed with regret, flowed through her.

"Don't pin any medals on me," she said. "Eva was murdered because I didn't get to her in time."

"You found her killer. Not everybody could have done what you did."

Colleen took a deep breath, let it out. "There isn't anyone in SFPD to take up the case? Mr. Copeland could make that happen, I suspect. Didn't you say he has friends everywhere?"

Christian Newell shook his head. "As far as Mr. Copeland is concerned, SFPD Homicide dragged their feet on Margaret. He wants a fresh perspective."

That gave her pause. But big-city police departments were frequently slow to respond. "Fresh perspective solving an eleven-year-old case. It could be tough."

Christian Newell leaned forward. "Between you and me, Ms. Hayes, Mr. Copeland simply wants someone to go through the case one final time, make sure there are no dangling items, so he can put it behind him. And he is prepared to pay you handsomely for your effort. There will also be a substantial bonus if the killer is actually found."

Colleen hadn't thought the word *substantial* would ever apply to her bank account again.

"Define 'substantial.'"

"Five thousand dollars is the amount Mr. Copeland threw out to reinvestigate the case. Another five if the killer is found. But I can tell you he'd be open to a discussion on another number—within reason, of course."

Five thousand just to start. Half a year's salary. She had about one percent of that right now, sitting in a Wells Fargo account. It had to last her until her first modest payment from H&M came in. She had never seen five thousand dollars in one place.

"Does Mr. Copeland really want to open old wounds? Because the best that's going to come out of this is that I solve an eleven-year-old murder. His daughter made a lousy mistake and paid too high a price for it. There were a lot of girls like that." Eva. Pamela. Margaret Copeland.

"Mr. Copeland is dying," Christian Newell said. "Lung cancer. He wants this matter put to rest so he can do the same."

Now it made more sense. "You say there's another daughter?"

"Alexandra. Alex."

"Tell me about Alex."

"You can meet her yourself—along with Mr. Copeland. Tomorrow night for dinner. At his house in Half Moon Bay." Christian raised his eyebrows. "Mr. Copeland has a private chef."

"I'm sure no one ever leaves one of his little soirées without gushing with praise. But I'm going to have to think about it. I don't want to fail a man who only has one shot left to find his daughter's murderer."

Christian Newell gathered his satchel up one more time and opened it. He extracted a white envelope thick with the dark outline of cash. "Mr. Copeland understands that you may have certain financial restrictions at the moment. He would like to advance you a retainer." He set the envelope on the dusty blotter, next to his business card.

The thickness of that envelope gave her wild ideas. Groceries, to begin with. Then, who knew? Maybe a second shot at changing Pamela's mind.

But she just didn't know, after last year, dealing with bikers, and a murdered girl, if she could handle it.

"I need to sleep on it," she said, handing Christian Newell the envelope. She wondered if she would ever see that much money again.

"Understood," Christian Newell said, standing up, pocketing the envelope. "But please call me tomorrow. And if there's anything I can do to change your mind, don't hesitate to ask."

She took a deep breath. She needed the work, but she didn't need trouble. If the police were involved, that could be a problem. She had to get through parole.

"I'll let you know tomorrow," she said.

CHAPTER TWO

The rain fell steadily the next morning as Colleen patrolled the derelict plant. Pebbles of water pelted the corrugated iron roof high overhead. H&M Paint was a drafty shell half the size of a football field, constructed of asbestos sheets and rotting wood milled when lumber was cheap and plentiful. The warehouse was dark, cluttered with rubble and leftover pallets of unsold paint, unsalvageable machinery, and junk. Puddles of water shone here and there on the concrete floor. The smell of mold hung in the air.

She hadn't eaten yet, hadn't showered, hadn't made coffee. She made it a point to do the morning rounds first thing. There wasn't much to eat anyway. She needed to get paid. She kept seeing that envelope full of cash Christian Newell had proffered last night.

Colleen directed her flashlight beam into the darkest corner of the plant as she walked past the former changing rooms, where the showers still worked—thankfully—and highlighted several 55-gallon drums of acetone that gave her uneasy nights. She'd remind the owners—again—to have them removed, along with the tinder-dry pallets stacked up against the wall nearby. Before some stray spark turned this old building into an inferno. But she knew how seriously they'd take her request. She was there for insurance reasons, to keep the premiums lower by having a guard on the premises.

She checked the remaining fire extinguishers located throughout the warehouse. There were six left. Their tags were still current.

Outside she pulled the hood of her Army Surplus rain poncho over her head. She continued her patrol at the dead delivery truck that sat on flat tires down by the water.

In the corner of the lot near the big Ford F600, the H&M Paint man on the side panel, with his friendly smile and jaunty wave, Colleen found a paper bag around the back that contained a couple of empty steel beer cans, and the wrapper to a corner store burrito—Chile Verde—along with some crumpled napkins. Recent.

Colleen stepped up on the wet running board of the truck, yanked open the creaky door to the cab. On the driver's seat she found a newspaper, folded in half.

La Prensa Gráfica. El Salvador. Dated last week.

She climbed in, nosed around, pulled the seat forward.

An old blue gym bag, spattered with paint. She unzipped it. Clothes, well worn, but clean. She went through the bag, looking for a weapon, anything illegal. She found a faded pair of jeans. Underwear. Socks. A letter fell out of a folded-up T-shirt, sans envelope, with a photo of a serious-looking young Indian woman with gleaming black hair, staring into the camera like a mug shot. Colleen tucked the photo and letter back, feeling voyeuristic, and couldn't help noticing a line written in a woman's hand, in Spanish, a language Colleen spoke well enough to understand.

The children and I miss you so much . . .

The gate buzzer went off like a claxon, echoing through the empty plant, shaking Colleen's thoughts loose. She put everything back, zipped up the bag, set it back behind the seat, hopped down, slammed the truck door shut, and jogged around to the front of the building with her poncho flapping.

A big man in a raincoat stood at the gate, obscured by the criss-cross of cyclone fence. He held an umbrella over his head. A white Ford sedan stood by the curb.

Colleen swore as a heartbeat twisted in her chest. Randy Ferguson. Her parole officer.

She got to the gate. Forced a smile.

Randy Ferguson looked like an ex-football player who'd gone soft twenty years ago. He had short gray hair combed straight back, light blue bloodshot eyes, and a nose that was starting to mottle with drinking. He was chewing gum, probably to mask his liquid breakfast.

"I haven't missed an appointment, have I?" Colleen said. "I've got you on my calendar for next Monday. Bryant Street."

He gave Colleen a smirk. "Home verification." He raised his eyebrows as he indicated the disused plant behind her. "This *is* the address you listed as your residence, right?"

Home verification. She was hoping to have an apartment soon. "Just for the short term. I'm waiting on a check. As soon as it arrives, I'll find an apartment."

"Just open the gate."

Colleen did. She took Randy up the outdoor stairwell, let him into the office, peeled off her wet poncho, shook it off, hung it up.

"This looks like an office," Randy said, dripping water in front of the desk. "An abandoned one at that."

"I'm back here." Colleen opened the door to the back room and flicked on the overhead fluorescent light. She stood by, more than a little anxious. Living here was a stretch per the Interstate Compact for parolees any way you looked at it.

Randy entered the room, stood with his hands in the pockets of his raincoat, and eyed the hot plate and Mr. Coffee plugged into an extension cord that snaked across the floor. Then he looked at the blue-and-white dish towel laid flat on the metal shelf over the huge sink, with a pot, single plate, and two cups and some mismatched silverware that had been left to dry. An ice chest on the floor doubled as her refrigerator.

At least she had folded the gray blanket neatly on her cot.

Randy gave her an ugly smile. "And what, exactly, makes you think this qualifies as adequate living quarters, Colleen?"

"I started my own security business. H&M is one of my clients. They like me staying here—added security. Call it killing two birds with one stone—until I get paid and find a place of my own."

"Doesn't matter."

"I've got everything I need: utilities, shower." She nodded at the hot plate. "Want some coffee?"

He shook his head *no*. "You have alcohol on the premises?"

No, she thought. *Why—did you need a quick belt?* "That would be a violation of my parole."

He squinted. "You have men stay over?"

Randy always brought this up. She fidgeted with the key ring hanging on her belt. "No."

He gave her a sideways look. "Women?"

Not this again. "No one."

"Didn't you have some kind of relationship with a woman in Santa Cruz? The one that filed a complaint against those bikers?"

Laura. "What does that have to do with my parole?"

"Let me see your arms."

She gave a sigh as she stood back and pulled up the sleeves of her Denver Broncos sweatshirt, no bra since she'd just gotten up, and the cold air, along with her heightened nerves, made her nipples poke through.

That caught Randy's eye.

"You should wear a bra."

She cleared her throat, stood back, crossed her arms over her chest. "Why don't we go back out into my office?" She wanted to get out of this room. The cot nearby. It didn't take a genius to see what was on Randy's mind.

He leveled a half-lidded gaze at her. "Right here is fine. Let me see your arms."

She let out an angry breath, held her arms out so he could see the crooks of them.

He examined her arms, holding them a little too hard. His fingers were rough and cold. "You're telling me a junkie can't find creative places to shoot up? I've seen track marks between toes." He let go of her arms. His smile turned oily as he nodded at her sweatshirt. "I have to make sure you're clean." His voice thickened. "Just down to your panties will do."

"No." She pushed her sleeves back down to her wrists, stumbled back until her calves hit the cot. "I don't think so."

"I need to do my job."

"I don't care what your *needs* are."

He slipped his hands in his pants pockets so that his raincoat spread open, revealing his groin. He was clearly aroused. Colleen flinched. "Look at you." He grinned. "Ten years inside, I bet you learned a thing or two. All those women? Not many men, though, huh? Just the guards. What say we mix it up and you do us both a favor?"

A rush of anxiety mixed with anger shot up her neck, making her cheeks flush. "Get out of here."

"Don't give me that. You're practically begging for it."

"You'll be begging to keep your job after I report you."

"Come on," he said, moving in. "What are we arguing about? You look after me. I look after you. You get to stay here. This is a win-win situation." He reached for her hair.

She smacked his hand out of the way with her left, taking him by surprise as she unhooked the keys from her belt loop and slipped one between her index and middle fingers. She raised her fist, the impromptu stiletto ready.

Their eyes locked.

"You've read my sheet," she said. "You know I'm good for it."

"You crazy bitch!" he gasped.

"That's what my ex said—right before I nailed him with the screwdriver."

Randy gulped.

"Okay," he whispered. "*Okay.*"

Randy fastened his raincoat, cinched it up. "I guess you can figure out how your home verification report went."

"Maybe I'll ask your wife."

"You think she's going to believe some cracked ex-con who stabbed her ex?" He laughed. "You can forget staying in SF, Colleen. Or California. You can forget ever connecting with your daughter. Your parole has been violated."

Colleen stood there, eyes blazing, fist still raised.

Randy glared back for a moment, then his face relaxed. "Too bad. You would have been done by now. I bet you would have even liked it."

He turned and left.

She dropped her fist. The keys rattled in her hand.

Randy strolled on through the office, whistling, and left the door wide open, rain blowing in as he stomped down the metal stairs. She prayed he would slip and break his damn neck but knew she wouldn't get that lucky.

She went out to the office, slammed the door shut.

And stood there for a moment, listening to the rain patter against the tall windows. She'd be transferred back to Denver. More time added to her parole. No chance of reconnecting with Pamela.

She needed a lawyer.

She sat down behind her desk and picked up Christian Newell's business card, tapped it for a moment, thinking.

She called his office and was put through.

"Mr. Copeland's offer," she said. "Does it come with legal assistance?"

"How so?"

She recounted Randy's visit and how she was in violation of parole for unacceptable living arrangements—leaving out the touchy-feely part, which she didn't want to discuss.

"Leave it with me," he said when she was through. "Stay out of Randy's way for the time being. With any luck you'll be assigned a new parole officer soon."

This having-friends-with-clout thing was okay.

"Thanks," she said. "I mean it."

"Mr. Copeland and his daughter Alexandra are looking forward to having you join them for dinner tonight."

If she'd any doubts about working for Mr. Copeland, they had evaporated.

"Does Mr. Copeland dine fashionably late?"

CHAPTER THREE

He watched the teenagers spill out onto Arguello Boulevard, leaving the three-story art deco building with its crisscrossed brick patterns shimmering on the edges of his vision.

He stood at a safe distance, across the street.

He watched the ninth-graders laughing, talking, smiling. As if the world was a sweet, wonderful place, full of fun and friends. They would learn.

And then he saw her.

Robyn. He knew her name. Blond hair feather-cut. Bare legs. Black platform shoes. Black pleated skirt, above the knee. White blouse under a dark blue sweater. White, white skin. Blue eyes. He could imagine.

Yes, he could imagine.

Even though his attraction to her wasn't something he initially wanted. It complicated things.

She was like that other one, years ago. *Margaret.* In Golden Gate Park that night. He tensed up at the memory.

Robyn would be easier.

In his dark warehouseman's jacket, with its leather shoulders, he wore his black watch cap pulled down tight on his head. His kinky black hair stuck out like wire, complemented by a bushy Fu Manchu mustache and sideburns. The snug cap kept his glasses firmly in place. He wouldn't lose his glasses again. He pulled both hands from the pockets of his jacket, touched the heavy black frames tucked under the cap, made sure they were secure. They were. It was something he did many times a day. Ever since that night, so long ago now, when his glasses had been knocked off and broken during the struggle with that woman. *Margaret.*

The price he had paid. A decade in Valley Oaks, talking, talking, talking with the doctors, finally convincing them he was cured. His father thought he could lock him away, silence him. But he couldn't. Not forever. His father would pay once again. For what he did to his mother.

His dear mother.

He watched them. He watched the ninth-graders leaving. He watched her. *Her.* A mixture of emotions swirled through him. She was someone he had to deal with. But he couldn't deny how she made him feel.

"See you, Robyn!" her friend shouted. The black girl. He didn't approve of that. There were plenty of white girls she could be friends with.

Robyn placed her fists on her hips and made a little dance motion and a funny face.

"Not if I see you first!"

Robyn couldn't hurt him. Not like the one who broke his glasses.

He watched Robyn walking toward Golden Gate Park, a few blocks from here, on her way home, putting one shapely leg in front of the other, her pleated skirt swinging.

He wondered if she would stop at the carousel in the park today. She liked to sit on the bench and watch the merry-go-round.

That would be the place to deal with her.

Trembling with excitement, he checked his glasses again. *Safe.* Looking side to side, he crossed Arguello Boulevard.

He would follow her. Just for a little while.

CHAPTER FOUR

"Mr. Copeland is expecting you, Ms. Hayes," a man with a British accent announced over the intercom. The speaker was mounted on a pole in front of a high stone wall on a private road flanked by tall pines that were swaying in the evening rainstorm blowing in from the Pacific.

Colleen thanked the man and quickly rolled up the driver's window against the rain. The beams of the Torino's headlights flickered with windswept precipitation while the iron gates clanked open. She drove through the entrance, getting her first view of Copeland Mansion. Against a blackish sky churning with clouds, there were too many chimneys to count.

Up the private road she passed manicured gardens where roses flew back and forth in the storm. In a long pebbled driveway, she parked alongside a white Jaguar XJ6 that sat next to a black Lincoln Continental. The brick mansion had a white portico jutting out, with columns on either side. Tall arched windows matched the elegance of the entry. Warm light radiated from within.

She checked herself quickly in the rearview mirror. Hair and makeup in place. She wore the silver magpie earrings she had bought for her daughter when Pamela turned thirteen. Pamela didn't want them anymore, had even given them away, but Colleen rescued them. She had spent close to a year in prison earning the money to buy them. She liked to think she was holding the earrings until Pamela changed her mind.

With the wind buffeting the car, she hopped out with her handbag, moving quickly in her black pumps for the protection of the entryway where she got out her brush and mirror and put her shoulder-length hair back into place. A puff of wind immediately undid her work. She was just about to ring the doorbell when one of the two tall front doors opened.

A real live butler stood before her, a compact Asian man, perhaps in his fifties. He wore black and had a kindly face.

"Please come in, Ms. Hayes."

She followed him down a hallway of dark oil paintings to a living room one could get lost in, with a view of the tumbling ocean through windows that nearly reached the sixteen-foot ceiling.

A man in a wheelchair sat with his back to Colleen. A bald spot showed through a burst of gray swept-back hair.

"Ms. Hayes, sir," the butler said.

"Ah, Ms. Hayes," a raspy voice replied. The wheelchair turned slowly around to face her.

Edward Copeland was a shadow of the man in the picture Colleen had seen in *The Chronicle* newspaper archives at the public library downtown that afternoon. That photo showed a vibrant countenance, elegant profile, and a determined, steely gaze. In that photo his hair was thicker and there was the hint of wry humor in his eyes.

The wry humor seemed to have survived.

Although Mr. Copeland was still imposing, his frame was slack-shouldered, and his head hung on his neck as if it were a weight to bear. His face was gaunt and pale. He wore a paisley silk robe over a shirt and tie. The cost of the gleaming brown shoes on his motionless feet would probably have paid the deposit on the apartment Colleen looked at last week.

"Thank you so much for coming, Ms. Hayes," he said. "What a ghastly night. I should have sent someone to pick you up. What was I thinking?"

"I actually enjoyed the drive," she said, and it was the truth. The coast road, away from the city, lashed by wind and rain, had given her time to think.

"Get our guest something to drink, Harold," Mr. Copeland said to the butler standing in the corner of the room.

"I think I'll wait for dinner," she said.

"That will be all, then, Harold," Mr. Copeland said.

The butler disappeared.

Mr. Copeland coughed, a deep hack that he recovered from slowly. "Please." He waved a shaking hand toward a deep leather Chesterfield sofa that faced the windows.

Colleen undid the blue wool jacket of her one suit and sat down, smoothing the hem of her skirt over her knee as she crossed her legs. Mr. Copeland may have been on death's doorstep but he noticed her legs.

"I gather that Christian gave you an idea of what I'm after, Ms. Hayes?"

"He did," she said. "I just don't want your expectations to exceed my abilities."

"I can already see that's not going to happen. The fact that you didn't want to take the case in the first place tells me it's important to you not to misrepresent yourself."

She appreciated that. "What I find surprising, Mr. Copeland, is that there's so little in the newspaper archives. A couple of articles tried to link Margaret's murder to the Zodiac Killer, but not until later." The Zodiac didn't write his first letter to the *Chronicle* until well over a year after Margaret was murdered. That's when he became a household name. And that's when Colleen had heard of the

Zodiac, while in prison. Clint Eastwood became an international star in a movie based on the Zodiac—*Dirty Harry.*

Mr. Copeland took a labored breath. "SFPD claimed they knew of the Zodiac as far back as 1965."

Claimed. "The articles written at the time of Margaret's death provide no real information, regardless. There's not a lot to go on. The investigation seems to have been dropped early."

Mr. Copeland shrugged and gave a sardonic smile. "San Francisco wasn't exactly a sedate place in 1967, Ms. Hayes. There was a bit of competition for print space."

Colleen still didn't quite buy it. The murder of a pretty young socialite commanded more attention. For some reason, Margaret didn't receive it. "Do you know of any friends Margaret might have had at the time? Boyfriends?"

Mr. Copeland gave a remorseful shake of his head. "We had lost almost all communication with Margaret by then. We know almost nothing, except that she was sleeping at some hippie pad in the Haight the night she was—ah—murdered."

Mr. Copeland said "hippie pad" as if it might be a location on Mars. "One concern I have is that some unpleasant information might come out—about Margaret."

"How so?"

Colleen knew there were serial killers who picked targets seemingly at random. But often the killer knew the victim, at least fleetingly. And there were times the killer knew the victim well, and there was a reason, however twisted, for the murder. "I just don't think we can rule out the fact that it wasn't some random event."

"I'm willing to accept whatever the truth is."

"Are you absolutely sure of that?"

"I'm dying, Ms. Hayes. It's time to wrap this up. Margaret's mother died the year after Margaret was murdered. Alex—her sister—has never quite forgiven me for not finding Margaret's killer and putting this family back on the right track. I failed. But the truth is: I was just a little unsettled myself by the whole business. I loved Margaret." Mr. Copeland gulped back something in his throat, then recovered. "I know you're not supposed to have favorites . . . but she was a wonderful, *wonderful* girl."

Colleen wondered what that felt like for his living daughter, Alex.

Mr. Copeland continued: "I want this taken care of before I cross the bridge. I want Margaret's killer found."

Colleen knew the precise feeling. She knew the vindication she felt when she had tracked down the killer of a young woman last year. When she looked in the face of the nasty specimen who had murdered Eva and knew his life was over, she had savored that grim satisfaction.

The only problem was, that feeling didn't last very long.

And now she knew it never did. The results of revenge could last forever, but the relief they provided was fleeting.

"How long have you got, Mr. Copeland? If you don't mind me being blunt."

"It's an excellent question. A couple of months, tops. Most likely half that much."

Then that was how much time she had. "What if—and I say *if*—I find your daughter's killer, Mr. Copeland. What then?"

Mr. Copeland's eyes looked deep into hers. "Then we bring him to justice."

She chose her words before she spoke. "Will that be enough?"

There was a pause while a blast of rain beat the windows.

"It will have to be," he said.

She would have to take him at his word. Because she knew what the alternative was—if simple justice wasn't enough. And she knew what that had done to her.

"Excuse me," a woman's voice said from the hallway.

Colleen turned to the entrance of the grand living room. Standing there was a woman in her mid-twenties who might have come straight from a modeling shoot. She was both shapely and statuesque, accentuated by the fact that she wore a slim beige tweed pantsuit, complete with vest, that showed off her figure and gave her a country look at the same time. Along with the suit, she wore a white shirt with French cuffs and a long collar that held a billowing dark gray tie with white polka dots. The gray in the tie was brought out by a pair of gray high heels. She had high cheekbones, languid eyes, and wavy blond hair combed over to the side, just below the ear, and curled above one thin, arched eyebrow. Her lipstick was light red. Colleen could even see a trace of it on the white filter tip of the cigarette she held up in two fingers. The elbow of her cigarette hand rested in the long fingers of the other. She looked like she was posing for a picture.

Colleen had no idea how long she had been standing there. She hoped she hadn't heard her father waxing on about how Margaret had been his precious one.

But she probably already knew.

"Father," the woman said, taking a sip on her cigarette. "Dinner's ready."

Colleen was more than a little surprised that she would smoke around her father, a man with lung cancer.

She turned to Colleen and blinked slowly as she seemed to study her.

"And you must be Colleen Hayes," she said, taking another soft puff, letting smoke curl up to the high ceiling.

CHAPTER FIVE

Colleen had just started on the roast beef when Edward Copeland broke into a fit of desperate coughing. In the mahogany-paneled dining room with opaque globe lights on the walls, he clutched at his throat, gasping. His eyes bulged.

Colleen shot up out of her chair, her silverware clanking on bone china, and rushed over to help. Harold, the butler, who had been standing quietly in the corner, quickly left the room.

"Father just needs his oxygen," Alexandra Copeland said to Colleen, taking a sip of red wine before setting the glass down on a white lace tablecloth. "Harold's gone to get it." She stood up, strode over to her father, put a hand on his shoulder.

"Deep breaths, Father. You've got this under control."

"I'm trying, damn it." He seemed to be sucking in nothing. His face was the color of alabaster.

"Soldier up, now." She patted his shoulder. "Harold's on his way."

Footsteps came pounding down the hallway, approaching the dining room. Harold appeared, holding a small green oxygen tank about two feet long with a length of plastic tube that ended in a facemask. He dashed over behind the table. Colleen and Alexandra moved aside. He set the tank down as Mr. Copeland eyed him, wheezing.

Alexandra took the plastic facemask from Harold in a business-like manner. "Head up nice and straight, Father." She fastened the mask over her father's face as Harold twisted the valve. The hiss of oxygen stiffened the tube. The red needle on the canister shot up.

Edward Copeland closed his eyes, leaned back in his wheelchair, and breathed deeply. His hands, which had been trembling on his thighs, relaxed. Color returned to his face. Harold fastened the tank into a bracket on the back of the wheelchair, came up with a nosepiece fixture, handed it to Alex. Mr. Copeland took a deep breath while Alex removed his facemask and replaced it with the nosepiece, which she slipped over his head and fastened into place, gently inserting the two cannulas into his nostrils.

"Is everything all right?" Colleen asked, feeling helpless standing by.

"It is now," Alexandra said, returning to her seat, sitting down. Pulling her chair in, she took a sip of wine.

Harold returned to the corner of the room, folded his hands behind his back, and looked straight ahead, as if nothing had happened.

"I'm extremely sorry about this, Ms. Hayes," Edward Copeland said in a rasping voice.

"Absolutely nothing to be sorry about," Colleen said, returning to her seat. "I can't help but feel my visit had something to do with it. Dredging up the past."

"It's the past we need to come to terms with," he said. "So I can leave all this behind in peace." He glanced over at Alex, picking at her food.

"Perhaps you should keep that oxygen tank on the back of your wheelchair at all times," Colleen said.

"He normally does," Alexandra said, looking up at Colleen. "He wanted to impress you." She raised her eyebrows.

Mr. Copeland gave a quick accusing glance at Alex before he spoke to Colleen. "I didn't want to play on your sympathies, Ms. Hayes."

"You're just a fool for a pretty face, Father." Alex took another measured sip of wine, set her glass down, picked up a fork. She looked at Colleen, giving her a sly wink before she cast her eyes back down and returned to teasing her food.

That look sent a small, illicit thrill through Colleen.

The hiss of oxygen pulled her back to the present.

"I'm sorry, Ms. Hayes," Mr. Copeland said, adjusting the nasal cannula of his oxygen feed. "But it means you might have to work a little faster than we thought."

"I'm prepared to do whatever it takes," Colleen said.

"Glad to hear that," Mr. Copeland said. "Let's drink to it. Harold, bring the brandy and snifters."

"See?" Alex gave Colleen a droll smile. "He's still trying to impress you. Boys will be boys."

And girls will be girls, Colleen thought.

CHAPTER SIX

The rain let up as Colleen took the Third Street exit off 101 into San Francisco and headed back to H&M Paint. The black outline of Candlestick Park jutted up, backlit by misty lights across the bay.

She parked the Torino out front, secured it with the club, grabbed her collapsible umbrella and keys, stood for a moment, looking around. No one. She let herself in through the gate and tread carefully across the debris-strewn asphalt, protecting her only pair of pumps. At the foot of the stairwell she removed the high heels and carried them in one hand as she stepped up the cold wet metal stairs. The icy wetness on the bottoms of her bare feet made her move faster.

In her "bedroom" she changed into jeans and sweatshirt and hung her suit on a wooden hanger, hooking it on an overhead pipe that snaked across the office. She turned on the space heater and directed it toward the damp outfit.

She pulled on socks, cowboy boots, and poncho and, armed with her five-cell flashlight and the section of pipe that doubled as a weapon, set off to do her rounds. It was starting to sprinkle again.

By the end of her patrol, she headed over to the delivery truck that hadn't delivered a thing in years, in the far corner.

Around the back, the bag of trash she'd found earlier was fuller. Flashlight beam down on the bag, she opened it with the knobby end of pipe. Another Tecate beer can and another burrito wrapper, Chile Verde.

She stood up, listening, scanned the area with the flashlight. Light rain needled through the beam. All she could hear was the backdrop of bay water, lapping against the bricks and rubble along the shore behind the plant. She marched to the truck's cab, shone the flashlight up into it, gripping the pipe in her other hand.

"Whoever is up there better come out. Right about now."

No response.

"I can call the cops, too. I don't imagine you want that."

She heard a squeak of springs, movement inside the cab.

"Okay, okay," a voice said in a Latin accent, deep, as if full of sleep. "I'll go. I want no trouble."

She stood back. "Open the door."

The door handle squealed. Slowly, the door opened.

A man with light copper-colored skin looked at her, blinking back the flashlight beam. He was propped up on one elbow on the bench seat, his jacket draped over him. He had obviously been asleep. He was about thirty, Latino, muscular, with a short back-and-sides haircut, and a jet-black pompadour combed back slick but tousled from sleep. He needed a shave about a day ago but was carrying it off pretty well. He had well-defined cheekbones and dreamy eyes. Despite the fact that he was sleeping in the cab of an abandoned truck, he was easy to look at.

"Who might you be?" Colleen said.

"Ramon." His hand went up to shield his eyes. "Can you take that out of my face, please?" He spoke English with an accent but spoke it well.

She directed the flashlight beam to one side.

"Thank you." He sat up at the wheel and rubbed his eyes as he threw off the jacket. He wore a paint-spattered long-sleeved T-shirt and painters' pants, once white, now touched here and there with color. Not too much, though. The sign of a good painter.

"How did you get in here?" she asked.

He jerked a thumb over his shoulder. "Hole in the fence."

Colleen turned, shone her flashlight out into the water, highlighting the hole in a section of fence. "That hole is a good six feet out. And the water's got to be a couple feet deep."

"Tell me about it."

"What are you—part fish?"

"Took my clothes off from the waist down. Shoes and socks, too. Carried them in my backpack."

She thought about him nude from the waist down and realized it had been too long since she'd spent the night with anyone.

"What do you think you're doing here?" she asked.

"The Hilton was full. Why?"

"I'm the night watchman," she said.

He grinned. "You're about the most fascinating night watchman I've ever seen."

She gave a smirk. "You're illegal."

"I'm from El Salvador. There's a war going on. No work to be had there."

"You always eat the same thing every night? Chile Verde burritos?"

"Saving money. Send it back home."

She knew from his letter he had a wife and kids.

"You married?" he asked.

"Now what does that have to do with you trespassing?"

"I don't see a ring on your finger."

"Not anymore." Then, "Look—I can't have you staying here. It's my job. It's what they pay me for."

"Then I'll pay you, too," he said, "to let me sleep in the truck. I'll come late, leave early. Just until the end of the week. That's when my job ends. We're painting an apartment building over on Valencia." His handsome face softened. She felt for him.

"Sorry," she said. "No can do."

"Okay." He rubbed his chin. "Give me a minute to get my shoes on and I'm out of here."

She stood there, looking at this Ramon, who was well built but didn't look very dangerous. Not nearly as dangerous as the animal that raped and killed Margaret Copeland, possibly still out there. And then she looked up, the rain coming down harder now, hitting her in the face.

She looked back at Ramon. He had one sneaker on, was searching for the other. Then she thought about how having Ramon around might actually be useful.

"Hold up," she said.

He did.

"Here's the deal," Colleen said, pulling the brim of the head of her poncho out to deflect rain. "You can stay until your job's done, end of the week, sleep in the truck. But I haven't seen you. If anyone finds out, you're gone."

"Okay," he said. "And that's it?"

She shook her head. "If I'm not here, you're my eyes and ears. You see anything weird going on, anybody hanging around, you let me know."

"How do I do that?"

She turned, pointed up to the building. "Office. Up there. Slip a note under the door." She turned back to face Ramon. "I'm especially interested if *la policia* stop by. Or a big *vato*, looks like a cop." She described Randy. "But anyone else, too." She raised her eyebrows.

"Got it."

"Don't get involved with anyone," she said. "Just observe and report. Stay low, keep your eyes peeled, and let me know if anyone stops by, hey?"

"Deal," he said, pulling off the one shoe. "You're a nice person— you know that?"

"You leave end of the week." She turned, headed back to the warehouse, the flashlight beam bouncing on wet rocks and bricks.

"Your husband must have been crazy," he said, "to let you get away."

She fanned the comment away. He was buttering her up. But he meant enough of it. Enough that she couldn't help but savor it.

CHAPTER SEVEN

"The Margaret Copeland case," Colleen said for the second time to the officer hunched over his keyboard. He was sitting behind a Plexiglas window in Room 475 at SFPD Headquarters on Bryant Street. His posture said he had become one with his chair long ago. Colleen stood before the counter, a manila file folder under her arm, with notes and papers she had gathered since her visit to SF Public Library. A line of people waited behind her.

The officer typed with two fingers. Eventually he pressed the *Enter* key on the computer terminal connected to a mainframe somewhere. Computers were everywhere you looked now.

Leaning forward even further to peer at what came back on the screen, he shook his head *no*.

"I know it exists," she said. Christian Newell had confirmed that, although he didn't have a copy.

"It's probably not in our computer system."

"The Copeland case is over ten years old."

"They're still converting the old cases."

"Can you check again, please?"

"I just did, ma'am."

"And I appreciate that," Colleen said, "but it's important. It's a cold case. And please don't call me *ma'am*. I'm not collecting Social

Security yet." She forced a smile but the joke seemed to have no effect on him.

He gave a theatrical sigh and shook his head.

"Is this going to take all day?" a man standing behind Colleen said in a gruff voice.

Colleen turned to the line of people building behind her. A big guy in a hard hat had spoken. He had a few days' worth of shadow on his fleshy face and a gut that said he was probably a supervisor, not a laborer.

"Hopefully not," she said, turning back.

"That would be nice," Hard Hat said with an edge.

She said to the officer: "Can you please show me what you just typed?"

"Jesus," she heard Hard Hat say behind her.

The red-faced officer gave an impatient sigh, stood up from his stool, turned the big computer monitor partway round so that the screen faced the window.

On an IBM 3270 with a black screen and lines of flickering green text, she read "NO RESULTS FOUND." Colleen checked the officer's search criteria.

"Ah," she said. "It's *Copeland*—with an E. Not *Copland.*"

The officer frowned, double-checked the scrap of paper that Colleen had handed him when this whole process had started. Then he turned the monitor back around, corrected his entry, and pressed the *Enter* key with his index finger, waited for a response. Squinted into the screen again.

"And what does it say?" Colleen asked between her teeth.

"Archived."

"And what does that mean?"

"It's a cold case."

Colleen stifled a sigh. "Can you please tell me who I would contact?"

"That would be in the report."

"Which I don't have."

"You'll have to submit a written request for a Xerox copy. Room 101. Downstairs." He pointed down, in case she didn't understand where *downstairs* was.

"And how long is that going to take?" Colleen asked.

"Within thirty days."

"*Thirty days?*"

"It feels like we've been waiting in this damn line thirty days," she heard Hard Hat say.

Colleen ignored him.

"This is kind of an emergency," she said to the clerk. "A member of the family is trying to settle affairs." True. "I really need to contact whoever is responsible for the case. Is there any way you could possibly find out?"

"Homicide."

"Right, Homicide—it's a murder case. But *who* in Homicide?"

"Don't know, ma'am." He shrugged, looked over her shoulder. "Next."

"I really want to thank you for going out of your way to help me," Colleen said with heavy sarcasm and turned, headed for the door.

"If I was her husband, she'd watch that mouth of hers," she heard Hard Hat mutter to the man in line behind him.

Colleen turned back.

"In your dreams." She saw the clerk on the phone now, which made her wonder. Was the phone call related to her visit?

* * *

"The police report still hasn't made it into their new computer system," Colleen said, the pay phone cradled to her neck. She was on the ground floor of the Hall of Justice, 850 Bryant. "And the clerk I spoke to wasn't about to do anything that resembled help."

"What we pretty much suspected," Christian Newell said on the other end of the line.

"So you never submitted a request yourself?"

"Twice. Never got a thing."

That made her pause. "Didn't you think that was just a little bit odd?"

"I thought it was SFPD bureaucracy at its finest."

"How long have you been working for Mr. Copeland?" Colleen asked.

"Just over a year. I've had quite a few things to take care of. I filed for the report but, as I said, never got it. Now that Mr. Copeland's health has taken a turn for the worse, it's become a priority."

"Where do I find your predecessor's files?"

"I've got them. A rat's nest, I can tell you. But no report on Margaret's murder. Nothing on Margaret at all, actually."

The family had probably wanted to put the murder out of their mind at the time.

"Go ahead and submit a request," Christian said. "You're down at 850 anyway, right?"

"Yeah, but we're talking thirty days—if I get anything at all."

"I hear you."

Who knew if Edward Copeland had thirty days?

"I'll file for the report," she said. "What about Randy Ferguson?"

"Working on it."

Well, that was something. She needed her parole officer off her back. But she was beginning to think Christian Newell wasn't perhaps the best at getting things done.

Room 561 was unlit and understaffed when Colleen stopped by. The officer at the desk was middle-aged, bookish, his thin frame lost in a dark blue uniform shirt that hung on him like he was a coat hanger. A silver seven-pointed star badge was pinned over his pocket.

"Inspector Jim Davis, please," she asked.

"Now there's a name you don't hear much anymore."

"Oh, really? Why's that?"

"Where'd you get it?" he asked. "The name?"

"Old *Examiner* article on a case he was working on."

"Well, you're about ten years too late. He took early retirement."

"Really? When?"

"Ten years ago."

Not long after Margaret Copeland was murdered.

"What if I had a question about a murder case?" she asked.

"Which one?"

"Margaret Copeland. November 21—"

"That one? Good luck. You'd have to talk to the officer in charge of it. It's a cold case."

"Who would that be?"

The clerk checked a schedule. "Lieutenant Bakken is the man you want."

"Is he here?"

He shook his head. "Out today."

Colleen took a calming breath. She handed him a torn-off piece of lined paper with "Margaret Copeland" written on it. Underneath was Colleen's name and the phone number at H&M Paint's office as well as her answering service. She didn't want to advertise that she was a private investigator if she didn't have to, so she didn't hand over her card.

The officer eyed the paper on his desk but didn't pick it up.

"Thanks," Colleen said. "Can you tell me anything about the case? Anything you might remember—if you were even here then?" He looked like he might have come with the place.

"And who are you, exactly?"

"Colleen Hayes. I was hired by the family to look into the case."

"You're a PI?"

"Not exactly."

"Not exactly?" He raised his eyebrows.

Damn. "Waiting on my license. In the meantime, I'm simply making a few inquiries for the family. They're settling affairs."

"I see. No, I don't remember much except it looked like this Margaret Copeland went off with some guy. The wrong guy, in this case. A lot of the girls were like that back then. Free love." He shook his head.

"So that makes it her fault?"

He smirked. "If she hadn't gone off with him, would she still be alive?"

"Maybe she was abducted."

"She could have put up a fight."

"Maybe she did." Colleen frowned. "I'd really like to speak to this Lieutenant Bakken. Thanks for all your help."

The paper on the desk didn't budge as she left. She thought it curious that the cop at the desk didn't give her the Zodiac as a reason Margaret was abducted. She thought that was supposed to be the official line.

Rattle cages. About the only thing she could do right now. She'd go to Room 101 next, get in line to file a request for the police report.

* * *

After Colleen left Homicide, the desk officer made a call. "Hey, Frank. Some woman was here, asking questions about the old Copeland case." He paused. "Yeah, she was just upstairs, too, trying to get a copy of the homicide report." Another pause. "Yeah." He picked up Colleen's contact information. "Colleen Hayes. No address—just a phone number."

CHAPTER EIGHT

"My husband's not home," Mary Davis said to Colleen, wiping her hands on a dish towel. She stood at the front door of a stucco house streaked with mildew on Paris Street, just up the hill from Mission, amidst similar junior fives built during the Second World War. It was late morning.

The street was crisscrossed with overhead wires. Mary Davis was middle-aged, thick around the middle, but not fat. A cigarette dangled from her lips. She wore a green apron with "Kiss Me, I'm Irish" on it and she had a curly red perm that was about as stiff as her attitude.

Maybe she was cool to Colleen because a younger woman was asking for her husband.

"It's a business matter," Colleen said, holding up one of her cards.

Ms. Davis threw the limp dish towel over her shoulder, took the cigarette from her mouth, and yanked the card from Colleen's fingers.

From upstairs, buzz-saw guitars and ninety-mile-an-hour drums blasted. Colleen could make out vocals that proclaimed that someone was a "fucking piece of shit." Punk rock, the latest musical offering.

"Steve!" Ms. Davis yelled over her shoulder. "Turn that down!"

A moment later, the music dropped in volume.

Ms. Davis took an angry puff on her cigarette as she read Colleen's business card. "Is he in some kind of trouble again? I made a payment on the furniture bill last week."

"I'm not a bill collector," Colleen said. "It's about an old case he worked on."

Ms. Davis squinted as smoke curled up her face, studying Colleen. "This better not be about that dead girl."

"Who?" Colleen said, feigning confusion. After a decade, was Margaret Copeland still an issue for the family of the man who had once worked the case? "No, something else."

"What *something else?*"

"I really can't say." Colleen nodded at her card in the woman's hand. "That's why it says *confidential* on the card." She gave a smile. "I have to promise my clients complete confidentiality. There is some money involved, though, for information."

Mary Davis took a puff. "How much money?"

"That would depend."

A door opened upstairs, letting more punk music seep out momentarily before it slammed shut. Footsteps thumped down the stairs.

A young man around twenty appeared, with slicked-back jet-black hair. He wore ripped jeans and a T-shirt with a Mustang pony logo. A pack of cigarettes was rolled up in one sleeve.

"Where's your dad?" Mary Davis asked him.

"Where do you think?"

"You better call about that job today, Steve."

"Yeah, yeah." He sauntered off to the kitchen, slamming that door, too.

The woman turned back to Colleen as she pocketed Colleen's business card in her apron. "Dizzy's," she said. "Down on Mission.

Tell him the shower's backed up again while you're at it." She shut the door before Colleen could say goodbye.

Dizzy's on Mission wasn't hard to find; the '50s-era neon sign outlined a man in top hat and tails clinging to a lamppost with drunken Xs for eyes.

Inside the dimly lit bar, the non-working crowd and a few people who probably should have been at work were hunched over glasses while the Giants played with the sound turned down on a fuzzy TV. Two men slammed dice cups. The jukebox was playing a song about a woman torn between two lovers and feeling like a fool. The only other woman in the place was the fireplug behind the bar serving drinks with a flat-line mouth, as if she were dispensing cyanide.

"Hey," a big guy in a Hawaiian shirt with flame-on toucans said to Colleen, spinning around on his barstool when she entered. He had a nose like a pomegranate and a beer gut to support the theory of how the nose might have gotten to that state. He looked like the class clown, grown up into bar jester. "You looking for me, sports model?" He gave a leer that was probably meant to be a winning smile.

"I am if your name is Jim Davis," she said. But he didn't look like the guy. From the ten-year-old photo in the *Chronicle*, Jim Davis looked more like an older version of the slender kid listening to punk rock up at the house on Paris Street. A lot like the man bent over an empty shot glass and half a beer in an otherwise vacant corner booth. That guy looked like he'd been beating his liver for the last decade.

"Bingo," the big man said.

Colleen strolled over, hands in the pockets of her leather bomber jacket.

"Jim Davis?"

Jim Davis looked up at her with watery eyes. He had a five o'clock shadow that was at least a day old. But most of all, he radiated sadness. It was deep within him, the core of his being.

"Do I know you?" he said defensively.

"Not yet." She smiled, introduced herself, got out one of her business cards, slipped it across the table. Jim Davis read it as he sipped his beer.

"Okay if I sit down?" Colleen asked.

He drained his beer, looked at her with raised eyebrows. She took the hint.

"Boilermaker?" she asked.

He shrugged, twisting his smudged beer glass.

A minute later she was back with a beer and bourbon for Jim Davis and a fizzy beer for herself.

Jim Davis downed the shot, smacked his lips, drank a swallow of beer, rubbed his nose. "So what's this about?"

"Margaret Copeland," she said quietly.

Jim Davis looked as if he'd been slapped. He drank a third of his beer. "Now there's a name from the past."

"You worked on her case."

Jim glanced over at the bar. The big man in the wild shirt had gone to the restroom.

Jim looked back at her, his voice low. "Until it was deep-sixed, I did."

Interesting.

Jim drained his beer and had that look like he was ready to get up and leave.

Colleen nodded at the empty glasses. "Ready for another?"

"Depends on where this conversation is going."

"Edward Copeland—Margaret's father—hired me to look into her murder."

Jim Davis sat back. "After all this time?"

"After all this time."

"Lucky you."

"Got some time to fill me in?" she said.

"The report is on file."

"Trouble is, it's going to take thirty days for me to get a copy—and that's if I get it. SFPD seem to be dragging their feet."

He gave a silent laugh, backed up with a weak grin. "That a surprise to you?"

"And what does that mean?"

"It means it might be best to mind your own business."

"I can do that some other time. Right now, I'd like to talk to you—the guy who wrote the report. And also find out what wasn't written down—if anything."

He stood up, wobbly, closed his eyes for a moment, found his balance. "Thanks for the drink."

She put her hand on his arm, dropped her voice. "I'm willing to pay to hear your side of the story."

He frowned, seemed to think about that, sat back down. "How much are we talking about?"

"Depends on what you have." They were conversing in hushed tones.

He dropped his voice to a near whisper. "The original report."

This seemed to be her lucky day. They eyed each other.

"You have it?" she asked.

He gave an almost imperceptible nod.

"Five hundred?" she said. Over two weeks' pay—if one were working.

He frowned, shook his head from side to side, held up two fingers.

She took a deep breath. She didn't have that much. She'd have to get it from Mr. Copeland, providing he even went for it. But she suspected he would. Time was the most valuable commodity to him right now. And the fact that Jim Davis had the original meant something.

"I need to make a phone call," she said. "When?"

"Give me an hour."

"Make it two," she said. She might have to run to the bank. "Here?"

He shook his head.

Then she realized. Dizzy's was a cop hangout. And ex-cops going nowhere. Jim Davis didn't want to be overheard talking about Margaret Copeland here.

Even a decade after the fact.

"So tell me where," she said.

Pulling a pack of Lucky Strikes out of the pocket of his plaid flannel shirt, Jim Davis shook one out, managed to get it into his mouth. He fumbled for a book of paper matches, tore one off.

"Manor Coffee Shop," he mumbled as he lit his cigarette. "Bring cash. I'll bring the report."

"Twelve thirty," she said quietly, checking her watch, then sipping beer. "By the way, your shower is backed up."

He nodded as he got his cigarette going, sucked on it so hard it crumpled.

From the back of the bar, the squeal of a restroom door preceded the big guy sauntering back to his stool at the bar.

Jim Davis stood up and, in a loud voice, said to Colleen: "My wife made a payment just last week! We're doing the best we can. You can't get blood out of a damn stone." He gave Colleen a drunken wink before he stumbled toward the door.

"Too bad, Jimmy," the big man said to him on his way out. "I thought maybe you were gonna get lucky."

"Story of my life, Frank. Damn bill collectors."

The door swung open and a scrap of gray light lit up Jim Davis as he staggered out on Mission, pulling a tail of cigarette smoke behind him. The door cut it off.

Colleen got up, leaving her unfinished beer.

"That asshole a friend of yours?" she said to the big guy in the shirt as she headed for the door.

"You have a nice day, now," he said to Colleen as she left.

Then he rubbed his face.

"Brenda," he said, throwing a dollar bill from the cash by his drink into the drink well. "I'm going to need some dimes for the pay phone."

CHAPTER NINE

"Hey, Jimmy, where you goin', man?"

Jim Davis looked over as he plowed up fog-strewn Persia Street, heading home. He was going to get that Copeland report the Hayes woman wanted.

He did a double take when he saw Frank in his Hawaiian shirt, sitting in the passenger seat of an SFPD black-and-white. Henry driving, in his blues. A couple more years until retirement for him. Then he'd be warming a seat down at Dizzy's, too, along with the rest of them.

"Hey, Frank," Jim said. "I hate to be the one to break it to you, but you're retired now—just like me."

Frank grinned. "I know, Jimmy, but I still need my squad car fix now and then. Where you going?"

"Home," he said. "Mary's gonna rip me a new one if I don't fix that shower."

"Oh, I thought maybe you might be plannin' to meet that spunky mama you were shouting at—down at Dizzy's. She did have a build, huh?"

Jim feigned confusion. "I guess."

Car crawling alongside him now. Henry watching him, too. Jim was starting to get a little edgy with the attention.

"Who was she, Jimmy?"

"Some bill collector," he said. "We're gonna lose the furniture any day now. I tell you, it's not easy getting by without a paycheck."

"Tell me about it, man. Hey, Henry and me got a couple of six-packs. And your namesake." Frank waved a pint of Jim Beam just above the door sill. "We're going down to Third Street, cruise the teeny bops." He gave a leer. "What do you say?"

Jim forced a grin. "In that shirt?"

Frank flipped the collar of his toucan shirt. "Call it undercover—just like the old days. Jump in. You need a break. I haven't seen a smile on that puss of yours in a long time."

"Nah, Frank. Not my scene." Walking faster now, wanting to get away. "You guys have fun."

"Come on, man, we're not gonna *do* anything. Just fuck with 'em."

Sure. Hassle the teen hookers. Take their cash, dope, scare their pimps, maybe squeeze a BJ out of 'em. Made him sick. Some cops. "If I don't fix that blocked shower stall, Mary's gonna have my balls, Frank."

"Shit, Jimmy, you're too nice to that woman." He turned. "Ain't he, Henry?"

"Straight up." Henry nodded, driving slow.

"I'll see you guys later," Jim said, breaking into an alcoholic sweat as he pushed faster up the hill. "Dizzy's later, right?"

"C'mon," Frank said. "Hop in. We'll give you a ride home. Before you have a heart attack."

"No worries, Frank."

He turned the corner onto Paris Street.

"You know, Jimmy—you're starting to hurt my feelings. What's the deal? Too good to drink with your old buddies now?"

Jim stopped. So did the cruiser. He'd have to play it smart with Frank. Be cool. Not raise suspicion. Until he got his hands on that money. Then he could take Mary to Tahoe, take a vacation. She needed one.

His eyes met Frank's.

"Come on, Jimmy," Frank said, flashing the pint again. "A quick blast before you have to deal with the little woman. It doesn't pay to jump too high for 'em anyway, man. Ain't I right, Henry?"

"Damn straight."

Jim eyed the flat. "Maybe just a quick one."

"Now you're talking, homeboy." Frank grinned ear to ear. "Hop in. Can't have the general population watching cops drink on the job."

CHAPTER TEN

Colleen nursed a cup of watery coffee at The Manor coffee shop for close to half an hour, where the Chinese waitress darted around in a pink dress, white socks, and white shoes. Then she ordered a hamburger, very well done, because that looked like the safest option with the state of the griddle.

By one thirty she hadn't come down with ptomaine poisoning.

But Jim Davis hadn't shown either.

Stood up?

Jim Davis had most likely headed home to get the police report. But he had been hammered at Dizzy's. He was a professional boozer. Maybe he had met a drinking buddy, wandered off.

Or maybe he had changed his mind.

Colleen let out a sigh. She had spent the morning running to Wells Fargo to pick up the cash Christian Newell had authorized to pay Jim Davis for the report.

She paid her bill, left a fifty-cent tip, and drove back to Jim Davis's house on Paris Street. The air was wet in the Outer Mission, fog that wasn't going to lift today. She turned on the windshield wipers.

* * *

"You again?" Mary Davis said, cigarette bouncing between her lips. "Can't you take a hint?" The front door began to close.

"Please hear me out," Colleen said, pushing against the door. "*Please.*"

The door slowly reopened.

"One minute is all you have," Mary Davis said, taking the cigarette out of her mouth, brushing her curly red hair back off her forehead.

Colleen looked up and down the street. "We should talk inside," she said.

* * *

"You did *what*?" Mary Davis said, arms crossed, sitting at the Formica kitchen table. Her cigarette smoldered in an ashtray. "I thought I made it pretty clear that the subject of the dead girl was out of bounds. I asked you if that was why you wanted to see Jim. And you told me *no*."

"You would have shut me down," Colleen said, leaning against the kitchen counter. It was visually busy with green and yellow tile from another era.

Mary Davis put her head in her hands. "Christ almighty."

"Look, I am very sorry. But when I spoke to your husband at Dizzy's, he agreed to meet me at The Manor coffee shop and talk about the case." She wasn't going to mention the report.

"And that makes it okay?" She looked up, her face streaming with angry tears. "You got a look at him. Does he seem fully functional to you?"

"Functional enough."

"And you've been married to him for thirty-one years?"

"We had an arrangement. There's some money involved." She raised her eyebrows. "There still is."

"No." Mary Davis shook her head. "We don't want your money."

"That's odd. Because I get the distinct feeling you're not exactly rolling in the stuff."

Mary gave her a hard stare. "Mind your own damn business. I told you—nothing to do with the Copeland girl."

"I get it now," Colleen said. "But you know, I don't think it was just about the money. I got the impression your husband really wants to talk about the case." Something was eating at Jim Davis. Perhaps he needed to clear his conscience.

"He'll talk about the Jolly Green Giant if you dangle a damn drink in front of him."

"Did your husband come home about an hour and a half ago?"

"No."

Now Colleen was starting to get concerned. "Maybe he bumped into a friend?"

Mary Davis let out an irritated sigh. "Maybe."

"If you tell me what you know, perhaps I can help."

"How the hell can *you* possibly help?"

"I've got resources, through my client. A lawyer."

Mary Davis shook her head. "Lawyers!"

"What was the reason your husband left SFPD?"

Again, Mary Davis shook her head. "No."

"Something to do with the Copeland case?"

Mary Davis looked straight at the ceramic sugar bowl in front of her. Then she stood up stiffly, picked up the sugar bowl, and, like a ball player on a bad day, hurled it against the wall past Colleen's head where it shattered, spraying the kitchen in white sugar. Colleen's heart hammered while pieces of sugar bowl settled on the floor.

"There's my answer." Mary Davis glared at her. "Now get *out*."

Colleen sucked in a deep breath and was just about to leave when the kitchen door flipped open. Steve Davis stood there. He jammed his hands in the front pockets of his ripped jeans.

"What the hell, Ma?" He glanced at Colleen for a moment, then back at his mother. "You okay?"

"Show this woman out," Mary Davis said through her teeth, getting a kitchen broom out of the pantry and already sweeping up the pieces of pottery and sugar in taut, short strokes. "And don't let her back in. Or you can just find your own place to live. It's about time, anyway."

Steve Davis showed Colleen out.

"I'm sorry," he said quietly. She turned to question him, but the door had shut and the lock turned.

CHAPTER ELEVEN

"I'll take it," Colleen said.

The by-the-week room reeked of Lysol. The bed sagged. The view from the window was a brick wall four feet across a grim light well. Downstairs she could hear some guy yelling at a woman to go out and get him his damn money.

But it was a place to live. Or, more to the point, an address Colleen could provide for address verification. Although it wasn't assured that the Thunderbird Hotel in the Tenderloin would qualify. But the apartments she had looked at required an application, would not be available right away, and had plenty of competition. And being an ex-con would not put her at the head of the line. She needed to get a "real" address ASAP.

"Forty a week," the manager said in a reedy voice. "In advance."

Colleen peeled off eight twenty-dollar bills, catching the manager's interest enough to make him quit chewing his thumbnail. "I'll take it for the next four weeks. I'll need a receipt." A month would show good faith to her parole officer.

"Where's your luggage?"

"Not here."

The hotel manager narrowed his eyes. There were significant lines under them. A worrier. "No guests after ten." He squinted. "And *no* soliciting."

"Is that what you told the guy downstairs?"

"You can always go somewhere else."

"I won't be here much anyway." If at all. She handed him the money, and then unraveled one more twenty. "And this is for you. If someone stops by to verify parole, you'll know what to say, right?"

"So it's like that," he said, taking the money, slipping the last twenty into a different pocket. "My apologies about the . . . solicitation thing." He held out the room key, dangling from a yellow plastic diamond.

"Maybe I should be flattered." She took the key.

* * *

The magnetic employee in/out board at the Community Assessment Service Center on Sixth Street showed Randy Ferguson was not in the office. That was fine with Colleen.

It was late afternoon.

"Can you see that Mr. Ferguson gets this?" she said, handing over a copy of her rental receipt to a heavyset woman in a bright plum Damask colored top behind the desk. "It's my new permanent address."

The woman took it, read it, raised her eyebrows.

"Good luck," she said, folding the paper, slipping it into Randy's message slot.

Good enough. She had no intention of ditching her current setup at H&M Paint, but this would hopefully show she had found a legitimate place to live.

In the back of her mind, though, she wondered what had become of Jim Davis. She needed to check back. But she didn't relish having to deal with Mary Davis again. She'd give it a little time. Better still, try to deal with her son, Steve, the punk rocker. He might be approachable.

Colleen drove over to Mission and Cortland where she parked in the Safeway lot. At a pay phone she dropped a dime into the slot and called the *San Francisco Chronicle*'s main number.

A woman with a nasal voice answered.

"Howard Broadmoor, please," Colleen said.

"He's out this week, I'm afraid."

Damn. "Is there someone else who might be able to answer questions about a series of articles he wrote about a decade back?"

"Which ones, ma'am?"

"About the Margaret Copeland murder—in 1967."

"And you are?"

"A friend of the family. Just trying to clear up some loose ends. But it *is* important. Isn't there anyone I can talk to?"

"Mr. Broadmoor is probably the only one who can answer your questions. If you leave your name and number, I'll have him call you."

Colleen left her name and number, thanked the woman.

She went inside the Safeway and stocked up on things she couldn't afford before she got the advance from Mr. Copeland. Real coffee. Cream. Bread, the kind you cut with a breadknife, which she also bought. Butter. A block of sharp cheddar. Fresh squeezed orange juice. All the things she did without for ten years in Denver Women's Correctional Facility.

Near the Safeway by Cortland Avenue, she picked up a used dorm fridge at an appliance store with a hand-painted sign over the door. The Latin guy who owned the store carried it to her car. And for a moment, life was good.

She filled the Torino all the way to F at a 76, something she hadn't done in quite a while. At sixty-five cents a gallon, it set her back more than ten bucks.

But this was money she hadn't earned yet.

It had only been five or six hours since Steve Davis had shown Colleen the door. Too soon to go back and try again. Hopefully Jim Davis would come home soon. If Colleen had learned anything about being inside ten years, it was how to wait.

She got on 101 South, headed for the Candlestick Park exit.

An official-looking overnight letter in the steel mailbox at H&M Paint addressed to her from SF Department of Adult Probation made her fleeting good cheer sink like a rock.

She tore it open, then and there, setting the sack of groceries on the weed-grown forecourt of H&M. She had a pretty good idea what was inside.

"Revocation of parole based on conduct that occurred during the period of supervision, in violation of the Interstate Compact."

She skipped to the bottom.

"Policy 1A-27 allows for the warrantless arrest of parolee: Colleen A. Hayes."

She took a deep breath, picked up her sack of groceries, hauled them up the metal stairwell. Then she came down, got the fridge. She still had her strength, all those years of working out inside.

CHAPTER TWELVE

"So now what, Christian?" Colleen said into the phone, her cowboy boots up on her office desk. She took a sip of strong, fresh-brewed coffee, softened by rich cream and two heaping spoons of brown sugar.

"I'll put in a call to the parole office," Christian Newell said on the other end. "But it's after hours. We won't hear anything until tomorrow at the earliest."

"You think the Thunderbird Hotel is going to work as a verifiable address?"

"We'll say it's interim lodging. Even if they don't accept it, it shows good faith."

"You don't know Randy Ferguson. I don't think the term 'good faith' exists in his vocabulary."

"Is there any way you can get him on your side?"

"Oh, there's a way, all right. He's made it pretty clear. But I'm not going that far."

The line crackled. "So he's one of those."

"Yep," she said, sipping.

"You should have told me."

"It's not something I felt like talking about."

"It gives me more to go on."

"I prefer to fight my own battles in that department. And, to be honest, I kind of thought you had already taken care of things. That was part of the deal."

"I *am* taking care of things," he said defensively. "In the meantime, don't answer the door. Especially if the people on the other side look like cops. You could be on your way back to Colorado while we're still trying to straighten this mess out."

"Let me know. I can't do squat stuck here."

When the sun went down, she did the rounds of the rubble-strewn plant, checking for any new disturbances. She patrolled the perimeter, walking along the water, finishing up by the dead delivery truck. No new garbage around back. She walked around the front to the cab, shone her flashlight on the door.

"*Hola?*"

Ramon wasn't there. She kind of wished he were.

She finished the rounds as it started to rain again, then went back upstairs, turned on her new transistor radio, dialed in some classical music, set the radio on the desk.

Time to call Mary Davis again? No. Too soon. She couldn't risk incurring Mary's wrath and cutting off all communication. She'd give her time to let the sugar bowl incident fade.

What had happened to Jim Davis? Had he simply blown her off? Or was it something more ominous?

CHAPTER THIRTEEN

Night was the time she could roam freely—free of others.

Tara stumbled along the darkened beach, the sun long gone, the sand heavy with moisture under her boots, boots two sizes too big. Her bare feet slipped around inside them, cold and grimy. Fog soaked her face. She'd been sleeping on the beach but had not found any peace there. The crashing waves, calming to some, were cannon in the distance to her, sounds from a war always waging inside her head. She climbed up the sandy bluff, using her hands and her feet, toward the old fort, past the Second World War gun emplacement. The concrete façade was overgrown with decades of hanging ivy.

Tara jumped when a critter moved. The dark eyes of a raccoon stared at her from the undergrowth.

She made her way down the other side, looking inland at the parking lot, the old Nike missile site, long since deactivated.

No cars. She was as free as she could be. These were the hours where she could gather back her sanity.

She flinched when she heard something in the distance. She stood up, wary. An engine.

Coming in from Skyline Boulevard.

Headlights appeared, bouncing across the uneven asphalt.

The beams stopped near the bluff and cut out, leaving white shadows in the backs of her eyes. The engine died. Silence. She could hear the sea again. The pounding of the surf.

A police car. Black and white. Like a giant skunk.

She saw two men get out. One a policeman. Another with a big belly. Even in the moonlight she could make out the birds on his Hawaiian shirt.

They hustled a man out of the back of the car.

The man protested, stumbling. "What are you guys doing?"

"Come on, Jimmy," the Hawaiian shirt man said. "Let's have a drink at Fort Funston—for old time's sake."

Jimmy seemed to come to his senses. "What are we doing here?"

"One more drink, Jimmy. Just like old times. Remember how we always came down here when we were boys?"

The man, Jimmy, had trouble moving but tried to pull away. The man in the Hawaiian shirt grabbed him by the arm.

"Come on, Jimmy."

"Get the hell away from me, Frank." He smacked off Frank's arm and spun, losing his balance, regaining it with a clumsy half-step, then staggered away.

The other man, the policeman, went after him, caught him, spun him back around.

Jimmy threw a wild punch, managed to catch the policeman in the jaw. But it was a sloppy effort, and although the policeman wobbled back, he recovered while the man in the Hawaiian shirt moved in, caught Jimmy.

"You're starting to piss me off, Jimmy. We're your goddamn friends, remember?"

"No, you're not. You're not my friends."

The man in the Hawaiian shirt held Jimmy's arm. "What the fuck? You and me known each other since we were eight. Eight!

Now, come to your goddamn senses. We're gonna have a drink, for old time's sake, and then we're gonna forget this nonsense. All right?"

They stood there for a moment, the man Frank still holding Jimmy's arm.

"All right, Jimmy?"

Jimmy finally nodded.

"All right, then. Enough of this bullshit. We're friends."

"Friends," Jimmy slurred.

Tara watched them, one on either side of Jimmy, a bottle dangling from the big Hawaiian shirt man's hand, leading Jimmy off. Up toward the cement bunker.

Not long after, the two men came back without Jimmy. Both men were puffing, the big man's forehead shiny with sweat, like they'd been working hard.

Tara watched the Hawaiian shirt man take a final drink from the bottle, then give a painful gasp before he hurled the empty across the cement where it shattered and spread.

"Fuck it, Henry," he said. "Let's get out of here."

They got in the skunk and drove off, headlights bouncing away.

Tara knew what had happened, even though people said she didn't know much at all. She went back to that concrete tunnel that formed the house for the big gun that once guarded them all from the Japanese. And saw what she knew she'd see. The man was curled up like a snail. Motionless.

She reached down and touched him.

"Jimmy?"

No movement.

And then she stood up, her mind aflame.

CHAPTER FOURTEEN

Christian Newell sat in his BMW a few doors up from 437 Colon Avenue, up on the hillside overlooking South San Francisco, listening to KCBS news talk radio. Watching the various front doors open, men leaving houses, getting into cars, going to work. Some walking down to Monterey Boulevard to take the bus.

He should've known a man like Randy Ferguson, with a City job, wouldn't be leaving his house any time before nine. One would've thought a house up in Westwood Highlands would be out of financial reach of a parole officer.

Christian tapped the stiff envelope in his hand on the steering wheel while the radio host on KCBS discussed Jimmy Carter's declining poll ratings, inflation creeping back up, getting close to seven percent.

The front door to 437 finally opened and out came his quarry.

He looked like two hundred and twenty pounds of asshole marinated in vodka. Wearing a snappy raincoat and sunglasses to boot, on a gray foggy San Francisco morning.

Christian sucked in a nervous breath and hopped out of the car with his envelope at the ready.

Randy Ferguson walked around to the driver's side of a white Ford LTD, bought and paid for by San Francisco City and County, just as Christian crossed the residential street.

"Randall Ferguson?"

The man turned, key in the door lock, gave Christian an ugly frown, a questioning look in his eyes behind the dark lenses when he saw the envelope in Christian's hand.

"These are court papers," Christian said, holding up the envelope.

"Shove 'em up your ass, you little faggot." Randy made no effort to take the envelope.

"Tonight's star prize!" Christian touched Randy Ferguson's shoulder with the edge of the envelope and let it fall. "I hereby anoint thee." The envelope fluttered to the asphalt.

"I'm not picking that up, cocksucker."

"Doesn't matter," Christian said in his court voice. "You've been served, bub."

Randy Ferguson lunged at him, a guy eighty pounds heavier, and Christian skittered across the street backwards.

"I'd give them the once-over if I were you," he said from a safe distance. "And if you have any sense of self-preservation, you are going to want to reconsider your behavior." Giving a lazy salute, he said: "Oh, and have a nice day."

CHAPTER FIFTEEN

"So it's safe to leave the compound now?" Colleen asked Christian, sitting across from her desk. It was late morning and the rain had let up although threatening clouds were blowing across the bay. Wind buffeted the industrial windows.

"If your parole officer has any sense," Christian said, straightening a white cuff, "he's going to reverse the nastygram he sent you and beg his boss to put someone else in charge of your parole."

That was a relief. But Colleen knew nothing was guaranteed. "What did you file charges for?"

"No charges. I filed a restraining order."

"Don't *I* need to file a restraining order?"

"Not a workplace restraining order. In fact, an employee cannot file such an order. But Mr. Copeland can, since you are one of his employees—technically—and this warehouse is your workplace—technically."

Colleen gave a wry smile. "Even to my untrained mind, that seems like a stretch."

"Doesn't matter. Randy Ferguson's finances are a mess. He's living above his means, a paycheck away from bankruptcy. He's not going to take on Mr. Copeland and his millions in civil court. And he certainly doesn't want anything that remotely smacks of harassing women to reach SFPD. He was brought up on a similar charge two years ago."

Interesting but not surprising. "Remind me never to play poker with you."

"It's not all bluff," Christian said. "That kind of thing is being taken more seriously now, especially in San Francisco."

"What can I say? Except thanks." She honestly hadn't thought Christian Newell had it in him. She just hoped it was going to work as he said it would.

"Don't worry," he said, "you'll return the favor."

That's what concerned her.

"Where are we on Margaret Copeland?" Christian asked.

Colleen tapped a Virginia Slim out of the pack she'd been playing with. Now that she had funds again, she was able to resume a bad habit. She stuck the long cigarette in her mouth. "Yesterday I was supposed to meet Jim Davis, the retired homicide investigator who originally ran the case, for a copy of the police report, in exchange for the two thousand dollars expense money you authorized."

"And?"

Colleen frowned. "I spent two hours in a greasy spoon drinking weak coffee. Davis never showed. I'm waiting to contact him again."

"What's stopping you?"

"I have to let his wife cool off. She was pretty emphatic that she didn't want her husband to have anything to do with the Margaret Copeland case. We're talking throwing-pottery-around upset."

"Well," Christian said, "it's a start."

Maybe. But Colleen didn't like the way Jim Davis had just disappeared. Sure, he was a drinker. They sometimes did those kinds of things. Maybe he got cold feet. She took the unlit cigarette out of her mouth and slid it back into the pack. She stood up, scooped the car keys off the desk.

"Now that I'm allowed back out on the streets, I'm going to head back over there and make a nuisance of myself. I've still got your two K. Hopefully, I'll need it to buy the report from Jim Davis soon."

"Keep me posted. I expect a daily update. Anything significant, let me know immediately—day or night. You've got my home number, too, right?"

"I do."

"Mr. Copeland is eager to hear any progress. He's going to be pleased with what you've done so far."

Colleen zipped up her bomber jacket. She was glad somebody was going to be happy with her progress. Because she wasn't.

CHAPTER SIXTEEN

Late morning, Colleen parked down Paris Street, noting a blue Chevy C10 pickup blocking the driveway of 355. It looked like Mary Davis had company. Maybe not a good time to stop by. Or maybe Jim Davis had finally come home. That would be a huge relief.

A few minutes later, a man in a Giants cap left the Davis house, bouncing down the stairs even though he was middle-aged and a good forty pounds overweight. Colleen knew him, in a sense. He'd tried to chat her up a couple days ago, sitting on a barstool at Dizzy's, when she went in to speak to Jim Davis. Jim had called him Frank. She watched him get into the pickup, fire it up, back out onto Paris Street, and head off.

Colleen got out of the Torino, headed to the Davis residence. She took a deep breath, rang the bell.

She thought she saw someone darken the peephole viewer.

The front door flew open. There stood Mary Davis, wearing a red bathrobe over a nightdress and white slippers with blue snowflakes on them. The drone of metal music floated from upstairs, quieter than the other day. Mary Davis's eyes were red and had been recently wiped. But the rest of her face radiated pure rage.

"You again!" she hissed.

"I am really sorry to bother you, Ms. Davis."

"Where is my husband?" Mary Davis practically spat the words.

So Jim Davis wasn't around. Colleen's spirits sagged. "I don't know. I was hoping to speak to him myself."

"When did you last see him?"

"Not since yesterday—when I stopped by. It was down at Dizzy's. I told you: we were going to meet at The Manor coffee shop, but he never showed up."

"And you haven't seen him since then?"

"No. And I take it you haven't either."

The rock-n-roll grew louder upstairs, as someone opened the door.

"Ma?" Steve Davis shouted down the stairs. "Who is it?"

"Just that *woman* who was here yesterday. And turn that garbage down."

The upstairs door shut. The music dropped in volume.

Mary Davis turned her attention back to Colleen, holding onto the door with a hand that vibrated with anger. "I'm going to say this just one more time," she said. "Leave us alone." She turned her head, eyed Colleen sideways. "Jim's got friends on the force. Got that?"

Colleen swallowed. "Maybe I can help you find him."

Mary Davis laughed out loud. "Yeah, you've been such a help already. You don't even have an investigator's license. Now get lost. Final warning."

"I'm—"

The door slammed in Colleen's face with such force that she reared back.

Back in the car, Colleen rolled down the window, lit up a Slim. She'd hit a wall with Mary Davis. Who had told her Colleen didn't have her PI license? That guy Frank? The one who'd just left? He looked like a cop. He hung out in a cop bar, with cop friends. He knew Jim Davis.

And then there was the resistance she got trying to obtain a copy of the homicide report. She thought she'd seen the clerk at 850 Bryant make a phone call when she asked for the report. She remembered talking to the desk officer in Homicide, too, room 561, asking about the case. She'd told him she didn't have a license. Could he have contacted someone? Frank?

She got out her file folder on the Copeland murder. In 1967, one of Margaret's friends from the crash pad she was staying at said Margaret had gone out for a walk late the night before she was found dead in Golden Gate Park. Colleen reread another article, which included a map showing where Margaret Copeland's body had been found near Stow Lake in Golden Gate Park.

She tossed her cigarette, started up the car. Fifteen minutes later, she parked at Stow Lake, a man-made affair with paddleboats for rent and an island in the center. It looked like something Pamela would've liked when she was a kid, before her dad had taken her innocence, and Colleen had taken his life. Colleen pushed the thought away. Thinking about her daughter only ended up bringing sorrow anymore. If Colleen could just reconnect with Pamela, perhaps they'd be able to move past that painful time. But Pamela didn't want to know.

At the boathouse she bought a box of Crackerjacks and asked the kid behind the counter if anybody ever heard anything new about the old Margaret Copeland murder that had happened nearby. The kid had a severe case of acne. He didn't know anything. He'd probably been in kindergarten at the time of the murder.

Colleen opened the Crackerjack box. "Is your boss around?"

"He comes in later."

She set a business card on the counter. "There might be some reward money for any new info on that murder."

Eating caramel corn and peanuts, Colleen hiked down to a grouping of shrubs and trees. Margaret's body had been found by a man walking his dog early in the morning when the dog had run into a secluded spot in the trees. The shape of a twisted tea tree, its thick branches sprawling low to the ground like giant limbs, matched the photograph in the article, although the tree had grown. This was the place. Colleen felt an involuntary shiver. The details of the murder in the newspapers were grisly, and this place had been hell on earth for Margaret Copeland.

Colleen stepped over and past branches, brushing foliage aside, and found herself in a damp green cavern. She stood there for a moment, a smell like eucalyptus filling her nostrils, and gazed around, looking around at the spiral of branches. She felt foolish when she eyed the ground, as if some evidence might still exist after all this time.

Eleven years ago, someone had dragged Margaret Copeland in here.

Beat her. Sexually assaulted her. Suffocated her with a plastic bag. Ended her life.

Colleen realized the half-finished box of Crackerjacks was dormant in her hand. She was no longer hungry.

She marched back up to the boathouse where there was a pay phone. She'd call the *Chronicle* again, see if Howard Broadmoor might have checked in. He'd written several articles on the Copeland murder over a decade ago. She tossed the Crackerjacks in a waste can, wiped her sticky fingers off on a napkin she had pocketed, and dialed the number.

"Your messages are still in Mr. Broadmoor's *In* box, ma'am," a nasal voice informed her.

Colleen thanked the woman, headed over to her Torino parked in the loop around the lake. She got in, rolled down the window. A couple with a young boy were out in a paddleboat. The man and boy were going at it furiously, grinning up a storm. Water thrashed and ducks quacked. Colleen was just about to light a cigarette when she saw an old gray-hair in a blue jumpsuit pushing a wire cart full of tools up to the door behind the snack shop.

She slid the cigarette back into the pack, got out of the car, and went back to the snack shop, where she caught him by surprise.

He started. He had fine slender features and crooked wire-frame glasses.

"Sorry," Colleen said. "You the manager?"

"Does it look like it?" He pulled a wrinkled handkerchief from his pocket and wiped his forehead.

"Maintenance?"

"You must be clairvoyant." He began to unload the cart, pulling a loop of green garden hose out and flinging it up against the building.

She gave him one of her business cards.

"Hayes Confidential?" he asked.

She introduced herself. "I'm working for the family of the girl who was murdered nearby in '67."

"You have a tight schedule," he said, getting out a pair of vise grips, fiddling with some kind of metal trap he'd picked up out of a cardboard box in the cart. It had a long metal contraption apparently made for snapping some small beast's back. "Only been what—eleven years?"

"I know," she said. "But here I am."

"And here you are." He gave her an appraising look before he wrestled with a spring that appeared to be seized up.

"I didn't get your name."

"That's because you haven't asked."

"Fine," she said with a smirk. "What's your name—if that's not too personal a question."

"Larry," he said.

"Great. Now that we've got that out of the way, Larry, were you working here back then by any chance?"

"Oh, sure," he said.

A flutter of enthusiasm lifted her spirits. "Remember anything?"

"Margaret Copeland was the girl's name. They never caught the guy. Later on, they said it might have been the Zodiac."

"You remember her name," Colleen said. "Margaret Copeland."

"You think I'm simple because I'm the maintenance man?"

"Now did I say that?"

"Not in so many words."

"I didn't even imply it, as a matter of fact."

"I guess not," he said, wrestling with the animal trap. It snapped shut and popped out of his fingers as he let it go. "God dammit!" The trap landed on the grass.

"So," she said. "What else do you remember about the murder?"

"No one wanted to listen to me then. Why now?"

"*Who* didn't want to listen?"

"SFPD."

Interesting. "Well, I certainly want to hear all about it."

He gave her the once-over. "You married?"

She attracted only the finest. "Dear man, I'm afraid so."

"Figures."

"You know, there is some reward money involved—not just for any old piece of gossip—but for information related to solving the case."

"How much?"

"That's a good question. The family hasn't told me yet."

"I see." He reached down to pick up the trap, started fussing with it again with his vise grips.

"You could lose a finger doing that."

"I know what I'm doing."

"Back to Margaret Copeland. You were working here."

"Right *here*." Larry pointed with his vise grips down at the ground. "Twenty-first of November, 1967."

He had a good memory. "What time?"

"Five in the morning."

"See anything?"

"I already told the cops. Nobody thought it was important."

She put her hands on her hips. *Learn to wait*, she told herself. "I'm listening," she said. "It's important to me."

"How important?"

"Well, we know I'm married," she said, going for the wad of cash in her pocket. She peeled off a twenty, held it up between index and forefinger. "But maybe this will ease your pain."

"That's it? Your reward?"

"This is just an incentive. To finish this conversation before the day's over." She reached over, tucked the bill into the top pocket of his jumpsuit.

He went back to fiddling with the trap.

"Green Ford Falcon," he said. "Parked right up there." He turned, nodded where her Torino was parked under a pine tree. "Only car up here at the time. Except for my truck."

Green Ford Falcon. "And how did that come about? You being here at five a.m.?"

"Came in early," he said. "Had to fix the generator before we opened up. Broke down the night before. Thought it was odd, that car, brand spanking new, parked up there like that. No one else seemed to think so though."

This was sounding like a decent lead. "Get a license plate?"

"No." He looked up.

She gave a sigh. "That's too bad."

"Because there wasn't one."

That sparked her interest. "You think someone might have taken the plates off?"

He squinted and pointed the vise grips at her. "I can see how your mind works. Suspicious. But maybe the car was new?"

"Do you recall seeing any paperwork taped to the inside of the windshield?"

"Didn't get that close. When I saw no one was in it, I went to work on the generator."

"When did the Falcon leave?"

"It was gone when I left. I didn't hear it leave. But I was futzing with the generator in the boathouse."

"And you told the police all this, right?"

"I did. And they couldn't have cared less. The guy I talked to didn't even write down a thing I said."

"You don't remember his name, do you?"

"Sure, I do."

She wondered if he was going to tell her. "Was it Jim Davis, by any chance?"

"No, Jim Davis was the one in charge of the case."

She nodded with approval. "You've got a mind like a trap, Larry. A lot better'n that thing that's about to snap your finger off."

He looked up again, smiling. "I do." He looked back down, focused on his task again. "Madrid was the cop's name," he said. "Like the city."

"It was on his name plaque?"

"You got it. 'F. Madrid.'"

"Was his first name Frank?"

He shrugged.

"You've been a big help, Larry." She got out her penny notebook and a ballpoint pen. "Let's stay in touch."

"How come you don't wear a wedding ring?"

* * *

For whatever reason, most likely because she was feeling encouraged, Colleen drove over to Mission Street to The Manor coffee shop. Maybe she'd get lucky. Maybe Jim Davis had forgotten what day it was, and was going to show up now, and bring the report, and tell her everything she needed to know, including the killer's name and address.

She ordered a cup of coffee and changed a dollar in dimes for the pay phone. She dialed the Department of Motor Vehicles and, after being transferred several times, learned what she needed in order to do a vehicle search. She jotted it down in her notebook.

Then she dialed SFPD Human Resources and said she was calling from Wells Fargo Bank, checking a job reference in regard to a home loan application for an Officer F. Madrid.

"Sergeant Frank Madrid retired from the force four years ago," the woman informed her.

Colleen would bet that Frank Madrid was the Frank in Dizzy's the day she went to meet Jim Davis. The same Frank that had left the Davis house earlier.

"I'm sorry," Colleen said. "Now that you say that, I do see that information right here on this application. You don't have a forwarding address, do you?"

"He didn't put his address on the application?"

"No."

"I'm going to need you to talk to my supervisor," the woman said with an air of suspicion.

"I'll call back. Thanks so much." She hung up, went back to her seat at the busy counter, loaded up her weak coffee with sugar and half-and-half. It was easy to nurse because it still wasn't very good. She fought having a cigarette to go with it. She was just getting up the courage to go back to Jim Davis's house when the Chinese waitress in the pink dress and white socks reached up and turned up the volume on the television that had switched away from *Hollywood Squares* to a local news update.

"We interrupt this broadcast for late-breaking news: a former SFPD detective's body has been found down at Fort Funston."

Colleen looked up at the TV. A pretty young woman with a dark feather-cut spoke into a microphone in front of the entrance of some kind of concrete bunker, presumably down at the beach. There were quite a few people in and around a wide tunnel that led to a sandy bluff beyond.

"The World War II gun emplacement at Fort Funston is a known hangout for San Francisco's growing transient population. It was here this morning that the body was found. The name is not being released at this time, pending notification of kin. Police are asking anyone who has any information to contact them. More news as it comes in."

Excited chatter erupted around the coffee shop. Speculation began. Transients. Suicide. Drugs. Double-cross. Gangs.

Colleen found that her coffee cup had been half raised to her lips, frozen in midair for a good thirty seconds. Although the detective wasn't named, she knew who it had to be.

She set the cup down on its saucer, paid, left a fifty-cent tip, and went out to her car, bracing herself for another face-to-face with Mary Davis.

She drove down Mission, up Persia, took a left on Paris. Numerous vehicles were parked in and around Jim Davis's house, including two SFPD black-and-whites, one in the middle of the street. Not the time to drop by.

But it confirmed her suspicion about who'd been found down at Fort Funston.

Not that there'd been much doubt to begin with.

A tidal wave of guilt flowed through her, knowing she might well have had a hand in Jim Davis's demise. She had planned to meet him regarding a case that SFPD apparently didn't want brought to light. And now he was dead.

Dead.

She drove by the house slowly, then headed back down Mission, where she managed to find a parking spot not far from Dizzy's. A black-and-white was double parked outside the bar. Colleen got out of the car and headed for the bar. She knew she wouldn't be welcome but she had to know what the hell had happened to Jim Davis.

CHAPTER SEVENTEEN

Dizzy's was two deep at the bar with patrons commiserating the death of Jim Davis. More than a few wore SFPD uniforms, guns on hips, glasses of beer or cocktails in their hands. Others watched a blurry seventeen-inch television over the bar where the newswoman with the dark feather-cut spoke about the body found at Fort Funston in a solemn tone. The backdrop behind her was the same gun emplacement, but with the day's shadows waning over it as rain took hold again.

"Still no leads on the tragic death of former SF cop Jim Davis," she said.

Now he had a name. Colleen felt sickened. She knew she had helped bring about this man's death. She took a deep breath, working to calm her nerves.

Now she had to see this thing through. It wasn't just about Margaret Copeland anymore.

On the corner stool, where he had been the day Colleen first entered, sat the big man—Frank Madrid she believed his name was—with the hard gut and drinker's nose. Today he wore a faded purple T-shirt that read "Riordan Crusaders" in cracked yellow letters and the same Giants ball cap she had seen him in earlier when he left Jim Davis's house and got into a blue Chevy C10. He eyed Colleen standing by the door, picked up a burning cigarette from the ashtray in front of him on the bar, took a puff, snapped the ash off, set it back down in the ashtray, not once taking his eyes off of her.

She was unwelcome, and it was more than invading an impromptu private wake. She walked over to the unoccupied section of the bar next to the big man on the stool, feeling his hard stare on her as she tried to get the server's attention. The bartender in the gray perm was busy pouring shots, drawing foamy beers and sliding them over the wet bar. Death was good for business. Colleen caught the woman's eye and she gave Colleen a nod. She'd be over in a sec.

"What the hell do you think you're doing here?" the big guy muttered.

"It's after five, right?" she said, turning to meet his gaze. She nodded at his near empty beer mug. "You ready for another?"

He shook his head angrily as he crossed his big arms. "Not if *you're* buying."

"That's funny. The other day you were looking at me like I was a pastrami sandwich."

"Don't flatter yourself."

The bartender came over and put her plump hands on the bar in front of Colleen. "What'll it be?"

"No, Brenda," the big guy said. "Not her."

The bartender looked over the big guy with a squint. "Say what, Frank?"

"*Not her*, I said."

"Is that so? Last time I checked, this was *my* bar."

Frank flicked his chin at Colleen while he swiveled on his stool. "She's the one who was in here the other day, giving Jim a hard time."

Brenda turned back to Colleen, blinked as she took her in. "So she was. I remember you now. Jim stormed out of here after talking to you. You're some kind of bill collector. You got a heck of a nerve, coming in here today, of all days—the day they found him."

"I'm very sorry about your friend." Colleen pulled one of her business cards from the breast pocket of her leather jacket, laid it on the bar. "I'm not a bill collector. I'm a private investigator."

"Now she's a private investigator," Frank said, grimacing, arms locked over his chest. "Who's she gonna be tomorrow? Loni Anderson?"

Hands still on the bar, Brenda frowned at Colleen. "Get lost." She pushed herself up and went down to the other end of the bar to take an order.

Colleen got out her pack of Virginia Slims, slid one in her mouth. She patted her pockets.

"Got a light, Frank?" she said.

"You know I don't."

She reached over, took the book of Dizzy's bar matches from in front of his ashtray, meeting his gaze, opened the book, pulled a paper match. Out of the corner of her eye, she could see Brenda talking to a couple of uniforms. Heads kept turning in her direction.

"That wouldn't be Frank Madrid, would it?" Colleen said, striking the match. It flared, sending a stink of phosphorus up her nose as she lit her cigarette.

"You are one nosy bitch."

"And you used to work with Jim Davis, right?" She blew the match out, reached over, tossed it in his ashtray.

He grabbed her wrist, lowered his melon head. "You know what happens to nosy bitches in my part of town?"

Colleen eyed his big mitt on her wrist, then his face. She lowered her voice to a whisper. "You know what I find strange, Frank? That you don't want to talk to me. Why is that? If Jim was your friend, why wouldn't you? Maybe I know something. Now let go."

Their eyes locked.

"*Now*," she said again.

Frank flung her wrist loose.

Two men came over. One was a young SFPD officer with a blond buzz cut and the other man a shaggy-haired guy about forty in a plaid shirt hanging out over his work pants.

"What's the problem here, Frank?" the cop said, eyeing Colleen.

"Nothing," Frank said. He thumped the bar with his fist. "Hey, Brenda. What do I got to do to get another drink? Throw you a fuck? Okay—if I have to." He laughed at his own joke.

The young cop came around Frank and up to Colleen. "I'm sorry you're getting this kind of treatment, but you better leave. People are upset about Jim."

"Me, too," she said. "Did you know him?"

"Don't be such a pussy, Rick," Frank said to the cop. "What the fuck would your old man say?"

Rick shook his head, spoke to Colleen. "Take a hint—for your own sake. And don't come back."

She wasn't going to get any joy here. Not today. But she knew enough to know something was wrong.

"I'm sorry about your friend," she said, stubbing out her cigarette in Frank's ashtray, letting it smolder. "I really am."

She left the bar, the smoke wafting out after her. It had started to drizzle.

CHAPTER EIGHTEEN

Back at H&M Paint, Colleen donned her poncho, grabbed her five-cell flashlight, and did the rounds as rain fell into darkness. Nothing new. No sign of activity at the delivery truck.

She finished off her patrol by walking through the plant downstairs, stepping around growing puddles, past the piles of rubble and pallets of paint that would never wind up on any walls.

Wondering how she was going to make contact with Mary Davis again.

Upstairs she heated a can of soup and listened to the local news on KCBS.

"SFPD have extended their investigation of the death of retired detective Jim Davis, whose body was found down at Fort Funston early this morning, to Golden Gate Park. They are anxious to talk to anyone who has knowledge of any transients who might've been seen in that area. In other news, the Giants lost 3-0 to the Padres."

Colleen took her transistor radio and her cup of soup out to the desk where she sat down and put her feet up. The sky over the East Bay was dark tonight, full of rain.

Transients beating up a retired policeman who spent his day warming a barstool at Dizzy's. It didn't make a whole lot of sense. Especially since Jim Davis was supposed to meet her at The Manor coffee shop, with a copy of the Margaret Copeland report, and collect two thousand bucks, money she suspected he surely could have used. How did he wind up down at the beach? Was he dumped there? By who? Transients, as everyone liked to call them, didn't own cars to haul people around in. Hard to think that Jim Davis just waltzed down to Ocean Beach in this weather. When Colleen left him, he was toasted, but it was the world-weary inebriation of a functioning alcoholic, not the wild bullet drunkenness of a spree drinker.

The phone on her desk rang, loud and clattering, making her jump. She answered it.

"I'm sure you've seen the news," Christian Newell said.

"Transients," she said in a dry tone.

"Seem funny to you, too?"

"Hilarious."

"So what's the next step?"

"Find a way back to Mary Davis." Colleen drank some soup. "Might have to wait a day or two, though. I just stopped by Jim Davis's former watering hole and was unceremoniously shown the door by his cop friends."

"That's it?"

She wasn't going to mention Frank Madrid yet. He was still a working hypothesis.

"I was nosing around down at Stow Lake earlier and might have found something—maybe."

"Now that sounds interesting." It was clear Christian was waiting for more information. When it didn't come, he said: "And?"

A green Ford Falcon, but again she kept it to herself. "At this point, nothing for public consumption."

"I'm not the public," he said. "I'm the person who hired you."

"I don't want you running off to Mr. Copeland with every little scrap. He doesn't need to get his hopes up."

"That's not your concern."

"Believe me, Christian. When something solid comes up, you'll be the first to know."

"I better be."

She suppressed a sigh. "Talk to you tomorrow."

"Call me this time."

"Right." She hung up and crushed out her cigarette before it was half finished. At close to forty cents a pack, smoking was getting to be an expensive habit.

* * *

Later that night, the gate buzzer went off.

Colleen put down her paperback, got up, hit the intercom button. "Security."

"Why, hello, security," a woman said in a smoky voice.

"Alexandra Copeland," Colleen said, sitting up. "What can I do for you?"

"We'll see," she said. "And call me Alex."

"Sure thing."

"How do I get into Fort Knox here?"

"I'll buzz you in. Stairwell on the right. Watch your step—it gets slippery. And make sure the gate is shut behind you, please." Colleen hit the buzzer, stood up. She ducked back into her windowless room, ran a brush through her hair.

Alex wore black leather slacks, pumps to match, and a motorcycle jacket tailored at the waist with a high collar with long points. The jacket was unzipped to a risqué level, revealing eye-catching décolletage. From what Colleen could tell, Alex wasn't wearing much under the jacket, if anything. The ambient light from the desk lamp lit up her pale skin and the coronet of her fluffy, styled blond hair. She looked like a punk Marlene Dietrich. Alex was an eyeful, no matter who was doing the looking.

"I love what you've done with the place," Alex said, looking around the office, holding her cigarette up fashion model style.

"My decorator wanted to try something different," Colleen said.

"You'll have to give me his number." Alex stepped over to the desk to tap ash out in an ashtray. She exuded a soft fragrance of something that cost several hundred dollars a bottle as she gazed down at the cover of the paperback Colleen was reading.

"Patricia Highsmith," she said. "Interesting."

"What can I do for you, Alex?"

"Got anything to drink?"

"Fresh ground coffee."

"Ah, yes," Alex said, alluding to Colleen's parole. Colleen knew the family had checked her out thoroughly. "Let's go out and get one. I'm gasping."

Colleen wondered what Alex was after. She compared her own blue jeans, cowboy boots, and blue Oxford shirt to Alex's ensemble. "Can I have five minutes to change?"

"Don't take too long." Alex flicked more ash into the ashtray. "I'll wait outside in the car."

* * *

"Want to trade cars?" Colleen said as she sank into the plush leather passenger seat of Alex Copeland's white Jaguar XJ6. She had changed into a crisp white blouse, a pair of new bell-bottom jeans and burgundy platform shoes, along with her trusty brown leather jacket that went with everything. To top it off, she wore her silver magpie earrings. Pamela's earrings.

Alex gave her a sly grin as she slipped the key into the ignition. Jazz oozed from the 8-Track.

"'So What,'" Colleen said.

"Sorry?" Alex said, turning to look at her quizzically.

"The song," Colleen said, nodding at the player under the polished wood dash. "Miles Davis. 'So What.'"

"Oh." Alex fired up the Jag. It responded with a throaty rumble. "I'm a little slow."

"Maybe just distracted."

Alex drove to the end of the street, spinning a tight 180, yielding a hint of squeal. The East Bay lit up as they turned around, then shot back past the paint factory along the water into the warehouse district.

"Why would I be distracted?" Alex said as she turned onto Third Street. The suggestion was that it might be Colleen doing the distracting. Colleen slipped her hands in the pockets of her jacket and sat back.

"Your father's dying," she said. "That would affect just about anybody."

"You don't know my father."

"No, I don't. But I know he hasn't got much time left. I'm sure that's hard."

"Not for me," Alex said coolly. "I was never his favorite. She was taken from him long ago."

"Maybe that makes it harder," Colleen said.

"All I care about is making sure my name is spelled correctly on the will."

They picked up speed, the warehouses whipping by.

* * *

The barman's bare ass showed in his leather chaps as he turned around to make change at the cash register. Alex passed a dripping gin and tonic to Colleen, the two of them packed in tight at the bar. The DJ was spinning Romeo Void's "Never Say Never." Clubbers spilled off the little dance floor in the corner of the back room and overflowed into the bar. Women outnumbered men a good three to one, but the men still didn't seem too interested. It was a same-gender dance scene.

"What do you think?" Alex shouted over the music, taking a slug from a long-neck beer.

"Beats the hell out of the last place I went to," Colleen said, sipping her drink. Ice cold.

"Where was that?"

"Some lovely little hideaway called Dizzy's."

A woman screamed and the two of them were mashed up against the bar momentarily by a young woman wearing a garbage bag as a dress and snakeskin platform boots. She had heavy makeup and hair by Crayola, favoring the purple and black crayons, curled in front of her face in what must've taken her, or her hairdresser, hours. But she was lithe and young and carried it off. Colleen lifted her drink up, to keep it from spilling, as did Alex.

The girl stared into Colleen's eyes with Dracula-grade mascara and blood-red lips.

"Want to dance?"

"It's my night off," Colleen shouted back.

"You'd never call me anyway," she yelled, gyrating back into the crowd, bouncing like a wave to the thump-thump-thump of the drums.

"Is she right?" Alex said in Colleen's ear in a voice fast growing hoarse.

"About what?"

"You know what," Alex said, crinkling her eyes. "Calling her."

Colleen turned her head. Alex's pretty face was inches away. She gave Colleen a slow wink.

Colleen went back to her G and T.

"I need something stiff to go with this," Alex said, turning to the bar now, flagging down the barman with the bare butt. He came up, leather military cap dripping with chains along the brim. "Tequila. Straight up." She turned back to Colleen. "Join me?"

Colleen held up her half-finished cocktail and shook her head *no*.

The shot of tequila was gone in one gulp. Alex slammed the shot glass on the bar. "Hit me again," she shouted at the bartender, and gave Colleen a peek-a-boo look. "You sure about that slammer, Security?"

"Better not," Colleen said. "I think I might be driving."

"You wish."

"Are you sure you can get back to Half Moon Bay after a couple of those?"

"The car knows the way," Alex said, then leaned in so close her lips touched Colleen's ear. They were soft and wet and hot, sending a shiver down Colleen's back. "Besides," Alex whispered, "I could always crash at your place."

Colleen was being played. But when you'd spent a decade on your own, within gray walls, keeping your thoughts and feelings locked down for self-preservation, a creature that looked and sounded and smelled like Alex Copeland, breathing in your ear, only made your heart run a little faster.

Colleen hadn't slept with anyone for close to a year.

Alex downed another shot of tequila.

"Come on," she said, taking Colleen's hand. "Dance with me."

"No," Colleen said, pulling away.

Alex reared back, gave her a look.

"Why not?"

"Because that's not what this is about."

"No?" Alex cocked her head sideways. "Why did you get all dolled up, then?"

"Because you look like a million bucks, and I didn't want to look like your auto mechanic."

"That would have been fine with me. I like cars."

"You can afford to."

Alex leaned back against the bar, elbows on it, chest out. "So what *is* this about?"

"You tell me," Colleen said, drinking. "You're the one who stopped by to check up on me."

"Check up on you?" Alex sounded just a little bit slurry as her voice rose. "What do I need to do that for? I've got Christian for that."

"Sure," Colleen said, setting her glass on the bar. "But he already called and I told him I was working on something I wasn't ready to discuss yet. And then he gave the family his update." She took a sip and eyed Alex directly. "But you want to know more. I don't blame you. I would, too. But I don't want everyone going off on a wild goose chase. Emotionally."

"An emotional wild goose chase?" Alex frowned. "Doesn't sound like me at all."

"Pretend all you want," Colleen said. "But death is hard. First your sister, then your mother, soon your father. You love that old guy, even if you are number two. I saw it when he was gasping for air. You were there for him, even if you were cool about it."

A brief look of hurt crossed Alex's face before she resumed her hard stare. "Think you might have read me wrong, girlfriend. My biggest worry is how I'm going to spend all his money."

"You're already doing a pretty good job of that," Colleen said. "No, it's because you want some peace between the two of you before he goes. And that means finding out what happened to Margaret."

"God, you're boringly down to earth. Doesn't it get a little tiring?"

"Not as tiring as playing games."

"Games."

"Kind of like the one you're playing now, pretending to be some spoiled brat with too much money. Yeah, you do a pretty good rendition—but it's not you. Not really. You don't want to get hurt again. Why should you? Your father already did that in spades. Maybe your mother, too—I don't know. Well, join the club. Anyone I ever got remotely close to only let me down. Sometimes my best days are when I don't have to talk to another human being. But your secret's safe with me." She smiled.

Once again, Alex's face softened. "An expert." She shook her head. "For the record, Christian doesn't tell me squat. I'm out of the loop. I have to find out what's going on by eavesdropping. Yeah, I heard him call Father, tell him how you had some information you couldn't divulge yet. No one even bothers to tell me what's going on. And she was *my* sister."

"I'm doing everything I can to find out what happened to Margaret. But I need to work my own way, not go off on a tangent on things that haven't been substantiated. I don't want you to get your hopes up."

Alex blinked as she took that in.

Colleen continued: "And when I do find something, you'll be first to know. In fact, I'm going to call *you* with my daily updates from now on. You can break the news to Christian." Colleen drained her drink. "How's that?"

Alex clinked her beer bottle against Colleen's glass. "Deal," she said softly, inaudible over the music. But Colleen could read her lips. And see that she meant it.

"Come on," Colleen said, setting her glass on the bar. "Let's get you home." She put her hand out. "Car keys."

Alex slid her hand into the pocket of her leather jacket, pulled out keys on a leather key ring, holding them up between thumb and forefinger. "Has anyone ever told you you're a wet blanket?"

"Only when I look into the mirror."

They headed back to H&M Paint, Colleen at the wheel. She took surface streets because she wanted to talk to Alex, who had a cigarette going, the open passenger window pulling the smoke out as they drove. Cool night air between rain showers swirled around the back seat, mixing with smoke as Alex exhaled.

"Tell me about Margaret," Colleen said.

"What's to tell?" Alex said, flicking ash out the window. "The perfect student. Skilled equestrian. Social butterfly. You name it."

"Until the summer of sixty-seven," Colleen said.

"Oh, yeah." Alex took a light puff. "Margaret derailed then. But she had plenty of company. Lot of nice kids came up to the city to play vagabond. Me—I'm only good for an evening at a time." She turned and smiled at Colleen. "I don't have the *cajones* she had."

"You have the smarts to stay alive," Colleen said. "Don't underestimate that little talent."

Alex smoked and shrugged. "Yay for me."

"Doesn't anybody know where Margaret was staying at the time she was killed?"

Alex took a puff and shook her head. "She came up to SF with a girlfriend early in the summer. Just turned eighteen. But they went separate ways. Father tried to keep track of her. Even though she was close, she was far away. The last we heard, she was staying at some squat on Frederick Street in the Haight. That was around July? Maybe August. All of my parents' efforts to lure Margaret back home came to zip. The harder they tried, the more she went off the deep end. Smoke. Pills. Acid. Whatever was in fashion. And then Mother decided, in her infinite wisdom, that we were not to contact her anymore. Not only that, Margaret wasn't welcome back home. Ever. The psychology being that Margaret would have to work for it. Be *accepted* back into the family."

"And that went over like a lead balloon."

"Mother's car spun out on Highway 1 less than a year after Margaret was murdered. Hopped a guardrail. She was thrown clear, but it was a long way down to the rocks. So I guess you could say she and Margaret were reunited, after all."

Colleen shook away the image. "I'm so sorry, Alex."

"Don't be. It's just a sick joke that I'm the only Copeland woman left standing. The one least deserving."

"Not from where I sit." But now she saw how important it was for Alex to learn what happened to Margaret. Come to terms with it so she could move on. "How old were you when Margaret was killed?"

"Fifteen. Three years younger than her. But I thought Margaret was about as cool as it got. And once she started playing 'wild child,' well, now I had a role model to live up to if I wanted to attract the old man's attention. Anything Margaret could do, I could do, too. That first weekend she took off, I stayed out all night for the first time. Wound up with some black dude at Hunters Point. I remember him calling the house, asking for me. Mother hit the roof! That was the reason Mother banished Margaret in the end. The more Margaret carried on, the more I copied her. Mother and Father wanted to nip me in the bud. But I had already started to blossom."

"What was the address on Frederick Street? Where Margaret lived?"

"Four one three Frederick was what we heard. But we were never sure. The police could never find anyone there who admitted to knowing Margaret."

"Did you have any kind of connection with Margaret?" Colleen asked. "Anything? Something your parents weren't privy to?"

Alex looked over for a moment, squinting as she took a puff off of her cigarette.

"It would be just between you and me," Colleen said. "It's important that I know all there is."

"She used to call me from time to time," Alex said. "Usually in the afternoon. When I got home from school and Father wasn't home."

"What would you talk about?"

"Nothing really. Never anything about herself. She would just ask how school was going, whether I was doing my homework. I wasn't. But I didn't tell her that. That's not what she wanted to hear."

"Do you know if she met anyone? Had anyone special in her life? A boyfriend?"

Alex screwed up her face in thought. Shook her head.

"You sure, Alex?"

Alex looked at her. "Well, she never said anything, but toward the end, it seemed like she was . . . I don't know."

"Her tone changed?"

"That's it—her tone changed. She was softer somehow. Dreamy almost."

A woman in love? Colleen wondered. "You think she met someone?"

"Maybe. She was more . . . hopeful. But then, right before she died, she seemed sad. Sad and angry. Like something had gone wrong."

Not much to go on. "It sounds like she was ruining her bad girl image with her phone calls."

"Yeah." Alex sipped on her cigarette and the open window sucked smoke from her lips as she exhaled. "But I loved it when she called. I never told Mother or Father. It was my thing. *Mine*."

Colleen saw a young girl, hurt, waiting for her parents' love. She turned off on Yosemite, drove down the street, pulled the Jag in front of H&M Paint.

They sat there, the engine throbbing in idle, looking at each other.

"You think of anything else," Colleen said, "please let me know."

Alex nodded.

Colleen cleared her throat. "What happened to Margaret wasn't your fault."

Alex frowned. "That's what I tell myself, but if I'd been a little more grown up, instead of acting out, things might've been different. I could have told my parents she was calling. Maybe I could have even got her to come back. But no, I was living vicariously through Margaret. And Margaret was still getting all the attention."

"Margaret made her own choices," Colleen said, hands on the wheel. "Don't let her make yours."

Alex tossed her cigarette out the window, leaned over, brushed Colleen's hair out of her face where it had fallen over her eye. "God, you've got pretty hair. And I bet all you use is some shampoo from the drugstore."

Alex's hand felt soft and warm on Colleen's cheek. "Whatever Safeway has on sale," she said. Gently, she took Alex's hand away. She took a breath.

"When was the last time you spoke to Margaret?" she asked.

Alex gave a heavy sigh, looked away.

"Alex," Colleen said, "I'm not judging you. It might help me find who killed her."

"She called me a couple nights before," Alex said, looking up, "before she . . ." It seemed Alex couldn't finish her sentence. "Out of her head on something. But coherent, too—you know what I mean?"

"A 'fleeting moment of clarity' is what they call it," Colleen said.

"Yeah."

"What did she say?"

"She wanted to come home," Alex said, looking at her nails, painted pearl white. "She said she had done something foolish, and that she had had enough."

"And what did you say?"

"I told her Mother and Father weren't home," Alex said, looking out the window. "They were downstairs, watching TV." She looked down at her hands, which were clenched together now. "She said she would try to call again in a day or so. Three days later they found her . . . in Golden Gate Park." Alex looked down. "I've never told anyone else that."

"You were upset. You'd been upstaged once too often. Didn't want it to happen again."

"Yeah," Alex said with a sigh. She looked up. "Some fucking sister I turned out to be. I could have saved her."

Colleen let Alex's confession sink in, wondering what to say. Sometimes, the best thing to say was absolutely nothing.

"So *now* what do you think of me?" Alex asked.

Colleen turned. Alex's eyes glistened. "You were fifteen, Alex. *Maybe* you could have prevented Margaret from making a terrible decision. I'm putting my money on *probably* not. It was Margaret's choice. To leave home. To go out that night. To make a lot of bad choices. But they were her decisions to make. Not yours."

Alex blinked, gave a tiny frown. "Thanks."

"You bet."

There was a pause.

"So I guess there's no extra room on that cot of yours, after all?"

Colleen swallowed, blushing. "This is about finding your sister's killer, Alex. Nothing else."

Alex's hand rested on Colleen's thigh, warm and soft. "You sure about that, Security? Because I get the distinct feeling you could be talked out of it."

Colleen took a breath, lifted Alex's hand off her leg, gave it a friendly squeeze. "Don't complicate things."

Alex sighed, sat up. "Once again, Margaret gets everybody's attention."

"Sure you're okay to drive?"

"Are you kidding? Your little heart-to-heart chats could bring anybody down."

"It's important to be good at something."

Colleen got out of the Jag, stood on the wet asphalt, the sky threatening more rain. Alex hopped out, came trotting around in her leather pants and million-dollar biker garb, and leaned over before she got in and pecked Colleen on the cheek. Colleen's head hummed with excitement and confusion. Whatever Alex was, she couldn't become a distraction.

Then Alex climbed into the driver seat, pulled it forward, waved, and set off at about ninety miles an hour, rubber squealing.

Colleen watched the sleek white car disappear.

She let herself in through the front gate.

Then Colleen heard a sound—something, banging—coming from the plant.

She stopped, listened.

Downstairs.

Little quills of anxiety sprang up her back.

CHAPTER NINETEEN

Colleen entered the plant quietly, and just as quietly, pulled the gate shut behind her. The debris-strewn lot resembled a lunar landscape in the moonlight.

She stopped, cocked an ear.

Voices. Echoing from inside the warehouse.

She stepped through bricks and rubble carefully in her new platform shoes, over to one of the big industrial windows, where she rubbed the heel of a fist in the grime coating a pane. Peered through.

There, in the dimness, the moving beam of a flashlight.

Run upstairs, call the police? How long would that take? Maybe it was just some punks, screwing around.

The beam of light shifted, followed by a scrape of wood. A pallet. A man speaking: *Put it over there.* He sounded older, not like a teenager.

She'd check things out discreetly, call the cops if need be. She took a deep breath and headed to the other side of the plant, the old employee's entrance, opposite the side to the stairs to the office. She stopped at a pile of waste, found a piece of rebar about a foot and a half long. More banging echoed from inside the building, people dragging stuff, the sound booming off the high corrugated-metal roof.

At the side entrance, rebar in hand, she stood, her limbs vibrating. *Calm down.* The door, normally locked, was open, the window broken. She turned back to the street, eyed the fence. The corner was obscured by a dumpster on the street. They had gotten in somehow.

She tiptoed into the plant amidst the clanging. Her eyes adjusted: two shadows moving behind a bouncing flashlight, not twenty feet from the 55-gallon drums full of acetone.

Her nerves shot into overdrive.

Two men. Throwing a wooden pallet onto a disordered stack. One guy was young, judging by his build and lithe movements, wearing a dark hooded sweatshirt. The other, holding the flashlight, was bulkier, a bandanna tied around his face bandit style. She didn't recognize either of them. The young man held up an oblong container and squirted liquid onto the makeshift pyre.

Barbecue starter.

"You can cut that out right now," Colleen said. "The cops are on their way."

Both men spun toward her.

"See those drums behind you?" she said. "Acetone. How bad do you want to be blown sky high?"

"She's bluffing," the big guy said.

"It's a paint plant, Einstein," Colleen said.

"Fuck you, bitch," the kid in the hoodie said, draining the bottle, tossing it on the pile as well. It clanked, bounced off somewhere.

"You need to mind your own business," the big guy said to her. He pulled something out of his jacket. Even in the shadows there was no mistaking the outline of the pistol. Guns had that kind of energy. He pointed it at Colleen. Her heart pounded as she ducked behind a vertical steel support beam. The flashlight beam swept over the big empty space, over wreckage of machinery, without catching her.

The big guy said to the kid: "Just do it."

She craned her neck around the post and saw the kid pull something from the front pocket of his sweatshirt. A book of matches. He yanked a match and, after a couple of dry scratches, got it lit, setting fire to the whole book. The flame danced in his hand.

"Hurry up," the big guy said to the kid. "We got to get out of here."

The book of burning matches floated onto the stack of soaked pallets. A daunting *woof* preceded blinding blue and orange flames that lit up the center of the warehouse, filling Colleen with adrenaline.

"Let's go!" the big guy yelled. The two men turned, ran in her direction, heading for the door. Colleen waited, grimacing as flames leapt hungrily in the darkness. The two men drew closer, the kid in front.

She came out swinging the rebar.

The kid in the hoodie dodged out of the way. Swearing up a storm, he dashed for the exit. Colleen swiveled round just in time to see the pear-shaped man coming toward her, gun up. She reminded herself how hard it was to hit anything with a pistol, even in broad daylight, let alone the dark, especially while running, under the threat of a counterattack. Heart thudding, she waited until he got closer.

He fired.

The shot ricocheted, echoing through the plant, stretching her nerve endings tight. She came at him, catching him by surprise, exactly what she wanted. Overweight and off balance, he skidded, crab-like. She caught his teeth with the rebar. An ugly crack traveled from his jaw down the steel rod into her arm.

"*Motherfuck!*" he grunted, a hand shooting up to his face. The gun went off again, wild and deafening up close, the report bouncing off the rafters. She ducked back, lunged in again, swiped him one more time, not a direct hit like before, but enough to knock the gun out of his hand. He snorted as the gun smacked the floor and disappeared into shadows.

Flames roared, licking up the pallets.

The young guy was long gone. The big guy staggered toward the doorway, one hand gripping his face.

She'd have to let them go. The fire had to be put out. Before the plant went up.

Flames panted, illuminating the darkness with wild shifting light. She tossed the rebar. It clanged off across the floor.

On the metal column she wrestled a dust-caked fire extinguisher free and lugged it over to the blaze. The pile of pallets was engulfed by fire, flames edging closer to the drums of acetone. No more than ten feet away.

Her pulse racing, she approached the fire. A wall of heat warmed her face. All her body wanted to do was flee. She sucked in a smoky breath and pulled the pin, squeezed the handle.

A blast of chemicals hissed, white fog subduing the monster briefly. But within no time the canister was empty and the flames crept back up to their former height, crackling with intensity. Tossing the empty extinguisher aside with a crash, Colleen hurried back to the former break room, trying to clear her thoughts. There was another extinguisher by the door. She checked them on her rounds. She found it, wrenched it off.

"What's going on here?" a voice yelled in Spanish.

At the doorway. Ramon. *Thank God.*

When he saw the flames, he came running into the warehouse. "I saw two guys running away."

"There's another extinguisher," she shouted in Spanish. "By the men's lockers. Hurry."

"Got it!"

She ran back to the roaring fire, pulled the pin, and used steady side-to-side strokes, working the base of the fire this time. Behind her, she heard Ramon. A pin popped and then he stood alongside her, bathing the blaze with retardant as well. She stopped shooting for a moment, ducked behind him, moved over, blocking the path to the drums. She resumed her attack. The burning pallets began to crackle and die.

"I'm almost out," Ramon said. "We'll need another one."

"Two, just to be sure," she said. But they had this thing on the run. She searched her mind for the location of the remaining extinguishers.

CHAPTER TWENTY

Colleen pushed the cyclone fence gates shut after the last SFFD engine backed out, the fire marshal's red Crown Victoria following it. Morning light struggled to break through the rain gray sky. Threading the chains back through the gates, she padlocked them, then walked over to reexamine the corner of the property by the street. A good-sized flap had been cut, big enough for a fat man to get through. A mix of emotions swirled through her—a little apprehension, a lot of exhaustion, but most of all, anger.

She had called SFPD, figuring she pretty much had to. She would also need reports for the building's owners, for insurance purposes. When SFPD arrived, they insisted on calling the fire department, since this was arson. The firefighters had broken a window to get their equipment into the building and hosed down the offending area to a fare-thee-well, leaving a pond of ashy muck that covered most of the factory floor.

She'd caught the fire early. And, thankfully, Ramon had been there to help put it out. But a burnt wet stench hung in the air.

The police officers who arrived were less than courteous as they logged Colleen's statement.

"How did you manage to put a fire like that out by yourself?" A serious young female officer with a blond ponytail and a squarish jaw had her pen posed over a notebook while her partner strolled around the sodden plant, hands in his pockets.

"I was lucky enough to catch them in the act," Colleen said.

"Seems so," her partner said, tapping an empty fire extinguisher with his toe. "I count six empty extinguishers."

Six included the dud that hadn't fired. But Colleen knew what they were thinking. She wouldn't be the first security guard to start a fire, then put it out, saving the day, and providing a little job security. But she wasn't about to tell them about Ramon. The last thing an illegal needed was attention from the police.

"Did you get my description of the two arsonists?" she said.

The blond cop flipped a page, checked her notes. "Right here." She looked Colleen in the face. "And you have no idea who the two men were?" She didn't attempt to mask her suspicion.

Colleen thought about telling her that she'd bet everything she had that at least one was a cop, or an ex-cop. But the tone of the woman's voice and the fact that she was SFPD prevented her.

She shook her head.

"No idea at all?" the woman asked.

"Just the way I described them."

"And you didn't see them getting away?"

"They ran out that door," Colleen said, nodding at the door with the broken glass. "I was kind of busy putting the fire out to chase them down. I did clock one with a piece of rebar."

The officer checked her notes. "Do you have any enemies?"

Colleen wasn't about to say. Not yet.

She watched the police leave, knowing they didn't quite believe her.

Ramon told her that he had seen the heavy man exiting the hole in the fence to a pickup truck, where a driver had pulled up and the young guy was getting in. The truck took off as the fat guy scrambled to get in.

"What kind of truck?" Colleen asked, an idea of one already forming in her mind. But she didn't want to put suggestions into Ramon's head.

A Chevy C10.

Her nerves tightened.

"A C10," Colleen repeated. "You're sure of that, Ramon?"

"*Sí.*"

"How can you be? It was dark at the time."

"It's the best truck you can buy. If had a million dollars—and a green card—I'd buy a Chevy C10."

"And what color was this one?"

Ramon shrugged his broad shoulders as he thought. "Dark blue or black—something like that."

"License plate?"

He shook his head no. "I only just saw the side of the truck from where I was. Before I came in to help you."

"Get a look at the driver?"

Ramon blinked his thick lashes in thought. Again, he shook his head. "A big man in a baseball cap."

She thought of the truck she had seen parked outside Jim Davis's house. And the driver. There was more than one dark Chevy C10 in San Francisco—and more than one driver in a ball cap. But she didn't need any more to know who'd tried to burn the plant down. And scare her off.

Frank Madrid. The ex-cop who'd taken the initial report on Margaret Copeland—according to Larry the maintenance man at Stow Lake. The same one giving her grief at Dizzy's, telling her to "mind her own business."

Did Frank Madrid have something to do with Jim Davis's disappearance? She'd need proof—absolute proof—before she fingered SFPD.

She stood in the morning light, her heart pulsing hard. She knew more than she did before. But she'd have to watch her back from now on.

Taking a cue from the arsonists, she dragged half a dozen pallets over to the flap they had cut in the corner of the fence and leaned them up to cover the hole, positioning them so that the weight was on the corner fence pole. It wasn't much but it would have to do for the short term.

Puffing, Colleen slogged up the outside stairwell, holding onto the handrail. In the office, reeking of smoke, she climbed up on the desk, reached into the pocket of her jacket, and pulled out the Colt Detective Special she had picked up from the warehouse floor, wrapped in a blue handkerchief. She uncovered it. It had a snub nose and a good-sized chip knocked out of the wooden grip, probably from where it had landed after she had smacked it out of the older arsonist's hand. Low velocity. Keeping it swathed in the handkerchief, she thumbed the cylinder release hatch, flipped it open. A whiff reminiscent of sulfur drifted up, acrid and sour. Four rounds left. She left the two empty shell casings in the gun and snapped it shut with a flick of her wrist. Over her head she pushed one of the asbestos ceiling tiles up from the hanging frame and hid the gun on the right adjacent tile. Resetting the original tile back in its slot, she squatted down on the desk for a moment, selected a pencil out of the Giants pencil cup, stood up, punched a small hole in the corner of the tile to mark it. She climbed back down from the desk and settled back in the manager's chair. Hands crossed over her stomach, she leaned back in the chair, looking up. She could make out the little pencil hole in the tile, right over the corner of the desk. The gun was evidence. She might even need it for protection. She closed her eyes and breathed through her nose, trying to relax. Smoke had saturated her hair and skin.

A fresh bout of rain pattered the windows. She was exhausted. But she had plenty to do today. It was still early.

She'd rest for a moment, make coffee, take a shower.

She had made an enemy. But she knew who he was.

She'd call that progress.

CHAPTER TWENTY-ONE

A long hot shower and two cups of French roast put the worst of the fire behind her. Colleen donned a fresh pair of 501s, a white V-neck T-shirt, and her white leather Pumas. She tossed her new going-out clothes that were now charred and stunk of smoke in the trash. She wrote up an incident report for H&M and called the head office and got hold of the facilities manager.

He was less than pleased.

"A *fire*?"

"Arson," she said, tapping ash into an ashtray at her desk. "SFPD were here. Fire department, too. I'm waiting on their reports."

She could hear him take a deep breath, as if to say, *What?*

"Maybe you should come out and look at the damage yourself," she said coolly.

He said he'd wait for her report and the police and fire reports. H&M would no doubt put in a claim, despite the fact that the plant was waiting for the wrecking ball. Colleen was babysitting a tear-down, but she'd still need to repair the fence, and the sooner, the better. The manager gave her the go-ahead and told her to take care of it herself, submit the bill with her next monthly invoice. Great, she thought, more capital outlay. But it was all in a day's work for Hayes Confidential. She reminded him about the drums of acetone. He said they were on the list of tasks. She decided it wasn't a good time to ask when her first invoice would be paid. Fortunately, she had Mr. Copeland's retainer.

Which meant she better get on with finding Margaret's killer.

She called her answering service at Pacific Bell. No new messages.

She flipped open the Yellow Pages and found local fencing contractors. She got hold of one and agreed to meet him at three p.m., telling him she thought it was a quick repair.

Then she called San Francisco City and County office of the Assessor-Recorder to find out who owned the building at 413 Frederick Street. Alex said Margaret had been crashing there around the time of the murder. The City told Colleen the name and she jotted it down. Then she dialed directory inquiries and got the owner's phone number. She called that, got an answering service, left a message saying she had a few questions when he had a moment.

Outside she fired up the Torino, feeling pretty fortunate to have nipped the fire in the bud. She didn't like to think what would've happened if she hadn't been there when it started. She shuddered at what might have happened had she been asleep when those two thugs started the blaze or if Ramon hadn't been around.

Someone was out to do her harm.

She pulled out on Yosemite, thinking that she should start parking on the premises proper, behind locked gates. That involved getting out of the car each time, unlocking gates, removing padlocks and chains, pulling in, reversing the whole procedure. And it had done nothing but rain lately. But so be it.

Colleen drove down to Fell Street to the Department of Motor Vehicles where she filled out an FFDMV-4 public information request form on Ford Falcons registered in the Bay Area.

The clerk had a receding dark crew cut graying at the temples. He said the report might take a while and generate a mountain of information; there were over 330,000 vehicles registered in San Francisco alone.

Colleen modified the form to Ford Falcons registered just in San Francisco in 1967. There was no option to search by vehicle color. She paid her ten-dollar fee and asked how long the search might take.

"You should hear something within a week or two. It will be mailed to your address."

The clerk wore a white short-sleeve shirt with a pocket protector and a neat line of pens, organized by color. The opposite kind of getup to her leather bomber jacket over a V-neck T-shirt and no bra.

He gave Colleen a shy smile.

She took a deep breath, filling her lungs and T-shirt, not too proud to use whatever leverage was available. "Any way I can expedite that, Ed?" His name was on his tag. "My right front fender was nailed by a hit-and-run driver and the insurance company won't cough up a dime. All I've got to go on is a mid-sixties green Ford Falcon. A '67, I believe."

"Let me see what I can do," Ed said, his face reddening as he made a note on the form and set it to one side. "Why don't you check back next Monday?"

"Why, thank you so much, Ed." She patted the countertop twice and gave him a wink. Then she strutted out of the DMV, adding just a little sashay to her walk.

CHAPTER TWENTY-TWO

The bell rang. He felt the excitement building deep inside as the double doors of Roosevelt opened and teenagers splashed out onto the sidewalk. They were animated, bubbling with smiles and chatter. He stood across the street, in front of the laundromat on the corner, knit cap down tight over his head. Instinctively he pulled both hands from the pockets of his jacket, touched the heavy black frames of his glasses tucked under the hat for the umpteenth time that day. The glasses were in place. He'd never forget that woman breaking his glasses that night. Margaret. That whore. She'd almost gotten away. He pushed the thought aside.

He wondered if Robyn had come to school today. Yesterday, her mother picked her up in a beat-up VW bug. It was her whore of a mother who needed a lesson taught. And his father. But her mother was too tall, too strong. So he selected Robyn.

He grinned.

And then his heart pounded when he saw her, with a big smile as she came through the door with her black friend. Robyn wore wide yellow bell-bottoms. All the kids were wearing clothes like that now. And her hair. Different today. Her blond hair was pulled into a ponytail for a change. Looking very grown-up. She looked older than most ninth-graders.

Again, she reminded him of Margaret, from so many years ago. That night in the Haight. He got an uncomfortable feeling. But he had done what he had to do.

He fought the urge to cross the street and take a closer look. Proceed carefully. Plan this out so he wouldn't be caught. The other day he had followed Robyn to Golden Gate Park, where he watched her sit on a bench. She liked to watch the merry-go-round before she went home.

He would stay in control today. Watch from a distance. Control.

Soon he would prepare. Chloroform. Handkerchief. Plastic dry-cleaning bag.

And then a screech of tires broke his concentration. He turned to see a blue Chevy C10 pickup truck pull over in front of the laundromat. The driver's door flew open and a big man jumped out of the truck, storming up to him. His large plaid shirt flapped over a T-shirt stretched over his beer gut.

"God dammit!" He cuffed him around the head, knocking his hat loose, making his glasses slip. "What the *hell*? A damn high school?"

He hunched down, gripping his hat, pulling it back down tight on his head, straightening his glasses. Damn Frank. Fat bastard.

"I wasn't doing anything, Frank . . ."

"Bullshit!" Frank pushed him, treating him like a child, a man over thirty. "Get in the fucking truck!"

Hunched over, he hurried to the truck, head down, where he climbed in, pulling the passenger door shut. Frank scrabbled up behind the wheel, his belly touching it, heaving the door shut with a slam.

"Hanging around a damn high school." Frank shook his head as he crunched the truck into gear, squealing off. "What would your old man say?"

"Don't tell him, Frank," he whined, hating himself for the weakness in his voice, but he had no choice. He had to play along. For now. "Don't tell my father. *Please.*"

CHAPTER TWENTY-THREE

Late morning, Colleen tuned in to KCBS news talk as she drove over to Paris Street to check in on the Davis household. She heard the name "Jim Davis" mentioned, turned the volume up. SFPD were questioning transients in Golden Gate Park and around the Fort Funston area. Colleen shook her head as she drove. Blame it on the transients.

On Paris Street she slowed down as she approached the Davis house. No blue C10 pickup parked outside today. No black-and-whites either.

Mary Davis wouldn't be ready to entertain her visit.

But her son—Steve? He might. He might have a lead on his father.

She peered up at the attic room as the Torino crawled by. That's where the rock-n-roll emanated from. But no lights. No movement. She drove around the block. Nothing.

Down on Mission, Colleen parked half a block down from Dizzy's. There was no need to advertise her presence. A few minutes later, she pushed through the swinging door of the bar, looking for Frank Madrid or anyone who might resemble her two arsonists.

Dizzy's was near empty. One poor soul was hunched over a drink, talking to it. At the pinball machine a guy with a scraggly beard banged and coaxed the thing as it rang and flickered with lights. The bartender, Brenda, looked up with surprise from the newspaper laid out on the bar before her.

"What the hell are you doing here?"

"I think I left my keys here the other night," Colleen said. "I was right over there." She nodded at the spot by the serving hatch.

Brenda looked under the bar, came up with a shoebox, fished through it.

Shook her head *no*.

Colleen thanked her, left, just as the pinball man swore, the machine buzzing on her way out.

She loaded up the parking meter and made herself comfortable in the Torino, turning up KCBS, watching Dizzy's from her vantage point, seeing who came and who went. The only time she got out of the car was to reload the parking meter with dimes and duck into a greasy spoon to order a burger and Coke and use the restroom.

She ate her lunch in the car, listening to an announcer hold forth about how the transients were ruining the city. She watched Dizzy's. The people who came and went were the kind of people who hung out in a bar like Dizzy's during the day. But no one she recognized. Like Frank Madrid. Maybe he'd had a late night last night, driving arsonists around. Ramon had said he'd seen a truck like his exit H&M at high speed.

At 2:30 p.m. she fired up the car and headed back to H&M to meet with the fence contractor she was supposed to meet at three.

By 4:00 p.m. he was still a no-show. Frustrated, she went up to her office and called. No answer. She called her answering service. No call from the fence guy. But Jonathan Marsh, the owner of 413 Frederick, had returned her call. He could talk to her after 5:00 p.m. and left a number.

That'll do, she thought.

CHAPTER TWENTY-FOUR

"No one by the name of Margaret Copeland ever lived in that apartment to my knowledge," Jonathan Marsh said over the phone. "But the house on Frederick had pretty much turned into a free-for-all during the summer of sixty-seven."

Colleen had her file folder open and was drawing a square on a sheet of yellow-lined paper under the beam of the desk lamp in her office. It was evening and the rain had eased to intermittent spatters against the office windows. "I'm sure you remember the Margaret Copeland murder."

"Indeed," Mr. Marsh said. She could tell by his voice that he was an older gentleman, with a throatiness creeping into his words.

"It's rumored that Margaret might have stayed there around that time."

"The police canvassed the neighborhood, but nobody knew of her. Not a surprise. Half of them were kids out of their heads every waking hour. And they moved a lot, here, there, and everywhere, some on a nightly basis. Margaret Copeland might've stayed a day, a week, or months, if she stayed at all. But no one knows."

"Can you tell me whose name was on the lease?"

"Well, I'm not supposed to . . ."

Colleen jumped at the man's hesitation. "The victim's family is trying to reach a point where they can finally put Margaret's murder behind them. I'm chasing down any possible leads the police might have missed so we can say we're through, once and for all. Margaret's father is terminally ill. He's not expected to live much longer."

She heard Jonathan Marsh take a deep breath, as if considering a response. "It was some little princess who skipped out on four months' rent. Did much more than that in damage to the property. Left the place like a garbage dump. Cost me a small fortune trying to find her, all to no avail. So, if you do manage to track her down, I want to know where she is. Off the record, of course."

"Deal," Colleen said.

"Lesley Johns was the name," he said. "No forwarding address."

"Eleven years later, she could be just about anywhere."

"I still have a box of her stuff."

Colleen felt a boost of encouragement. "You know, it would probably come to nothing, but I wonder if I could take a quick look—off the record."

She could almost hear Jonathan Marsh thinking about it.

"I'm up at Lake Tahoe right now," he said. "I'll be back in San Fran Thursday."

"You pick a time and I'll be there."

"Make it around noon on Thursday." He gave her an address out in the avenues. She jotted it down on the inside of the empty box she had drawn.

"I'll be there. Thanks again."

"Don't get your hopes up," he said.

She wouldn't.

She set the phone down in its cradle, contemplated the pack of Virginia Slims on the corner of the desk. She hadn't had one all day, not even while staking out Dizzy's. Fresh rain started to pelt the windows. It was getting dark outside and that hole in the fence was still a hole.

Colleen pulled on her poncho, gathered her flashlight. On the way out the door, she picked up her trusty iron pipe. During her perimeter check, she found no new evidence of anybody breaking in. The pallets over the hole in the fence didn't appear to have been moved. She checked the dead delivery truck down by the water.

No sign of Ramon.

Ramon had stuck his neck out to help her save this worthless structure, and she hadn't really thanked him. And he was easy to look at. He'd be gone in a couple days, back to El Salvador. To his family. She trudged back up the metal stairs, peeled off her poncho, sat at her desk.

She needed to call Alex, give her an update. Then she wanted to head back to Dizzy's, do a little more surveillance.

Then the gate buzzer rattled through the office, shaking her thoughts loose. She hit the intercom on the wall by the door. "Security."

"Hello there, Security."

Alex. Sounding just a little husky so early in the evening. She probably wanted an update on Margaret.

"I'm upstairs." Colleen got up, hit the intercom, let Alex in. "Watch your step, stairs wet, all that."

Colleen met Alex at the door, feeling dowdy in her jeans, V-neck T-shirt, and bomber jacket, when stacked up against Alex's ensemble, a dark blue one-piece flared trouser suit with capacious bell-bottoms and a matching blue floppy hat on her head, drooping over one eye. All topped off with a short gray fur. Stones shone around her neck. In her hand she carried a paper bag that obviously contained a bottle.

"I was just about to call you," Colleen said, holding the door.

"Sure you were." Still playful, but a slight edge. She came in, leaving a whiff of sexy perfume. "Daily updates, right?"

"Wouldn't have done me much good to call though. You're obviously not home."

"Your powers of deduction are stellar." Alex's pretty nose wrinkled. "What is that *smell?*"

Burnt warehouse. "Long story."

"I see." Alex went and stood at the windows, looked out at the Bay Bridge.

Colleen took a seat behind her desk, one foot up on it while Alex stared out the window. "I thought you young Bohemians wouldn't be caught dead going out before midnight."

"It's midnight somewhere." Alex turned around.

"How's your father?"

Alex yielded a tight sigh. "Been on oxygen most of the day."

"Sorry to hear that."

"Tell me some news, Coll."

"Okay," Colleen said, lighting a cigarette. "I've learned that, although the landlord at 413 Frederick Street doesn't remember Margaret, and has no trace of her on a lease, there might still be something."

Alex turned from the window. "Something like what?"

Colleen weighed what to tell Alex. She felt like she had to give her something. "He's still got a box of effects from the woman whose name was on the lease back when Margaret was—ah—murdered. I'm to meet with him Thursday and look through it. Probably nothing to get too excited about."

"Okay," she said, nodding. "Anything else?"

"Nothing concrete."

"It sounds like there's something you're not telling me."

"Like I said last night, I'm not happy telling you something that doesn't pan out. So please, just sit tight and let me move ahead."

Alex came over, pulled out a chair, sat down. She set the bottle in the bag on the edge of the desk.

"You can tell *me*, Colleen. I'm not Father."

"I don't want you—or your father—getting your hopes up."

"Maybe I *want* to get my hopes up."

"You're paying me to figure this out—not feed your insecurities."

"*Feed my insecurities?* Don't treat me like a damn child."

"Then stop acting like one. I told you I'd give you updates, but that doesn't include every single thing I'm chasing down."

"If I want to hear every little thing you're doing, that's up to *me*. Not you."

It had been a long day. Colleen took a puff, blew a smoke ring. "I'm sorry you feel that way. If you can't handle a simple rule, feel free to hire someone else."

"Hey!" Alex said, alarmed. "Calm down. I didn't mean it."

Colleen let out a breath. "Neither did I. I had a lousy night. I know this is awful for you. And it's being dredged up again after eleven years."

Alex nodded at the bottle. "How about a little joy juice?"

"I hate to pee in your cheerios, but a condition of my parole is no booze on the premises. I'm already pushing it by just living here."

"It figures." Alex stood up, picked up the bottle in the bag by the neck, came around to Colleen's side of the desk, stood there. "Not that *you* need a reason to be a wet blanket."

"I am a wet blanket. Soaking wet."

Alex came closer, brushed a strand of hair out of Colleen's face. "We can go out for a drink, if you like. I can ask you to dance and you can turn me down. Sound like fun?"

Colleen could almost feel the heat from Alex's fingers. She set her cigarette down in the ashtray. "You're a client, Alex."

"Right. Which means you have to do what I say. So I'll wait while you change. Or I can help you pick something out." She continued to play with Colleen's hair. "You've got such nice hair."

Colleen's face was warm. She gently moved Alex's hand aside. "Believe it or not, I have something I need to do tonight."

Alex picked up Colleen's cigarette, smoked. She leaned back on one hip, scrutinizing Colleen. "Really?" She took a sip on the cigarette. "Or are you just not sure?"

A flash of irritation nicked Colleen. "And what is *that* supposed to mean?"

"Boys or girls, Colleen? Or both?"

Colleen sat up, took the cigarette from Alex's fingers, smashed it out in the ashtray, left it smoldering. "Now *that's* definitely none of your damn business."

"A-ha! Maybe we have a masquerader in our midst."

Colleen stood up. "Tell you what, Alex: I'll focus on Margaret. Maybe you can spend a few minutes with your father—while he's still alive. If you can squeeze it in with your club-hopping."

Alex stood there, hurt, her eyes turning glassy. "Fuck. You. I was just trying to be friends. I figure we could both use one right about now."

Colleen flinched, put her hands on her hips. "Sorry, Alex. I'm tired. And there's some shit I really don't want you part of right now. For your own good."

"Shit like what?"

Jesus. "I didn't want to tell you, but this place was broken into last night. SFPD were here. The fire department, too. So excuse me if I don't want to go hang out with the In Crowd tonight."

"Somebody broke *in*? Christ! Is *that* what that smell is?"

"I hope it's not me."

"You mean someone tried to set *fire* to the place?"

Colleen let out a sigh. "Don't tell your father. Or you're off the daily update list."

"Christ, Colleen. That's serious! You need to be careful."

"Yep." Colleen raised her eyebrows. "You, too. Probably not a great idea to come around for the time being."

"So it's something to do with Margaret?"

"I don't know," Colleen said.

"But you think so. You think someone is trying to get at you for looking into Margaret?"

Colleen found herself nodding again. "I don't have enough to confirm that yet. See how much fun this is, Alex? You not knowing what I don't know for sure either? I'm trying to shield you from this—you *and* your father. You don't need to know what doesn't definitely pertain to Margaret."

"Okay," Alex said. "Point taken. But if someone is threatening you, that's not cool. Maybe Christian can help."

The less people knew of what she was up to, the better. "I've got this one covered, Alex. Let me just do what I need to do first."

"Okay." Alex gave a crooked smile. "Next time just tell me, please."

"Don't stay out late," Colleen said. "Don't drink too much. Please don't drink and drive. Etcetera. Etcetera."

"Now you sound like Margaret."

A sudden chill ran down Colleen's back. Maybe *that* was the connection. Alex wanted her big sister back. And Colleen fit the bill. And then some.

"The lecture is now over," Colleen said. "Let's talk tomorrow."

Alex took her bottle and left, clumping down the metal stairs.

And Colleen felt herself getting confused. And then a bunch of the things she just didn't want to feel. Not right now.

Maybe she was just shattered. The thought of climbing into bed.

But she tore off a paper match and lit another cigarette instead, stood in her crummy office for a moment, in her broken-down warehouse, the perfect backdrop to her fucked-up life. She smoked her cigarette all the way down this time, savoring the rich burn of the second half, smashed out the butt, grabbed her keys, went out, pounded down the metal stairs, got in her car, and drove back to Dizzy's.

CHAPTER TWENTY-FIVE

Dizzy's glass brick window was lit up with yellow light and movement from within. As Colleen drove by, she saw what she was looking for—a dark Chevy pickup parked outside. The same one she'd seen parked in Jim Davis's driveway yesterday. Colleen stopped in the street, craned her neck, examined the emblem on the fender.

C10.

Frank Madrid's truck. The one used last night to spirit away the two arsonists.

All she needed to know for now.

She kept driving, turning left on Persia, heading up to Paris where she took a right, then slowed down as she passed the Davis house. Lights on downstairs. Mary Davis was probably home. A light on upstairs, where Steve Davis battered his eardrums.

She headed back down to Mission, crossed over, stopped at a Bank of America closed for the night, where there was a pay phone out front. She left the car running, hopped out.

A young Latino with a pompadour and a shiny black leather jacket was walking smartly up Ocean Avenue.

"I'm wondering if you can do me a favor," Colleen said.

He stopped, gave her the once-over. "Depends."

"I'm going to dial a number here, and all you need to do is ask for Steve. If he's there, hand me the phone. If he's not, say goodbye, hang up."

"Why can't you do it?"

Colleen gave a smirk. "If a woman answers . . . well, let's just say she doesn't need to know I'm calling."

"Got it," he said. "What's in it for me?"

She held up a five-dollar bill. "A drink on me."

"Cool." He took the bill, pocketed it.

She dropped a dime in the slot, dialed the Davis house, waited for the ring, handed the guy the phone. He took it, cradled the phone to his ear, eyeing Colleen while the phone rang.

A woman answered.

"Yeah," he said. "Is—uh—" He looked at Colleen for confirmation, eyebrows raised.

Colleen mouthed the word "Steve."

"—is *Steve* there?"

There was a pause.

After a moment, he said, "Okay, thanks." He clicked the phone off, handed it back to her. "Looks like your Steve stepped out on you."

She took the phone, hung it back up. "Story of my life," she said.

* * *

"Who was on the phone, Ma?"

"No one," Mary Davis said, resuming her seat in front of the television, in the armchair next to Jim's empty one. On TV, Mork was making fun of a man's loose toupee.

"I've seen wavy hair before but never seen hair wave!" Robin Williams' character quipped. The audience broke up in a cacophony of canned laughter.

They still hadn't caught Jim's murderer.

Steve stood just outside the living room in the darkened hallway. His hands were jammed in his back pockets.

"No one, Ma? Like a wrong number?"

"Just someone for your dad," she said.

"And you told him he wasn't here?"

Mary Davis nodded, her jaw firm. On the coffee table, a cigarette smoldered in an ashtray.

"Why didn't you just tell them the truth?" Steve said.

"Well," she said. "He's not here, is he?"

"They'll find him." Her son came into the living room. "They'll find Pop's killer."

She picked up the cigarette in the ashtray, tapped it, took a puff. "Oh, do you really think so?" she said in a hard voice.

"All the friends he's got? On the force?"

"You're going to learn a thing or two about friends, Steve," Mary Davis said, smoking. "That, when push comes to shove, they're not always worth that much."

"I'm gonna make sure," he said, bringing one hand out of his back pocket to tap his chest. "I'm gonna make sure they catch Pop's killer."

This from a kid who lived in his room, listening to noise all day, couldn't find a job. In his twenties already. If he had any friends of his own, they weren't worth much more than Jim's.

"Did you hear me, Ma?"

"Yes, son." She smoked. Mork made another idiotic joke. But the audience loved it.

Steve went to the hall closet, returned wearing his denim jacket.

"You're going out?" she said. He'd been pretty good about sticking around, keeping her company. But his dad was dead a couple of days now, and he wasn't going to hang around his mom forever. She stifled the hurt.

"You okay on your own for a while, Ma?"

She smoked. "Sure."

"Just for a little while, Ma. I need some air."

"She hasn't tried to contact you, has she?"

"Who, Ma?"

Oh, but he was a terrible liar. Mary Davis turned her head, narrowed her eyes, and gave her son a flat-lined smile as she tapped the cigarette in the ashtray. "You know who. That woman. The so-called investigator."

"Oh, her."

Mary Davis smirked. "Right—her."

"No." Steve went upstairs, rummaged around in his room, came back down.

"What did you go upstairs for?" she asked.

He held up his car keys.

"Thought you were going for a walk."

"Think I'll drive around for a while."

"Don't you dare go down to the beach." She didn't need him trying to find the spot where they found Jim. She wasn't superstitious but both of her boys in the same place where one had died was not good.

"Got it, Ma."

"Stay out of trouble. Hear me?"

"Right." He headed to the front door, opened it. It stayed open for a moment, then she heard him say, quietly, "Love you, Ma." Before she could answer, he pulled the door shut behind him and was skipping down the front stairs.

Her eyes watered. He hadn't said that since he was a little boy. She smashed her cigarette out in the ashtray, wiped her eyes, flipped off the TV, and just sat there.

* * *

Frank Madrid left Dizzy's and got into his pickup. He fired up the truck, gunning the big engine, then spun a U right in the middle of Mission, headed up to Persia. He better drop in on Mary, make sure she was doing okay. She'd cope if World War III broke out, but she was taking Jim hard. She was still in love with that loser. He never could figure it out. But he owed her. And he needed to keep a close eye on her and Steve, make sure things were under control.

Waiting for the light on Persia to turn green, he heard a familiar engine roar down the street. And if it wasn't little Stevie Davis in his matte black Mustang, the hood shaking with the tricked-out 289 small block, misfiring like a mother. Punk couldn't tune up an engine if his life depended on it.

Frank watched Steve turn right on a red, a California stop, fat tires squealing as he shifted up, picking up speed, charging down Mission.

Now where was *he* going? Supposed to be looking after his mom. They had a deal.

Damn punk.

Frank spun another wide U, right in the intersection, mashed the pedal down flat, went after the Mustang.

Just like his dad, Steve was. A pain in the ass. A fucking pain in the ass.

CHAPTER TWENTY-SIX

Back home at H&M Paint, Colleen did a quick perimeter check, verified that the fence hadn't been breached, then called her answering service. No new messages. She climbed up on her desk, retrieved the .38 she had knocked out of the arsonist's hand. She took it into her "bedroom," slipped the gun underneath her pillow, undressed, climbed into her cot with its crisp, clean sheets and three blankets, pulled her head in like a turtle, and went into immediate hibernation.

Sometime later, she awoke from the deepest sleep she could recall in weeks, with no idea where she was, or what time or day it was. The phone was ringing in the office next door.

She climbed out of her cot, pulling a blanket over her bare shoulders, and stumbled into the office. She'd left the desk lamp on, since the break-in. The clock said it was just past midnight.

She answered the phone, half expecting to hear Alex's inebriated voice. Bracing herself to turn her down again, without hurting her feelings. Stay strong.

"Security."

"Is this the investigator?" a young man's voice said. She knew the voice, even with the street noise behind it, young people laughing. The muffled sounds of primitive rock-n-roll. A bar, a club.

"Yes," Colleen said. "Steve Davis, right?"

"Right," he said, sounding distracted. Nervous.

"What is it, Steve?"

"Did you try and call me earlier? At my house?"

"I did. I need to talk to you. But I didn't want to upset your mother."

"Okay."

"Okay *what*? You want to talk?"

"I guess."

Yes! She was coming awake fast. She flipped open her file folder, got a pencil ready, sat down in the office chair with a squeak. "I'm all ears."

"No," he said. "Not on the phone. I'm at the Palms Café. Over on Polk. I'll wait outside. By the pay phone."

CHAPTER TWENTY-SEVEN

Steve Davis hung up the pay phone outside the Palms Café, lit a Marlboro, took a deep drag. His heart was pulsating, but he had to see this through. That investigator woman said she'd be here in fifteen–twenty minutes.

"Hey, Stevie."

The voice caught him by surprise, made him spin around.

Frank Madrid. *What the fuck?* Steve took a nervous hit on his cigarette.

"Hey, Frank," he said, stamping his feet on the sidewalk as if he were cold and needed to move on. Good thing Frank hadn't caught him on the phone with Colleen Hayes. "What are you doing down here?"

"About to ask you the same thing." Frank came up to him, gut out in a T-shirt under his open work shirt. Probably couldn't get the damn buttons done.

"Just hanging out," Steve said. Inside the club, the band was in between numbers. Someone did a drumroll.

"*Here?*" Frank said. Several others milled around outside as well. A couple of skinny guys decked out in tight leather and spiky haircuts. "In this fag neighborhood?"

Steve smoked, nodded at a girl—totally wasted, in a torn Sex Pistols T-shirt—trying to get her purse shut. Showing some side boob.

"If she's a fag, Frank, count me in."

"Plenty of 'em around here, Stevie, all I'm sayin'. Polk Street is their turf." Frank gave a nod of approval at the girl, then patted Steve on the shoulder with his big meaty paw, a little too hard to be friendly. "Thought you might be keeping your mom company tonight. She needs you at a time like this."

"I'm doing my bit," he said, smoking. "I just needed some time off for good behavior."

Frank's hand still on his shoulder. "Your old man gets killed by vagrants and that's all you can come up with? '*Time off for good behavior?*' Christ, Stevie, I expected a little more out of you."

Steve bit down on what he wanted to say. "Yeah, Frank, you and everybody else."

The band started up inside with a bellowed *one-two-three-four*, followed by buzz-saw guitars and pounding drums. The singer started screaming that John Wayne was a Nazi.

"Jesus, Stevie. How can you listen to that shit? Go on home already. Be with your mom."

Stevie took a puff. "In a while." He was getting tired of Frank's hand on his shoulder.

"Remember that little situation we took care of for you, Stevie?"

Getting caught receiving stolen property. "How can I forget? You only bring it up every time I see you."

Frank gave him an ugly smile. "You might want to watch your lip, pal."

Steve's heart rattled as he took another puff. "Want to get your hand off my shoulder, Frank? In a neighborhood like this, people are bound to talk, right?"

Frank shook his head. "Always the smart mouth."

"You follow me here? Or are you out cruising for guys?" He grinned.

"I know what you're going through, Stevie. Your dad was my best friend. My partner. It's like losing a brother."

Steve wondered about that. No, he didn't wonder. He knew about Frank.

Frank dropped his voice. "Your old man ever talk to you—about the old days?"

"Nonstop."

"Well, that makes you one of us, Stevie. The son of a cop is as good as, in my book. And I'm sure he told you about the code. We don't talk out of school. None of us. No, sir."

Frank was staring directly into his eyes. Hard.

"Hell," Steve said. "I stopped listening to my dad's shit a long time ago. Never-ending. After a while I'd just nod my head, so as not to hurt his feelings."

Frank rubbed his face. "That woman hasn't tried to contact you, has she?"

Steve took an uneasy hit on his cigarette. "What woman?"

Frank squinted. "That investigator. Colleen Hayes. Your mom said she's been to the house a couple of times—asking nosy questions."

Steve did his best to feign confusion as he sucked in smoke. Then he said: "Oh—*her*." He shook his head. "*I wish* she'd call." He raised his eyebrows. "She's not bad, huh?"

Frank smiled. "She'd put you in the hospital, pal."

Steve smoked. "But it'd take the docs three days to get the smile off my face."

Frank laughed. "Stick to the teeny-bops. Man, I wish I was in your shoes. There's gonna come a day when you don't know what you had."

Like my father, Steve thought bitterly. *I had one of those not too long ago.* "Hell, she's out of my league, Frank."

Frank nodded, his face serious. "You're a good guy, Stevie. And you got your old man's friends to look out for you."

Did he? He knew what his dad had told him, in drunken confidence, about Frank. Some fucking friend he was.

Frank patted his shoulder one more time, this time gently. "Go on home now, buddy. She needs you. You can scramble your brains this weekend. Your mom'll be better by then. Do me a favor. And I'll remember I owe you one."

It really wasn't right, he knew, leaving Ma alone. Frank wasn't gonna let up until he left anyway. Steve didn't need that woman Colleen showing up while the two of them were standing there having a heart-to-heart that looked like it was going to go on all night. And she might show any minute. He couldn't risk that.

"Yeah," he said, flicking the tail end of his cigarette out on the street where it skidded and popped red embers. "I hear you." He got out his car keys. "I hear you, Frank."

* * *

Not long after, Colleen drove past the Palms Café. No Steve Davis waiting out front by the phone. She circled the block, made sure there weren't any suspicious cars, parked half a block down, got out of the Torino. Grating music wafted down Polk. She crossed over, headed toward the club. A couple of head bangers in black leather were making some kind of illicit trade out front, not too discreetly, although they probably thought they were.

Still no one at the pay phone next to the black door. Colleen gazed up and down Polk.

Maybe Steve Davis was inside the club.

She went inside, punk music deafening. Kids jumping up and down like pogo sticks. Some of them doing a facsimile of playing football in the middle of the dance floor, crashing into each other, knocking each other back and forth. One girl in a torn yellow T-shirt diving off the stage, landing in a crowd of kids who, thankfully, caught her, dipping to the ground. The place was hot and damp, like a locker room.

No Steve Davis.

"Five-dollar cover," the guy at the door said, not that she could hear him—reading his lips. He was wearing one black glove.

"I'm just looking for a friend," she yelled. "I was supposed to meet him outside."

"It's still five bucks," he shouted.

She got out her money, unclipped it, peeled off a five, held it up like it might be used toilet paper. The guy took it.

She wasn't too shy to go into the men's room where one poor slob was heaving his burrito dinner into the sink. No Steve.

She went back out, stood at the bar, ordered a shot, despite parole. The shot went down fast. She pushed the empty shot glass at the bartender. He poured another. She downed that, too, went outside, got back in her car, smacked the steering wheel with the heel of her hand, and let loose a few choice expletives.

Then she waited.

* * *

Two a.m. Colleen watched the punk rockers stumble out of the Palms Café.

Steve was a no-show. It would not have bothered her so much except that she sensed he really wanted to talk.

She drove back home, wide awake. She parked inside the gates, went through the rigmarole, grabbed the flashlight from under the seat, did a quick check of the fence where the hole was. Had the pallets been moved? No, she didn't think so. She'd do a quick patrol before she hit the sack.

She headed back to the far side of the facility, the employee entrance, when she heard water running. Inside the plant.

CHAPTER TWENTY-EIGHT

Colleen let herself into the side door of the paint plant, unlocked now because the window was smashed in, and heard water splashing from the locker room. Using her flashlight to step around the indoor pond left by SFFD, she snaked along the old wall separating the main plant from the changing rooms and cafeteria and such. As she got to the locker room, she heard the shower running. Flashlight down, she pushed open the door and went in, treading quietly.

A candle in a glass jar on the floor flickered by the last shower stall, sending shimmers of light up the white tiles. It was one of those votive candles you could buy in the Mission, with a Virgin Mary decal on it. She seemed to be protecting whoever was taking a shower in the otherwise near darkness. Steam wafted from the open stall as water splashed off a moving body. Colleen powered off the flashlight.

She had a pretty good idea who was in there.

And it made parts of her body warm, parts that had been cold too long.

And then the bather broke into song, a deep voice singing in Spanish.

There was a little rancher girl . . .

And she stood there, interrupting a private moment, and savoring it, realizing how much Ramon must miss his home, even if the one he sang about was a mythical one, like in the song. But she missed the same home. She wanted to go back, even though it didn't exist.

Steam floated out of the stall, over the dancing candlelight, as he sang about lost love.

My heart will always follow, wherever you may roam . . .

There was no time like the present.

She set the flashlight down softly, and slowly, quietly, undressed.

She stood up, completely naked, the San Francisco air chilled by rain making her skin prickle and goose bump. As well as the anticipation of what she was about to do.

She picked up the flashlight, turned it back on, shone it on the far wall, above the quivering light of the candle flame.

Ramon stopped singing.

"Who's there?" he said in English. "Colleen?" He said her name in two words, unnatural syllables for his language. She'd never heard her name pronounced like that before. She liked it.

"Yes," she said, pleased that he didn't startle. He wasn't that kind of guy. "*Si.*"

"I hope you don't mind," he replied in Spanish. "I needed a shower."

"Why did you stop singing?"

A moment went by, the water spattering.

And I will always be there, when you are far from home . . .

She tiptoed down to the end of the locker room in her bare feet, the cold tiles heightening expectation, and she turned and shone the light on him.

His back to her, water ran off his muscled body, a body sculpted by hard work and whatever genes had made it the work of art it already was. His butt looked white compared to his tanned back and legs.

"*Date la vuelta*," she said, the flashlight directly on him.

He turned, slowly, his hands covering his groin. She could see the dark hair around it.

Then he saw that she, too, was naked. His eyes widened. His mouth parted.

She focused the flashlight on his hands covering himself.

"Show me," she said.

He gradually removed his hands. He was already growing hard.

She set the flashlight down on its side so that the beam lit up the shower stall. And then she walked in, the warm water caressing her skin as she reached for him.

CHAPTER TWENTY-NINE

"I'm supposed to head home today," Ramon said.

Those words made Colleen stop stirring her coffee. She picked up two cups and took them over to where Ramon sat on a sheet on the floor, a blanket draped over his lower half. Her inadequate cot had been stripped of its bedding and a makeshift double bed had been hastily constructed after their prolonged shower. The floor hadn't bothered either one of them in the slightest.

She squatted down in just her sweatshirt, handed him a cup of coffee. The space heater whirred. The warm air felt good on her bare backside.

"Back to El Salvador?" she said, sipping the rich coffee. It should have tasted perfect after a night of frenzied lovemaking, but the reality of Ramon leaving so soon brought her back down to earth. "Of course. Your job is finished."

"We're done with the painting." He drank, looked up at her. She saw a hint of hopefulness in his dark eyes. Was he thinking what she thought he was thinking?

Stay on a little longer? Didn't she want another taste of what they had consumed last night?

But last night was a reprieve, nothing more. They had both just grabbed something that felt good. Ramon had a wife and three kids. He didn't need an entanglement. And God knows she didn't either. Half of last night was a reaction to Alex. Colleen was still trying to figure that out.

Colleen hadn't slept with a man in ten years. There had been a woman, last year, and that was tender, but there was nothing like being with a man. Especially one who looked like Ramon, hardened with labor and desire.

"El Salvador is a long way," she said.

"Three thousand miles."

"Well," she said. "I wish you a safe trip."

His face fell. "I could stay a while longer. Fix that fence for you . . ."

She shook her head. "Not a good idea, Ramon."

"Why not?"

"Apart from the fact that you've got a family?" She gave a wry smile. "Because I've got my hands full and I don't need your tush in the way."

"Hands full how?" He narrowed his eyes. "Problems . . . with the people who started that fire?"

"No," she lied, looking away.

"I'm not sure I believe you."

"Well, it doesn't matter. I can't have you here anymore."

"You might need my help again."

She shook her head again, drank coffee. She couldn't have Ramon risking his neck for what might happen. Frank Madrid. And whoever else was involved with this unraveling mess.

Ramon sipped coffee. "Was I that bad last night?" He grinned. "In the shower?"

"You were that good," she said, winking, setting down her cup. "That's why we're going to do it one more time." She got on her knees, pulled back the blanket covering him. "Then you're on your way."

CHAPTER THIRTY

Jonathan Marsh lived out in the avenues, in the part of town they called the Sunset District. This was residential San Francisco, sand dunes when the 1906 quake hit, now street after street of two-story junior five stucco houses, cars rusting with the sea air that blew in from Ocean Beach. Not much in the way of trees, not like the pretty city further inland, just plenty of overhead wires, crisscrossing plain fog-strewn avenues.

Jonathan Marsh's garage door was open when Colleen pulled up to a neat white house with red trim. A gray-haired man in his sixties was bent over a workbench. A turquoise blue 1955 Ford Thunderbird occupied the tidy garage. Colleen got out and headed directly there, not bothering with the front door.

The man wore a blue cardigan and pressed trousers. He was working on the metal flap of a heat register with a screwdriver, trying to free up a hinge that had been painted shut.

"Mr. Marsh?" she said.

"Miss ahh . . ." He didn't look up. "I'm sorry . . ."

"Hayes," she said, setting a business card down on the workbench. "Colleen Hayes."

"Yes," he said. He focused on his task but pointed over his shoulder at the workbench on the other side of the Thunderbird. "Over there—help yourself."

She walked around the sports car and found a cardboard box with *Lesley Johns: 413 Frederick, 1967,* written neatly on the side in black marker.

She stood at the bench going through the box. Jonathan Marsh had been right when she spoke to him on the phone. There appeared to be absolutely nothing of value in this box—some keys, a golf ball of all things, correspondence held together by a thick rubber band, a transistor radio, and an old toothbrush.

She undid the bundle and sorted the letters: an old PG+E bill in Lesley Johns' name, past due, more than a few letters requesting payment for various items, all in her name. Colleen got out her notebook and pencil and went through the personal correspondence.

Anything that had been addressed to Lesley Johns had been opened. She assumed Jonathan Marsh was looking for any trace of his former tenant, a forwarding address or a phone number. Colleen did the same, opening each letter, first checking the author, verifying that it wasn't Margaret Copeland. Feeling voyeuristic, she jotted down names and addresses to follow up on. But with eleven-year-old letters, the words *long shot* rang loud and clear.

Toward the bottom of the stack, she found a small pink envelope, the kind a woman might send a thank-you card or personal note in.

It was addressed simply to Alex, no last name, at her parents' Half Moon Bay address. A virgin five-cent stamp was stuck in the upper right corner. No return address. It was penned in pretty cursive handwriting.

Colleen's nerves tingled with apprehension.

She slipped the note out. Pink parchment paper.

My dearest Bobo,

You can't believe the crazy things that have been going on in this crazy city! All I can say is that I need a break from this endless chaos. I have had enough.

    I spoke to Father Guy and he said you have been acting up, dear little sister. No, I don't care about the colored boyfriend the way mother and father do—in fact, there's something beautiful about black skin and white skin together—but you're far too young to even know about such things. There are men out there who will tell you what you want to hear and break your heart. Take it from me.

    Our private phone calls make me realize how much I miss you.

    That's why I am coming home this weekend, like it or not. I haven't been invited to Thanksgiving so, in order to preserve everyone's sense of dignity, since I know all those stuffed shirts we call relatives will be there, I'm coming Saturday, after everyone's gone.

    And I'm going to straighten you out, young lady!

    And maybe, just maybe, you will do the same for me.

Love you and miss you so much,

Margaret

Colleen gulped back the beginning of salty tears as she verified the date on the letter. November 20, 1967. One day before Margaret was murdered. If only she had been able to make it home for Thanksgiving.

Colleen couldn't help but think of her own daughter, Pamela, in that damn commune now, not far from here. It felt as if she was gone as well. One more time Colleen recalled the day when she came home early from Gates Rubber in Denver, found Pamela crouching in the corner of her darkened bedroom. Shivering in a T-shirt, hugging her knees. Eight years old. Eyes glazed over. Colleen had suspected. And done nothing.

She bent down, tried to hug her daughter. But it was like holding a stone. Pamela pushed her away. Continued to push her away. Even to this day.

Colleen let go, gave her daughter space she would never yield.

"Your father?" she asked quietly.

There was a pause, then a single, frightened, angry nod.

Five minutes later, her ex lay sprawled on the kitchen floor in a pool of blood, clutching at the screwdriver buried in his neck. Frozen.

She had suspected something was wrong.

If only she had acted sooner.

If only she had not acted out of rage. Selfish rage.

If only Pamela would forgive her.

With a thickness in her throat, Colleen slid the letter back into the envelope. She put the rubber band around the rest of the correspondence, placed that back in the box with the golf ball and keys and toothbrush, and put the lid back on the box.

And she went back to where Jonathan Marsh was still futzing around with his heat register.

"Yes?" He didn't look up.

She showed him the letter.

"It's nothing," he said.

"Remember where and when you found it?"

He squeezed his eyes in thought. "Tucked away in one of the rooms. In a drawer in one of the built-in cabinets. I found it when I was cleaning the place out. Eleven years ago?"

"So it was written but never posted."

"Seems about right."

"Mind if I take it?"

"Remember our arrangement."

"If I find out where Lesley Johns lives, I let you know."

"Correct." Jonathan Marsh went back to his heat register.

She slipped the letter that Margaret Copeland had written to her sister, Alex, one that had never been mailed, in the breast pocket of her bomber jacket, and walked back out to her car. The sun was fighting to get through the rain clouds but it was a losing proposition.

She got into the car, lit up a cigarette, took a puff. Two. Three.

She tossed her cigarette out, rolled up the car window, and headed down to the beach, where she took the Great Highway south toward Fort Funston, thinking about how close Margaret Copeland had gotten to not being murdered.

CHAPTER THIRTY-ONE

On the way to Fort Funston, Colleen pulled off the Great Highway into a small parking lot on the beach where there was a pay phone next to the public restrooms. Half a dozen cars were parked facing the booming Pacific, and even though clouds churned low and rain spit, a few die-hard surfers were out, battling the waves. One lanky kid with a tanned face and long white blond hair sat on the tailgate of a beat-up pickup truck, zipping up his wetsuit. Fine sand blew across the parking lot, heading inland, dusting the Great Highway.

Colleen found a dime and dialed retired Lieutenant Daniel Moran's number in Santa Cruz. Her intention had been not to get him involved. But she needed his assistance. And he owed her. The operator came on the line and told her to deposit thirty-five more cents. She had change ready and slipped the coins into the slot. A wave crashed.

His wife, Daphne, answered the phone. She didn't sound particularly happy to hear from Colleen. Not surprising, considering the events that brought Colleen and Lieutenant Moran together in the first place, last year. The result of that shaky alliance was the arrest and conviction of a corrupt Santa Cruz homicide detective, the death of a local drug kingpin, and a girl with no name interred in a cemetery north of Santa Cruz. Eva Unknown. After all of that hell,

Colleen still had not been able to reconnect with her daughter. Pamela had joined a commune that kept Colleen at arm's length. But the truth was, her daughter just didn't seem to want to know her anymore.

Moran was out in the yard gardening. Daphne reluctantly went to get him.

Colleen heard him pick up the phone as a gust of wind blew her hair into her face. She pulled it away, flipped up the collar of her leather jacket.

"What can I do you for, Hayes?" Moran said. She pictured the man, in his mid-sixties, medium build, dark hair cut short, pushing his glasses up his nose with his finger. His voice sounded older, wearier. That case had taken much of the strength he'd had left.

"I need to find someone who fell off the face of the earth eleven years ago," she said.

There was a pause. "I take it this has to do with Edward Copeland?"

"It does indeed."

"So you took the gig."

"I almost didn't. But I have this obsession with regular meals." The truth was, it was more than that, but she didn't want to discuss it.

"Better bring me up to speed, Hayes."

She filled Moran in on the case.

When she was done, there was another brief silence. "This has gotten out of hand, Hayes. I was just trying to throw a little work your way. I thought it might simply be a matter of you filing for a police report and checking a few addresses and such. But it's turned into a rat's nest. A dangerous one. Jim Davis killed?" She could almost see Moran shaking his head.

"I've just hit a snag," she said. "Nothing I can't handle."

"You want my advice?"

"My clairvoyant side is telling me you want me to let the case go."

"That's *exactly* what I'm saying. SFPD aren't going to stand by and let you implicate them in some kind of cover-up. The death of Jim Davis doesn't sit right. Just like his early retirement for disability."

"Disability? Is that what happened?"

"Oh yeah. Right after the Copeland thing, eleven years ago, he was given a package. You can call it early retirement, disability, whatever you like, but Jim Davis was shown the door."

She had suspected something. "He stepped on some toes."

"And he was a boozer. Just like me. That's how I met him. Years ago, when we were both sent away to dry out."

Neither one of them made it.

"Best thing for you, Hayes, is to tell Mr. Copeland that you don't have the authority to take this any further. Which happens to be true. Then, get your license, guard your paint plant. Do you hear what I'm saying?"

"Loud and clear. But I'm not ready to hang it up. Not yet."

"The writing's on the wall. Learn to read."

"I think I might wait for the movie."

"You sure this doesn't have something to do with your Jane Doe? The one up at Four Mile Beach?"

Eva Unknown. Possibly. "All I'm asking is for you to make a phone call," she said. "Help me find what became of the girl who leased the place where Margaret Copeland was crashing. She might have a record. That house on Frederick was Party Central. Maybe she got popped for dope or something."

There was a pause while a salvo of waves pounded the surf behind her.

"Maybe," Moran said. "But does the phrase 'needle in a haystack' mean anything to you?"

"She might know something about Margaret that can help me figure this out."

"Possibly," Moran said. "That's it?"

"That's it," Colleen said. "If nothing comes of it, I can tell Mr. Copeland I did what I could. Then I'm done."

"Not sure I believe you."

Neither did she. "That's because you have trust issues."

Another pause while Moran cleared his throat.

"What's the girl's name?" Moran said.

"Lesley Johns."

She heard him scratch it down. "You got a number where I can reach you?"

She gave him her number.

"If anything comes of it, someone'll call. But, be forewarned: it's not likely."

"I really appreciate this," she said. "Really."

"Good."

"How's retirement?"

"Did you know that gardening is the number one pastime in this country?"

"No, I did not."

"They can keep it. Watch your back, Hayes."

CHAPTER THIRTY-TWO

A wet wind blew in from the ocean as Colleen walked across the sand, her shoulder bag swinging, toward Fort Funston—the 1940s concrete bunker that had been built to protect California from the Japanese attack that never came. The location where Jim Davis's body had been found. Three days ago now. SFPD still hadn't arrested anybody, although they were apparently questioning many, focusing on Golden Gate Park, where the allegedly infamous transients were taking up camp. It seemed the police, TV, and radio were going to blame everything on them. The hippies were passé.

Against a bluff she found the bunker. It was monolithic, built into the hillside, a huge cement visor over a tunnel leading through to the other side of the mound where it opened up to reluctant daylight trying to break through churning clouds.

She hiked over the dune.

Ice plant hung around the edges of the fortress-like structure, softening the appearance. It looked futuristic, weird, yet somehow organic. The circular rusted iron track that a massive gun had once rotated on was still visible, covered by sand and creeping vegetation.

In the bunker, the concrete was cracked and wet, and the walls were layered in graffiti. A urine smell hung in the air.

She found a small grouping of flowers and a modest wreath leaning against the wall of the tunnel near where Jim Davis had been
found. The flowers were weather-beaten and windblown. Trash had
collected around the wreath. Colleen walked over, stooped down,
pulled a torn section of wet newspaper and a fast-food wrapper from
the wreath, then noticed the card. The ink had run. "From your
comrades at SFPD. Fallen but not forgotten."

She unlatched her shoulder bag, got out her file folder. In the
stiff breeze she double-checked an article she had cut out of the
Examiner. The theory was that Jim, in his drunkenness, had somehow managed to make his way down here and had fallen foul of one
of the homeless people who roamed the beach and park at night.
Jim was a drinker and an accident waiting to happen. A morality
tale of an article.

And one that didn't make a lot of sense.

His car was still in his garage. Drunks might be irrational and
self-destructive, but they didn't venture several miles down to
Ocean Beach in treacherous weather, out by the sand dunes, on
foot.

Unless somebody helped them.

She'd seen Jim herself the morning before he disappeared. They
had made an arrangement to meet at The Manor coffee shop and,
although Jim was half in the bag, he'd exhibited that weary bearing
common amongst heavy drinkers. A functioning alcoholic. Colleen
knew all about it. Her father had been one.

Jim wanted to meet with her; she knew it. Not just to bring the
police report he had written eleven years ago on Margaret Copeland,
in exchange for cash, but also to explain. Come clean. About
Margaret's case. The older Colleen got, the more she realized she
should trust her intuition. It was the best bellwether one had when
the supposed facts didn't add up.

A gust of wind almost blew the newspaper article out of her hand. She caught it, shoved it back in the file folder, slid the folder back into her shoulder bag.

There was really no point coming down here. She stood up, turned to go, looking out at the waves crashing in, restless, unsettled.

Over the rise of a plant-speckled dune, a movement caught her eye—someone ducking down. Just a glimpse but enough to leave an imprint in her mind. Wild long dark hair, blowing sideways in a squall of wind. Slight frame, angular. Haunted dark eyes. Mouth open.

A crazy person. A woman. A transient.

Go with your instinct.

"Hey!" Colleen shouted, heading for the dune. "Where are you going?" She made an effort to sound friendly, something she had to work at as a rule.

At the top of the dune, she saw the woman loping away. She wore a long, ragged khaki-colored coat that flapped in the wind.

Colleen cupped her hands around her mouth and called again.

The woman stopped, hunched over, turning slowly, eyeing Colleen, holding her coat together. Like a wild animal, gaunt and frightened. She was probably middle-aged, but her skin looked like leather.

Colleen dug into her pocket, came out with her pack of Virginia Slims. Held it up.

"Cigarette?" she shouted, one hand still around her mouth.

Stooped over, the wild woman watched Colleen, motionless. Shook her head no.

Colleen shoved the cigarettes back in her pocket, came out with a pack of Juicy Fruit. She held that up between thumb and forefinger and wiggled it. "I got gum."

The pack of gum held the woman's stare for a moment. Two moments.

She nodded.

"Come and get it," Colleen said.

She shook her head.

"Tell you what," Colleen shouted. "I'll leave the gum right here." She bent down, stuck the pack into the sand next to an empty beer bottle. "It's right here—next to the bottle."

The woman watched.

"Come and get it. I'm going over inside that tunnel to look around. You'll be safe."

Taking in her words.

"Okay, then." Colleen turned, hastened down into the cement tunnel again, and stood by the wreath. Waited while the wind blew, bending the plants, craning her head around to see.

Just when Colleen thought she might be crazy, too, for talking to strangers, the woman's head appeared, then the rest of her, still holding her coat together. She came over the rise of the dune. She saw Colleen, a safe distance away now, and grabbed the pack of gum.

Colleen's hands went back up around her mouth. "Were you around when that poor man was found dead up there? In the tunnel?"

The woman stared at Colleen with a troubled look, blinking, as if not sure how to answer.

"You were, weren't you?" Colleen said.

The woman frowned and gave a single nod, then turned to go.

"Wait!" Colleen shouted. "You hungry?"

Slowly the woman turned back around. Of course she was. A nod confirmed it.

"What do you like? Sandwiches?"

Nods. Colleen saw a gap of missing tooth.

"What kind?"

No answer. More staring.

"I'll be back in a little while. With some sandwiches. I want to talk to you. I promise I won't hurt you. I hope you like the gum. It's my favorite."

The wind gusted the woman's hair into her face. She pulled it away.

Then she turned and was gone.

* * *

Thirty minutes later, Colleen returned with a paper sack from a corner convenience store near the zoo, with two sandwiches, one pre-wrapped in cellophane—cheese on white bread and a square hamburger on a soft bun, the kind heated up in a toaster oven. It was still hot, radiating. Also in the bag was a carton of milk, a can of Coke, a bag of potato chips, and a couple of paper napkins. To balance it out, there was a shiny red apple.

Colleen didn't find her wild woman waiting at Jim Davis's memorial. She gave a deep sigh.

She climbed up on the sand dune where she'd seen her will-o'-the-wisp woman take the pack of gum. She stood, holding the bag of food, looking up and down the shore. With the bleak weather, the wind spitting rain, the beach was near deserted. Just a young man with a girl down there, walking along the sand, dodging waves as they held hands. Love conquered everything. Well, maybe hormones did. She thought of Ramon for a moment.

No sign of the wild woman. Colleen squatted and carved out an indent in the sand and set the bag of food there. She stood up, hands in her pockets, and scoured the beach one more time.

Then she walked back into the protection of the gun emplacement and smoked a cigarette. She checked her watch, went out to the sand dune, went back into the cement tunnel, thought about another cigarette, put it off, had one anyway, followed it with a stick of gum from the fresh pack she'd bought at the store when she went to buy sandwiches.

After more time than was probably necessary to realize she wasn't going to show, Colleen left, headed back down to the parking lot that used to be the old Nike missile site. She'd check back on Wild Woman later.

CHAPTER THIRTY-THREE

The sky was turning dark as Colleen drove down Paris Street, making one in the afternoon feel like early evening. The light was on in Steve Davis's bedroom. She was tempted to walk right up and knock on the front door. He'd stood her up last night at The Palms.

She held off. She had no need to get into another spat with Mary Davis just yet. The woman had enough on her mind. Too soon.

Down on Mission, she found Frank Madrid's truck parked in front of Dizzy's. She wondered if there was a guy in the bar with a bandage on his face, thanks to the rebar she had applied to it when he and his punk friend tried to set fire to H&M.

She drove back down to the beach, swung by Fort Funston one more time. The sack of food she had left was gone. That meant one of two things: her wild woman had shown up, taken the sandwiches, and now hopefully trusted Colleen more, or the raccoons or someone else had gotten a free meal. She'd come back tomorrow.

She drove home.

In her office she called her answering service. Howard Broadmoor from the *Chronicle* still hadn't returned her call. There wouldn't be anything from Moran yet. It was too early to call Alex.

So she sucked in a breath and called the Davises. The ploy she had used last night, having some male call, wasn't going to work twice in such a short period of time. And she had no stand-in this time any-way. She'd wait until Steve answered.

Mary Davis answered in one ring, her voice brittle and nervous. "Yes?"

Colleen hung up, feeling like a rat. She smoked a cigarette, waited ten minutes, called again. The same breathy *yes* was followed by more silence.

"Whoever this is can go to hell." Mary Davis slammed the phone down. Colleen smoked another cigarette, waited twenty minutes, and, feeling like a bigger rat, called again. Maybe Steve Davis would get the hint.

"Hello?" Finally, Steve Davis. "Who *is* this?"

"You stood me up last night, Steve," she said.

He dropped his voice. "I was there. I couldn't stick around."

"Okay," she said. "That makes me feel better. When can we meet? I'll fit into any time and place that works for you."

She heard Steve take a breath. "It's not a good idea now."

In the background Mary Davis said in a sharp voice, "Who's on the phone, Steve?"

"Look, Steve," Colleen said. "You're the one who called *me*. You set it up."

"I made a mistake," he whispered.

"No, you didn't. You've got something you want to tell me. And I want to hear it."

"Who the hell is it, Steve?" Mary Davis snapped in the background.

"Ma, will you just go away already? It's personal."

"I want to know who it is, damn it. The same person who's been calling and hanging up? What the hell are you up to? It's that woman, isn't it?"

"It's just a girl I know!" Steve's hand went over the receiver. There was a long, muffled exchange that ended in shouting and the slamming of a door. Finally, he came back on the line.

"I got to go," he said.

"Where and when do we meet?" Colleen said.

"Get a clue, already. Can't you see I've changed my mind?"

"Unchange it."

"Look, I can't help you. I thought I could. But I can't."

"Someone threaten you?"

He gave a laugh of false bravado.

"Who?" she said. "Frank Madrid?"

"I'm hanging up the phone now."

"Your father was murdered," she said, her voice full of venom.

There was a long pause. "I know," Steve said. "The transients at the beach . . ."

"Spare me the bullshit. It's something to do with that case your dad worked on. Eleven years ago. He was going to talk to me about it, and I was all set to meet him but—wouldn't you know it?—some *transients* at the beach killed him for no good reason after he decided to just wander down there instead of meeting me. No coincidence there, huh?"

"You don't know any of that," he said.

"I know enough," she said. "And my gut's telling me the rest. Just like yours is telling you. That's why you wanted to talk to me. But someone scared you off. Who? Ten to one it was Frank Madrid. And it's got to do with the Margaret Copeland murder. How am I doing?"

"You don't know what the hell you're getting into."

"Oh, I have a pretty good idea, Steve. And I rattle just like you do. But when push comes to shove, I don't let scumbags like the ones who killed your father get away with it. Maybe it's a character flaw.

Now you've got to ask yourself one question: How are you going to feel when I figure this out *without* your help and nail the killer your dad wanted to nail? And the one who killed your dad? How you gonna feel then? Proud of yourself? You're a young guy. You've got a good fifty years to walk around, looking at your shoes, telling yourself how you should have stood up to those vermin instead of letting your old man down. Your mother, too. Because she's going to carry this around with her, too."

And for one blissful second, she thought Steve was going to change his mind.

"I'm sorry," he finally said, "but don't call back." He hung up the phone, leaving her ears buzzing with dial tone.

Colleen exhaled a sigh of exasperation. She had just been dealt a two when she was pretty sure she was going to get a decent card.

But if it was meant to deter her, it wasn't working.

CHAPTER THIRTY-FOUR

Late afternoon, thick fog rolled across the nearly desolate playground. From the trees he watched Robyn trot right by the carousel in her platform tennis shoes and wild big-checked bell-bottoms. She wasn't stopping to watch the merry-go-round today.

He swore under his breath.

The merry-go-round sat idle and empty in its elegant circular rotunda, the varnished, painted creatures stone still, frozen on their brass poles. No riders today. Fog almost like rain. He should have known. Known she wouldn't be stopping to watch today. Bulbs of light shone fuzzy in the vapor.

It had been a risk to follow her and he had miscalculated. He gripped the bottle of ghetto chloroform in the pocket of his black warehouseman's jacket, his annoyance boiling into anger. In the other pocket he had a handkerchief ready. The top half of a plastic dry-cleaning bag was neatly folded in the breast pocket. Now he let both bottle and handkerchief go, removed his hands from his pockets, pulled the black watch cap down tight over the sides of his glasses, securing them firmly over his ears. That repeated motion reminded him of what he had done all those years ago. Not far from here. He rubbed his bushy mustache in frustration.

He was ready *now*. Ready to punish his father. Once again. The man never seemed to learn his lesson.

Then he saw Robyn, her blond ponytail bouncing as she hoisted her Charlie's Angels backpack up on her shoulder, turned, picked up the pace, dashing across the playground, moving quickly. It was chilly and she wanted to get home.

Then he realized.

She was taking the short cut up to Kezar Drive, up through the trees on the hill.

Not a bad spot to take her down. Maybe this wasn't a dry run after all.

Maybe he hadn't miscalculated. There was an element of magic about the act of hunting a quarry. It wasn't all black and white. It was a dance.

It wasn't for everybody.

He darted along the path flanking the playground, following her but staying close to the trees. The lack of people would make him obvious if she were to turn around and see him.

He was puffing with the effort, with the adrenaline.

With the excitement.

She would be sorry. Her mother would be sorry.

Oh, Father, you will be sorry.

He got to the rise in the path as he saw a white platform sneaker disappear into the trees fringing the last of the hill. Up she went. He wouldn't have thought she'd risk dirtying her nice clothes. But what did she care? She'd let her bitch of a mother clean them for her.

She was half his age and quick. But he was quick, too, when he wanted to be.

And he was driven. Driven by a passion few could grasp.

Steam from his face and fog misted up his glasses as he climbed into the trees, the mud of the path smearing wet under his shoes. He slipped, landed on a knee against the gnarled root. Buzzed with pain. *Damn it!*

He got up, panting, one knee muddy and throbbing, grabbed his handkerchief, gave his glasses a quick wipe, secured them back on his face back under the watch cap. He saw her checked bell-bottoms climb over the cement retaining wall onto Kezar Drive. Oh, but he was angry now. He was livid now. There was no stopping a man on a mission. He'd get her. He'd find a way. He was ready. He clambered up after her.

He made quick time. Yes, he had missed a prime spot, but there were still opportunities along Kezar Drive. Traffic, but still places to pull her in. One had to be flexible in this kind of endeavor. It existed on another level, had its own rules. Rules he understood. She didn't.

"Hey, Robyn! Watcha doing, girl!"

What?

On Kezar Drive, he scrambled out onto the sidewalk, staying close to the trees, peering out.

With irritation he saw Robyn, not fifty yards away, talking excitedly with her friend, the black girl from school with her hair in puffs either side of her head. She had seen Robyn, called out to her. Now the two were chatting, happy, hands gesturing. Blah, blah, fucking blah.

His heart pounded. He had been on the cusp.

He sank back into the bushes, watched the two girls cross Kezar Drive against the blare of a car horn, to the other side of the street, where the apartment buildings began. Laughing and joking.

Damn her. Damn her whore of a mother. Damn his father. The situation had turned on him. Well, if they thought he was going to be made a fool of, stopped by a little thing like this, if the world thought he would be stopped, if his father thought he would be stopped, they had another thing coming. He would take her down. And she would pay. Her mother would pay when she found out what had been done. And his father, oh, he would pay.

CHAPTER THIRTY-FIVE

"Father's not doing well," Alex said.

Phone cradled to her neck, Colleen toweled off her hair. She stood by her desk in her underwear, watching rain clouds roil in the night sky. It was getting late, past eight o'clock.

"I'm so sorry to hear that, Alex." And she was, even as she tried to keep the worry out of her voice so that it didn't transfer over. "If it helps, I can tell you what I've got so far. You know how I feel about sharing information if it's not ready, but . . . if you think it might comfort your father . . ."

"Colleen—ah—do you think you might see your way to coming down here and talking to him in person? The phone is so impersonal. And Father is about as old school as it gets."

Colleen checked her watch.

"Give me about forty-five minutes," she said. Half Moon Bay was down the coast, Highway 1. The two-lane road followed some sharp curves and it was raining. "Maybe an hour. I'll be as quick as I can."

"Thanks so much, Colleen." Alex sounded like she was choking back tears.

Colleen opted for her dark business suit, the only suit she had, with her silver bird earrings and black pumps, no nylons.

She drove down 101 and took 92 to Half Moon Bay instead of 1, taking the curves too fast, the Torino having more muscle than agility. Once she got into Half Moon Bay proper and headed up the coast into the darkness, she rolled down the window. The fresh air felt good.

* * *

"This way, please, Ms. Hayes," Harold, the butler, said.

The compact, middle-aged Asian man, wearing a crisp white shirt, black bow tie, black pinstripe vest and trousers, led Colleen up a flight of stairs carpeted with a red Persian runner. A huge stained-glass window on the landing offered a fragmented glimpse of the expansive yard behind the mansion. Beyond that, the dark Pacific.

Colleen followed Harold down a long hallway to a huge corner study that overlooked the back grounds. Like the rest the house, it was paneled with dark oak and carpeted in reds and golds. Flames danced in a stone fireplace. Frosted globe lights on the walls cast an additional warm glow.

The quiet hiss of oxygen emanated from the corner of the room.

Behind a large desk, his back to Colleen, sat Edward Copeland in his wheelchair, facing a picture window. Alex stood beside him, a hand on his shoulder. Tall trees swayed in the night wind. The back of Mr. Copeland's head showed neatly combed gray hair, indented where the band of an oxygen mask was secured.

Alex turned, gave Colleen a nervous smile. Alex wore a black knee-length dress with a white pointed collar and white cuffs on short sleeves. Her shoes were two-toned black and white, to match the dress. Colleen wondered if she ever looked like she hadn't just come off the runway. Alex's eyes flickered with apprehension.

Colleen smiled in sympathy.

"Colleen's here, Father."

Mr. Copeland's head turned.

"Splendid," he said in a raspy voice. His thin arms struggled to turn the wheels of the chair. "Excellent."

"Let me." Alex took over, turned the chair around so Mr. Copeland could face Colleen.

"I'm not dead, yet," Mr. Copeland replied, straightening his oxygen mask below his nose. His face was flushed with the minimum effort he had exerted. Silk pajamas showed beneath his paisley robe. No formal outfit today. He was doing the best he could.

"I do apologize for my slovenly appearance, Ms. Hayes," he said. "And for you having to come upstairs to my little cave—especially after driving all the way from San Francisco in this weather. It's not so easy for me to get downstairs anymore."

"It's no trouble at all," Colleen said, unhooking her bag from her shoulder.

"We need to install that wheelchair lift on the staircase, Father," Alex said.

Mr. Copeland gave a weak but wry smile. "My daughter loves to play this game, Ms. Hayes: the one where I'm going to live forever."

"Not forever, Father," Alex said. "Just long enough to install a wheelchair lift and make good use of it for as long as possible."

"Then the workmen best get started now and work round the clock," he gasped.

Colleen couldn't help but notice Alex's affectionate tone toward her father. She liked what she saw.

Mr. Copeland motioned at Harold. "Harold, get something to drink for our guest, who is still standing and shouldn't be. I'll have a brandy. A large one."

"Make it a small one," Alex told Harold. "A *very* small one. And a *large* glass of water."

"And for you, Ms. Hayes?" Harold bowed in Colleen's direction.

"I'd love a glass of white wine," she said.

He nodded deferentially, turning to Alex. "Miss Alex?"

"We don't have any powdered rhino horn on hand, do we, Harold?" Alex winked at Colleen, making her blush.

Harold cleared his throat. "Not today, I'm afraid."

"Nothing for me, then."

Harold exited the room.

"I do wish you wouldn't be so disrespectful," Mr. Copeland said to Alex.

"It's called levity, Father. And we could all use a bit more of it."

Colleen sat down in one of the buttery soft leather wingback chairs on the guest side of the desk and opened her bag. She fished out her file folder, the cover marked with notes, phone numbers, and scribbles.

Drinks appeared. Harold floated away. Colleen took a sip of white wine. It was not at all like the stuff you got in the dairy case at the corner store.

Alex stood behind her father again, a hand on his shoulder. Mr. Copeland turned his head to address her. "Will you kindly leave Ms. Hayes and me alone for a few minutes, Alex?"

Alex flustered. "I'm the one who called Colleen. I want to hear what she has to say, too."

"Not now, girl," he said gruffly.

Alex fluttered her eyelashes uncontrollably, and Colleen could see her hiding a wave of hurt. She would always be a child to him.

"With all due respect, Mr. Copeland," Colleen said, "I think it's important that *both* of you hear what I have to say—even though much of it is still unconfirmed."

"Do you now?" She could see Mr. Copeland inhaling deeply on the oxygen, clearly piqued, and trying not to show the effort involved in breathing.

"I'll be blunt. Things are moving, but everything is taking longer than expected. As much as I hate to say it, that means you may not be here to see the end results. But Margaret's murder is going to be resolved one way or another—and Alex may be the one who sees the investigation to completion."

A silence fell over the room. Outside in the sprawling yard, wind blew the trees to and fro.

"Very well." Mr. Copeland waved his hand. "Sit down, Alex."

"I don't think so, Father," she said, patting his shoulder. "You're doing more than enough of that for the both of us. I do wish you'd get off your lazy duff once in a while."

"Hysterical," he said. "Stand, then." He nodded at Colleen. "Tell us what you've learned, Ms. Hayes."

"I wasn't ready to share this yet but, under the circumstances . . ." Opening her file folder on the desk, she began with the green Ford Falcon parked near the murder site the night before Margaret's body was found. "The maintenance man out at Stow Lake says he reported the vehicle to SFPD, but that they didn't seem interested. I'd love to see if the Falcon made it into the report. I'm still waiting for a copy. But that is still close to a month away, if my request doesn't get 'dropped.'" She told him about attempting to meet Jim Davis.

"It's terrible about that poor man," Mr. Copeland said.

"It's a little more than terrible," Colleen said. "I was supposed to meet with him the day before he was found dead. You might remember Christian authorized additional expenses—to pay him for a copy of the report."

Both Mr. Copeland and Alex observed her with grim stares.

"But wasn't the man a terrible drunk?" Mr. Copeland said. "An accident waiting to happen?"

"That may be how the newspapers like to put it, but Jim Davis was a functioning alcoholic. It doesn't make sense that he would wander down to the beach and be set upon by transients when I was about to pay him two thousand dollars. And I got the distinct feeling he had something to tell me."

"I see."

She spoke about her attempt to connect with the Davis family. The lead on Margaret's old roommate. The arson fire at H&M Paint. The blue Chevy C10 pickup truck. "Add the Ford Falcon into the mix and you've got a lot of doubt about Margaret's murderer being the Zodiac."

"*Doubt* being the operative word," Mr. Copeland said. "It's a function of the human mind to try to make order when there is none, Ms. Hayes. You can't be faulted for it, but it's likely your very intelligent brain is trying to make sense of things that perhaps make no sense."

That took her aback. "I can't get anyone to work with me: reporters, police—no one. In fact, SFPD feel like the opposite of cooperation."

"SFPD are doing what they do best—sloppy work. And you don't have a license, so no one is taking your requests seriously."

"Supposedly disconnected events. But there's a linchpin that binds them together."

She had their attention now.

"Frank Madrid," she said. "Owner of the pickup uncannily similar to the one spotted outside the H&M plant during the fire. Also seen outside Mary Davis's house on multiple occasions. He's also Jim Davis's former subordinate and partner. And he didn't seem to think that the green Ford Falcon without license plates near a murder site warranted writing down."

Mr. Copeland appeared to mull that over while Alex shifted her weight to her other foot and frowned.

"So this is the path you're pursuing?" Mr. Copeland said. "The ex-partner of the man who did shoddy work eleven years ago when my Margaret was murdered?"

"My Margaret, too," Alex said quietly, squeezing his shoulder.

"Yes, yes." Mr. Copeland focused on Colleen again. "So SFPD did substandard work then and probably have not changed their ways. City employees." Mr. Copeland took a breath, with effort, let it out. "I'm not so sure you are on the right track, Ms. Hayes, I'm sorry to say."

Colleen felt she was getting resistance for some reason other than her progress. "I did say I wasn't ready to share what I'd found."

"And I can see why."

"Father!" Alex said.

"Ms. Hayes is a big girl, Alex. She can take it. She's being well paid to. Perhaps hiring someone who doesn't have a license and has her own problems with law enforcement may have been too optimistic on my part."

"Father—Christian did his due diligence on Colleen. And we *all* decided that she was just what we were looking for."

"Christian did have reservations," Mr. Copeland said.

"I know I'm on to something, Mr. Copeland," Colleen said.

"Based on *what*?"

"The facts will tie together. I just need a copy of that police report. And I'll get one—eventually."

Mr. Copeland spoke to Alex. "Would you leave the two of us alone, *now*, Alex?" He gulped a breath of air. "If it's not too much trouble, of course?"

Alex gave Colleen a look. "Yes, Father."

A few moments later, Alex's heels echoed purposely down the hall.

Colleen sensed bad news.

"Just give it to me straight, Mr. Copeland."

"My health has taken a serious turn for the worse, Ms. Hayes. I thought I had more time. A couple of months. Well, change that to weeks. The doctors are still being very generous, in my opinion. I've got a lot of work to do in order to settle my affairs."

Colleen cleared her throat. "I'm so sorry to hear that, Mr. Copeland—I really am. But I thought settling Margaret's murder was one of those affairs."

He waved her comment away. "Alex can't handle this by herself. Dredging up Margaret's murder? Taking on SFPD? Making enemies? She's a child. A lovely, spirited young woman—but still a child. It will be all she can do to take over my estate without squandering it on her ne'er-do-well friends."

"Surely that's what a trust is for."

He squinted at her, as if it was none of her business, which it wasn't. "There are ways around such things, Ms. Hayes, and believe me, if anyone can find them, it's Alex."

"From what I've seen, Alex is more than capable. And I think it's important that you share this tragic experience and resolve it together. Even if you have to take my word for it that it will be resolved."

Mr. Copeland gave Colleen a knowing squint, along with a smirk. "Has she gotten to you, too, Ms. Hayes?"

Colleen felt the warm blush on her cheeks as her face reddened. So *that's* what was bothering him. Mr. Copeland continued. "She's very good at that, Ms. Hayes: wrapping people around her little finger. The problem is, she's not much good at anything else."

"I think you might be underestimating her."

"She's my daughter. I've watched her for a quarter of a century—much longer than you. I know *exactly* what she is—pretty, vivacious, charming, seductive, but about as deep as a puddle. Just like her mother was."

Colleen found herself shaking her head. "Alex is the one who insisted I come down here tonight to talk to you. She cares a lot more than you think."

"Probably because she wanted to see *you*," he said. "Everything she does ultimately comes down to her own childish wants and needs. It's all about Alex. It always has been. She will always let me down."

"Are you sure you're not talking about Margaret?"

Mr. Copeland nodded sagely. "Touché. Very well. Let's leave it this way, Ms. Hayes. Today is Friday. Spend the weekend on Margaret, then write it up. And then we'll call it done. You keep the five thousand. You've done excellent work and I'm more than impressed. But Alex is going to have a lot on her plate sooner than we thought. She doesn't need this hanging over her head as well."

Colleen took a deep breath. "If you mean you think she doesn't need *me* around, Mr. Copeland, I can assure you there's nothing going on between the two of us."

The old man nodded, clearly embarrassed. "Thank you for being so forthright. There have been, well . . . I worry that someone will take advantage of her. Especially when I'm gone. Not you, of course," he added.

Colleen let that drop. "Margaret is as important to her as she is to you." More, perhaps, she thought, recalling Margaret's unsent letter. "From what I see, Alex isn't done grieving. She needs to see Margaret's murder solved if she's ever going to get past it."

"I value your opinion." He began gasping, which turned into a sudden attack. Colleen rose from her chair, hurried over. His lips had turned pale blue. She dialed his oxygen up. He settled down to even, if shallow, breaths. When he stabilized, she handed him his glass of water, and he took it and drank a deep draught. She took the glass from him and set it on his desk.

"Thank you again, Ms. Hayes," he said. "You have until Monday. Then make something up to keep Alex happy. Just between us, eh? I'll have Christian pay you a bonus."

"I don't care about a damn bonus! You're paying me more than enough as is. I just don't want to drop this case."

"Well, you're going to have to."

Colleen let out a sigh. "Is there any other reason you're dropping the investigation, Mr. Copeland? Something I should know about?"

"No. It's just that I thought I had more time. But I don't. Mine is almost up." Their eyes connected. "Thank you, Ms. Hayes. Now, I've kept you far too long. Please send Alex up on your way out and tell her I'm ready for bed. And thank you again for making the journey down here tonight."

There were times you couldn't cover any ground. There were times you lost it. This was one of those.

Colleen found Alex in the entryway at the bottom of the grand staircase, sitting like a statue in a chair that belonged in a museum. Legs crossed, hands folded, poised, in her black and white ensemble, she was stunning. But frown lines furled her pale brow.

She looked up as Colleen descended the stairs.

"He wants to see you," Colleen said. "He's ready for bed. I turned up his oxygen, by the way."

"Thanks, Coll." Alex stood up, smoothed out her dress. She looked up, meeting Colleen's gaze with steely blue eyes. "So what did you two talk about?"

Colleen frowned. "He thinks you and I are having a *thing*."

Now it was Alex's turn to redden. She put her hands on her slim hips. "What a damn prude! Not to mention *hypocrite*. Do you know how many 'secretaries' he's been through over the years? Right under Mother's nose. Mine, too! Ever since I can remember. Margaret detested it. And now he's worried about a couple of women doing a better job of things when all he did was send them packing when he got bored or when Mother eventually put her foot down?"

"It's his generation. And we're not doing any such thing. You have to let him know as much, Alex."

"Isn't it awful to be blamed for something you didn't do? Perhaps you should have just gone for it." She smiled, this time lasciviously.

A bolt of annoyance shot through Colleen. "Shut up. He told me to stop working on the case."

Alex's smiled dropped. "He did? But *why*?"

"From his perspective it looks like you and I are playing footsie under the table when I should be working and he's running out of time. And that only feeds his fears that you're just his little girl who can't handle the grown-up world. He doesn't think you can see it through."

"Jesus Christ." Alex let a huge sigh escape. "What a fuck-up."

"He wants me to wrap it up by Monday. But I'm going to need more time."

"Please don't stop."

"I won't, Alex."

She reached over, squeezed Colleen's hand. "You're the best unlicensed PI a girl could have. I'm sorry about that crack."

"You can't help it." They traded cautious smiles. "Better get upstairs."

Soon as she got in the car, Colleen pulled a cigarette from the box on the dash, lit it with the car lighter, and took several deep drags.

She didn't want to tell Alex that she was going to solve this case even if she was cut off completely. Even if Alex told her to quit.

She owed it to Jim Davis.

She drove home taking Highway 1, the coast road, savoring the cool night air. A scrap of moonlight broke through the clouds and flickered off the ocean.

She'd missed dinner. She reached into the pocket of her jacket for a stick of gum, thinking about her wild woman walking along the sand dunes by Fort Funston. She'd try to connect with her again tomorrow.

In Pacifica she noticed a pair of headlights in her rearview mirror.

She squinted into the rearview. The vehicle was well enough behind and in the dark, she couldn't make out much. But it was large, a sedan of some sort.

How long had it been following?

CHAPTER THIRTY-SIX

The car stayed behind Colleen through Pacifica. Passing a school and the commercial buildup, she eased her foot off the gas, slowed down to fifty, below the posted limit of fifty-five.

So did the car behind.

It started to sprinkle again, and she turned the windshield wipers on low. A gas station sign lit up the dark sky ahead. She put her turn indicator on, pulled over into the gas station, and waited, the engine running.

A moment later, an off-white Ford sedan rolled by, slowing long enough for her to see tinted windows. The tip of a searchlight poked out of the driver's-side window.

An unmarked patrol car.

It picked up speed and disappeared.

An attendant in a brown jumpsuit came jogging out of the gas station office, wiping his hands on a rag, and she waved him away to let him know she wasn't buying gas. He turned around and went back inside. She pulled over next to a dumpster, away from the pumps, and got her Bay Area map from the door pocket. Unfolding it, she flipped on the dome light to look for an alternative route back to San Francisco. It was back the way she came. She folded up her map, put it away, flicked the interior light off, and pulled out to the highway, checking the road in both directions.

On her right, pulled over on the shoulder up ahead, was her cop, taillights fuzzy in the drizzle. Waiting.

Colleen turned left, headed back south on Highway 1. She kept to the speed limit, one eye on the rearview. The rain picked up. She turned the wipers on full.

She saw the car's red taillights sparkle through the rain running down her rear window as the car spun around and headlights appeared. Following her. She told herself to stay calm.

Past the high school she cut a hard left without signaling, skidding onto Sharp Park Road. She climbed quickly into the hills, gunning the big V-8. The Torino roared toward the summit. But every time the road straightened out, she saw square headlights in her rearview.

The next time the car disappeared behind her on a bend, Colleen flipped off her headlights. She stepped on the gas, headed toward a four-way stop where the 35 Summit Road crossed, in total darkness. The pinnacle crawled with fog, visibility reduced to a few car lengths. Straight across led back down to the freeway to San Francisco. No headlights either direction. Colleen drew a deep breath and barreled through the stop sign, cutting another hard left, onto 35, sending her into a fishtail. The right rear tire caught roadside and spewed gravel. Colleen eased off the throttle, let the car straighten out. Tires gripped the road once more. She turned the headlights back on, mashed the pedal, despite the fact that she couldn't see more than fifty feet in front of her. Fog billowed past, lit up by the short reach of her headlights.

The cops behind her, or whoever they were, would hopefully assume she'd taken the alternate freeway route, the quickest way back.

Had someone at SFPD learned of her connection to the Copelands? She didn't need the Copelands implicated, especially if she was going to push ahead on her own.

She put both hands on the wheel and stared into the fog.

CHAPTER THIRTY-SEVEN

By the time Colleen got back to H&M, it was close to midnight. Her heart rate was elevated from the high-speed drive and her thoughts were tense. She'd lost the tail but she suspected they knew where she lived.

In the office, the smell of dead smoke still hung in the damp air. She took off her suit jacket, threw it against the chair. She lit up a cigarette, fluffing her damp hair out as she called her message service.

No new messages. Damn.

She stepped out of her pumps, picked them up, took them and her jacket into her room and changed into her jeans and cowboy boots and put on her poncho.

And did the rounds, more than discouraged.

The fence was as she'd left it, the pallets still leaning up against it. She felt more like a sitting duck now. When she got time, she'd take a crack at fixing it herself.

She went through the effort of moving the Torino inside the gates. She didn't need any more bad news. Someone—ten-to-one SFPD—had their unfriendly eye on her.

When she was done locking up, she checked the wooden mailbox on the front gate. Just because she always did at the end of her patrol.

And, to her surprise, found an 10x13 manila envelope. Nothing written on it. She picked it up. Held it.

She could tell there was a file folder inside. The file folder was thick with sheets of paper.

And she forgot all about the police, or whoever they were, tailing her. Her heart thumped for another reason. She wanted to tear the thing open then and there but caught herself, looking up and down Yosemite. No one around.

She headed back up to her office, where she got the space heater out of her "bedroom," plugged it in by the desk. She sat down in the manager's chair and opened the envelope clasp. She pulled the file folder from the envelope.

Laid it on her desk. Opened it.

San Francisco Police Department, Department of Homicide.

Investigative Report.

November 23, 1967.

Written by Detective James Davis. The original report. Not a copy. The only person she suspected owned this was Jim Davis. And since Jim Davis was no longer alive, that meant his son, Steve, had probably managed to get hold of it, and, after last night's failed rendezvous, and her phone call, must have relented and dropped it off.

No note, no contact information.

It was too late to call the Davis household. That place was a minefield anyway. All she knew was that, now, she had what she needed. A wild thought came to her, that she might wrap this up while Mr. Copeland was still breathing. And that would make things that much easier for Alex.

Colleen laid the report back in the folder for a moment, got up, put water on for coffee. It promised to be a late night.

CHAPTER THIRTY-EIGHT

The homicide report written by Detective Jim Davis was dated two days after Margaret's body was found in Golden Gate Park and put her murder between November 20–21, 1967. The cause of death was listed as "Homicide (suffocation)." The location was listed as the one Colleen had visited at 50 Stow Lake Drive.

"Upon responding to the above location, R/Os Evans and Madrid reported taking the statement of a Stan Paul, a cab driver who resides at 1042 Fell Street, San Francisco, who reported finding the victim while walking his dog at approximately 5:30 a.m."

The victim was reported as wearing "one white go-go boot" and showed signs of "extensive physical trauma" with "her legs twisted around," suggesting "sexual trauma." The direction of the body was listed. The condition of the victim's nails was described. The state of the victim's clothes—short Afghan coat, miniskirt, tie-dye T-shirt, white underpants and "hippie headband"—were detailed, and their location—11 ft. away from the victim—was given. The times that the crime lab and coroner were called were listed, as were their names.

The single-spaced report was nearly three typed pages. It was signed by Detective James Davis, officers Frank Madrid and Robert Evans, and a lieutenant whose name Colleen could not make out as the signature was on top of the typed name, but all were accompanied by badge numbers. The time of report completion—9:45 p.m.—was listed.

Attached was a copy of the coroner's report.

Colleen had seen two other homicide reports in her time and this was the most detailed one she'd read. Jim Davis was—or had been—thorough.

But nowhere was there any mention of a green Ford Falcon, as supposedly stated to Reporting Officer Frank Madrid by Larry Dunmore, the maintenance man at Stow Lake.

She smelled a rat.

Colleen got up, placed her hands on her hips, and stretched back to crack out her spine. It was late, almost one a.m. She refilled her coffee cup, lit another cigarette, and sat back down, picking up the autopsy report, knowing she would have to fortify herself. She had caught a glimpse of the photograph of Margaret Copeland's brutalized body earlier when she pulled the paperwork out of the manila envelope and now had to face it head-on.

She wasn't the squeamish type, but just looking at Margaret Copeland's leg—the one not wearing a white boot—raised up to almost a sitting position and twisted over her abdomen, leaving her groin wide-open and defenseless amongst the leaves and pine needles, filled Colleen with repulsion. She couldn't help but notice that Margaret's chipped toenail polish matched that of her long fingernails.

Colleen felt cowardly placing her hand over the photograph as she read around it, which included a rape victim examination account: injury to lips, injury to throat, bite marks, injury to arms, injury to wrists, injury to nails—as if that made any difference— injury to thighs, injury to ankles, and then a detail of the vaginal area, with a long list of scratches, bruises, abrasions. Specimens listed included swabs: introcoital, vaginal, anal. Blood, loose hair, pubic, matted and combings.

Enough.

She put the report facedown. She didn't need to read any more. She knew what had happened. She just needed to find out *who* made it happen.

And why certain things were missing. Like a green Ford Falcon. And Larry Dunmore's testimony.

Stomach contents showed no recent evidence of opiates, stimulants, or ethanol, but a RIA—radioimmunoassay—blood measurement showed 327 micrograms of entactogen—lysergic acid diethylamide—LSD—in the victim's system. An asterisk pointed to a footnote at the bottom of the page that stated that as little as twenty-five mcg of entactogen was capable of producing potential deleterious psychedelic effects and that 300 units was sufficient to produce severe perceptual, visual, and psychoactive disturbances. The fact that LSD dissipated from the bloodstream within twenty-four hours of ingestion suggested the victim's initial dose was in fact much higher.

Significant levels of chloroform were also detected in the blood and tissues by gas chromatographic/mass spectrometric analysis and traces were found in the victim's lungs, as well as on her face, indicating that Margaret was subdued with chloroform during the prolonged attack.

Cause of death was listed as smothering, as opposed to suffocation—which was what was recorded in Jim Davis's police report. Suffocation referred to general deprivation of oxygen, a footnote explained, whereas smothering indicated the closing of the external repository orifices either by the hand or the introduction of a foreign substance such as mud, paper, cloth, plastic, etc. Jim Davis may not have known that. Colleen hadn't.

Although Colleen did not understand half of the technical details of the coroner's report, Margaret Copeland's last twenty-four hours were nonetheless painfully clear. She had been tripping her brains out on acid and been taken advantage of by someone who knocked her out with chloroform, beat her mercilessly, sexually abused her, and smothered her to death with a dry-cleaning bag. Colleen attempted to blink away the horror the girl must have gone through. She ran her fingers through her hair and thought of Eva Unknown in her pauper's grave in Santa Cruz. Colleen had tracked down Eva's killer with a perseverance fueled by wrath.

She felt the same drive now.

Hoping she had passed the worst of the report, Colleen pushed on.

Stomach contents as stated were devoid of food or alcohol; however, two foreign objects were discovered—both small pieces of plastic. Curious.

A grainy photograph of the two pieces on a sheet of paper next to the tip of a sharpened pencil established their size, showing them to be small, innocuous fragments of black plastic, one three millimeters in length, the other two millimeters. Both pieces were of a similar width, 2.5 mm high, with a thickness of less than 1 mm. The exact material was cellulose acetate, a lightweight and relatively inexpensive plastic.

That didn't seem to make any sense at all. Except that people out of their minds on drugs might be likely to put funny things into their mouth and chew on them. But still, something wasn't right there.

Getting out her pad of yellow-lined paper, Colleen made notes. Unfortunately, tomorrow was Saturday, but perhaps she could find Millard Drake, the forensic analyst who had signed Margaret Copeland's autopsy report.

She checked her wristwatch. Almost two in the morning. She wasn't going to sleep tonight, not with the image of Margaret Copeland's body, left like trash in the park for the coyotes.

There were just some things you couldn't unsee.

CHAPTER THIRTY-NINE

Colleen sat in her office, drinking her second cup of coffee of the morning, mulling over the reports left in her mailbox. She'd done the rounds of the plant, and all was secure.

Much had fallen into place. But one thing hadn't. She flipped open the coroner's report one more time, called the San Francisco Medical Examiner's office.

It was open seven days a week, but general enquiries by the public were only handled Monday to Friday during normal business hours.

Colleen dialed Directory Assistance. Millard Drake, the forensic analyst who had written Margaret's autopsy report, did not reside in San Francisco. Colleen tried Oakland, Berkeley, Marin, Palo Alto, and a couple more Bay Area cities before she completely exasperated the operator. Colleen thanked the woman and hung up.

What she really wanted was to see the evidence. Actually *see* it. Those two odd pieces of plastic found in Margaret Copeland's stomach—she couldn't get them out of her mind.

She called Christian Newell, the Copelands' lawyer.

"What if I wanted to see the crime scene evidence from Margaret's case?" she asked.

"What kind of evidence?" he said suspiciously.

"Her clothes, personal effects."

"Aren't you supposed to be winding this thing down?" Christian said. "Mr. Copeland asked me to settle up affairs with you. I'll mail you a check."

"Whoa," she said. "What's your hurry? It's only Saturday. I have until Monday morning."

"You can keep the fee. You don't need to work on this anymore."

"I still have a couple of items to clear up. Then I'll write it all up. I want to get the report professionally typed up. How about end of the week?"

Christian Newell sighed. "I'll pencil you in for middle of the week for the report. Wednesday. Courier it to me. There's no need to bother the Copelands anymore. Have a nice weekend."

Have a nice weekend. It was a strange new language these Californians were speaking these days, one that meant absolutely nothing.

It was time to call Moran again.

Moran was out in the yard gardening. His wife, Daphne, gave a loud theatrical sigh when Colleen asked for him, put the phone down with a distinct *clunk*.

A moment later, Colleen heard someone pick up the phone.

"No update on Lesley Johns, Hayes," Moran said. "I told you someone would call if anything came of it."

"That's not why I'm calling," Colleen said. "But I do have another favor to ask."

"Related to the Copeland case?"

"I want to look at some physical case evidence. There's something that doesn't make a lot of sense." She brought Moran up to speed.

"This has gone too far, Hayes. You're treading on dangerous ground."

"I'm fine."

"I disagree. You say Mr. Copeland told you to wind it down. Take the money and run."

"That's what I tell myself," she said, "but I can't do it." She thought of Edward Copeland. And Alex. And, in her heart, she thought of Jim Davis, who might still be warming a barstool down at Dizzy's if not for her. Finally, she thought of Margaret Copeland, who never got justice. "I just can't walk away."

Moran gave a weary sigh. "You should have been a cop, Hayes."

"It's a little late for that," she said. "Unless they've changed the rules on hiring ex-cons."

She heard Moran take a breath. "Got a pen?"

Thank God. She had one ready. "Shoot."

"Call this number. Use my name discreetly. Be prepared to hand over some cash. And when you see what you need and are still stuck, think seriously about what I just told you."

"I really appreciate this," she said, jotting down a San Francisco phone number.

"And if you decide you still aren't going to take my advice and walk away, call me again. I need to convince you to drop this thing."

She didn't need a sixty-five-year-old man who'd been to hell and back risking his neck for her again. "Will do."

"I doubt that."

CHAPTER FORTY

Colleen couldn't meet Moran's contact until tomorrow—Sunday. That was how much time the man needed to finagle a way for her to see the physical evidence from Margaret Copeland's murder—if he could find a way. She understood it wasn't on the up and up. And it was going to cost pretty much everything she had left over from her retainer. But she was excited. He'd call when he was ready.

Which made it one long Saturday. It rained. Despite Christian's advice to wind things down, Colleen called the Copeland house. She needed to check in on Mr. Copeland anyway and pass along a warning. She asked for Alex first.

"Ms. Copeland's not home, Ms. Hayes," Harold said. "She said she might not be coming home until late, if at all."

Colleen felt a pang of disappointment at Alex for not keeping her father company. And, just perhaps, a hint of protectiveness, wondering who she might be with. She ignored that. "Can I trust you to pass something along, Harold?"

"Absolutely, Ms. Hayes."

"Someone followed me home last night, not long after I left your place. I think it might be related to the case I'm working on for Mr. Copeland."

"I understand."

"I don't want to alarm anyone, but please tell Alex to keep her eyes peeled. You, too."

"I will, Ms. Hayes. Thank you."

"How is Mr. Copeland today?"

"I had to call the physician. But I think he's stabilized for the time being."

"I wish there was something I could do."

"What you're doing is important."

"You do know that he's asked me to stop investigating the case, don't you, Harold?"

There was a pause. "I don't think you should stop—although it's not my place to say."

"I appreciate hearing that, Harold."

* * *

Late afternoon, Colleen called Steve Davis. It only took one call for him to pick up the phone this time, instead of his mother.

"I just wanted to say 'thanks' for the package," Colleen said.

"So you got it okay."

"I'll get the reports back to you when I've made copies."

"I don't want to see them again."

"They belonged to your father," she said.

"And look what happened to him."

"It's important they go back wherever you got them," she said. "In case someone else knows about them, and sees they're missing." Someone like Mary Davis. And anyone else who might know. It was a risk Steve Davis didn't need to take.

Steve seemed to give it some thought.

"Got it," he said.

"I can meet you," she said. "I'd prefer not to be seen in your neighborhood with you—for your sake."

"Mabuhay," Steve said. "Eleven o'clock tonight." He hung up before she could reply.

She had time to kill. She'd pay a visit to Fort Funston, see if she could find her wild woman.

* * *

The rain had taken a break by the time Colleen parked at Fort Funston early evening. She got out of the Torino, locked up, scoured the substantial parking lot that had once been host to a Nike missile site. Teenagers in cars, drinking beers. The smell of dope wafted her way. A couple of vans were parked, with fat mag wheels, their sides painted up with fancy murals. Conan the Barbarian with a bare-breasted vixen over his shoulder stood out on one. Led Zeppelin's "Black Dog" thumped from inside. Just another Saturday night in any American city. Only out here they had the drama of the crashing Pacific. If anybody was paying attention to that.

No police cars. She was keeping one eye in the rearview mirror at all times now.

Colleen picked up the sack of McDonald's, flashlight, zipped up her bomber jacket, and headed up to the sandy bluff, holding the bag close. It radiated heat in the bitter wind spitting rain. She turned on her flashlight as she approached the World War II gun emplacement. The concrete and hanging vines glimmered in the misty beam. She checked the tunnel. No one around. Too cold and wet for anyone to come up here to get high or make out. Jim Davis's flowers were gone. A few dried petals lay in the windblown sand.

She stood in the tunnel where the old giant gun once sat, built to heave shells at approaching Japanese ships, with a report so loud it could shatter the windows of nearby houses. A battle that, thankfully, never came to our shores.

Colleen waited, the flashlight pointed down at the ground. Hugging the warm bag, she pressed herself up against the cement wall to stay out of the wind. The aroma of onions and French fries made her mouth water.

And then, over the tip of the dune, here she came—Colleen's wild woman, windswept hair blowing. A quiver ran up Colleen's spine. She didn't move at first, not wanting to startle her quarry. Like stalking a deer.

And then the rest of the silhouette appeared. Haunted, thin.

Colleen stepped out slowly.

"Hi there," she said gently, as if talking to a child. Colleen held up the bag with one hand, shone the flashlight on it. "Look what I brought." Taking a couple of steps forward, Colleen set the bag down on the sandy cement and then stood back. "Burgers and fries. A drink, too. I hope you like Coke."

The woman first looked at Colleen, then the bag, then back at Colleen. Uncertain.

"Go ahead," Colleen said. "It's for you. I'm glad you came."

The woman scuffled up, grabbed the sack, scurried back to the safety of the dune. She squatted on her haunches, eyeing Colleen from a safe distance. Colleen saw Wild Woman's shoulders loosen.

"Eat up," Colleen said. "Before it gets cold."

The woman set the bag on the sand, opened it, looked inside, constantly checking to make sure Colleen wasn't about to make a move. She removed the drink, plugged in a straw. She extracted a clump of fries and stuffed them into her mouth, chewing with her mouth open. Then she dug into the sack, came out with a hamburger wrapped in paper, then another. One in each hand. She held one out to Colleen.

"No, thanks," Colleen said, "I already had one. Well, two actually." She smiled. "Nobody can really have just one, can they?"

Wild Woman gave a cautious smile, unwrapped a hamburger, bit off a third in one bite. It was soon gone, the wrapper fluttering off into the wind, and she started in on the other, stuffing fries into her mouth between bites. When the second burger was gone, she sat down in the sand and fed herself fries at a slower pace, taking a break to suck up soda.

Colleen kept the flashlight beam on the ground halfway between them, a long oval, enough so that they could share some ambient light.

"I'm Colleen."

The woman took a slurp of Coke.

"What's your name?" Colleen asked.

No answer. The woman ate some fries. Colleen wondered if she was mute.

"You were here that night, weren't you?" Colleen said. "The night that poor man was found dead." She nodded at the tunnel. "Back there."

There was a long pause while Wild Woman sat, open-mouthed, frozen, mid-bite. Finally, she nodded once.

Colleen's stomach twisted in queasy excitement. Closer. Getting closer.

"Did someone bring him here?" she asked, trying to sound casual.

Nod.

Colleen's heart thumped.

"How many? One man?"

Shook her head from side to side.

"Two?" Colleen asked.

Nod. Two men had brought Jim Davis here.

Colleen swallowed hard, deliberating over her words.

"You didn't notice if they wore uniforms, did you?" she asked. "Blue uniforms?"

Wild One held up one finger.

"So one man was a policeman? But not the other?"

Head nod.

"The man who wasn't a policeman—was he a big man? Like this?" Colleen turned sideways, made a motion with her hand, animating a big beer gut over her slim belly.

Nod. *Yes.*

Colleen's blood pressure rose. There was only one man she knew who fit that description. "Was the man who died alive when they brought him here?"

Nod.

"But not when they left?"

No movement. Frozen, mouth open, showing food mid-bite. She was afraid to say what she saw. Who wouldn't be?

"I'm not here to get you into trouble," Colleen said. "I just need to know what you saw. The man they brought here had a family."

Wild Woman seemed to take that in.

"What's your name?" Colleen asked again. "I told you mine. It's Colleen."

No answer. She wasn't eating anymore. Colleen was losing her. She would make a rotten witness anyway.

"Did they kill him?" she asked.

Wild Woman stared, then nodded once. She leapt up, leaving the rest of her food uneaten, and darted off into the shadows.

The blood pounded between Colleen's ears.

CHAPTER FORTY-ONE

Colleen heard booming rock music as she walked down Broadway, where the Mabuhay, the old Filipino nightclub turned punk venue, was wedged in amongst the nudie bars and rip-off nightclubs.

Down at the Fab Mab, she felt noticeably out of place in her bell-bottoms, cowboy boots, and bomber jacket amongst the kids in ripped jeans, torn shirts, and leather jackets dripping with chains and held together with safety pins. Mohawks and spiky haircuts abounded. Safety pins had made it through a few ears and cheeks as well. She checked the line waiting to get in. No Steve Davis. She got in line. Whoever was onstage was making the walls shake as a singer bellowed about someone being his *sex bomb, baby, yeah* over a relentless dirge.

Inside the Mabuhay, the mosh pit was in full swing, kids slam-dancing like drunken football players. Colleen pushed her way through, looking for Steve, throwing up an elbow when one body in motion collided with her. Onstage the band played low-slung guitars in a deafening attack. She settled in against the bar, ordered a beer, checked her watch.

Ten past eleven.

Twenty minutes later, she ordered another beer, hoping Steve wasn't going to bail again. She needed to get his reports back to him. She also wanted to learn more about his father.

And then she saw him, getting his hand stamped by the bouncer at the front door. Looking remarkably subdued compared to the rest of the crowd, in a faded denim jacket over a white T-shirt and jeans, short black hair slicked back. His dark eyes were intense.

He saw her right away. She wasn't that hard to make out in this crowd. He walked straight through the slam dancers in the center of the floor, pushing one aside on his way up to the bar.

She raised her beer bottle. "Glad you made it." She had to shout in order to be heard over the music.

Steve sidled up to the bar, ordered a shot, downed it. He turned around, leaned against the bar, crossed his arms over his chest. He radiated tension.

"Anyone follow you?" she asked.

He shook his head *no*.

"I've got your reports in my car," she said. "I didn't want to walk around with them."

"Okay," he said, "let's go."

She was a little surprised at his urgency but she set her half-finished beer down on the sticky bar. It was painfully loud anyway.

Outside, he lit a cigarette. Colleen nodded up the street, where her car was parked near the Broadway tunnel, deliberately out of the way in case someone was following her.

They walked, crossing Columbus. Carol Doda's flashing nipples lit up the Condor Club on the corner.

They turned up the side street where she had parked, stopped at her car.

Steve took a puff of his Marlboro, nodded in admiration. "'72 Gran Torino. Sport Roof. Not too shabby."

"Don't look too close. It's got its share of dings and scratches."

"Doesn't matter. It's got a Cleveland V8." Steve smoked, exhaled. "Four hundred and twenty-nine cubic inches. Three hundred and seventy-five horses."

"That's why I picked it up cheap, with gas at sixty-five cents a gallon."

He eyed her with what appeared to be newfound respect. A woman driving a serious muscle car.

"You know cars," she said.

For the first time, Steve smiled at her. Half smiled. "I knew all the models before I could barely stand. My dad would pull me to one side, so I couldn't see the badges or emblems—not that I could read them anyway—and he'd say, 'What kind is that, Stevie?' And I'd say, 'T'underbird.' Couldn't pronounce 'Thunderbird.' But I knew the lines of the car all right." He smoked, eyes distant in some memory. "Knew 'em all."

"You like Fords," she said. "Same here."

"'*First On Race Day*,'" he said. "My old man used to say, 'No, Stevie. It's: '*Fix Or Repair Daily*.' But then, why are all the cop cruisers Fords? Because they're the best. He used to take me out in his LTD, put me on his lap, let me drive. I remember one time—" Steve stopped, took a tight drag on his cigarette, let the smoke billow out hard. "Fuck it." He stood there, like a boy, looking at the sidewalk now. "Fuck it, anyway."

She nodded in sympathy. "I can't imagine what it's like for you, or your mom." She went around to the trunk to give him a minute to be on his own, opened it, got her shoulder bag, came back with it. She pulled a manila envelope from the bag and held it out.

"You don't know what a help these were, Steve."

He took the reports, shrugged. "You make copies?"

"I did," she said. "Let's go somewhere and talk. I have a couple of questions."

"Where?" he said, smirking. "One of the girlie bars?"

"We can talk in the car. You can admire the genuine simulated wood dash."

"I don't want to leave my mom on her own for too long. She's not sleeping."

Neither was he, judging by the rings around his eyes and gaunt look to his face.

"I'll walk you to your car, then," she asked. "We can talk on the way."

"Whatever." He took one more drag, flipped his cigarette out in the street, turned, headed off, slapping the manila envelope on his leg as he walked.

She caught up. "Thanks to those reports, I'm finally getting somewhere on Margaret Copeland, that girl who was killed eleven years ago. Your dad kept those reports for a reason. He wanted the case solved."

"Yeah," he said, smacking his leg absentmindedly with the manila envelope. "It was a big deal to him."

They walked.

"Your dad took early retirement not long after the Margaret Copeland murder—for disability, right?"

He stopped at a matte black '65 Mustang half a block from the Mabuhay. The club was throbbing with noise. A crowd milled around outside. "They called it a couple of things, but he was let go. They gave him some story about his drinking, but Dad kept a lid on his boozing then. He was just one of those guys who stayed an inch off the ground. Well, so do half the force. All cops drink. He was a good cop. Everyone said so. He made detective early." Steve got his keys out.

"How long after the Margaret Copeland case was he let go?"

"A few months?" Steve said, rubbing his eyebrow. "It was some bullshit they made up. *Stress.* At first, he pushed back. Then he got a special payment to grease the wheels. Something they pulled out of a hat. He paid the house off with it, so me and Mom would be set, he said. It was like he knew he wasn't going to live that long. After that his drinking got out of control."

"Did he ever talk to you about the case?"

"Not to me. But I'd hear other people talk about it. Kids at school. I'd hear their parents. Never my mom and dad, though. They *never* talked about it with me around. But one day, when Dad was loaded, I asked him."

"And he told you?"

"Just that the case was sidelined because of some bigwig."

That was the first she'd heard of that. "Any idea who?"

Steve shook his head sadly. "Next day he asked me never to breathe a word. Said the subject was off limits. Wasn't gonna let me have to carry *that* around. I could tell he was sorry just for telling me what little he did."

"But he told you about the reports?"

"No. But I knew where he kept them. In the garage. In the rafters. I was a nosy kid."

"I think you just wanted to know what was going on and cared about him. You think your mother knows where the reports are?"

Steve thought about that a moment, squinted. "I'm not sure. But I did hear her talking on the phone the other day. Someone was asking her whether she thought my dad had them. They were lost, I guess. She said she didn't know. But my mom plays her cards close to her chest."

Colleen cleared her throat. "Who was talking to your mom on the phone?"

Steve looked Colleen in the eye, then looked away. "I don't know about this conversation anymore. This might've been a mistake."

"No one will know you told me, Steve."

"We don't talk about my mom." He sat back on the rear fender of his Mustang. "That's where I draw the line."

"Understood—but this is important. Do you think it was Frank Madrid on the phone?"

Steve looked away. There was the equivalent of silence while horns honked on Broadway.

When Steve didn't answer, she said: "Frank's an old friend of the family—isn't he?"

Steve returned her gaze. "My old man never liked him, not really."

"But they were partners."

"When Frank got promoted. There was talk about how he pulled that off. But that's a whole different ball of wax. *You have to work with a partner,* my dad said. *Sometimes it's the hardest part of the job. They can be bigger assholes than the guys you're supposed to catch.* Frank wormed his way in—always coming around the house, sucking up to Mom. She didn't like him at first. I remember right before they let my dad go, I was nine or ten, listening at the top of the stairs. I heard Frank talking my dad into taking that fucking package. Dad didn't want to do it. He wanted to bust that case. He was a good cop. Frank said Dad had to take one for the team or people'd make life difficult. He understood how Dad felt, but it had to be done. I remember not long after that Dad talked to me—he was getting loaded more and more—and he said, 'Stevie, if a man says he's your friend, don't just take him at his word. You make sure, son.' And I knew he was talking about Frank."

"So it was Frank who was able to get your father a lump sum payment?"

"Somehow. When Frank swung that, it changed my mom's mind about him. She was never crazy about Dad being a cop to begin with, but she knew what it meant to him, so she kept it to herself. But when they dangled that money, well, that was all she wrote. Mom pushed Dad to take the package. She said the writing was on the wall and he should just quit and take it before they found another way to get rid of him, and then he might not get anything. So Dad threw in the towel. Started his next career, warming a barstool down at Dizzy's."

So Frank Madrid knew the right people. Or the wrong people. "Any idea how Frank managed the payoff?"

Then Colleen saw an SFPD black-and-white crawling down Broadway, other side of the street. *Damn.* "Don't look now, Steve."

Steve turned, saw the cop car, pushed himself up off the Mustang. "Holy fuck," he said, thrusting the manila envelope at Colleen. "Take this."

Colleen took the envelope, keeping it low, slipped it into her black leather shoulder bag, flipped the flap shut.

The black-and-white stopped in the middle of Broadway. A lean middle-aged cop with a pencil mustache and pointed bald head sat at the wheel, looking at the Mustang, then at Colleen and Steve. Another cop sat in the passenger seat.

"Hey, Stevie," the cop shouted, loud enough to carry across Broadway. His arm was resting on the door sill. "I thought that was your ride. What you up to, man?" He saw Colleen, gave her a wry smile.

"Hey, Don," Steve shouted back. He shrugged, jamming his hands in his pockets. "Nothing."

Colleen eyed the vehicle number on the door. She made a mental note: *226.*

"*Nothing?*" the cop named Don said from the cruiser. He eyeballed Colleen's body up and down, gave her a nod of approval. "She doesn't look like *nothing* to me."

Colleen wanted to slap his face.

Don flipped on the hazard lights, got out of the cruiser, hitched up his pants, strolled across Broadway, putting a hand out to stop cars.

"Be careful, Steve," Colleen said quietly as Don approached. "He's an asshole."

"Let me handle it."

Don maneuvered between two parked cars and stepped up onto the sidewalk and stood in front of them, long legs apart, one hand on the butt of his gun in the holster, the other on the handcuff case of his duty belt.

"So?" he said to the two of them, giving a playful frown that was anything but. "*Nothing?*"

"That's what I said," Steve said.

Don crossed his arms. "You know, Steve, if it was my old man just died, I might be home with my mother, not out running around."

"Sorry, Don," Steve said. "What I meant to say was, 'It's *none of your fucking business.*'"

Don rubbed his bony face. "So it's gonna be like that?" He gave Colleen a malicious stare. "Who are you?" He turned to Steve. "She's not the one been snooping around, is she?"

"Also, none of your damn business," Steve said, fists clenching, harboring a young man's temper, easily lost.

Colleen put her hand on Steve's arm, tried to convey a message to shut up and play along.

"We bumped into each other and decided to go for a drink," she said to Don. "You know . . ." She dropped her voice, let it slide into as much innuendo as possible.

"Is that what they call it now?" Don said. "You got to be ten years older than he is."

"More like fifteen," Colleen said, wanting to punch his lights out but giving him a sly wink, glad to steer the conversation away from anything related to Jim Davis.

Don gave her a look of contempt. "You know, Steve, I'm really sorry about your old man. I was a friend . . ."

"Bullshit," Steve said, vibrating with anger. "All you and Frank and the others ever did was buy him too many drinks and put him down."

"Let me tell you something, Stevie. No one ever had to encourage your dad to drink too much. He managed just fine on his own."

"Get fucked," Steve hissed. "You never respected him, because he was twice the cop you'll ever be. He had you guys figured out. Don't you have something better to do? Like go down to Hunters Point, hit on the teenybopper hookers? I know all about that shit."

Colleen put her hand on Steve's arm again, gave him a *shut the hell up* look. Then, to Don: "Give it a rest. Can't you see he needs a break? We were just going for a drink."

"Classy." Don turned to Steve. "I *do* have a lot of respect for your old man, Stevie—whatever you think. I'd like to see a little more out of you. Maybe you can start by taking care of your mom, instead of *her*." He shook his head, turned, headed back between the parked cars, putting his hand out to stop traffic. He got into the black-and-white and set off with a squeal of tires.

When the patrol car was down the street, Colleen said to Steve, "How well does this Don know Frank Madrid?"

"Everybody knows Frank." Steve smoked.

So maybe Don didn't know exactly what Colleen was up to. But he might still report back to Frank. "That guy could be trouble, Steve. Watch out for him—and Frank. Frank is onto me." Colleen retrieved the envelope. "Go home, and when you are sure—*absolutely* sure—no one is watching you, not even your mother—put these back in the rafters in the garage where your dad left them."

Steve took the envelope, smoked his cigarette. "You think they're on to me, too?"

"If not, they might be soon. Like you say, your mother could know about the reports. It's hard to think she wouldn't, unless your father kept them from her. And from the phone call, it sounds like Frank suspects she does. So you need to get them back in place, pronto, before someone finds them gone. Because if someone thinks you've been helping me . . ."

Colleen left the sentence unfinished.

Steve smoked, gave a nod.

Colleen said, "If Frank asks you about tonight, you say that I bumped into you outside the Mabuhay, asked you to go for a drink, but we got interrupted by Don, and you went home. You didn't tell me anything. That puts it on me and leaves you in the clear. Got that?"

Steve smoked, letting it sink in. "Yeah."

"You did the right thing, Steve, sending the reports my way. Your dad would be proud of you."

"Who knows?" he said, dropping the cigarette on the sidewalk, stubbing it out. He gave her one last look, turned, headed out into the street with the envelope to get in his car.

Colleen listened to the Mustang start up with a rumble, then watched it jerk out onto Broadway with a screech and thought about the Margaret Copeland case being shut down because of some bigwig.

CHAPTER FORTY-TWO

"You got an appointment, honey?" the fat man said, phone cradled to his ear, slumped back almost horizontal in a worn leather office chair that was testing the limits of its construction. Behind a desk piled high with file folders, loose court papers, fast-food containers, and at least two coffee mugs, in an office with linoleum floors that suggested former laundromat, sat—or lay—Al Lennox, president of Out Now Bail Bonds. What Colleen could see of him, around stacks of papers, was a mound of flesh in a huge wrinkled blue shirt with a yellow tie hanging off to one side like a noose.

"I called yesterday," she said, not sure how much to divulge since their business wasn't quite legit.

"You and about a million other people, sweetheart." The sole of a brown loafer stared her in the face, as the shoe rested on the desk. The chair squeaked.

Several others waited in straight-back wooden chairs around the office, leafing through old magazines or simply looking anxious. One woman told a little boy to shut the fuck up. It was Sunday morning, and Saturday night in San Francisco had generated plenty of fresh business for the courts and its satellites like Out Now Bail Bonds around the Hall of Justice.

"I'm Colleen Hayes," she said quietly.

"Oh, you're the one whose old man got popped for the DWN?"

"DWN?"

"Driving while naked." He laughed. "You bring your court paperwork, honey?"

"I'm a friend of Moran's."

The chair squealed mightily as the bulk in it rose up like a whale breaching. Al Lennox came into view, round face red with blood pressure, and scruffy salt-and-pepper hair. An untrimmed mustache complemented the look. The sloppy knot of his tie hung halfway down his shirt.

The chair came to rest.

"I remember now," he said. He hung the phone up in an unexpectedly delicate motion. "I was on hold anyway." He leaned forward on his elbows. It seemed an effort for him to get that close to the desk. He managed to fold his pudgy hands.

"You bring the money?"

Colleen glanced around the office. A poster of Hawaii failed to offer much relief. At the other desk, a black man even larger than Al Lennox—but one who had transformed his mass into muscle and wearing thick glasses and suspenders over a short-sleeved white shirt—was helping an elderly woman in a blue hat fill out paperwork. His desk was the polar opposite of Al's, meaning it was organized and you could see more than half its surface.

"I did," Colleen said.

Al Lennox raised his eyebrows and held his hands up, as if to say, *Well?*

Colleen picked up her bag from the floor, retrieved a white envelope that contained twenty-five twenty-dollar bills. She leaned forward, found an empty spot on Al's side of the desk, tossed the envelope over. She sat back, crossed her legs, smoothing her blue skirt over her knees. This caused Al's attention to wander for a moment. But he was soon digging through the contents of the envelope, his lips moving as he counted bills.

"And you got the same amount for my contact, right?" he said.

Colleen frowned as she set her bag back down on the floor beside her straight-backed chair. "I don't believe we discussed that on the phone."

He nodded and she could see his tongue working underneath his upper lip, moving the push-broom mustache around. "The good news is, it's a go—the evidence inspection. The bad news is, he's not gonna do it for the standard amount. Not something like this."

No one else in the office seemed the slightest bit concerned in their conversation. The only one having a problem with it was Colleen.

"So we're talking another five hundred?" she said, incredulous.

Al Lennox confirmed with a single nod.

"That's not right," she said.

"I'm sorry, honey. But in this line of work, things are variable. If you need to think about it, fine. I'm here, seven days a week."

What could she do? If she wanted to see Margaret Copeland's case evidence . . .

"When do I get to see the—ah—evidence?"

"Today, if you want."

Today had a lot of appeal. She just didn't have the money. She had run-around money but, until H&M paid her invoice, or Mr. Copeland sent a check, five hundred dollars might as well be a million.

"I'll have to write you a check," she said. "The banks are closed today."

She saw him squint as he scrutinized her face. *Trust her?* A decade behind bars could make her hard to read when she chose to.

"Hell, you're a friend of Moran's," Al Lennox said with a smile. "That's as good as any bank."

Colleen picked up her handbag again, got out her checkbook.

"Do I make it out to Out Now Bail Bonds?" she said.

"Make it out to me personally."

"I'll need a receipt," she said. "For my expenses."

"What have you been smoking?" Al Lennox gave a smirk. "My work is guaranteed. I don't stay in business by shortchanging customers, honey. Not with my kind of clientele."

As she wrote out the check and deducted the balance in her register, she saw that Hayes Confidential was now running a negative surplus. She'd heard the governor use the phrase on the radio the other day.

She stood up, dropped the check on Al's side of the desk. She didn't think she could watch him struggle like a seal trying to get onto a dock for a fish.

Al examined the check, nodded, let it flutter to the desk. "I'll call the guy now." He picked up his phone, dialed a number, put the receiver to his ear. After a brief phone call, he gave her an address on Potrero.

"Lenny Coltrane is the man you want to see." Al consulted his watch, a big shiny gold thing. "He works the day shift." Al turned to the black man working with the old woman at the desk next to him and said, "Peanut, when you're done there, how about getting us some burritos?"

CHAPTER FORTY-THREE

"You got five minutes," the short, stocky evidence officer said, dumping two cardboard boxes with Margaret Copeland's case number on them onto a Formica table in the examination room that doubled as a break room. The overhead fluorescent light buzzed.

Just to make sure that his instructions were clear, Lenny Coltrane held up his wrist, showed Colleen the time on his watch: 2:58. "We'll call it three-oh-five." He gave an oily smile. He had thin lips, pale skin, and brown eyes set far apart. "Then you're done looking."

They were in the long-term evidence storage facility on Potrero Boulevard, next to one of the garages, down the street from SF General. Property/Evidence Supervisor Coltrane sat down on the opposite side of the table and lit up a Lucky Strike, blowing a smoke ring, staring at the candy machine.

It should not have been a surprise that Colleen would not be left alone with case evidence. But it was. It didn't matter, she supposed. She needed to see what those pieces of plastic were, the ones mentioned in the autopsy report. They might trigger a breakthrough in the investigation.

"Time's a wasting," Coltrane said, as if reading her mind, showing her his watch again and taking another puff of his non-filter cigarette. A hacking cough took over for a moment. He covered his mouth with his cigarette hand.

"So it is," Colleen said, standing at the table, taking the first box from the stack down, setting it in front of her. It was light so she started on the other one, removing the lid.

The yellow evidence sheet lay on top. She removed it, placed it by her side, gave the list the once-over.

One Afghan jacket. A pair of white plastic boots. A miniskirt. A tie-dye T-shirt. Panties. Personal effects. Miscellaneous.

All of these items were encased in heavy-duty plastic bags, with case and exhibit numbers written on each bag.

The underpants were the first item.

She held up the baggie with the once white cotton panties to the fluorescent light. High cut, modest compared to the rest of the hippie garb. One side was torn away and the material smeared with mud and blood long since faded. Nothing more to be learned from these.

Next, she removed a larger baggie that contained the tie-dye T-shirt. Ribbed cotton, wild colors, albeit faded now, mostly blue and purple, all in a swirl, with a jarring streak of dried, rust-colored blood across the bottom. She placed that to the side as well.

The miniskirt was yellow with a matching looped-through belt. Likewise soiled.

The boots took up the lion's share of the box.

She held the bag with the boots up to the light. They were cracked with time, moldy, and caked with dried muck. One boot was much worse off than the other, very muddy, and heavily blood-smeared. She assumed this was the one that Margaret had been wearing when she was found, the one that had taken the brunt of the attack.

She set the bag down, began to pull open the Ziploc fastener.

"Uh-uh-uh," Coltrane said, admonishing her.

"What?" Colleen said in surprise. "I can't take a quick look?"

"No way, José," Coltrane said, smoking. "What did you figure?"

"I figured I'd get a hands-on look for my thousand dollars."

"*A thousand bucks?*" he said, eyes popping. "Is that how much that fat bastard charged you?"

"Five hundred apiece," she said. "Right?"

Coltrane's face fell. "To hell with that!"

"You'll need to take that up with Al." She tossed the items back in the box, pushed it angrily to one side.

While Coltrane muttered and shook his head, she started in on the second, lighter box.

"Where's the Afghan jacket?" she said, checking the inventory list.

"Doesn't fit in a box," Coltrane said, as if she were dense. "It'll be in a storage closet somewhere."

"I'd like to see it," she said.

Coltrane stuck the half-smoked cigarette in his mouth, held up his wristwatch. Three-oh-three. "If there's time. And there won't be."

"This is complete and utter bullshit."

He held his hands up to the ceiling as if the situation was beyond his control.

Colleen swore, opened the second box.

The personal effects included a near empty pack of Rizla rolling papers, a Muni bus transfer, an opened roll of Lifesavers, shriveled and brittle, a small, wrinkled cellophane wrapper of some sort, a crumpled dollar bill, and a dime. A pair of tarnished earrings, Egyptian Ankh symbols. To finish off, a leather necklace with three turquoise blue beads and a bloodstained tie-dye headband.

"No purse?" she asked.

"Do you see one?" Coltrane said, frowning. He was still annoyed about how much Al Lennox had charged for this private viewing.

"Kind of like the coat," she said flatly.

"Your time's almost up," he said, puffing.

The last baggie that lay in the bottom of the near empty box was small and labeled "Miscellaneous." It contained what appeared to be the two small broken pieces of black plastic mentioned in the autopsy report. They had been found in Margaret Copeland's stomach. Colleen took the bag out, felt the fragments through the thick clear plastic with her fingers and thumb. A shiver went through her own stomach at that point, touching these mysterious items that had somehow found their way into the poor girl's belly.

"You got one minute left," Coltrane said. "One lonely minute."

She held the bag up. "I need a closer look at these."

Coltrane shook his head, smashed his cigarette out in an overflowing amber glass ashtray.

You might as well be hung for a sheep as for a lamb.

Colleen opened the small Ziploc bag, reached inside.

"What the hell do you think you're doing?" Coltrane jumped up. "You'll get your fingerprints on those!"

"Oh, lighten up," she said, touching the fragments. "It's not going to matter at this point. This case is eleven years old."

He grabbed for the Ziploc bag now encasing Colleen's hand and she took the opportunity to make the biggest fuss possible, yanking her hand out of his way, "accidentally" knocking the larger box of evidence onto the floor, along with the ashtray full of butts. Ash flew as the ashtray shattered. She made sure that the Miscellaneous bag tumbled to the floor as well.

"Jesus Christ!" Coltrane shrieked. "That's exactly why I didn't want you to fucking open that!" He fell to the floor, scrambling for the bag.

"I'm really sorry," Colleen said, palming her hand to her mouth.

"Fuck!" he hissed, standing up with the baggie that had contained the fragments. "One of 'em's gone!"

"Maybe it's under the candy machine." With the other evidence all over the floor, it was a reasonable deduction. Colleen was betting he'd buy it.

He checked his watch. "We need to get out of here."

"I'll help you look for it."

They both got down on the floor and peered under the candy machine. A year's worth of dust and trash.

"Crap," he said. "Nice goin'."

After a brief, fruitless search, they both got up off the floor, dusted themselves off. She helped him collect the fallen box of evidence and restore the items.

"You'll find it," she said.

"You better hope so."

And if he didn't, who was he going to tell?

"This is the last time I do Al a favor," he said, showing her out.

Colleen doubted that.

"Have a nice day," she said.

Outside it was starting to rain again as she picked up the pace and made for the Torino parked at a meter. She got in behind the wheel, double-checked for anybody following. Clear.

Then she raised her hand to her mouth, spit out the chip of broken plastic she had secreted under her tongue, into her palm. She felt a dark connection, knowing that Margaret Copeland had done something very similar, eleven years ago, but in reverse.

She stared at it.

It had been found in Margaret's stomach.

She shuddered.

What the hell was it?

CHAPTER FORTY-FOUR

Monday morning, armed with a Virginia Slim, a handful of dimes, and a cardboard cup of coffee that set her back thirty-five cents, Colleen made her calls standing at a pay phone by the forecourt of a Shell station at Sixth and Mission. A panhandler offering to wash customers' windshields at the mini serve island was eyeing her Torino parked under the billboard advertising *Dallas*, a new prime-time drama from CBS.

"Millard Drake, please," she asked the receptionist at the *San Francisco County Examiner*'s office.

"Mr. Drake retired last year, miss."

Colleen asked for his address.

"I'm sorry but I can't give that information out."

"Oh, that's too bad. I was hoping to get his check in the mail today. It's the first payment on his annual annuity. I'll make some calls. Thank you very much for your help."

"I'm sorry," the woman said. "Who did you say you were with?"

"Wells Fargo Annuities Department. The check was returned. Wrong address."

"I suspect it wouldn't be any harm, in that case."

Colleen had her pencil ready, poised over her penny notebook on top of the pay phone next to her coffee.

The second call was to the Copeland residence in Half Moon Bay. Harold the butler answered. Alex was home. He put her through.

"I was just thinking about you, Coll," Alex said.

That was nice to hear.

"Any news?" Alex asked.

"Actually, yes," Colleen said. "But I'm going to need a little more time."

"It's Monday morning. Didn't Father give you the weekend to finish?"

"Christian and I agreed until midweek to complete the paperwork."

"You're like one of those Gila monsters."

"That doesn't ever let go once it latches on?" Colleen smoked and tapped ash into the air. "In some ways. How's your father?"

"With the doctor, as we speak. On oxygen twenty-four seven. Soon as I'm done talking to you, I need to call the supplier, refill our order."

"Any plans to move him into a hospital?"

"A good idea but not in his wishes in the least. My other chore— and I shouldn't use that word—is to hire full-time nurses. As soon as possible. You don't know anybody, do you?"

"I wish I did." And she did.

"Well, it's good to speak to you all the same," Alex said. "That wasn't too risqué, was it?" she said with a playful edge. "I wasn't being too forward, I hope?"

Colleen laughed, the first laugh in days. "No. But you might not think it's so nice when you learn the reason I called."

"What is it—your mysterious reason?"

Colleen took a deep breath. "I need to borrow some money. Before a check bounces."

"Oh, is that all? And here I thought it was something serious."

How nice it must be not to have to worry about cold hard cash all the time. "I ran into an unexpected expense with your sister's case. I know I'm not technically employed anymore but I'd like to keep my head above water until I see it through. There shouldn't be anything else. And I'm willing to cover it myself, once I get reimbursed by H&M Paint."

"Don't be so damn ridiculous, darling. How much do you need?"

"Five hundred would get me out of the jam I'm in today. Another couple hundred would cover me until the ghosts at H&M finally decide to pay me."

"Well, unfortunately, I don't keep that much cash on hand. I'm sure you're shocked. But I've got to run some errands later and will run to the bank as well. I can meet you tonight."

Colleen let out a sigh of relief. "You just saved my bacon."

"Should I bring it over later?" she said in a low voice. "Your place? Hmm?"

"Not a good idea."

"I see," Alex said coolly. "You just want my money."

"It's not that," Colleen said. "I'm worried it's getting a little dangerous around there."

"Harold did say you called to warn me about someone possibly following."

"Please take it seriously. I can come down there. Maybe catch a glass of that knockout Chardonnay Harold serves."

"I need to be up in the city later anyway. Met me at Peg's Place."

"Peg's Place being a bar, I take it."

"Not just any bar."

"What time?"

"Ten-ish?"

Colleen wouldn't get her money into the bank until tomorrow. It would have to do.

"I'll be there," she said. "And thanks again."

"Just don't think you're gonna get lucky," Alex said with a laugh, then hung up.

CHAPTER FORTY-FIVE

The choppy ocean waves outside Mendocino seemed more desolate than those just a couple of hours south in San Francisco. Driving north along Highway 1, past the old lighthouse and the picturesque nineteenth-century village built out on the bluff during the logging boom, Colleen saw a different world than the one she'd left behind that morning. It was one separated by windblown trees and rural cattle ranches stretching out to the rugged, foggy coast.

Last she knew, her daughter, Pamela, still lived not far from here, in a commune near Point Arena, in an old farmhouse that looked idyllic but was quite the opposite. Colleen had been turned away with more than just a cold shoulder—a restraining order, to be exact. To stay away from her own daughter. None of that would've mattered so much had Pamela not ultimately spurned her as well. Didn't want to know her own mother. The fact that Pamela was brainwashed by religious extremists with shaved heads and orange robes didn't placate Colleen. She'd seen the rage in her daughter's otherwise vacant stare. Much of it was directed at the world at large, but much of it was reserved just for Colleen. And had been for years.

When Colleen had killed her ex all those years ago—in her own fit of rage—it was because of what Pamela's father had done to their daughter when Pamela was a child. But Pamela never saw it that way. Denial? Colleen's selfish, angry reaction over Pamela's needs? Was Pamela angry at the fact that Colleen never saw the abuse until the day she stabbed her ex? There was a year, when Pamela was seven, when she was quiet, moody. Sullen. Colleen had initially read that as Pamela being old enough to sense her parents' dead marriage. More than dead, a sham, forced on them when Colleen got pregnant at seventeen. Neither one of them wanted each other after a few meaningless minutes in the back of Roger's Camaro. But he was determined to do the right thing, like the martyr he was, and insisted they get married. And made sure everyone knew of his sacrifice.

They all suffered for it—when Colleen thought Pamela was somehow exempt. Fool. As it turned out, Pamela paid the highest price. The chasm between Colleen and her ex, silent and mutual, where they were more than willing to ignore each other, allowed his sick behavior to go undetected. How Colleen wished she had gone it alone, raised Pamela solo. Wallowing in her own misery, she never saw what was happening right under her nose to her own daughter. And, as a mother, she should have.

And now, Colleen had to accept it.

So she was anxious to see if Pamela was still living at the Moon Ranch commune, if nothing else. But checking meant violating the restraining order and thus the terms of her probation.

A decade in prison had forced her to learn patience. She would have to wait until an opportunity appeared, and then she'd move to reunite with Pamela. She would look for one when she was done with Margaret Copeland.

Just north of Mendocino, the low Torino crawled up a rocky dirt road past towering redwoods where Colleen found an old Victorian overlooking the Pacific. Built nearly a century ago, its dilapidated charm was slowly being restored by its new owner, Millard Drake— the man who had written Margaret Copeland's autopsy report.

Colleen pulled over next to a weather-beaten Jeep Wagoneer, its faux wood paneling turning white with salt air. She shut the engine off and heard the whish of the wind through the trees and, behind her, the distant boom of the ocean. And then from inside the house, the pounding of a hammer. She got out of the car. In her skirt suit, the air was chill. A sizable German Shepherd bolted off the wrap-around covered porch and charged at her, barking like a fiend.

Colleen jumped. "Nice doggie," she said, as calmly as possible.

The dog stayed, but blocked her path to the house, growling in a way that made her spine tremble.

A screen door slammed and an older woman emerged, wearing a tool belt slung over baggy overalls. Her gray hair was pulled back and, despite her advanced years, she moved as someone who was fit. The dog kept snarling.

"Good boy, Roscoe," she said. "Go to your place now."

Roscoe immediately terminated his snarling assault, turned around like a lamb, and trotted back up the old wooden stairs to the porch where he lay down and watched Colleen with his head on his front paws.

"How can I help you?" the woman said in a cool tone. She had an educated East Coast accent.

Colleen had a business card ready. "I was hoping to talk to Mr. Drake. I'm researching a case he worked on many years ago."

The woman took Colleen's card in her rough hand. A Band-Aid wrapped one thumb. She read the card, looked up. "You drove up from San Francisco? You didn't think to call first?"

"I thought about it, Ms. . . ."

"Drake," the woman said as if Colleen might be slow.

". . . Ms. Drake, but, to be perfectly honest, I didn't want to be turned away. It's that important to the family I'm helping." She could say *helping*, because, as of today, she wasn't getting paid to work the case anymore. And it sounded better.

"This wouldn't be about the Copeland case, would it?" Ms. Drake asked, raising her eyebrows.

"It is," Colleen said. "As you may be aware, the case was never solved. Mr. Copeland is terminally ill. It would mean a great deal to him and his daughter to gain any fresh insight into the murder in order to put the matter behind them before he passes."

Mrs. Drake tapped Colleen's business card on a knuckle, frowning. She shook her head, handed the card back. She turned, headed back to the house.

"There would be a reward leading to any new information," Colleen said. There was no such thing, but Colleen could figure out something.

Mrs. Drake stopped, turned back around.

"We are *not* interested." She marched to the house.

"Can you please tell me why?" Colleen called after her.

Mrs. Drake stepped up on the porch.

"Anything you tell me would be kept in complete confidence," Colleen said.

There was a pause before Mrs. Drake went inside. The door closed behind her. The lock snapped shut. Head on paws, Roscoe watched Colleen from the porch.

Damn.

Colleen checked her watch. It was a good thing she'd had a big breakfast. She might miss lunch. She went to the Torino, got in, rolled down the window, lit a Virginia Slim. She'd wait them out.

By the time she was finished with the cigarette, she saw a curtain move. A figure, eyeing her. If the Drakes called the police or the sheriff, she'd have some explaining to do.

Colleen turned on the AM radio. CBS news talk crackled with static. She punched the other chrome presets. Same story. Poor reception up here. She turned the radio off and sat back.

If the cops came along, she'd leave. But she was running out of options. Or, rather, Edward Copeland was.

Half an hour later, the curtain shifted again. Mrs. Drake's silhouette. The curtain fell back into place. A moment later, the front door opened.

Mrs. Drake appeared, stood on the porch, hands on hips.

"Make it quick," she said, turning around without waiting for an answer, heading back inside the house.

Colleen found Mr. Drake, a stick of a man, also in his later years, sitting at a workbench, studying architectural plans. The interior of the house was down to the studs in places and in others showed the faded opulence of what it once was, with ornately trimmed woodwork and Victorian ceiling stencils. It looked to be a labor of love to bring this structure back to its former condition but that seemed to be what Mr. Drake and his wife were doing with their retirement.

Mr. Drake turned in his chair with what appeared to be an effort to examine Colleen as she entered the half-finished back room facing a hillside of pines and tall redwoods. His features were gaunt and his skin an unhealthy white, although his pale blue eyes were steely behind gold-rimmed grannie glasses. He wore a roomy plaid shirt and a New England Patriots ball cap. If he weighed more than a hundred and thirty pounds, Colleen would have been surprised. She suspected some illness had the better of him. Perhaps that was why the Drakes had relented on seeing her— sympathy for the dying Mr. Copeland. The airy room wasn't warm at all.

"My wife tells me you want to talk about the Copeland case, Ms. Hayes?" He had the same refined accent his wife did but not as pronounced.

"Yes," Colleen said. "Thank you for agreeing to meet with me."

"I haven't promised anything yet," he said.

"As I told your wife, anything you tell me will be kept in the strictest confidence."

"Good, because if anything comes of this discussion, I'm denying it. I will not testify in any court, either. Eleven years ago, I was instructed not to discuss the case."

Interesting. "Understood," she said. "You signed the autopsy paperwork."

"I did." His eyes were momentarily drawn to hers. "Where are my manners?" Bracing himself with a hand on the back of his chair he stood up and tottered over to an old wooden ladder-back chair with a skill-saw on it. He soon had the saw off and the seat dusted with a rag. Millard Drake's legs were as thin as posts. Colleen headed over to help him bring the chair back to the workbench, but he stopped her, dragging the chair by himself across the rough wooden floor and maneuvering it into place for her.

"Thank you," she said, sitting down.

He raised his head and shouted past Colleen's shoulder. "Alice? Are you thinking of putting the kettle on?"

"No, please," Colleen said. "I don't want to trouble you."

After a lengthy pause, Alice Drake shouted from another part of the house, "Tea or coffee?" as if she might be busy putting out a fire.

Millard Drake gave Colleen an inquisitive look.

"Coffee, if I have a choice," Colleen said.

"Coffee!"

"Just a moment!" his wife snapped.

Soon they were drinking mugs of rich coffee loaded with cream and sugar, and Alice Drake had left the room as icily as she had entered it.

Colleen set her cup down on the workbench and got her file folder out of her shoulder bag. The file was growing thicker, more recently with her hastily scribbled notes from that morning's visit to the evidence facility. She got out the copy of the autopsy report Mr. Drake had written eleven years before.

"No need for that, Ms. Hayes. Margaret Copeland was one of the more memorable cases."

She shut the file, rested her hands on top of it. "It seems very thorough."

"I miss my work."

"There's no semen."

"I beg your pardon?" He blinked in surprise.

"In your report, I mean," she said. "Every other bodily fluid is listed. Locations, color, volume, state—except for semen. Kind of a given for a rape, no?"

"Perceptive." Millard Drake took a sip of coffee, cradled his cup. "That's because there wasn't any."

"You don't think that's odd? In a case where a man—it *was* a man who killed Margaret Copeland, I assume."

"It had to be. The physical strength alone shown during the beating, even with the fact that he subdued her with chloroform—oh yes. It was a man."

"Was he wearing a condom? There's no mention of any of the lubricants sometimes found in them."

Millard Drake shook his head. "If there had been, it would have been in the report."

"And wouldn't it be odd for him to wear a condom in the first place? Somebody who exhibited such a wild, uncontrolled temper?"

Millard Drake gave an approving nod. "Exactly."

"So, I guess I don't understand."

"Margaret Copeland's murderer wasn't wearing a condom. Or, if he was, it had absolutely nothing to do with what he did to her. Because, although he violated her in the most depraved and psychologically sick manner possible, he never consummated their union sexually. He couldn't, most likely."

Colleen considered that. "Impotent?"

"Perhaps. But more likely inhibited. So much so he couldn't follow through. Repressed rage. Something of that nature. Happens all the time with that kind of crime. Rape is never about sex. But it is always about control. And anger. And murder is the only way some men—thankfully very, very few—can reach any sort of a fulfillment. In this case, this was one enraged killer."

"You think he might have been stalking her?"

Millard Drake lifted his cup to his lips with both hands, drank. "Perhaps. Although there was no evidence of what is called *regret*. No covering up of the body after the act, no cushioning or hiding of the limbs or head—all the things one sees when a victim is well known to the killer. Although he did pose her right leg in a manner that highlighted her humiliation. If he knew her, he probably didn't know her well. As I say, anger was driving him."

Colleen recalled the hideous positioning of Margaret Copeland's leg with a slight shudder. "If he didn't know her well, why so much anger?"

"Anger at someone else. Misdirected." Mr. Drake gave a thoughtful frown. "Anger at a parent is very common."

Colleen nodded as she considered that. "SFPD have suggested Margaret Copeland was a Zodiac victim."

Mr. Drake sipped coffee and shook his head. "The signature of this killing doesn't support that. A completely different ritual. The plastic bag over the head—rare. The use of chloroform. The Zodiac tended to simply shoot his victims. Or stab them. Nothing elaborate, really. And take the cocked leg—very unusual. In all my years, I've never seen anything quite like it. And haven't since. It makes me think the murder was a one-off."

Colleen took that in. "Your analysis is so insightful. I can't help but wonder why it wasn't written up."

"Oh, but it was."

"It *was?*"

He nodded toward the other part of the house where his wife was banging a pot on a stove with gusto. "Doctor Alice Drake, former Chief Forensic Psychiatrist at Atascadero State Mental Hospital— where Margaret Copeland's killer should have been. She wrote it up as a research paper but SFPD weren't interested."

Colleen couldn't do anything but frown.

"Alice was quite unhappy about it," Millard Drake said. "There was plenty of evidence, especially with Detective Davis's report, and with the psychiatric profile Alice worked up, the case could've been solved. *Should* have been."

Colleen just came out with it. "It's as if SFPD didn't want to hear about it."

"I can't say—except that the investigation was dropped quickly, then thrown into the Zodiac file." He gave her a wry squint that told her he was being diplomatic at best.

"Time for your medication, Millard!" Alice Drake shouted from the kitchen.

Colleen had to take a chance.

"I won't keep you," she said, "but I do have one last question." She reached into the pocket of her blue suit jacket and came out with the small round pill case she had picked up in a drugstore after she'd left the evidence facility. She held it out, flipped the lid, showed Millard Drake the plastic fragment.

He looked at it, his eyes bulging behind the round lenses.

"Where on earth did you get that?" He eyed Colleen suspiciously. "That's evidence!"

"I'm trusting you not to tell. I plan to return it when I'm done."

He took a deep breath, pulled his hat off, ran his fingers through his thinning hair, put his hat back on.

"Well," he said, "it has been sitting around for eleven years, I suppose."

"That's what I thought. What do you think it is?"

"No idea," he said. "Except that it must have been important to Margaret Copeland. She swallowed it shortly before she died."

"How do you know that? That she swallowed it *shortly* before she died?"

"It was in her stomach. She hadn't eaten in almost a day. It would've been in one of the intestines if she'd swallowed it much earlier. But there was another piece, too, correct?"

"One is all I managed to get hold of. Why do you think Margaret swallowed it?"

"One moment." He sat up in his chair. Again, he shouted over Colleen's shoulder. "Alice—would you mind coming in here for a moment?"

Impatient footsteps thumped into the room. Alice Drake stood there with a floral apron on over her overalls. Her fists rested on her hips. Not a patient woman.

"Ms. Hayes here was asking about the plastic fragments found in Margaret Copeland's stomach," Millard Drake said.

"What about them?" Alice Drake said.

"Why you think she might have swallowed them?"

"It's all in my paper," she said. "Although as hypothesis, admittedly." Her voice softened. She looked at Colleen. "Considering the emotional and mental state Margaret Copeland must have been in during that hellish experience, and the fact that she was out of her mind on LSD—not to mention chloroform—it made total sense that she would've grabbed whatever little scrap of normalcy lay around her and that it would somehow find its way into her system. She was trying to take a pill, if you like—to make her nightmare go away."

Colleen pondered that for a moment. And didn't quite buy it. But she wasn't a pathologist or psychiatrist. She had an Associate's degree in English she'd earned in prison.

"Thank you," she said. "This is all very helpful. The Copelands will be most grateful."

"You're welcome," Alice Drake said in a cold tone, then left the room.

Colleen closed her pill case, put it back in her pocket, put her file back in her shoulder bag. She stood up, extended her hand to Millard Drake. They shook.

"I'll be more than glad to tell you whatever I find out," she said. "If you want to know."

"Of course, I want to know."

"I only ask that you not talk to anybody about this until I'm ready?"

"Nobody's wanted to talk about this for eleven years, Ms. Hayes. A little longer isn't going to make any difference."

CHAPTER FORTY-SIX

Colleen took Highway 1 out of Mendocino south, along the coast, heading back to San Francisco. Past Little River she approached the 128 turnoff that proceeded inland, the fastest way back. Highway 1 might be scenic but it was winding and slow.

She punched a chrome button on the AM dash radio. Reception was slightly better. KCBS radio news talk included callers ranting about the brewing problems in Iran. President Jimmy Carter had his hands full. The static made the grating chatter even more grating. She pressed another button, got Dr. Don Rose, with his silly horns and noisemakers. An old '60s song came on, one she used to love. Two minutes of mindless fun. She watched the 128 turnoff sign come and go, as she stayed on the coast road. She told herself it was because she was in no real hurry to get back. She wasn't due to meet Alex until later tonight. She needed time to mull over what she had just learned from Millard Drake and his wife. To her right, the waves swelled before crashing up onto the shore.

But if she was being honest with herself, she knew why she had missed the turnoff. Why she had come up to Mr. Drake's without calling ahead. Moon Ranch lay just south of here. A no-man's land somewhere between this world and one Colleen didn't understand.

One where Pamela, her daughter, was staying, last time Colleen had stopped by.

It had been two months since she'd last tried to see Pamela. That visit had been followed by a restraining order served by the Unification Church. Violating that order meant Colleen would fail her upcoming parole review. Things were already shaky.

But by the time she neared Point Arena, midafternoon, Colleen began to second-guess herself. She decided to stop and call ahead, see if Pamela was still living at Moon Ranch. She pulled the car over at a tiny coffee shop covered with weather-beaten shingles, used the restroom, bought coffee, lit a Virginia Slim at the pay phone outside, dropped a dime, and called Moon Ranch.

"Unification Church," an indifferent voice said.

"Good afternoon," Colleen said, smoking. "This is FedEx. We have a delivery scheduled and I wanted to confirm the recipient will be there to sign before someone comes all the way out there." Moon Ranch was out on the headlands, a ways off the main road.

"What is it? And who is it for?" Not the friendliest of conversations.

"A registered check for Pamela Hayes." That should get their interest. The church was always looking for ways to bleed their followers.

Line static crackled.

"Just a minute." The phone was placed on a hard surface. A muffled conversation followed that Colleen couldn't make out. Then someone else picked the phone up.

"Who is the check from?" an older man said.

"The estate of Thelma Hayes," Colleen said. "I believe it's an inheritance settlement." What a laugh. Colleen's mother had left nothing but a pile of debt.

"What time do you expect to be here?" the man said.

Colleen checked her watch. "Forty-five minutes?"

"Someone will meet you at the gate."

"Just to confirm, we will need Pamela Hayes's signature," Colleen said.

"She will be there to sign. We'll meet you at the gate. Do *not* attempt to enter the premises." The phone was hung up with a clatter, leaving a dial tone. Colleen took a drag on her cigarette.

It sounded like Pamela was still at Moon Ranch—what she wanted to know. She could head back to SF.

But now Colleen wondered what condition her daughter was in.

She had to know. A quick look. From a distance. She wouldn't try to make contact. Just make sure Pamela looked like she was holding up.

Colleen stepped out her cigarette, drained her coffee, went out to the gravel parking lot in front of the coffee shop, the wind chimes tinkling in the cold ocean breeze.

She needed to draw the church members out of the house up to the gate. But they knew her. They knew her car. There was the restraining order to consider.

Across the street at Beep's, a faded drive-up with outdoor tables, she noticed two teenage boys in a green 1950s Dodge pickup truck, eating hamburgers. The driver had a thick streak of dark hair hanging in his face. His partner had a headful of blond waves.

The thump of rock music pulsated from the truck as Colleen approached. She went around to the driver's window. It was rolled down. Sammy Hagar sang about his bad motor scooter.

"Hey," the driver said, slurping on a soft drink.

Colleen held up a twenty-dollar bill. "How would you and your buddy like to make a little extra money?"

* * *

Afternoon fog swept inland across the bluffs as Colleen guided the Torino carefully down the bumpy dirt road toward Moon Ranch. The white two-story farmhouse that served as the members' quarters disappeared intermittently in billowing vapor. After parking in the cover of some Monterey Pines at the top of the ridge, she got out. This was as far as she could go and not be arrested.

She got her binoculars out of the trunk, stood in the trees, wishing she had her jeans and sensible shoes, not her one good skirt suit and heels. She focused on the ranch. The gate was festooned with the usual warnings and topped with barbed wire. She checked the house through the binoculars.

Then she heard the rumble of an engine coming up the dirt road she had just taken. Colleen turned to see the two teenagers bobbing along in their pickup. The driver, eyes hidden by his dark hair, gave a single lazy wave as they bounced past.

The truck bobbed down to the gate, made a three-point turn, stopped, the engine running, while the kid with the blond hair hopped out and stood by the gate, holding an empty envelope. He looked around, uncertain, hunkered down in the cold in just a Mr. Bill T-shirt. Exhaust pumped from the truck's tailpipe.

Colleen watched the farmhouse through the binoculars, coming and going in the fog.

The front door opened.

Three people emerged. They came out from under the porch. Two men with shaved heads and orange robes, each man flanking a smaller woman in a white robe.

Pamela.

Colleen tightened up the focus of her binoculars, following the trio as they descended the porch steps and walked along the dirt road to the gate.

Pamela's beautiful red hair was still shorn back to a tufty, uneven crew cut. Her narrow face was pale. Her lips were parted. A vacant expression hung.

But she was still alive. Her weight looked about the same as it had a couple of months ago. Her robe was clean enough, from what Colleen could see. She wore sandals.

The man to the right of her carried a length of something. A stick, a pipe. The man on the left had a rifle slung over his shoulder, looking surreal with the orange robe. They weren't fooling around. For all their talk of peace, the church members were easily provoked. A newspaper reporter who had written an exposé had found a live rattlesnake in his mailbox.

Colleen followed Pamela's face as the three members approached the gate. She wondered if Pamela felt any differently about her since her last visit. Did she still hate Colleen for killing her father?

Secretly, she wondered if Pamela might even miss her. Half as much as she missed her.

She saw Pamela and one of the men chatting as they made strides. Pamela smiled at something the man said, her eyes blinking shut momentarily as she laughed. Just seeing that small gesture crushed Colleen's spirit like a boulder rolling over a newly sprung flower. A mix of emotions flooded through her. Had she really wanted Pamela to be miserable? Trapped? Wasn't it better that she was at least content enough to smile, if nothing else? Wasn't that better than feeling like a prisoner, which is what she was in Colleen's eyes?

Colleen let out an involuntary sigh of exasperation.

She lowered her binoculars.

Pamela was okay. Mission accomplished.

The three people were about halfway to the gate.

Colleen came out from behind the tree, stuck her little and index finger in her mouth, under her tongue, gave a quick sharp wolf whistle. The kid in the Mr. Bill shirt looked up. She gave him a nod before ducking back into the trees. He tossed the envelope, jogged back to the passenger side of the truck, climbed in. The truck ground into gear and clambered up the incline.

Pamela and her two guards stopped, watched the truck leave with a questioning look.

The truck crested the ridge, took off, the driver giving Colleen one final wave.

Pamela and her two orange-robed escorts looked at each other, no doubt confused. Then they turned back around, headed to the farmhouse. Colleen watched though the binoculars. At one point Pamela turned, looked at the gate with a frown of confusion, before turning back. Colleen watched them enter the house. The house ebbed into late afternoon fog that was growing thicker, darker.

Another deep sigh escaped Colleen's lungs as she put her binoculars away, got into the Torino, started it up with a rumble.

She knew all she was going to know about Pamela for now.

She'd concentrate on Margaret Copeland.

CHAPTER FORTY-SEVEN

Peg's Place was what they called a "woman's bar"—meaning there wasn't a man to be found. If one came in, it was a delivery. Or by accident, or to gawk or cause trouble. And they didn't stay long. The bouncer, a two-hundred-and-twenty-five-pound woman with a pompadour, wearing a black leather vest over a white T-shirt, no bra, made damn sure of that, greeting everybody at the door with a firm smile and a nod.

The lights were soft and low when Colleen arrived at ten p.m., the clientele well dressed and well behaved, chatting quietly at the bar or in booths at a volume that reminded Colleen of bells tinkling. In the corner at a piano, a woman with short jet-black hair sang, "I Hadn't Anyone Till You." It was a far cry from the Mabuhay.

Alex waved at Colleen from the back of a blue velvet booth. But it wasn't necessary. Colleen had spotted her the moment she came in. Alex was sitting with several other women, huddled around champagne glasses in a haze of cigarette smoke and laughter. Her blond hair was gelled tight at the sides and curled up goddess style at the back. Her white skin was contrasted by blood-red lipstick.

Alex scooted over the lap of a woman so that Colleen could sit next to her. The woman made a pleasurable face when Alex did that, and the other women laughed.

"Right here, you." Alex patted the seat next to her and twinkled with her eyes. Colleen sat down and Alex's warm leg brushed hers, something Colleen didn't hate. Alex showed a hint of black lingerie under a mock leopard fur coat.

"Is this the friend you been telling us about, Alex?" a striking black woman in a leather cap asked.

Alex introduced Colleen around the table. One other woman had long flame-on red hair that had been immaculately brushed. Her name was Antonia and she looked at Alex in a way that said she knew her pretty well. She wore a tight white tank top with a red star on it. Another woman wore a shirt and tie, had a man's haircut, and a shy smile to soften her look. She actually stood up to shake hands with Colleen while Alex pulled a near empty bottle of Dom Perignon from an ice bucket and poured the dregs into a glass that had been sitting empty. She pushed it in front of Colleen, waved the bottle at a waitress. "Another one of these bad boys, Liz."

"You got it."

"Well, don't just look at it, Colleen!" the black woman said.

"I'm savoring," Colleen said, twirling the glass. "I'm used to straight out of the bottle with a paper bag around it."

One woman laughed.

"Let's toast our fifth wheel," the woman in the shirt and tie said, eyeing Colleen.

All five glasses were raised.

"By all means," Colleen said. "Let's toast *me*. I spliced a chain-link fence early this morning." And she had, mostly, with a pair of pliers and some advice from the Ace hardware man. Glasses clinked. A fresh bottle arrived and was popped. Glasses were refilled. Cigarettes were lit and witty conversation spilled out. And for thirty lovely minutes, it was like listening to Dr. Don Rose—light and fun and worry free. A reprieve. But she soon drifted away from the conversation and saw Margaret Copeland, twisted up in Golden Gate Park. How did those plastic fragments wind up in her stomach?

After another glass she said, "I have to run."

Alex's face dropped. "So soon?"

"What I said about that fence? I didn't actually finish. I need a clear head for tomorrow. But it's been wonderful to meet everyone."

"I have something for you," Alex said. "I need to pee. Come with me."

"What's this, Alex?" Antonia Redhead said, raising her eyebrows. "Secrets?"

Blushing, Colleen followed Alex into the women's restroom. She didn't see a men's restroom anywhere. There was one other woman, drunkenly splashing water on her face.

"Why are you leaving so soon?" Alex said to Colleen, applying lipstick in the mirror. "You just got here."

"I'm trying to stay on schedule, what's left of it. Not that your friends aren't fun and everything."

"Uh-huh," Alex said, puckering her lips in the mirror. "And what does *everything* mean?"

"It doesn't mean anything."

The woman washing her face came up for air, yanked a paper towel from the dispenser, dried her face slowly and deliberately.

"Do you have some kind of prejudice against dykes, Coll?"

The woman stopped mid-facewipe and eyed Alex and Colleen in the mirror.

Colleen felt her blood pressure rise. "For Christ's sake, Alex. Do you really have to ask me that?"

Alex turned as the woman continued to stare. "I think your face is dry now. You can leave." The woman coughed, balled up her paper towel, tossed it, quickly exited the restroom.

Alex gave Colleen a piercing stare in the mirror. "So? Are you, or aren't you?"

Colleen let out a frustrated sigh. "What fucking difference does it make? I like people—sometimes. *People.* Maybe I'll tell you more when I know you better. I like you—and your friends—just fine. I happen to like you a lot, Alex. That's one of the reasons I'm still on this case. But right now is about Margaret—not you. How many times do I have to tell you?"

"So I'm shallow? For thinking about myself?"

"I never said that. And you're not. But you are being a little selfish. What about your father?"

Alex gazed at the floor. "I just wanted you to meet some friends. Let your hair down. You need it."

"And I did. And it makes me wish I was a little more fun to be with. But I'm not, Alex. I'm not one of the pretty people. I spent ten years in prison. I'm trying to keep my head above water, so I can reconnect with my daughter. Margaret has my attention right now, not you. Hanging out in bars with the *in* crowd takes second place."

Alex blinked Colleen's comment back. "I didn't know you had a daughter, Coll."

"I guess Christian didn't tell you everything then, did he?"

"How old is she?"

"Nineteen."

"What's her name?"

"Pamela."

Alex pursed her lips. "You must have been a kid when you had her."

"I was young and stupid—that's for sure."

"What about her? Where is she? Why can't you see her?"

"Not now, Alex," Colleen said. "Some other time. I'm almost out of time on Margaret."

"So you're just leaving? To do what? Go sit in your dingy little warehouse? It's late. Come on! It'll do you good."

"You know why I came. Don't make me feel beholden to you."

Alex grimaced. "Sorry." She opened her coat, which revealed not much except for a bodice and suspender belt, and came out with a wad of bills. The denomination *100* was clear, at least on the top one. "Here. I don't want you to feel *beholden*. I was just looking forward to seeing you again. It hasn't been easy for me, either, you know. I loved Margaret for the short time I knew her. And it's all been coming back like a storm."

Colleen took the money, tucked it in her side pocket. "I can tell there's a whole lot more cash here than I asked for."

"So?" Alex went back to the mirror, puckered her lips, examined them. "No one's counting. You're in a jam. I've got plenty to spare. And I want you to keep going, even if Father doesn't."

Colleen caught Alex's soft look in the mirror. "Thanks."

"And when there's a lull, I want to hear all about Pamela."

"Deal."

"Any progress on Margaret?"

"Yes," Colleen said. She relayed the information on Millard Drake.

Alex shook her head in the mirror. "Margaret must have been out of her mind with fright. Why else would she have done that? Swallowed those pieces of plastic?"

"I don't know. *Yet*. But I'm going to find out."

Alex's eyes were growing moist. "Poor Margaret."

Colleen gave her a moment to recover. "How *is* your father?"

Alex gulped as she stood up straight, checked her hair. "The doctor said today he probably has a week, at most. That if there's anybody he wants to see, this would be a good time to call them." Her voice was starting to crack.

Colleen took a deep breath. "All I can say is that I'm so sorry."

"I know." Alex gave Colleen a weary smile in the mirror.

"I'm going to find who killed Margaret. I'm going to do it before your father passes. So *you* can tell him."

Alex's eyes and hers locked in the mirror.

"That would mean a lot," she said.

"I want to say when. But I can't. But every day I get closer. I feel like I know Margaret in a way. I knew someone just like her once."

Alex stared back in the mirror, eyes shiny. "Who?"

Colleen shook her head. "Another long story. For another time. When we have time."

"I'm not what you think I am, Colleen. Some lightweight. But *that man* treated me like a child all my life, and I'm going to miss him anyway, just like I miss Margaret. So I like to have a good time and forget about it all sometimes." She turned around, faced Colleen. "It's better than feeling sorry for myself. Who the hell wants that? Life's too short."

Colleen resisted an urge to brush a strand of hair off Alex's cheek. "You know what, Alex? I like your strategy. I've got stick-in-the-mud down like no one else. Do you think those friends of yours have drunk all the champagne?"

Alex gave a weak smile. "Probably."

"Then we'll just have to go back and order another bottle. You can put it on my expenses."

Alex grinned. "Now you're talking."

She moved in, quick, grabbed Colleen's cheeks between her warm palms and planted a kiss on Colleen lips, softly, gently, and Colleen didn't stop her. It was pure electricity that radiated down Colleen's gut to her groin.

It lasted for a while. Then Alex let go, pulled back.

"That's for nothing," she said, giving her a slow wink. "Let's go tie one on."

Colleen's head buzzed with champagne and excitement and confusion. She had a feeling she would remember that kiss for a while, if not forever.

But she wasn't going to repeat it. Not until Margaret was taken care of.

CHAPTER FORTY-EIGHT

It was well past last call before they filed out of Peg's Place, smoking and joking. Two a.m. Not the best time to be on the roads after a few glasses of champagne plus a few more, but it was too late for that. Colleen rolled down the car window for the fresh air, lit up a cigarette, cranked up the radio. KFRC, the station she'd been listening to earlier that day on the way back from Mendocino. The oldies just kept coming. "I'm a Believer," "I Got You Babe," "Ticket to Ride." Sailing down Geary Boulevard in the Torino, big block V8 growling, reminding herself from time to time that she'd better keep her speed under, or at least at, the limit.

Alex had a point. Sometimes you just needed a little time off. Besides, clearing the slate sometimes helped one to think.

The Torino made it back to Yosemite Street in one piece. It was a pain, getting out of the rumbling vehicle, unlocking the gates, pulling the Torino in, getting out, pulling the gates back into place, but she knew better than to leave the car out on the street anymore. Who knew when Frank Madrid or his pals might drop by? All the while some old song blared on the radio, one that she just loved when it came out because it was complete nonsense. She was in the mood for it now. She found herself singing along as she laced the chain back through the gates and padlocked them back up.

Striding over to the Torino, doing a sidestep to the song's oddball ending—a twanging '60s sitar after two minutes of boogie-woogie piano—she flung open the car door, reaching over to switch the ignition off.

"And that was 'Judy in Disguise (With Glasses)' whatever the heck *that* means," the DJ said. "Actually, the story goes that the song was written as a parody of 'Lucy in the Sky with Diamonds,' the Beatles tune that was also a hit in 1967 . . ."

Well, wasn't that fascinating? But it actually kind of spoiled her fun, making sense where there had been none, which was the way Colleen liked that song. She switched off the ignition, silenced the radio, leaving the distant rush of the elevated freeway behind her and the bay in front to fill the empty space in her ears, which were buzzing from champagne. Rolling the window back up, she grabbed her flashlight and shoulder bag, her head following a split second behind. She reminded herself to go easy on the Dom Perignon next time.

Almost two thirty in the morning. She'd do her last perimeter check then and there, in her one good suit, the hell with it, although she'd have to watch her heels around the rubble. She grabbed the flashlight she kept under the front seat and made the rounds.

The semi-repaired fence was fine. She'd get back to that. She ambled down the west side of the perimeter toward the old delivery truck where her short-lived beau had once slept. She knew he wasn't there but she stepped up on the running board anyway. If he had been around, she would have dragged him to the showers and made him do her dark bidding.

Colleen patrolled the rest of the plant, the cool night air clearing her head. Downstairs in the warehouse, she stopped outside the break room and waved the flashlight across the slowly evaporating pool of water that SFFD had created the other night after the fire. All clear.

She exited the building, stepping around a pile of debris in her good shoes.

The sound of an engine came echoing down Yosemite. Colleen stopped. Turned to the street.

An SFPD black-and-white came crawling into view. It stopped, sat there, waves of heat rising off the hood.

Colleen flicked on her flashlight, shone it on the fender. Number 226.

"I'm not afraid of you," she said, more to herself than anyone else.

The black-and-white rolled on.

She was running out of time.

Upstairs, she got her keys out, let herself into the office, and pulled the roll of cash Alex had lent her from her jacket. She kicked off her shoes, got out of her suit, hung it up on a wooden hanger on the pipe running along the ceiling of her "bedroom," before going back out into the office and dropping herself into the desk chair. Still buzzing. She would sleep tonight. She lit one last cigarette and dialed her answering service while she flipped through the wad of hundred-dollar bills. A lot more than the seven she had asked for. Bless you, Alex. Now she could keep going on Margaret. She put the money in the desk drawer.

She called her answering service.

No messages, ma'am.

In just her underwear, cigarette dangling from her mouth, Colleen climbed up on the desk and pushed up the ceiling tile with the pencil mark on it. To the right lay the arsonist's .38. She got it down. She'd keep it close by, in case she had unwelcome visitors.

Next, the pillbox. She sat back down in the chair, smoking, opened the case and examined the plastic fragment. Broken either end, smooth on the sides. Were those teeth marks? Had Margaret Copeland chewed something larger, broken it into two pieces? The material was plastic but seemed strong. She was leaning toward some part of an automobile. She thought of the Ford Falcon. Had Margaret broken a piece off the interior of the murderer's car?

If only there was more to go on.

She set the fragment back in the pillbox, closed the lid, set it in the center of the desk blotter. Maybe the answer would come to her in a dream.

She tried not to think of what had happened to Margaret when she swallowed it.

Colleen sat back in the chair and put her bare feet up on the desk. Smoke her cigarette, decompress.

Judy in Disguise.

With Glasses.

Of course!

Colleen sat up, wide awake now. Cigarette butt smoldering between her fingers, half forgotten, she scrambled for the pill case again.

CHAPTER FORTY-NINE

"I believe it's called cellulose acetate," Colleen said to the Asian man in the white lab coat bent over the counter, examining the black plastic fragment with the aid of a pair of tweezers.

Cellulose acetate was the name given to the material in the autopsy report.

"Zylonite," he said, looking up, blinking at Colleen from behind thick-lensed glasses. "Zyl for short."

"Zyl," she said.

Colleen stood on the customer side of the counter in Taraval Eyewear, on the street with the same name, just off 19th Avenue. The first phone calls she had made that morning as soon as the business day had begun had told her that Sai Chong was the most knowledgeable and helpful optician she was likely to get hold of at short notice.

He set Colleen's fragment down carefully in the center of a blue plastic tray, turned around, pulled a pair of frames from a display rack. They were turquoise blue. He held them up. "Zyl—extremely lightweight."

He placed the glasses down on the tray sideways so that one temple—the part that went over the ear of the wearer—rested alongside the fragment Colleen had brought in. In this manner it was clear that the fragment was part of a narrow portion of a temple from a pair of spectacles.

"See?" he said with a satisfied smile. "You were correct. Eyeglasses."

The ding of a bell announced a customer coming in through the door of the shop, a woman in a scarf and raincoat.

He acknowledged the woman who had entered. "Be with you in a moment, madam."

"How many opticians are there in San Francisco?" Colleen asked.

"Opticians and ophthalmologists combined?" Mr. Chong made a face, eyeing the ceiling in thought. "Well over a hundred. Many people come to the city to be fitted for eyewear. Plenty of work. Plenty of competition, too." He smiled, used the tweezers to put the fragment back in Colleen's pillbox, which he handed to her. "Have a good day."

One hundred. "What if I told you this piece was from a pair of frames at least eleven years old?" Colleen said. "Then how many opticians are we talking about?"

He gave an impatient snuffle. "Eleven years ago? Not so many opticians in San Francisco then. But Zyl was as widely used then as it is now."

"So," she said, "not a specialty optician?"

He nodded at the woman waiting but said to Colleen: "Difficult to say. Excuse me."

CHAPTER FIFTY

The line at the DMV on Fell Street was a snake of discontented people by the time Colleen got there later that morning.

Two clerks were on duty, one the guy she wanted to talk to—Ed, of the pear-shaped build and plastic pocket protector. His graying crew cut had recently been buzzed. He looked like one of the Friday haircut brigade. She had to let the pimply teenager behind her, clutching his driving exam, go first so that she could be next in line to see Ed.

Finally, her turn came.

"Hi, Ed," she said, stepping up to the counter. She gave him a little wave. "How's it going today?"

"Well, hello there," he said, blushing. He reached into an in-and-out tray and came back with a thin greenbar computer printout. "I put this aside for you. I thought you were going to come in yesterday."

"I wanted to, Ed," she said, "but something came up." She had intended to stop by yesterday, but the trip up to Mendocino to talk to Millard Drake had taken priority.

"Well, here ya go." He handed the report to her, hand shaking slightly. "Your search on Ford Falcons."

She surveyed the green and white computer printout quickly before she left the counter. She didn't want to have to get back into another twenty-minute line.

"Excuse me, Ed," she said, "but I notice there are no addresses listed for the vehicles in this report."

"That information is only provided to law enforcement agencies. Are you with a law enforcement agency?"

"I am not."

"The names of the vehicle owners are there, though." He raised his eyebrows so that she got the hint. She could always look them up.

"So they are," she said.

There were nine Ford Falcons registered in San Francisco in 1967. She had some legwork to do.

"Thank you so much, Ed." She gave him a sideways smile before leaving the counter, generating some serious blush on his part.

"Anytime," he croaked.

"Do you really think you'd ever stand a chance with a woman like that?" Colleen heard the woman working the counter next to Ed say.

Colleen spun around and went back up to the counter. A woman in a pixie haircut looked at her in surprise.

"I think Ed's a catch," she said to her. "I just love crew cuts." She patted the countertop, gave Ed a wink, making him turn crimson, turned, left the DMV.

The DMV on Fell was located on the end of the Panhandle, the strip of Golden Gate Park that extended from the main park itself—like a panhandle. The drive along JFK into the park, past the Conservatory of Flowers, with its delicate construction of thousands of panes of glass, and the de Young Museum, provided a pleasant break, but by the time she got to Stow Lake, it was raining again. She parked, got out, and opened up a two-dollar umbrella.

The snack shop wasn't open yet, but the door to the maintenance room behind was. Light spilled out onto the wet grass. Colleen knocked on the doorframe but found no one. She went back around front to the snack bar where she scanned the man-made lake with the man-made island in the middle. Deserted. It was the middle of the week, too early for customers, and raining.

At the shore a little dock moored half a dozen two-person peddle boats, about as many rowboats and, at the very end of the dock, a single red boat where a large sheet of opaque plastic shifted around over the outboard motor at the rear, accompanied by vibrant cussing.

"Knock, knock," she said walking toward the red boat.

The plastic sheet lifted up. Larry, the elderly maintenance man in his blue jump suit, stared at her from behind his wire-frame glasses.

"Hey, Larry," Colleen said. "Working on an engine?"

"No—my performance art."

"It does mean you have to keep all the customers waiting."

"My art comes first."

"Well, I have a question—if you can drag yourself away from whatever it is you're doing."

"Shoot." The plastic sheet went back over his head and he turned around and resumed clanking around on the motor as rain pelted on him.

"I'm talking to a giant sheet of moving plastic."

"I can do two things at once, you know." Larry banged away on the engine.

"Okay," she said. "Twenty-first of November, 1967."

"Yep." More banging.

"You came into work early that day to fix a pump. It was still dark. You saw a car parked. Not far from where Margaret Copeland's body was found."

"Yeppers." Clanking around under the plastic sheet.

"Green Ford Falcon, no license plates."

"I'm getting this distinct feeling of *déjà vu*," Larry said, knocking something. "We've had this conversation."

"You don't remember what exact model the Falcon was by any chance?"

"Are you serious?"

"I thought you had a superior intellect."

"I do. But I don't remember model numbers or eleven-year-old license plates. I just happened to notice there *was* no license plate."

"Good enough," she said, huddling under the umbrella as the rain came down. "Let's play a game. This one is worth twenty bucks if Larry gets it right."

He stopped tinkering but was still bent over the engine. "You have my attention."

"Cast your mind back to that morning. You just came in to work. You're a little ticked off because you had to come in early. You notice a car parked on the loop around the lake. That's odd. Too late—or too early—for kids making out. Far too early for customers. And normally there's nobody parked here at night. But there's a green Ford Falcon."

"I'm visualizing." Rain pelted his plastic sheet.

"Was the front of the car facing you? Or the rear?"

There was a pause. "Rear."

"Did you see it from the side at all? Could you tell if it was a two-door? Four-door?"

"Not sure."

"You're not sure?"

"I just said so, didn't I? It was sporty looking. I remember thinking, who would leave something like that out here in the middle of the night? But I don't remember how it was sporty. It just was."

"Maybe it had more than one exhaust pipe? One on either side? Take a minute and think."

He stopped moving for a moment. "You know what? It might've done, at that. But I can't be one hundred percent sure. But I think it might've well have had two chrome exhaust pipes."

"You've got a pretty good memory," she said. "I suspect it might have, too. Remember if it had a vinyl top? They were just coming into fashion then. Or did it have a hardtop? A green hardtop?"

The opaque plastic bundle stood up straight, turned around. The plastic moved, shifted away so that she could see his face again.

"Vinyl," he said. "Black. You didn't see them much then. I remember now."

"You sure?"

"About as sure as I can be. And that's pretty sure."

"One more question."

"This is kind of fun."

"No license plate—was it because someone removed it? Maybe there was a plastic plate from a local car dealer where the license plate normally is?"

"Like a brand-new car?"

"Exactly. One that didn't have plates yet."

He stood there, blinking, holding the plastic sheet over his head while the rain fell. "I think I would've remembered that. But I don't." He shook his head. "Sorry."

"That's okay, Larry. You've told me most of what I needed to know."

"You're good."

"No," she said, "I think you are."

"It's just too bad the police never wanted to know."

"Isn't it just?" she said.

The cheap collapsible umbrella was better than nothing, but it didn't prevent her jeans from getting soaked. She fired up the

Torino, cranked up the heater, sat behind the wheel shivering until hot air turned the car into a sauna, steam misting the windshield.

Colleen got her ballpoint out, went down the list of the nine Ford Falcons on her DMV report.

Three 1967 Ford Falcon Sport Coupes had been registered in San Francisco in 1967. The Sport Coupes featured twin exhausts and vinyl roofs. She didn't have an address but she had names. That was almost the same thing.

She redirected the heater vent to the inside of the windshield and waited for it to clear.

CHAPTER FIFTY-ONE

"You say this is about a claim on my Falcon?" the woman in the blue rinse asked, reading Colleen's fictitious business card that proclaimed her to be Carol Aird, claims handler with Pacific All Risk Insurance.

Rain tumbled off the umbrella Colleen stood under on the stairs of a junior five out in the avenues. She gave an appropriately somber nod. "I'm pretty sure a mistake has been made," she said. "I'm just doing my due diligence and following up."

"Someone filed an accident report, you say?" the woman said.

"In Los Angeles, on the third of last month."

"Couldn't have been us." The woman shook her head. There was a hint of Midwest twang in her voice. "We haven't been to LA recently. And that car rarely leaves the garage."

Colleen tempered her excitement. She wanted a quick look at the car.

"Just as I suspected," she said. "It would be a huge help if I could ask you a few questions? Just so I can clear this up and move on?"

"My husband won't be home until after work," the woman said. "He handles these things."

"I understand," Colleen said. "You have my card. Please tell your husband that if you get a call from SFPD, to have them contact me if any charges are filed." Rain pelted her umbrella.

"Wait!" The woman's eyes rounded in shock. "Are you saying the police might file charges?"

"Well, I certainly hope not. That's why I'm trying to clear this up before there's an issue. It's obviously a mix-up. You weren't even in Los Angeles last month. There's no way you could have been involved with a hit-and-run—is there?"

"A *hit-and-run?*" The woman's mouth dropped.

"Someone claimed your car ran a stop sign and hit their car. It's obviously a mistake."

"You better come in and see for yourself," she said, standing back, holding the door. "But you'll have to take your shoes off."

"Thank you." Colleen entered the house onto a clear plastic floor mat, pulling off her pumps. She had gone back home to change into her business suit, in order to be more presentable when asking pushy questions. She stepped onto the blue shag carpet in her bare feet, twiddling her toes. The walls of the house were painted blue. She noticed a definite color theme.

The woman had a kindly face. From the living room the murmur of a soap opera drifted out. She clasped her hands together. "I'm dying to know what this is all about."

Colleen extracted her folded-up greenbar DMV report from her shoulder bag, unfolded it, turned it to show the housewife the 1967 Ford Falcon Sports Coupe that was registered to her.

"That's Binky, all right."

"*Binky?*"

She gave a shy grin. "Would you like to see her?"

"Yes, please. Then I can get this cleared up."

"Follow me."

Colleen followed her to the hall doorway of a small junior five built in the '40s—two bedrooms, bathroom, living room, kitchen/ dining area, all on one level. Solid construction, even for a starter house; no cutting corners back then. The woman opened the door leading down to a pristine garage.

Tools hung on a pegboard, organized by size, over an immaculate workbench. The washer and dryer were perfectly aligned with each other. What was it with people who lived out in the avenues?

But the star attraction, taking up the center of the garage, was a pristine 1967 Ford Falcon Sport Coupe. It gleamed with polish. The vinyl roof was a deep rich black, unlike so many that weren't kept up.

But the car itself was baby blue. Colleen let out a sigh.

"May I take a closer look?" she asked.

"Help yourself."

Colleen examined the rear of the car. Twin pipes. But the paint had a deep patina of wax. Years' worth. "It obviously hasn't been in any recent accidents," she said. "It looks practically new. But it's eleven years old."

"I hardly ever drive it. And Bob—my husband—babies it."

"It's a beautiful color," Colleen said. "Did you have it repainted at some point? Many of these came in green."

"No," she said. "This is the original color. We test-drove a Mustang, and then I saw Binky on the lot, and I said to Bob, 'That's the one!'" She blushed again.

"Your husband likes to indulge you."

"He's a keeper. Do you still need to leave a message for him?"

"No," Colleen said, getting a pen out of her bag, drawing a line through the car on the greenbar printout, striking it out. "That won't be necessary. Thank you so much."

Outside, she dashed to the Torino in the rain, the umbrella bobbing over her head. She had two '67 Falcon Sport Coupes left. The
next one on her list had been registered to a local politician at the
time of Margaret Copeland's murder. She recalled Steve saying that
his father had quit because of some bigwig. This sounded
promising.

She'd watch her step.

CHAPTER FIFTY-TWO

Colleen pressed the buzzer and stood at the intercom by the stone gate of a mock Tudor house the size of a small castle in Sea Cliff, her collapsible umbrella flapping ominously over her head. The rain was still falling steadily and now, out by the ocean, the wind blew with menace.

Assemblyman Patrick Skinner lived alongside people of similar social stature. Although no competition for the Copelands' residence in Half Moon Bay, the house was impressive, with views of both the Golden Gate Bridge and the Presidio.

A woman answered. She had a Latin accent. Colleen announced herself as Carol Aird, claims handler.

"I called earlier," she said. "You said Mr. Skinner was home and might spare a few minutes to clear up a matter regarding an auto insurance claim?"

"That's right, Ms. Aird. Do come in."

The gate hummed and let Colleen in as a gust of wind pulled her two-dollar umbrella inside out. Down a stone walkway, a dark wooden front door with a diagonal antique nail pattern on it opened and a middle-aged Hispanic woman in a maid's outfit greeted her.

"This way, please," she said, offering to take Colleen's dilapidated umbrella. She had a perfect poker face.

"It's in a sad state," Colleen said, handing her the umbrella. "Maybe just do me a favor and toss it out."

"Of course," the maid said coolly as she took the umbrella and showed Colleen into a study, seating her at a small divan by a fireplace. No fire had been built and the room was on the chilly side. "Mr. Skinner will be with you in just a minute." She exited the room, leaving the door open.

Colleen stood up to examine the many photos on the mantelpiece and walls. Assemblyman Patrick Skinner was a big-boned, hearty-looking man of Irish extraction, with a head of thick red hair in his younger days, and a broad smile. He had been photographed with his arm around, or shaking hands with, many prominent people and people who appeared to be prominent. There was even a photograph of him and several other men on a golf course with Richard Nixon.

But what caught her eye were photos of his son, Kieran. The Skinners had three children—two daughters and a son—and Colleen was able to pick him out easily. That was because there was a preponderance of photos of Kieran in comparison to his sisters and mother. Black-and-white pictures of a little dark-haired boy blowing out candles on a cake, playing with a toy car with one of his sisters, then in a Cub Scout uniform. A substantial recording of his early life. Later on, the photos switched to color, with Kieran wearing a fencing outfit, standing at the tiller of a sailboat, in front of the Vatican in Rome, and many other locales. But one thing remained constant throughout—the detached, empty look in his eyes, which were set in a narrow, rawboned face, at odds with his father's.

And the fact that Kieran Skinner wore thick glasses from an early age.

The photos seemed to stop around the twenty-year mark. Why was that? By Colleen's calculations, Kieran Skinner would be in his early thirties now. In addition, pictures of his mother, a small dark-haired woman who tended to look past the camera, unsmiling, stopped after the late sixties.

This looked promising.

Out in the hallway, descending the stairs, came the sound of heavy footsteps. Colleen turned to the door, readying her best smile.

Patrick Skinner entered the room, all two hundred–plus pounds of him. He wore a double-breasted gray suit, white shirt, and green stripe tie. His reddish hair had turned to a dashing gray but was just as full as in the photographs. His big ruddy face beamed with a smile that was disarming.

"Ms. Aird!" he said as if they were long-lost friends, coming over to throttle her hand in a shake that probably worked like a charm on the campaign trail. She gave him one of her business cards and he offered her a seat, after which he sat down in a crewel-embroidered chair to one side of the divan. "And how can I help you today?"

"I'm sorry to take up your time," she said, "but I'm trying to clear up a matter for a client."

"Your client being . . .?"

"I'm with The Pacific All Risk Insurance Company."

"Never heard of them." He frowned. "What do they want from me?"

"Well, there was a recent claim made, referencing a vehicle registered to your son."

"Can't be." He screwed up his eyebrows. "Kieran doesn't own a car. Hasn't for years," he added with a jovial smile.

That surprised her. A young man from a well-to-do family might own more than one car. Since she was lying about everything else, she simply pushed ahead. She unhooked her shoulder bag and removed a file folder and extracted a letter on 24-pound bond paper from several she'd had typed up at a local temporary agency. One for each Falcon. The letterhead was a copy of the lawyers who had handled Colleen's court case in Santa Cruz last year. It xeroxed well enough to create the right impression if one didn't look too closely. "I'm afraid"—she pretended to reread the letter—"that a green 1967 Ford Falcon belonging to a Kieran Skinner was involved in an accident last month in Santa Monica. A hit-and-run . . ." She held up the letter, in case Patrick Skinner wanted to see for himself. When he didn't, she slipped the letter quickly back in its folder, but left the folder open on her lap.

"How odd." Patrick Skinner grimaced as he put one hand to his face, suitably confused. "Have any charges been filed?"

"Not yet," Colleen said. "I've been assigned to investigate first. But it sounds as if a mistake has been made. I hope we can sort things out before we go off on some wild goose chase and the police are called in."

She saw a telltale flicker of concern cross Patrick Skinner's face at the word *police*.

"Good thing, too," he said. "That car was sold eleven years ago—before we even got plates on it."

"Aha," Colleen said. "It *was* a mistake then."

"The new owner should have registered it."

She nodded. "Who did you sell it to?"

"Why, back to the dealer—Serramonte Ford."

"May I ask why?"

"You may indeed." Patrick Skinner dropped his voice to a discreet level. He rose from his chair, went over and shut the door to the study, returned to his seat, pulled the knees of his trousers up as he sat down and leaned forward to speak to her. He was a good actor, and it was an act.

"That car was a graduation present for my son, Kieran," he said. "Only he was not one hundred percent honest with us about actually graduating from Riordan." He gave a big grin. "He's got the gift of BS, like his old man, and he flat out lied to us. Can you believe it?"

Colleen smiled. "So you took the car back when you found out your son hadn't actually graduated from high school?"

Patrick Skinner nodded. "I did indeed. Took it back. 1967, it was. That taught him to make things up. I have no idea who Serramonte Ford sold it to after that, however."

Colleen shut the file folder and slid it back in her shoulder bag. She slipped the bag over her shoulder, stood up. "Thanks so much for clearing this up, Mr. Skinner. I'm very sorry to have disturbed you."

"Oh, just one thing." Patrick Skinner frowned again, as if he were slow witted, which of course he wasn't. "May I see that letter? The one you had out just now? From your company?"

Colleen's heart skipped. "Why, of course." She unhitched her shoulder bag, got her file folder out, extracted the fake letter, handed it to him.

He took it, read it, shaking his head. "Unbelievable."

That's what she was worried about.

"But I do believe we've cleared the matter up." She reached for the letter.

He held it up, away from her. "Mind if I get a copy—for my records?"

"Why, of course not. I'll see that you're sent one as soon as I get back to the office."

"No need," he said, smiling. "I've got my own Xerox machine."

Her stomach dropped. "You do?"

"Upstairs. My secretary is out at the moment. I'll just run off a quick copy myself—if you don't mind." Big beaming smile. "I'll be right back."

"Of course."

Patrick Skinner bounded out of the room with her counterfeit letter. She could hear him jogging up the stairs.

She'd seen all she needed to of the sitting room. She'd wait in the hall.

When she did, she heard two people talking upstairs, in voices that soon became heated. One of them was Patrick Skinner. She wandered over to the bottom of a carved staircase where she could hear better.

She still couldn't distinguish what was being said beyond the fact that the other voice belonged to a young man. Kieran Skinner was her guess. She took a few steps up the stairway, cocked her head.

"You best be keeping your nose clean," she heard Patrick Skinner say.

"I've done nothing—unlike some people I can mention."

"Don't tell me you're back on that, after all these years. I won't tolerate it. I can always send you back, boy."

"I'll take care of this!"

Lighter footsteps came hurtling along a hallway upstairs, and Colleen's heart leapt. She flew down the stairs to the doorway where she composed herself as she studied an elegant bouquet in a cloisonné vase on a side table. She pretended not to notice the young man storming down the stairs.

"Who the *hell* do you think you are, accusing me of hit-and-run?" he said. "Do you have any idea who my father is?"

Colleen turned nonchalantly to see a man in his late twenties or early thirties, wearing a wrinkled yellow bathrobe that only amplified his lean stature, his stick legs, his bare, boney feet, toe nails that needed cutting. His gaunt face was the same as the one she had seen in the photos in the study, albeit a decade older, and he had grown a bushy black Fu Manchu mustache and thick sideburns as if to compensate for his weak chin. His wild dark hair stuck out in an uncombed frizz. He looked like a reject from a porno flick. Thick-framed glasses amplified his unyielding dark eyes.

He stood on the bottom step and gripped the banister with a vibrating hand.

"Carol Aird," she said with a smile calculated to upset him further. "You must be Kieran Skinner. Nice to meet you." She walked over, put her hand out, and was not surprised in the least when he did not take it.

"Nice to *meet* me?" He stepped down onto the floor. "Then why are you harassing me?"

"I do apologize. It was just some confusion. It's been cleared up."

"Tell those assholes you work for we'll sue."

"O-kay." She nodded sagely. "I'll be sure to do that." Again, she returned her winning smile.

A second set of footsteps came thumping down the stairs, more deliberate than Kieran's. Patrick Skinner appeared with Colleen's letter in his hand, his plastic smile replaced by an angry scowl.

"How dare you talk like that to a guest in my house," he said to Kieran. "Apologize immediately."

Kieran's eyes shot to the floor. "I just . . ."

"I have no interest in hearing what you were *just* doing," Patrick Skinner growled. "Apologize. And get out of my sight."

Kieran Skinner looked down at the floor. "I apologize," he said through his teeth.

"It's no problem," she said. "I understand how frustrating something like this can be."

He turned, walked up the stairs with a furtive scowl, eyeing her.

"Here you go, Ms. Aird," Patrick Skinner said, pushing Colleen's letter back at her, staring at her with sharp eyes. "Please contact my attorney for any further questions."

"That won't be necessary." Colleen took the letter, placed it back in her shoulder bag.

The maid reappeared as Patrick Skinner headed back up the stairs. "I'll show you out," she said. She had obviously overheard the exchange.

Outside, the rain had eased up, but the wind hadn't. Colleen gauged how long it would take her to get to her car without an umbrella before she was soaked again.

But she didn't much care.

She'd just scored a direct hit.

Kieran Skinner wore glasses. Kieran Skinner had a powerful father who was covering up for him, a man he seemed to carry a deep grievance against. She recalled what Millard Drake, the forensic analyst who had signed Margaret Copeland's autopsy report, had said about repressed rage. Kieran Skinner once owned a car that was supposedly returned for some silly reason, a car that Colleen bet was the same one Larry the maintenance man at Stow Lake had seen eleven years ago, parked near the murder site where Margaret Copeland had met her demise.

A dark satisfaction washed through her gut.

It was finally coming together.

CHAPTER FIFTY-THREE

"Who do I make the check out to?" Alex asked Colleen, poised over her checkbook. The two of them were sitting at a corner table in the Cliff House, the sandy shoreline of Ocean Beach off to the south stretching into misty fog. Seal Rock peered through the haze directly in front. Gulls hunkered down en masse. The bar was half full, with quiet conversations muted by soft jazz drifting out of hidden speakers. Ferns abounded. A dampness hung in the air.

"'One Step Ahead Temporary Agency,'" Colleen said, tapping ash from her Virginia Slim into the ashtray. "They've been doing some work for me." She took a sip of her white wine and set the glass down on its coaster. "They'll be making the phone calls."

"And when do you think we'll know something?"

"Close to one hundred opticians and optometrists in San Francisco? I'm told a team of three hitting the phones can get to all in a day—maybe two. Sort out who was in business eleven years ago, narrow the list down. With that, and a little luck, we can hopefully find the perp's optician. Whoever might have done an emergency order for a pair of glasses shortly after November the 21st." And Colleen was hoping that order was for a young Kieran Skinner.

"One Step Ahead," Alex repeated, swiping her hair behind her ear as she wrote out a check. She wore a purple and lavender paisley blouse made of the finest polyester money could buy. A floppy black wool hat hung on the chair by her bag. She tore off the check, dropped it in front of Colleen, next to the open pillbox that contained the fragment of Zyl.

"When do they start?" she asked, pulling the stick of celery from her Bloody Mary and biting off a miniscule piece.

"As soon as I get this to them," Colleen said, picking up the check. "This afternoon—thanks to you." Folding the check in half, she slipped it in the side pocket of her suit jacket. The tone of the conversation had been tense and drawn, a far cry from the flirtations they had shared the night before. But she hadn't forgotten the other Alex.

Alex used her celery stick to stir her drink, then lifted the glass to her lips and guided the straw into her mouth before she took a very large drink. Her head shook slightly and she closed her eyes. Colleen knew she had to be hurting from last night's champagne bout at Peg's Place. On top of preparing to lose her father and the overdue grief being dredged up over her sister, Margaret, Alex had a full plate.

And now this. The possibility that Margaret's murderer was not only out there, but nearby. Soon to be known, with any luck. As much as she wanted to know, needed to know, the tension had to be nerve-racking.

"This all hangs on the fact that your suspect ordered glasses," Alex said. "In San Francisco after . . . Margaret . . ."

Colleen nodded, taking a puff of her cigarette. "It *is* a gamble. Maybe he had a spare pair and didn't need an emergency order. But"—she tapped ash—"maybe not."

Alex closed her eyes for a moment, as if to relax, then reopened them. "It would make sense that his optician would be in the same city where his family lived."

Colleen showed Alex her crossed fingers.

"Will an optician give out that kind of information, Coll?"

"The callers at the agency will be posing as a relative."

Alex gave Colleen a crooked smile. "What an evil mind you have."

Colleen took a sip of her Chardonnay. "I try."

"A woman of many talents," Alex said.

A small jolt of electricity flowed between them.

"And then you'll have what you need to nail this bastard?" Alex said.

"I already have his car at the scene where . . ." She left the sentence unfinished.

"But there must have been more than one green Ford Falcon in a city the size of San Francisco the night Margaret was murdered."

"Not one without registration, sold back to the dealer shortly after it was purchased, right around the time of the murder. I'm verifying all that now."

Alex sipped her Bloody Mary. "So his father wanted to cover his tracks."

"He has the clout to do it."

"Does he have any kind of record?"

Colleen drank some wine. "No. I checked at City Hall. Nothing. No employment record that I can find. Odd."

"It's as if he's spent ten years being invisible," Alex said. "Hiding in his room."

Colleen nodded. "Indeed."

"And then there's this," Alex said, touching the small box containing the fragment.

"Not enough to put a murderer away but, with the car, and, hopefully, the glasses, we'll have enough."

Alex touched the fragment almost reverently with her fingertip. "To think that this was the last thing Margaret . . . did." She moved her hand away, as if startled.

"Yes," Colleen said quietly.

"Why, Colleen?" She touched it again. "Why *this*?"

Colleen tapped some more ash. "Your sister knew what was happening to her, despite the drugs in her system. She wanted her murderer caught. And this"—Colleen indicated the fragment in the pillbox—"was how she did it." Colleen shivered inwardly, thinking of Margaret Copeland in her last few moments. She saw a desperate woman facing death, struggling with Kieran. Breaking his glasses. Doing what had to be done, hoping it would connect with someone down the line. After her death. "She swallowed evidence. Hoping that someday, somehow, someone would find it and piece it together."

"Like you did, Colleen."

"Don't pin any medals on me yet, Alex. I'm going by instinct."

"You mean *feel*," Alex said, drinking, putting her chunky glass down, rubbing her eyes.

"Sometimes it's all you have." Colleen shut the pillbox, slipping it in her other pocket. If she had followed her gut when her ex was violating Pamela, she would have known much sooner. Maybe even put an end to it before it did so much damage to her daughter. Before she killed her ex. Spent a decade in prison. Drove Pamela away from her.

"And when do *I* know?" Alex said, opening her eyes. "Who *he* is?"

"Soon."

"I want to know who this bastard is *now*, Colleen."

Colleen shook her head.

"She was *my* sister."

"This is the only way it can work, Alex." No vigilante stuff. She had seen that. Done that. "Believe it or not, I'm doing you a favor."

Alex squeezed her eyes shut and pressed her temples with her fingertips. "You don't know what it's like—to be so close after so long. Knowing that *you* know who he is. But not know myself."

"I can't imagine what it must be like for you, Alex. It's just that I don't know for sure—yet."

Alex's eyes jerked open. "I want to see him dead."

"Precisely why I'm not telling you yet," Colleen said, taking one more drink of her wine, setting it down, gathering her bag. "Not until we're one hundred percent."

"And what if it isn't?" Alex said. "What if you don't find enough evidence to convict this animal? Who's been hiding under our noses for eleven years? Protected?"

Colleen reached over, took Alex's hand, squeezed it. Alex smiled, squeezed back.

"We'll cross that bridge when we get to it, Alex." She released Alex's hand, checked her watch. Running late. She stood up, hoisted her bag over her shoulder. "Soon. Please give my regards to your father."

Alex's remark about Kieran hiding in his room for ten years gave her pause. After she dropped the check off at One Step Ahead so they could start calling opticians, she made a phone call.

To Millard Drake, the forensic analyst. She had promised to keep him up to date.

And she had a question for his wife, Alice, former Chief Forensic Psychiatrist at Atascadero State Mental Hospital. Although Colleen didn't agree with her hypothesis—that Margaret had swallowed the fragments in a symbolic act to put off some kind of mental torment during her murder—she had a question for her.

She spoke to Millard Drake, who was surprised to learn that the fragments were pieces of glasses, most likely the killer's. But not that surprised.

"It makes sense," he said.

"If any of this does," Colleen said. "I'm wondering if I might speak to your wife for a moment, Mr. Drake."

Alice Drake was put on the line. Her tone was aloof. Colleen now understood that the woman's cold bearing was more unintentional than not. She sensed she could trust her.

"I'm wondering if I can ask you a huge favor," Colleen said. "And a confidential one."

"What is it?"

"I'm looking for someone who might have been in a facility from the time shortly after Margaret was murdered until fairly recently."

"Why?" Alice Drake said icily.

"It's related to this case. I understand you don't want any part of it but I think I have a possible suspect. But one without a history since Margaret's murder."

"And you think he was locked up for a period of time?"

"Call it a hunch."

There was a long pause while Millard Drake hammered in the background.

"Very well," Alice Drake said. "What is the name?"

CHAPTER FIFTY-FOUR

Frank Madrid parked his C10 in front of the clubhouse in the dark gray afternoon, zipped up his 49ers windbreaker, pulled his ball cap tight down on his bald head, and hopped out of the pickup truck.

Rain was spitting over Lake Merced, a patch of it heavy, needling the surface of the water in spots, the remainder hitting the golf course sporadically. Frank squinted down the green. There he was, big man Skinner, swinging a golf club, too tight a swing, followed by the chop of the ball. The man was keyed up, tense. The weather wasn't helping, but Frank knew that wasn't the reason.

It had to be his fucking kid again. Kieran. That sad sack pervert. Why else would Skinner be out here on his own? Where there were no walls?

Frank strode down the side of the green in the partial cover of trees, his heavy black work boots squishing in the wet grass. He wasn't about to run for the likes of Assemblyman Patrick Skinner. Not anymore. He'd done more than enough for the man over the years. As he got closer, he saw Skinner in his blue Adidas raingear outfit, white piping, shoes to match. How much did that fucking cost? Titleist clubs, too—well over a grand. Frank jammed his hands in his pockets, walked over to the middle of the green.

"You picked a hell of a day for a round of golf, Pat." Frank pulled a pack of Winstons, slipped one into his mouth.

Patrick Skinner turned abruptly, in his Cascade rain hat, chin-strap tight under his square jaw, cinching his well-fed face. Giving Frank a disapproving frown as Frank bent down over his Zippo lighter and got his cigarette going. Didn't approve of smoking on the course. Well, tough shit. If he was going to get Frank out here, on a day like this, ask another favor, the man could go pound sand.

Patrick Skinner must have read the look on Frank's face because he said: "I appreciate you stopping by, Frank." He pulled the cover off his golf clubs, slipped the club in hand into the bag, wiped the head off with a little towel, then covered the clubs back up.

Frank Madrid smoked. "You wanted to talk?"

Assemblyman Patrick Skinner pulled a weatherproof glove off his hand, unzipped the pocket of his rain jacket, reached in, came out with a folded-up copy of a letter. He handed it over to Frank.

Frank read the letter, beads of rain blotting the ink.

"And who are Pacific All Risk Insurance?" Frank said, handing the paper back.

Patrick Skinner folded the letter up, put it back inside his jacket. "Whoever they are, they don't have a case open against Kieran's old car. That's because they don't exist."

"So who sent you the letter?"

"Some supposed claims investigator who called herself Carol Aird gave it to me. In person. She didn't want to. She doesn't exist either."

Jesus. Frank took a deep suck on his cigarette. "What did she look like?"

"Five seven, five eight. Dark eyes, hair. Nice build. Mid-thirties. Smart and professional but a tough lady."

"Colleen Hayes." Frank shook his head. "Now she's on to you."

Skinner gave a painful frown. "Maybe."

"No *maybe* about it, Pat. She found out what she needed to know—that Kieran owned that damn car."

Skinner grimaced. "Where do we stand on Jim Davis?"

"SFPD are interviewing transients, zeroing in on a couple, building a case."

"Can't you get involved, speed it up?"

"I'm retired."

"But you have friends."

"Not as many as I used to."

"But no one suspects that it was anything more than some stupid drunk who wandered down to the beach, shared his bottle with the wrong people?"

"So far, Pat, we're clear." Except for Colleen Hayes, Frank thought.

"You should have just had a word with Jim. You shouldn't have killed him, Frank."

Frank Madrid took an angry puff. "You think I didn't try? Jim wouldn't listen. He always felt pushed aside on the Copeland case. It ended his career."

"He was taken care of. Fifty grand's worth."

"It wasn't that. Jim was a Boy Scout. He never dropped a case. When Hayes came nosing around, he was finally gonna get his chance. He was ready, Pat. I couldn't change his mind. That day we picked him up. He was going to take us all down, if he had to. I couldn't talk sense into him. I *had* to get rid of him. You think I liked it?"

Patrick Skinner rubbed his wet face. "So now what?"

"You need to get that kid of yours back into a hospital, pronto. The Margaret Copeland thing was dead and buried—so to speak. But Hayes digging her up is bad news."

"Kieran's been out almost a year now," Patrick Skinner said. "With no trouble."

Frank sucked smoke. Kieran was a time bomb, waiting to go off. "Then why is he hanging around high schools, Pat?"

Patrick Skinner frowned in confusion. "What high school?"

"Roosevelt."

Patrick Skinner blinked. "When?"

Frank took a drag, thought, exhaled. "Few days ago."

"What was he up to?"

"Just gawking at the girls. I drove by, noticed him, sent him home with a warning."

"And you didn't bother to tell me?"

"In case you haven't noticed, Pat, I've kind of had my hands full. And I didn't think it was that big a deal, considering everything else." Frank flicked some ash off into the rain. "Fact is, some of those young chicks are worth looking at. But now, with Hayes nosing around, you need to get him out of the way. At least for the short term."

"It's not going to be that easy."

"Maybe he never should have left in the first place."

Patrick Skinner grimaced. "He couldn't stay inside for the rest of his life. His doc said he was making real progress."

The man wasn't going to listen. The truth was staring him in the face, and he didn't want to know. "You know, Pat, there are other private facilities. I know a guy who runs one in Colorado."

Skinner reared back, clearly offended. "Are you suggesting we put my son through some fanatical, illegal boot camp?"

"A buddy of mine's daughter was hanging out with lowlifes, using needles. Four weeks in Colorado—she's back home, going to church with her parents on Sunday again. It's worth a shot."

Skinner shook his head. "I don't know."

Weak bastard. Couldn't even see the fucking monster he had bred, the punk going to send them all to prison.

Patrick Skinner pulled the cover off his golf clubs, pulled a short wood, covered the rest of the clubs back up, reached into his left pocket, came out with a golf ball, teed it up. "I'll call his doc, try to get Kieran back into Valley Oaks for observation. But in the meantime, get rid of her, Frank. She's the real problem."

He was waiting for this. "You know, Pat, you say get rid of somebody like it's the easiest thing in the world." Frank sucked in a lungful of smoke, blasted it out. "It's not."

"Get some help."

"There's only a few of us left. I only have so much influence."

"You going limp on me, lad? Now's not the time for that. Just do as I say, and that'll be the end of it. Otherwise, we all risk going down."

Frank smoked. "Old man Copeland's about to kick any day now. Once that happens, this whole thing will fade away."

"Not her, Frank. She's not the type to let it go. I can see it in her face."

He might be right about that. But Frank had had enough. Eleven years' worth. Patrick Skinner could clean up his own mess. "Sorry, Pat. Jim was the end of the line."

Skinner glared into his face and gave a wry smile. "Nice try, but you're dreaming, lad. I'm running for Senate next year. Got a damn good shot at it. I've done you many favors. And will continue to do so—once I'm a senator."

"There's a limit, Pat."

Patrick Skinner looked him straight in the eye. "Who was it who came to your rescue when you were caught with your pants down, Frank? Who was it who smoothed things out with the chief? You could have lost your job. Taking kickbacks from underage hookers?

And not just cash ones?" Skinner shook his head, unable to hide his contempt. "Hell, you could've gone to prison, Frank."

"I've never forgotten."

"Well, it seems your memory may be fading just a tad. I won't be left out on my own." He raised his eyebrows.

Pat had him by the short and curlies. For life. Frank took a deep drag of smoke. It was bitter. "Have you thought about givin' him up, Pat? Maybe it's time Kieran finally took responsibility."

"And ruin my chances of making the Senate?" Patrick Skinner showed his perfect teeth in a scowl. "Get rid of her, Frank." He turned around and lined up the shot before Frank could answer. "Make it happen."

Frank flicked his cigarette off into the wet grass, turned away, jamming his fists back in his jacket pockets. He trod back to his truck down the middle of the green, the wind and rain blowing around him. Behind him he heard the chock of a golf club hitting the ball.

CHAPTER FIFTY-FIVE

Four-fifty Sutter was a landmark art deco medical building in downtown San Francisco with a lobby that dazzled the eye with its bold geometric Mayan patterns in gold, bronze, and silver. It wasn't a surprise that an upscale family like the Skinners would patronize an optometrist here, with a sweeping view of the city from the twelfth-floor waiting room.

"Ms. Lindsay?" a slender young woman with long prematurely gray hair said. She had just exited the back office and stood at one end of the counter with a thick file folder under her arm. Not far away, an older man in a lab coat, with a salt-and-pepper goatee, helped a woman try on frames that appeared to have wings on the side.

"Yes," Colleen said, setting the office copy of *Ladies Home Journal* back on the table and standing up, smoothing out her skirt, strolling over to the counter.

"We finally found the order you asked about," the woman said, holding up a yellow carbon copy of a medical form.

"Excellent," Colleen said. "May I?"

The young woman handed the order to her. Colleen read it, standing at the counter.

An order for a replacement pair of spectacles for Kieran Skinner, dated November 22, 1967. The day after Margaret Copeland's body was found in Golden Gate Park. The word *RUSH* was highlighted with an exclamation mark and a double circle around it.

Colleen's excitement was offset by the chilling thought of Margaret's final moments.

"This is just what I need," she said, handing the order back. "May I have a copy for my records, please?"

"May I ask why?" the woman said, holding the order form with both hands between thumb and forefinger.

Colleen feigned a pleasant laugh. "Oh, it's a birthday surprise. We're going to do a roast. We're gathering a few mementos of the times Kieran kept the family on their toes and this was one of them. He managed to break his glasses the night before Thanksgiving, when the family was due to set off on a ski trip to Tahoe. They actually had to delay the trip and it's become family lore." It was such ludicrous BS, she hoped the receptionist might buy it.

"I don't see why not," the receptionist said, turning to make a copy at the Xerox copier behind her, the kind of thing Colleen was seeing more and more of. There hadn't been such machines when she went to prison a decade ago.

The woman placed the copy on the countertop.

"Thank you so much," Colleen said, reaching for the copy just as the man in the lab coat turned from where he was helping the woman with her winged spectacles.

"I'm sorry?" he said with an air of suspicion. "*Who* are you again?"

"I'm Carol Lindsay," Colleen said, "Mr. Skinner's new secretary."

"And he sent you down here for a copy of an eleven-year-old receipt?" The man's incredulous tone bared his disbelief.

Colleen gave a wonderful laugh. "Believe me, I have plenty of other things to do—as I'm sure you do as well."

The man said to the receptionist, "Perhaps you better verify this with Mr. Skinner first."

"Certainly, Mr. Park." She reddened at her obvious transgression. "I won't be a moment."

"Absolutely," Colleen said, taking the copy anyway, keeping it down by her side, and returning to her seat, sitting down. Meanwhile, the receptionist was leafing through the Rolodex on the counter, no doubt searching for Patrick Skinner's telephone number.

Not good.

Colleen picked up her shoulder bag from the floor by her chair nonchalantly, opened it, slipped the order form into it, then quickly checked her watch, as if taken by surprise. "Oh, no! I forgot to feed the parking meter!" Standing up, she slung her bag over her shoulder and quickly left the office.

"Where is she going?" she heard the man with the goatee say behind her. "Did she just walk off with the copy of that order?"

"Oh, my," she heard the receptionist say. Then, louder, calling after Colleen, "Miss Lindsay?"

"Call Security," the man said.

Colleen didn't dare risk waiting for an elevator. She dashed for the stairwell. One floor down she learned that there was no access back into the building from the stairwell. Next floor, same thing. *Damn.* She stepped out of her high heels and, holding them in one hand, the banister in the other, she made eleven speedy concentric loops down the stairs in her bare feet to the lobby, hoping that door wasn't locked as well.

It wasn't.

Breathing a sigh of relief, she slipped her heels back on and emerged from a gold-paneled door with Mayan sun patterns on it into the lobby. She was winded and filmed with sweat.

She hurried for the exit doors to Sutter Street, not making eye contact with anyone.

CHAPTER FIFTY-SIX

Evening rain mortared down on the high roof of H&M Paint as Colleen stepped out of one of the shower stalls in the old locker room downstairs. Toweling off, she wrapped her newly purchased fluffy bathrobe around her, thinking briefly of that night with Ramon. It no longer seemed real, as if it never happened. And, in a way, it hadn't. It was over as soon as it started. By design.

She pocketed the .38 she kept close by these days and made her way back upstairs in her unlaced sneakers and bathrobe, hanging heavy with the gun in the pocket on one side. A new umbrella protected as much of her as possible from the rain. She was halfway up the stairs when she heard the phone ring. She hurried up to her office, answered the phone.

"Ms. Hayes?" It was Alice Drake, her refined accent neat and tidy.

"Yes." Colleen kicked off her sneaks and warmed her feet by the space heater.

"I have some information about your errant person of interest," she said.

Colleen's blood pressure rose. This might be more "good news."

"I'm all ears, Ms. Drake."

Kieran Skinner had spent the better part of a decade in Valley Oaks, a private, upscale psychiatric hospital in Napa that apparently resembled a spa more than a mental facility.

"He was admitted in December of 1967," Alice Drake continued, "and, apart from brief trips home for Christmas and such, lived there until last year. He was one of the critical care 'in-house' patients. Which means he wasn't allowed to leave. Kept under lock and key. A gilded cage, to be sure, but a cage all the same."

Colleen had hit more pay dirt. This only confirmed what she had concluded, that Kieran was a sick man.

"Can I ask how you know this?" Colleen asked.

"His private doctor was a former colleague. I am told that Kieran was treated for schizophrenia and psychopathic behavior—prone to violent sexual fantasies and fits of uncontrolled rage. But that he was evaluated as cured last year."

If there had been a shred of doubt in Colleen's mind, it was gone.

"So this is the one you think killed poor Margaret Copeland," Alice Drake said.

"I think so," Colleen said. "I think so."

"My God," Alice Drake said. "And he was tucked away all those years."

"Seems that way," Colleen said. But not for much longer.

"Good luck to you."

She thanked Alice Drake, hung up.

So, Kieran Skinner was cured, was he?

Not from what she saw during her brief interaction with him. And he hadn't paid for his crime. He'd been safely removed, and now he was back.

Colleen smoked a cigarette, wrote up her phone conversation with Alice Drake on a sheet of paper.

Then she studied her work, spread across her desk.

Jim Davis's police report. The autopsy report. The fragment of Zyl in its drugstore pillbox. The Xerox copy of the rush order for Kieran Skinner's replacement glasses, dated November 22, 1967. And now, proof that Kieran Skinner had been in a private mental facility for a decade.

On their own, not enough. But together, a winning combination. She *had* him.

She called the Copelands' residence in Half Moon Bay, to share her "good" news.

Harold answered. "I'm afraid Miss Copeland is not home at the moment, Ms. Hayes."

Disappointment trickled through her. "Do you know where she went, by any chance, Harold?"

"Up to the city, Ms. Hayes." He cleared his throat. "Actually, I thought she might be with you."

"And how is Mr. Copeland?" Colleen said, attempting to recover the disillusionment in her voice.

"A nurse is with him twenty-four hours a day."

"Will you please tell Alex I called? I have some important news for her."

"Absolutely."

Colleen hung up, dissatisfied. She had promised to tell Alex the news first, so that Alex could be the one to tell her father. It was a promise she wasn't going to break.

She tried to savor her success, alone. The space heater cooked her legs.

The phone ringing again jarred her out of her slumber.

"Security."

"Why, hello, Security," Alex's breathy voice said. There was a tinkling of piano and the murmur of animated conversation in the background. Colleen felt immediate relief.

"Let me guess," Colleen said. "Peg's Place."

"We're keeping your seat warm," Alex said, sounding a little drunk.

"I just got out of the shower."

"Ooh la la," Alex said.

Colleen laughed. "What I mean is, give me time to get ready to get over there. I've got some news."

"Really, Colleen?" Alex's voice grew shaky. "Good news?"

"I'm not sure how good any of this is, but, yes—it's what we've been waiting for."

"You've got him?"

"I can tell you who he is, at least," she said.

She heard Alex's breathing, unsteady.

CHAPTER FIFTY-SEVEN

Colleen quickly changed into a new pair of long flared black slacks, ankle boots with a mild platform, and a crisp white cotton blouse with long pointed collar. She topped the ensemble off with a new slim-fitting black leather bolero jacket with long, fashionable lapels. Not bad. After making off with the eleven-year-old rush order for Kieran Skinner's glasses this afternoon, she'd hit Macy's on her way through Union Square, grabbing clothes off the rack and buying them outright, not even trying them on. Her old business suit was beginning to take her shape.

Outside, thankfully, it wasn't raining, although she carried her new umbrella along with her trusty flashlight down the metal stairwell. The gun was stashed in the ceiling. Too risky for an ex-con to lug *that* around in public. Her precious file folder and the fragment of Kieran Skinner's glasses were tucked away in the ceiling tiles, along with the gun.

She went through the rigmarole of getting the Torino out from behind the gates. She was eager to tell Alex what she knew. Alex could tell her father and, hopefully, they could both come to terms with Margaret's death. It felt cathartic to be able to help Alex move past a tragedy that had been hanging over the family for more than a decade. She locked the gates back up, the Torino rumbling in the driveway, and headed off.

There was little traffic this time of night. She headed toward Third Street, to get onto 101 and into town. Lighting up a cigarette and rolling down her window to enjoy the momentary lapse in the rain, Colleen stretched back in the bucket seat and cracked out her spine, feeling a real release. There was still a lot of work ahead but she had hit a milestone. She flipped on KFRC. Wild Cherry was urging some white boy to play that funky music. She turned it up.

Then, in the darkness behind her on Yosemite Avenue, she caught a pair of headlights in the rearview mirror, half a block behind. She had not seen anything when she left H&M.

She turned a tight left on Third, an industrial thoroughfare, bouncing over streetcar tracks, heading toward the freeway, keeping her speed at thirty-five.

The headlights made the same turn behind her. Apprehension flared up her back.

She squinted to make out the vehicle in the rearview, but it was far enough behind to make it tough. But she saw two square headlights, higher than a passenger car. A pickup truck.

A Chevy C10?

Six blocks later, she turned sharp right on Paul, off course, and watched the pickup behind her make the very same turn. Any normal traffic should be heading for the freeway, not some desolate warehouse district at night.

Without signaling, she cranked a hard left, down a street lined with darkened warehouses. In the rearview mirror she saw the pickup truck continue straight down Paul, no longer following her. She couldn't tell the model of the truck but it was dark.

Getting paranoid in her old age? She breathed a sigh of relief.

At the end of the street of warehouses, she turned again, waited at the light on Third, back on course for the 101 on-ramp and then into town. A few cars filtered through the intersection, freeway bound.

And, lo and behold, in the rearview mirror, a pair of high square headlights emerged from the street adjacent to the one she had just snaked off a few moments ago.

The pickup had taken a parallel street to her and was now back.

In the rearview she saw the pickup pull over to the curb half a block behind her. Didn't want her to see they were following.

A lone figure sat in the pickup. Frank Madrid or she'd eat her hat. She saw him put something up to his face and the coil of a wire. CB Radio? Calling someone?

Colleen's heartbeats throbbed between her ears.

The traffic light before her was still red. She needed to turn right to catch the freeway.

To her left, rumbling down Third Street toward the wide inter-section, a semi approached, groaning in low gear. Colleen sucked in a breath, stomped the gas, unleashed the Torino's big block V8. Her tires squealed as she cut the steering wheel hard right, fishtailing into the intersection where she finally caught asphalt, shooting onto Third favoring two wheels.

The 101 on-ramp came quickly.

And there it was again in the rearview, the pickup, doing its best to keep up. A clump of vehicles ahead of Colleen was moving at the legal limit. She shot around a Volvo on the right, up on the shoulder, then back out into traffic, earning generous honks all around.

The pickup truck did the same but careened from side to side. It didn't have her center of gravity.

She mashed the pedal and the traffic became a blur. The Torino squealed past cars and trucks, darting in and out. The V8 roared as she shot onto 101 South, headed for San Jose now. The opposite direction of where she wanted to go, but now she had to shake her tail.

Down by the airport, she veered off the freeway, tires screeching, and maneuvered back toward H&M, taking surface streets, heading back into town from a different direction. Her fuel indicator was down a good notch after all the wild driving.

She needed to get her evidence together *now*. Hand it over to someone she could trust. Moran. She wouldn't risk going to see Alex tonight. Frank Madrid might follow somehow. Colleen had a hidey-hole, the welfare hotel she had prepaid to justify proper lodgings for parole. She'd stay there tonight.

Turning on Yosemite, she flipped her headlights off. She trawled down the desolate street in relative darkness. She pulled into the driveway of a wire and cable warehouse just before H&M, where she parked behind a delivery truck, out of sight. She killed the engine, got out of the car with her flashlight, moved quickly to the front of the property by a ramshackle, collapsing gate. Peering out, she breathed deeply, in an attempt to ease the agitation.

Just one lonely streetlight, casting a grainy oval of dim light onto the middle of the forsaken street.

She got her keys out, ready, and was about to make a dash for H&M when she heard the growl of an engine from the other end of Yosemite.

She ducked back into the shadows behind the fence.

A boxy white Ford sedan trolled by this time, a chrome light sticking out of the driver's door. An unmarked police car. Tinted windows. The same one that followed her the other night from Pacifica?

How many cops were involved? She knew Frank Madrid, and the two who tried to torch the warehouse, and possibly that Don character she'd run into with Steve Davis.

She raked her head around the fence, saw the car head down to
H&M.

It stopped at the gates.

A man in a mid-length coat got out of the car, went over to the
gate, leaned on the buzzer. She could hear it from where she stood,
distant but clear in the night air. When there was no answer, the
man looked around, went back to his car.

The searchlight on the car lit up, moved about, scanning the front
of the plant. Then it shut off, leaving a flickering imprint where the
light had been. She saw the car go to the end of the street where it
made a wide U-turn, came back, then park in darkness on the other
side of the street.

Staking her out.

Her heart rate ratcheted up.

She turned, hoofed it back behind the wire warehouse, up to the
shore where scummy water lapped onto trash and discarded lumber
and bricks. She followed the shoreline down to the fence that
reached out into the bay next to H&M. Where Ramon had found a
hole a few feet out where one could get through.

She stripped down to her new blouse and jacket, left her new
slacks, socks, and boots with the little metal studs on the ankles
folded up on top of a crate and flicked on the flashlight, keeping the
beam low.

At the shore she scanned the cyclone fence reaching into the
water.

There it was.

A gap in the fence, carefully pulled open either side. Thank you,
Ramon.

She waded out, testing each step cautiously, to ensure nothing
sharp lay underfoot. The water was good and cold, and she fought
the shivers. Up to her knees now. It smelled like oil and waste.

CHAPTER FIFTY-EIGHT

Up in her "bedroom" Colleen dried her frozen legs with a towel, shivering mightily, until she warmed up enough to pull on fresh socks and jeans. She left her white blouse with the pointed collar and black bolero jacket on, slipped on her white leather Pumas, and climbed up on the desk where she pushed the ceiling tile aside. She gathered her file folder, the Zyl fragment in its pillbox, and, after thinking about it, the .38 Detective Special. A risk to carry, but she might need it.

Everything went into a plastic garbage bag. She slung that over her shoulder.

Outside, she peered down the metal stairs. The unmarked car had been across the street, a few car lengths down, in the shadows. She took the stairs quietly, staying flat against the building to keep her profile minimal. She had to get out without being seen.

Back on the ground, she darted over to the fence in a crouching run. Over by the pallets stacked against the repaired hole, she saw the unmarked sedan parked across the street. Still staking her out. A case of nerves rippled through her. She shook them off, headed back toward the shoreline in a stooping run, back to the break in the fence out in the filmy water.

She shuddered at the prospects of another soaking. But one more time she stripped off, put her clothes inside the garbage bag, along with her shoulder bag. She drew a sharp breath as she held the garbage bag overhead with one arm, her flashlight in the other, and waded back out into the freezing water.

* * *

Colleen didn't think she'd ever actually have to sleep in the Thunderbird Hotel, where she'd paid a month's rent to satisfy parole. Fleabag wasn't the word. But it was better than the back seat of the Torino, which she'd stashed in a lot around the corner. She didn't need anyone spotting the car on the street.

She checked into her room with its dizzying odor of disinfectant and plenty of neighborly racket from people who probably didn't work days, if they worked at all. She settled in, then hiked down to the lobby to the pay phone. She called Peg's Place.

Alex Copeland and her friends had left. Damn. She did want to bring Alex up to date and knew that Mr. Copeland was running out of time. She called her answering service. No new messages.

It was well after midnight. She considered not calling the Copeland residence, but the urge to speak to Alex won over.

After three rings a woman answered. She was part of the round-the-clock nursing shift.

"So sorry to bother you," Colleen said. "But I was hoping to catch Alex. It's kind of important."

"Ms. Copeland called not too long ago to check in on her father and to say she would probably not be coming home tonight, ma'am."

"I see," Colleen said, a hammer of disappointment pounding from within. She wondered where Alex had wound up, recalling the faces of her pretty friends. Alex wouldn't have a problem finding a sympathetic ear if she needed one. "Thank you so much," she said, hanging up the phone, trudging back up to her hotel room, full of frustration.

Downstairs a man yelled at a woman to get him some ice. Next door "Life in the Fast Lane" throbbed through the walls, along with the acrid tang of marijuana.

CHAPTER FIFTY-NINE

"What do you think?" Colleen said, flipping up the collar of her leather jacket against the biting wind blowing in from the ocean.

Retired Santa Cruz detective Dan Moran pushed his glasses up his nose and handed Colleen back her file folder.

"It's good work, Hayes," he said. "Damn good." But his thick dark eyebrows furrowed in concern.

"Then why do I sense a 'but' coming?"

"Because it's not enough to nail this Kieran Skinner."

The two of them were standing outside the Santa Cruz Boardwalk Casino, the clatter and inanity of the arcade games being played at full volume wafting out. The two of them watched the wind blowing the waves to and fro beyond the pier. The sky had cleared enough today so that a few brave souls in wetsuits were paddling out on surfboards on the swelling waves.

"Not enough evidence?" she said. "I've covered everything."

"It's circumstantial at best," Moran said, frowning. "It relies on an inference to connect it to the Copeland murder."

Colleen gave a sigh.

"The Falcon is new evidence," she said.

"Which you have yet to find," Moran said, raising his eyebrows above his black-framed glasses. "No telling where that car is now, eleven years after the fact. Could have been crushed for scrap. And, even if you do find it, what do you have?"

"Larry, the maintenance man at Stow Lake. He'll vouch he saw it the night of the murder."

"Testimony taken over a decade later. Memories are faulty, Hayes, and, as good as you say his is, a jury is still going to be doubtful. And if they aren't, you have a car parked near a murder. Skinner's lawyers are going to argue that there could be a lot of cars parked near any murder."

"Okay." She grimaced. "How about the rush order for Kieran Skinner's glasses?"

Moran shook his head. "Kieran Skinner could have sat on his spectacles during Thanksgiving dinner. We both know he didn't, but I can hear his lawyer now. He or she—or, more likely, *they*—will make you look like a fool if you try to make *that* the reason he should spend the next twenty years in San Quentin."

Colleen pulled the pill case from her pocket. "What about the *pièce de résistance*?"

"Evidence you stole? Prove it's where you said it was—in the evidence box. That clerk is going to cover his tracks and deny he ever met you."

Christ. There was one other fragment, but it had spilled on the floor of the break room when she engineered her "accident" to steal the piece she had. It might never be found.

"I've got Doctor Drake," she said, "who wrote the coroner's report. I've got evidence that Kieran was tucked away in Valley Oaks for a decade."

"Fair enough," Moran said. "But you can't prove Margaret Copeland broke Skinner's glasses, swallowed a chunk so you could come along eleven years later and nail him for murdering her. You, Hayes—an ex-con who killed her own husband."

"For molesting my daughter."

"Your biggest enemy in all this, Hayes? It's not Kieran Skinner. It's not even his father, the assemblyman on his way to the state senate—although he is going to take you down any way he can. It's the rogue cops and ex-cops in SFPD who don't want you to get to square one. From what you've told me, there are at least three of them. Add Assemblyman Skinner and you've got formidable opposition."

"They killed one of their own—just to cover it up."

"Exactly my point. They are not going to let you win this, legally—or illegally."

Colleen took a deep breath as she put the pill case back in her jacket pocket. It seemed so small now, that little piece of evidence.

"I know he did it," she said.

"And you've convinced me, too, Hayes. Anyone can see the case smelled funny from day one—when SFPD dropped it, then later blaming it on the Zodiac—all because Patrick Skinner threw his weight around. But you can't fight City Hall."

Again, she sensed Moran had more to say.

"*Unless?*" she said.

He gave a wry smile. "Unless you have some direct evidence."

"Like?"

"A good old-fashioned confession, Hayes. Along with what you have, that might swing it. Let me call an associate of mine. FBI. Maybe he can help. It's a pretty strong case you make, after all. But it's going to be tough. Don't get your hopes up."

"What you said about SFPD," she said. "A few bad apples, right? There must be someone there who wants to see this solved."

"You can try. But tread warily."

"And here I thought you were going to pat me on the back and say what a great job I did."

"You *did* do a great job, Hayes. But you think you're at the tail end." He shook his head. "What you've got is a promising start." Moran pushed his glasses up his nose. "You've still got a long way to go."

It would be crazy to walk away now. She needed to see Mr. Copeland nod with relief. She needed to see Kieran Skinner's face when they sentenced him. She needed to see the look of release on Alex's face.

She needed to see Frank Madrid pay for killing Jim Davis.

"Can we still trade cars for a couple of days?" she asked. Her Torino was not only bright red but red hot, as far as SFPD was concerned.

"Why?"

"I want to head up to Point Arena to see if I can make contact with Pamela. At the commune."

"Bull." Moran actually laughed. "You're planning on following Kieran Skinner around."

"From a safe distance. Don't tell me you wouldn't do the same thing."

Moran shook his head. "Just bring it back in one piece, Hayes." He reached into the pocket of his checked jacket and came out with a set of car keys. "And don't tell Daphne. She'd kill me."

"Did you know that Kieran means 'Little Dark One' in Gaelic?" Colleen said, taking Moran's car keys, handing him hers.

"Go figure," he said, taking the keys to the Torino.

"And could you hang onto this for me?" She held out the file folder with all of her collected paperwork and notes, and the plastic pillbox with the Zyl fragment.

He looked at it for a moment, took the folder, slipped the pillbox into his jacket.

"Be careful, Hayes."

Out on the water, a surfer turned his board toward shore and stood up in his black wetsuit. He caught the crest of a rough wave, riding the curl as it plunged toward shore. The wave grew in size, wild and out of control. A frothy whitecap appeared underneath the board and the surfer stepped forward, arms out, and she thought she heard him give a victory whoop. But then the wave exploded and he flipped backwards, the board vertical for a second before both man and board disappeared. A complete wipeout. But a moment later, after the wave passed, his head appeared, and he swam to his board, climbed back on, and paddled back out.

CHAPTER SIXTY

"I don't want you leaving the house for a few days, Kieran," his father said, standing at the window with his back to him. His father was wearing a gray suit. His waking life was spent in a gray suit. The two of them were in his father's office upstairs, with the view of the Golden Gate Bridge breaking through thick fog.

Like those clouds, Kieran's head was swirling. Something was going on. He knew it. He'd overheard his father on the phone earlier. It sounded like he was speaking to Doctor Herrera, Kieran's doctor up at Valley Oaks.

His father was going to send him back.

He'd spent ten years in that place. *Ten years.* He couldn't spend another day.

He needed to pay his father back. Now. For what he did.

"Why?" he asked.

"Why?" his father echoed, head turned partway, eyeing Kieran. "I think you know why, lad."

A wave of shame washed over him.

"Because that woman is looking for me?" he said, his voice breaking. It wasn't really a question.

"She's not looking anymore," his father said, giving him the fish eye. "She's found you."

Kieran winced. The subject they never really talked about was coming up. Ever since that day, eleven years ago, when they never really talked about it for the first time, the power of these conversations only seemed to intensify. If they just would never talk about it again, perhaps he could finally start to get better. He used to think that time would soften the past, that it would fade. Didn't they say "time healed all wounds?" Well, it wasn't so. He remembered that night, clearly now. It would come back at him like a wild bullet from time to time. It did now. Parking by Stow Lake. Lugging her doped-up body down to the trees. She was stoned on acid and the chloroform he'd used to knock her out. Carrying her. She was his. For a while.

Then, in the trees, she came to, after he'd undressed her. After he . . .

She rose up, unsteadily, managed to hit him. A lucky punch. She knocked his glasses off. Off. Stepped on them as they fought in the shelter of the trees. Middle of the night. Broke his glasses. Broke his glasses! Well, he took care of her. Broke her. Dosed her with more juice. A plastic bag over her head to finish her off. Took care of her. Taught his father a lesson, too.

But getting away, with broken glasses. Not easy. He could have been caught. His damn father.

The past never let go. His wounds were as deep as ever. Thanks to his father. All those years in Valley Oaks. An upholstered prison, but still a prison.

"Do you think she knows?" he asked, meaning Colleen Hayes. A hard question to ask, because he was almost admitting to what happened that night, eleven years ago.

His father's head remained sideways, one eye staring. "Oh, she knows, all right."

"But it's okay to go for walks," he said, his voice shrill. "To Baker Beach?"

His father shook his head. "You've been relapsing," he said. He spoke to the sea now. "Hanging around schools."

Kieran's face burned. He'd been caught. Watching Robyn. Frank must have told him.

"Just the one time," he said, his voice reaching a high pitch. He forced it back down. "I just happened to be walking by."

"Well, that's why you're staying inside the house for a few days." His father clasped his hands behind his back. "It's for the best, Kieran."

"Fine!" he snapped.

"I know it hasn't been easy since your mother passed, son."

Passed. Kieran had to stifle his anger with a snort. Try: *killed herself.* Because of your philandering. You weak, weak bastard. Suffocated herself to teach you a lesson. And now you're doing it again.

"Promise me you'll stay in," his father said. "Just for a while. Until I get something settled. Promise me that. Will you?"

He squinted in annoyance. "Yes. Fine. Okay."

"Good lad." His father came over, gave him a pat on the arm.

Kieran needed to get away. Before his father sent him away again. Pay him back. Once and for all. Because he never learned his lesson.

* * *

"Where are you going, Kieran?" Grace, the Skinners' maid, stood at the front door, blocking his way.

"Just out for some fresh air," Kieran said. His father had left for City Hall so he only had Grace to deal with. But Grace kept a sharp eye on him.

Her middle-aged Latin features took on a suspicious frown.

"Your father said—"

"Oh, right," he said, holding up his paperback. "I'm not leaving the house, Grace. Just going out back—on the patio."

"Oh." She broke into a smile of relief. "But it's cold out there . . ."

"I don't mind." He shrugged. "I could use the fresh air."

"Would you like some tea? It's almost time for your medicine."

"Yes, Grace. I'll take it out back. Thank you."

He took the stairwell downstairs to the family room, plunking out a discordant chord on Grandpa's old roller piano the way he always did before heading outside to the flagstone patio.

Angry clouds roiled low over the Pacific. But it wasn't raining at the moment so he had an excuse to be out here. He knew Grace was watching. He set his book down on a patio chair and built a fire in the fire pit, stacking the wood in a cone, getting it to light.

Minutes later, huge, wild flames flapped in the breeze as he took his chair and pulled it close to the pit, putting his feet up on the stone ring. He opened his book to where he'd left off but couldn't concentrate. No matter how hard he tried, the words always seemed to float away unread.

Today had to be the day to take Robyn. His time was running out.

The sound of Grace coming through the den alerted him. He'd been waiting for her.

"Here we go, Kieran," she said, setting down a mug of tea and handing him a small ceramic dish with a yellow capsule in it.

She stood there for a moment, hands folded, watching Kieran sip his tea.

"It's good, Grace," he said, holding up the cup. "Nice and strong."

She arched her eyebrows, nodding at the pill dish.

"Oh, right." He picked up the dish, tipped the capsule into his mouth.

"You sure you're warm enough out here?" she said, rubbing her hands together.

He zipped his dark jacket collar up to his chin and gave her a thumbs-up, along with a smile.

"You're looking well today," she said. "It's good to see."

"Thanks for the tea." Kieran winked. Soon she was heading back upstairs.

He spit the yellow pill into the fire.

He didn't have much time before his father sent him away.

He finished his tea, threw another couple of logs onto the fire. It crackled and roared. Upstairs he heard the whine of the vacuum cleaner. He got up and took his paperback into the den and sat in an old leather chair.

And waited.

The vacuum cleaner shut off. He heard Grace thumping down the stairs quickly to the den. He opened his book to a random page and pretended to read. Grace appeared at the door.

"Oh, you're in here," she said with a relaxed sigh.

"You were right, Grace." He didn't look up from his book. "It's cold out there."

"Told you." She smiled, headed back upstairs. He heard her unplug the central vacuum attachment, and then she padded up to the second floor. She'd be doing the bedrooms next.

He had a window of opportunity.

Minutes later he was back outside, this time snaking around the side of the house, staying close to the wall where Grace wouldn't see him if she happened to look out the window.

At the front of the house he heard the vacuum start up again upstairs. He retrieved his black watch cap from his jacket pocket, pulled it down tight on his head, made sure his glasses were well secured under it. He double-checked his other pocket. The bottle of ghetto chloroform he had purchased from his contact in the Fillmore was wrapped neatly in a fresh handkerchief. The top of the dry-cleaning bag was folded in the breast pocket. He took a deep breath, opened the wrought-iron gate—quietly—slipped through, pulled the gate gently shut behind him.

The squeak of an upstairs window caught his attention.

"Where do you think you're going, Kieran?" Grace shouted in that singsong voice he detested.

He turned, looked up at Grace eyeing him, a smirk on her face.

"Just going for a walk, Grace. Stretch my legs."

"No." Her head shook slowly from side to side. "Don't even think about it."

God damn bitch. Damn woman telling him what to do in front of the whole world, like he was some child.

"Don't make me call your father," she said, a taunt to his ears.

He exhaled a deep breath.

"Fine!" he said, adding the word *bitch* under his breath. He turned around, stormed back through the gate, slamming it hard, let himself in through the front door, stomping over to the bottom of the stairs. Grace came down, stood on the landing.

"Why don't you come upstairs and have a rest, Kieran?" she said, standing at the landing.

"Because I don't want a fucking rest, Grace. Is that all right with you? Or are you going to call my father and tell him I won't take a nap?"

She grimaced, took the remaining stairs deliberately, holding onto the handrail. She reached the last stair, stood eye to eye with him with the extra step. "There's no point in getting testy with *me*, Kieran. I'm only doing what your father asked."

"No one's getting testy with you, you cow."

"What did you just call me?" Anger flared across her normally impassive face as she leaned forward, inches away. "I'll slap your face, you spoiled brat!"

"Go ahead. You'll be looking for a new job by this afternoon. Help wanted: Aging Mexican maid, pear-shaped, no longer able to draw the sailors from Camp Pendleton into the brothels of Tijuana. Not even for the donkey show."

Kieran grabbed the back of her neck with his bony hand and cinched it hard while he calmly wrapped the other around her throat. Her eyes popped as she grasped at his wrists.

"Calling my *what,* you fat little wetback?" He squeezed her throat. "Calling my *what?*"

She grunted, eyes bugging.

"Let me tell *you* something, Grace: If you even *think* of calling my father, I'll be calling immigration before you can say 'deported.' It won't matter where I am. That phone call will be the very first one I make. I promise you. Now how does that sound? *Eh?*" He squeezed. She choked. "You'll be on the next bus out of California. You and your little greasy *niños* and that toothless gardener you're married to. You can scrabble for a living in that hellhole south of the border. One phone call is all it takes. One thin dime." He raised his eyebrows. "I guarantee it."

Grace's frantic eyes pleaded for him to let go.

"Do we have an understanding, Grace?" he said calmly.

She nodded desperately.

He threw her back. She landed, her butt hitting a stair with a thump. She sat up, legs apart, massaging her neck, looking at him as if he were mad. "*¡Estas loco!*"

"Speak English, for Christ's sake."

"You're not well, Kieran. You need to see the doctor again."

"Don't tell me what I am, Grace," he said. "Now, I'm going out for a walk and that's all there is to it. I'll be back before my father returns. Nothing for you to worry about. Now, is that clear, or do I need to make that phone call? To the boys from *inmigración*?"

She massaged her neck, swallowed. "No."

"Of course not. And remember, if you call my father while I'm out, I will make it a point to drop a dime on you and your family wherever I happen to be. You may count on it. Now, do we have it all clear and copasetic, *amiga*?"

She put her hands down. "Yes."

"I'm just going out now. Finish your vacuuming. I'll see you later."

She nodded. "Yes, Kieran."

"Good girl."

That seemed to take care of things. It didn't do for the help to get uppity.

He headed out the front door.

A few moments later, he set off down Sea Cliff Avenue, checking that his watch cap was fitted well to his head, securing his glasses in place.

* * *

Colleen waited in Moran's Pinto until she saw Kieran Skinner turn on 27th Avenue. She was beginning to wonder if he would ever show. This was the second day staking him out. Kieran wore a knit watch cap, his dark glasses tucked under it. His jaw was set tight but he still managed to maintain a blank expression. His bushy Fu Manchu mustache and sideburns gave him an ominous air. She fired up Moran's Pinto, the little engine rattling, and tossed her cigarette out into the street. She cranked up the window. She was ready, in her 501s, white V-neck T-shirt, and white leather Pumas. Her old leather bomber jacket lay on the passenger seat.

She followed Kieran, slowing now and then to keep a half block between them. Four blocks later, he crossed Geary Boulevard, the main thoroughfare from the Richmond District into the city. He stopped at a bus stop, waited, pulling his hands out of the pockets of his jacket every so often to adjust his cap over the sides of his glasses. He did that a lot. She pulled over next to a corner store, the engine pinging, waited.

A red and white 38 Muni bus pulled up in front of Kieran Skinner, took off, and he was gone. Colleen pulled out on Geary, hitting a red light as the bus sailed on through. She'd follow it.

CHAPTER SIXTY-ONE

Kieran hovered inside the laundromat across the street from Roosevelt, waiting for the bell. The washing machines and dryers churned away, along with his tangled thoughts. He rarely liked what he was thinking.

But Robyn was one of the things he had to do. Her whore of a mother made it so.

The school bell ringing across the street shook him out of his mental disarray.

Peering through the laundromat window, he watched the double doors open. Kids began to file out. He recognized some of them from Robyn's ninth-grade classes. The odd teacher, but no Robyn.

What if she hadn't come to school today? His heart thumped. He was running out of time.

But then, there she was. He gave a deep sigh of relief.

Today Robyn wore her big checked bell-bottoms again, showing off her slim hips. Short denim jacket, red sneakers. Blond hair blow-dried and fluffy, Farrah Fawcett style. Looking very grown up. A big smile on her pretty face as she said goodbye to her black friend, before she turned with a delightful swirl and headed up Arguello, her folder under one arm, her Charlie's Angels backpack over one shoulder.

She was walking home today.

She was going home through Golden Gate Park. She liked to watch the carousel on her way home. He knew this from following her.

He'd get her in the park. Like the other one.

His body tingled with excitement. He checked that his cap was tight on his head, keeping his glasses securely in place. He banged into a plastic chair on his way out of the laundromat.

Outside on the sidewalk, he suddenly felt warm, even though it was overcast and cool. His breathing deepened as he looked around. No blue pickup truck. No fat pig Frank. He was free as a bird. Nothing to stop him.

Maybe it was a sign. That today was the day. He felt a power course through him.

He set off, tailing Robyn, but staying on the opposite side of the street.

* * *

Colleen watched Kieran skulk down Arguello, hunkered down in his knit cap, hands jammed in the pockets of his black warehouseman's jacket. Traffic clogged the street, parents picking up kids from school. If she followed him in the car, she might be unable to pull over and park if he ducked in somewhere. He was moving fast, as if following someone himself. She fired up the Pinto, rattled down Arguello, keeping track of Kieran's black watch cap bobbing. He bounded across the four-lane Geary Boulevard. He touched the watch cap. He was wound up tight.

She sensed she was on to something that wasn't right. Maybe it's because he was heading in the direction of Golden Gate Park.

Where Margaret had been murdered.

CHAPTER SIXTY-TWO

Kieran followed Robyn up to the edge of the park. Arguello became a hilly street crossing into a canopy of trees.

Robyn stopped to gaze in the window of a corner grocery store painted bright red.

He was tempted to cross over, approach her, start a conversation. That would make it easier to get close, when the time came. He braced himself, keeping his eyes down.

She went into the store. *Damn it!* He crossed over to Fulton, the street that ran alongside the park, and waited at a bus stop. Head down.

He'd speak to her when she came out of the store.

A few moments later, she emerged from the store, something in her hand.

A small pink envelope. Out of the corner of his eye, he saw her rip it open, pour some of the contents into her mouth. He watched her swallow, the fine gulp of her slender neck. She was wearing a gold chain. It hung over a dip of vanilla-colored skin above her sweater under her denim jacket. He could see the indentation of one of her small breasts for a moment as she tipped the envelope up to her mouth.

He caught himself. Here she came, crossing the street.

Hi, how are you? That's what he'd say. Get her to trust him.

She brought the envelope down, approached the light, waited for it to change, then crossed over, coming straight toward him. *Straight toward him,* making his heart thump.

He said nothing.

She walked by, humming, the movement of her backside pulling his gaze as she headed up Arguello where the street twisted into the park. His body prickled. He hadn't said a word. She disappeared from view. In his jacket pocket, he stroked the bottle of chloroform wrapped in the hanky.

She'd stop at the playground to watch the merry-go-round. He'd talk to her there. It would seem more natural anyway. He couldn't let her get away like she did the other day.

The candy she'd been eating gave him an idea. He swooped back across the street, ducked into the corner store where he bought two packs of Pop Rocks. Back out, he darted across the street against the blare of a car horn. He sprinted into Golden Gate Park, pushing up Arguello into the hilly part overgrown with trees. He felt invigorated. Soon his task would be done. At the top of the hill he saw her checked pants as she disappeared down the other side into the park proper. Back on track.

He shadowed her past the Conservatory of Flowers. Its ornate white framing and glass panes threw the park back to another century. Crossing JFK, he trailed Robyn to Koret Playground. Children were climbing ropes, swinging on big boats suspended like giant swings, one boat alive with kids singing, *Working at the car wash, car wash,* over and over. Robyn stood, watching them. Although he couldn't see her face directly, he knew she was smiling. She liked simple things like that.

She strolled over to the carousel, where organ music pumped out of the round structure with its elegant columns, housing the early 1900s merry-go-round. She stopped, holding her folder in front of her, taking in the graceful whirl of the ride. All sorts of exotic animals were represented, real and otherwise—ostriches, unicorns, tigers, dragons—painted in a myriad of bright shiny colors. Kieran kept back by a tree, watching furtively.

When the merry-go-round slowed, Robyn walked to a bench, sat down. She placed her folder and backpack next to her, crossed a leg, which made her look very grown up. She reminded him again of that girl from so many years ago, the one whose name he couldn't always remember. Margaret. But Robyn would be different. Smaller, more controllable. She would be quick.

The merry-go-round came to a halt. People filed out of the round pavilion and those who had been waiting boarded, and soon the music was flowing again as the carousel spun.

Robyn bobbed one foot to the music, and it caught his eye like a magnet pulling an iron filing. He studied the fine movement of her leg, so natural, and he wondered how she looked without so many clothes. How she smelled.

He gulped back his excitement. He was getting off track. This was the time. He would introduce himself, and she would trust him.

Chest tight, he walked over to the bench on stiff legs.

"Hey, Robyn," he said. "I didn't know you came here."

She turned from her seat, looked up at him, her lips parted in surprise. There was a trace of candy in the corner of her mouth. She blinked, her light blue eyes disappearing in between sensuous flutters. She squinted, rearing back slightly.

"Who are you?"

It was the first time she had ever spoken to him. She had a sweet voice but it was high. He had always imagined her sounding older. It was a bit of a disappointment. The chain around her neck held a small gold crucifix. It set off the whiteness of her skin. She wore a blouse under her V-neck sweater. Her skin was pink and flawless. Soft looking.

He caught himself. That wasn't the point of this. The point was to teach his father a lesson.

"You don't remember me?" Kieran said, laughing, trying to sound natural. "I'm Gary—a friend of your mom's."

Her eyes blinked in confusion. "I don't remember."

"I work at City Hall."

"You do?" Robyn smiled a cautious smile of small white teeth. So innocent.

"She talks about you all the time," he said.

"She does?" A bigger smile now. Good.

"You bet! She says you love Charlie's Angels."

Robyn tried to suppress a childish grin as she picked up her backpack to show him. "Roxanne says it's kid's stuff. But I still like them."

"Oh, Roxanne—your friend from school, right?"

"Yep."

That had to be the black girl she was always with. He didn't approve of that. But that wasn't important right now. "Well, I think Roxanne's got it wrong, Robyn. *Charlie's Angels* is cool." He nodded at the merry-go-round, throwing puffs of organ music out into the park as it spun. "Just like that is."

She gave him a shy smile. "Isn't it?"

"It was built in 1914. There's not another one like it in the whole wide world."

"It's so neat."

"It is *neat*. I like to walk through here on my way home, just to check it out."

She looked at him for a moment, and then she smiled.

"Me, too!" she said.

He casually pulled an envelope of candy from his back pocket, as if he had just thought of it. He tore the top of the envelope away.

He held the envelope out. "Want some of these, Robyn?"

"You have strawberry Pop Rocks?" she said, surprised.

He looked at her with a smile. "What other kind are there?"

Another big smile. "I know."

"Put your hands out," he said.

She cupped her hands and he poured half the pack into her pink palms. She scooped them into her mouth like a much younger kid.

He sat down next to her on the bench, leaving a couple of feet of space between them. He checked around to see if anyone was watching. So far, so good.

They ate candy and listened to the merry-go-round and she wiped her hands off on the edge of the bench. He didn't think that was very ladylike and almost said something.

The merry-go-round slowed.

She picked up her folder, a manila Pee Chee with the athletes playing tennis, football, running. She had drawn long hair and mustaches on two of the runners in blue ballpoint. She collected her backpack. "I have to go."

A twitch of anxiety made him sit up straight.

"You have plenty of time, Robyn. Your mom has to finish up some stuff at work."

"She does?"

"Did I forget to tell you? She's going to be late. Hey, I know! Why don't we go for a ride?" He nodded at the merry-go-round. "My treat. What do you say, Robyn?"

She turned to gaze at the merry-go-round, her blond hair falling over the collar of her pale blue denim jacket, shiny, giving him a nostril full of sweet shampoo scent, then she turned back to him, frowning. "I better not."

But she wanted to, he could tell. She just wasn't sure. About him. "Stupid me!" He gave an animated frown and hit his forehead with the heel of his hand. "Your mom told you not to do things with strangers! What a *maroon*." He'd heard Bugs Bunny say that. Kids liked Bugs Bunny. "I guess I didn't think of myself as a stranger. But you are absolutely right." He stood up, forcing himself not to check whether his knit hat was on straight. "Well, it was *neat* meeting you again, Robyn. I think I'm going to ride the merry-go-round anyway. I've always wanted to. And today's the day. Please tell your mom I said *hi*. I'll see her at work tomorrow."

Her frown faded, leaving an uncertain smile. "Okay . . . Gary."

Chest thumping, he turned to walk over to the ticket booth. If she walked away, he'd follow her.

Then, with a gush of relief, he heard her soft footfalls behind him. "Hey, Gary . . ."

Yes! He turned slowly, swallowing hard, forcing composure.

"Hey, Robyn. What's up?"

"Just one ride," she said. "Then I better get home."

"Cool."

"But I get to ride my own animal. No sharing."

He couldn't stop from grinning, even as an eyelid flickered. "Of course. Which one do you have in mind?"

"The unicorn," she said with a shy smile. How could she be the daughter of such an immoral woman?

"Good choice! We better hurry, in case someone else grabs it."

The man behind the counter gave him the steel eye as he paid for the tickets.

They climbed up on the circular deck and he helped Robyn onto the unicorn, with its white pearl paint and huge glass sequins down its mane. His hand just brushed the hem of her checked bell-bottoms as he stood back.

"Nice pants, Robyn."

He climbed on the horse next to her and felt in his left pocket. The handkerchief and bottle of chloroform were there. Why did he keep thinking they wouldn't be? He checked his watch cap again. Tight around his glasses.

"Why do you keep doing that?" she asked.

"Doing what?"

"Grabbing your hat."

"Do I?" He reddened.

The merry-go-round set in motion and the music churned around their heads, sending his thoughts asunder. He tried to focus on the paintings of old scenes and flashing mirrors overhead but things felt out of control. His winced as the green of Golden Gate Park blurred around him and gripped the pole tightly with both hands. How could anyone possibly enjoy this? Being flung up and down like a damn yoyo? But he looked over and saw Robyn smiling, one hand going to her chest above her cross in a dainty *oh-my* gesture as she cocked her head just so. Soon he would be finished with her. She wouldn't be putting on any airs then.

*　*　*

Colleen lost Kieran past the Conservatory of Flowers, when he took a path that forked off JFK Drive into the other side of the park. What bothered her was that he appeared to be following a teenage girl in wild check bell-bottom pants and a denim jacket. Something wasn't right. What a time to lose him.

She pulled over and parked the Pinto facing against traffic along-side the Hall of Flowers. She got out, went to the trunk, opened it, looked around, pulled the .38 from her bag, slipped it into the pocket of her beat-up leather jacket. She slammed the trunk, dashed across the street, set off down the path Kieran had taken.

It crossed a street and split into two.

Her forehead was growing moist.

She took the path to the right. When she got to the tennis courts, Colleen couldn't see a sign of Kieran or the girl. Uneasiness crept over her. She asked a couple of middle-aged jocks playing tennis if they had seen anyone like Kieran. They hadn't.

Then she heard, a few hundred feet away through the trees, the musical whistle of an organ, like a fairground.

"What's over that way?" she asked one of the men, who was just winding up to serve. He stopped, eyed her with annoyance.

"The merry-go-round," he said tightly.

Maybe they went that way. She took the path in the direction of the music, breaking into a run.

* * *

"Let's go for another spin, Robyn!" Kieran said, forcing joviality but trying to stay casual. The few minutes on the ride had unsettled his wits and made his head spin.

"I need to get home," Robyn said, not looking at him, collecting her folder and backpack from the stone ticket booth where she had left them with the man.

That was fine with Kieran. He didn't need another ride on that damn thing. But he couldn't let Robyn get away. He'd broken through. He had to get her into the trees.

"Thanks for the ride, Gary." She gave a tense smile and turned away quickly.

"Wait, Robyn! I'll walk you home."

"No, it's okay."

"I insist. It's not safe."

"Okay." But she headed off ahead of him, walking quickly in the direction of Kezar Stadium.

His anxiety returned; he was about to lose her. All that work.

He set off after her.

Robyn was looking straight ahead when he caught up. She wasn't smiling.

Damn it, he thought, scurrying along, accidentally adjusting his watch cap. He pulled the last envelope of Pop Rocks from his back pocket, held it up. That caught her eye.

"Who's your buddy?" he said.

"No thanks."

He handed it to her as they walked. "Come on."

"Okay." She took the envelope.

"Here, I'll carry those while you eat your Pop Rocks." He nodded at her backpack and folder.

"No, that's okay," she said. She stood, ripping open the envelope, her hands full.

They were past Sharon Meadow, near a good clump of leafy trees. Plenty of privacy there. He'd steer her that way.

* * *

At the merry-go-round, Colleen saw no sign of Kieran or the girl. She scanned the playground. Nothing. She hoped she hadn't gotten things wrong. There was a lawn bowling green across the way.

She'd check there. But she stopped at the stone ticket booth by the carousel where she asked the man if he had seen her daughter, describing the girl with the check pants, and her brother, describing Kieran.

"They were supposed to meet me here," she said, looking at her watch.

"Those two?" he said with what she thought was an air of suspicion. He nodded past the playground. "They just got off the ride. They went that way. He's her uncle, you say?"

Colleen felt a blast of relief, albeit temporary. "Yes—why do you ask?"

"Just wondered."

Colleen turned, saw a meadow off past the playground, through some trees, heading toward the Haight.

*　*　*

"Cut over here, Robyn," Kieran said as he walked behind her along the trees toward Kezar Drive. She was moving quickly, in no mood to be with him, it seemed. The tension mounted in his temples. His head was starting to hurt. He needed to finish it. *Finish it.*

"Mom says to go this way," Robyn said. She hadn't touched her candy.

"But *this* way's quicker, Robyn," he said. "Your mom won't mind."

She pushed ahead. "I don't know."

She was so close. Her hair. Her skin. But she was getting away. He turned as he walked, getting his bottle and handkerchief out. It was time. He uncapped the bottle, spilled a generous dose of chloroform onto the material, a sharp whiff of chemicals coming at him, thinking that was actually kind of funny for a moment,

Robyn not knowing. She had no idea what was in store. She'd learn to snub him. He capped the bottle, slipped it back in his pocket.

He looked around. No one. *Ha.*

"Robyn, jeez—will you wait up?"

"I have to get home!"

"There's no need to shout. I just want to chat as we walk. Slow down, will you?"

"I said 'I have to get home,' Gary!"

"What's the matter. Don't you like me?"

"Leave me alone!" She picked up speed.

"Don't you tell me what to do!" A surge of adrenaline fueled his legs and, with his larger size, he was soon upon her from behind, locking her neck with the crook of his left arm, bringing the handkerchief over her mouth with the right. The envelope of Pop Rocks flew to the ground.

She actually smacked his handkerchief arm out of the way for a moment, letting loose with a high-pitched squeal that pierced his ears and annoyed him beyond belief. Shrieking like a child! He thumped her face with the heel of his fist and stifled another scream with the handkerchief back over her mouth. "Just be quiet, Robyn. It's fine." She was no match for him. No match at all. She'd learn. It would take a moment for the chloroform to do its work. But this stuff was ghetto, potent, made in some back room.

He dragged Robyn, kicking and moaning, into the bushes, where there was a nice little clearing. Empty bottles, cardboard on the ground, a used condom next to it. She was putting up a fight but quickly losing strength. He yanked her hard. He was getting excited. He was getting physically excited. Yes he was. That was her fault. He found himself laughing.

"Just stop it, Robyn! Honestly!"

She tried to shout but it was wobbly.

"Do you know your mother is fucking my father?" he said through gritted teeth.

* * *

Nearby, Colleen heard a girl scream in a high voice. She bit down hard and ran along the trees toward Kezar.

CHAPTER SIXTY-THREE

Colleen's heartbeats thumped double time as she searched along a bank of pittosporum. She was sure the scream had come from nearby. But Kieran and the girl were nowhere in sight. How could she have let them get away?

Then, through the trees and bushes, she heard the girl shout.

"No!" Her voice was slurry. "Let me go!"

Frantic, Colleen pushed her way through the bushes, where tree branches formed a secluded enclosure.

"Gary, stop!"

The girl writhed about on rumpled cardboard and newspapers, her checked pants muddy. Kieran Skinner squatted in front of her, holding her down with one hand. He had a damp rag of some sort. A handkerchief. He pulled her blond hair out of her face with his little finger. Her eyes rolled. She seemed nearly unconscious. He tipped a brown bottle into a wadded section of the rag, soaking up liquid.

He had doped her. And was planning on taking it further.

Colleen reached into her pocket, pulled the .38.

"Stop right there, Kieran."

Still squatting, Kieran jerked his head around. His mouth dropped when he saw Colleen.

"You!" he shrieked, jumping up. "What are *you* doing here?"

She brought the gun up as she entered. She couldn't fire with the girl so close.

"Get up, sweetheart," Colleen said to her. "Get out of here. Now."

The child tried to raise herself up but gave a disoriented shriek when she saw the gun.

Colleen lowered the gun to ease the girl's fears. "I'm here to stop him, not hurt you. You're safe. But go. Head over by the merry-go-round. Get someone to call the police. The man at the ticket booth."

Kieran dropped back down, tipping the brown bottle into the handkerchief again, a wild grin breaking out. Colleen brought the gun back up, aimed it directly at him with a shaking arm.

The girl tried to get up but slipped and fell.

"It's over, Kieran," Colleen said, readying the gun.

Behind his thick glasses his eyes darted back and forth. His bushy mustache wiggled as he worked his mouth. He moved the handkerchief over the girl's face.

"No," he crowed. "I think *you* better leave, eh? Too much of this will kill her. Yes, it will. And it will be your fault. *Your* fault! Now just put that down!"

Colleen lowered the gun again but inched forward, heart pounding. Discreetly, she pulled the hammer back with her thumb, the click tightening her nerves.

"Just move back!" Kieran hissed. "Now!"

The child moaned, lolling under the suspended handkerchief. His eyes darted over to her, and Colleen took another step.

His eyes shot back to her.

"Just get back!"

"What are you going to do, Kieran?" she said. "Hurt her and you're dead. Dead," she said again. "I'll make sure."

His eyes flickered wildly as the tip of his tongue appeared.

Another step. A few feet away now.

Kieran lowered his head and suddenly leapt at her, butting her chin with the top of his head. It knocked her senses loose. Jaw splitting, Colleen tumbled back, onto the ground, bringing the gun up as the wet handkerchief came in at her, covering her mouth. It stunk of some sweet chemical. Kieran's hand pressed down on her face, his other hand grabbing her throat. He held the handkerchief firmly over her nose and mouth.

"Got you, now, you bitch!"

Her head started to spin.

Colleen breathed what smelled like bleach and sugar before she stopped herself. But her head rang deeply, compounded by Kieran's head butt.

"Wait until I'm done with you!" he squealed.

The rag was pressed so tight it hurt. Her senses swam.

Concentrate.

She managed to swing her gun arm up. She cracked the side of Kieran's head. He yelped and the gun tumbled out of her hand. Kieran grunted, falling away. Colleen's ears shimmered. Her vision shook. She brushed the handkerchief off her face and climbed up, stumbling.

The bottle and handkerchief lay on the ground, moving around with her blurred vision.

Kieran lunged in with both hands, grabbed her throat before she could react. Colleen clutched onto his wrists and pulled. He locked onto her.

Focus. Don't weaken.

He squeezed. Something in her throat felt as if it snapped. Panic seized her. She choked and fought. He was driven by some insane, powerful fury. The same fury that he had directed at Margaret.

Their eyes met. His watch cap was twisted halfway off. Wild frizzy hair stuck out. His pupils were tight and black behind thick glasses, staring directly into her eyes. She saw his latent rage rising like a tide.

"I'm going to enjoy this," he whispered. He gave a weak smile, curling up the corners of his mouth. "I'm going to enjoy *you.*"

That day came back to her in a jarring flash, the day she killed her ex, buried a screwdriver deep into in his neck after she came home and found her daughter crouching in the corner upstairs, half naked.

That anger had never really left her.

Maybe she and Kieran had that in common.

She sucked in what strength she had left and brought a knee up into Kieran's groin, savored the solid connection it made as his eyes rolled back in his head. He gulped air as he released his grasp on her throat and fell down to the ground, rolling into a fetal position, grabbing between his legs.

"You fucking *bitch!*"

Colleen scrambled, flew at him, her head swirling, kicking him, kicking him again, on top of him now, holding his collar with her left fist, punching. Over and over. Her head was swimming.

And then he was still, hat gone, eyes shut, face bloody, glasses gone. She stopped, gasping. She wondered for one horrific moment if she had killed him.

And then he started wheezing, blood spluttering from the corner of his mouth.

CHAPTER SIXTY-FOUR

Colleen grabbed the .38 from the ground, reset the hammer, stood up in the hollow of the trees. Her head spun like the merry-go-round that jangled nearby. Then the blur began to ease. She staggered forward, regaining her balance.

She stared down at Kieran Skinner. He lay flat on his back, arms clutching himself, wheezing through bloody lips. His mustache was sopping with blood on one side. His glasses had come off. One lens was shattered. The irony of the broken glasses filled her with a mixture of horror and dark satisfaction.

This time there would be a different outcome.

Hunched over, one hand on a knee to brace herself, she waved the gun at him.

"Stay down," she panted, "or I *will* . . . put a bullet in your leg."

He rolled over onto his side and vomited. A sick stench filled the air.

She forced herself to stand up straight. She heard the girl choking, crying.

Colleen stepped back, the gun on Kieran. She focused.

The girl had fallen trying to get out the enclosure. Clambering up, she slipped, fell back on her butt. Her denim jacket and checked pants were smeared with mud. But she was coming to. A sense of

relief overwhelmed Colleen. She didn't know how much chloroform the girl had been given but she also knew that a little went a
long way.

"How are you feeling?" Colleen gasped, eyes darting over to
Kieran every few seconds.

"My head . . ." The girl put a hand up to her disheveled blond hair.

"I bet it hurts like sin. Are you hurt anywhere else?"

"I . . . I don't think so."

"Good. What's your name, sweetheart?"

"Robyn. Robyn Stiles."

"I'm Colleen. In a minute, when your head clears, you're going to
go over to the carousel, find someone who works there. Tell them
what happened, call the police. Think you can do that, Robyn?"

"I . . . think so. What about you?"

"Right behind you. Go. Call the police."

Colleen had reservations about calling the cops. With the connections Kieran's father no doubt had, and the way the police had
been harassing her, calling them filled her with apprehension.

But what choice did she have? And, from what she saw, Frank
Madrid and his crew were a few renegades. She had to bank on it.
She'd call Moran as soon as she could.

Robyn nodded slowly, looking over at Kieran, then back at Colleen.
Colleen noticed that Robyn wore a wide white belt on her hip-huggers.

"Before you go, Robyn," she said, "give me your belt."

When Robyn left, Colleen stood up fully, the belt in one hand,
the gun in the other. Kieran sat up, puke glistening in the corner of
his mouth. She zigzagged over, pushed him back down with the
bottom of her sneaker.

"On your stomach," she panted. "Hands behind your back." Her
head was returning to normal, albeit with a wicked headache. "Any
bullshit and you get a dose of chloroform."

"My father will sue," Kieran said, but rolled over onto his stomach on the crumpled newspaper. "My father will sue."

"Hands behind your back, Kieran."

"You won't get away with it," he muttered. But his hands went behind his back.

CHAPTER SIXTY-FIVE

"What happens now?" Colleen asked, signing her statement. She sat at a table in a windowless interrogation room on the fifth floor at 850 Bryant, where she'd spent most of the afternoon and early evening since SFPD arrested Kieran Skinner. Her throat hurt when she spoke, where Kieran had choked her, as if something might be caught in it. As she initialed the pages, her wrist throbbed. Her whole body ached from the tension that had been released from the fight, as if she might be coming down with something.

SFPD Detective Owens, sitting on the other side of the table from Colleen, said: "What happens now is that I review the statements and write my report." He wore a well-worn brown suit, his tie loosened at the collar of a rumpled white shirt, had a Prussian crew cut graying at the temples and the beginnings of jowls. But he seemed to be on the up and up—thorough, if nothing else. "I plan to have everything over to the DA by tomorrow morning so they can charge Skinner. It's going to be a late night. I'm also going to need the evidence you say you have. I can't even locate the original Margaret Copeland report right now."

Wasn't that a surprise? Colleen felt ambivalent about giving her file away, along with the fragment of Zyl. But it wasn't her case anymore. SFPD would need what she had to further their case. She would have to trust them.

Moran had come up to the city after Colleen had called him, brought Colleen's file and pill case containing the Zyl. He had made his own statement to SFPD as well.

"What exactly is Skinner going to be charged with?" she asked.

Owens sat back, picked up a pencil, tapped the eraser on her statement. "We're holding him for aggravated assault and battery for now."

That didn't sound like much.

"What kind of a sentence does that carry?" she asked.

Owens twisted the pencil. "Assault is a wobbler—meaning it can be a misdemeanor or felony. The former carries a maximum of one year. A felony, up to three. But we're talking two charges—assault is the attempt, battery is the actual act. The DA might think the intent of the assault could actually be the more significant, as you caught Skinner and put an end to whatever he was about to do to the girl."

"I think he was about to kill her."

"Possibly."

"He's done it before."

Owens frowned. "That's a whole different ball of wax. One yet to be proved."

"Attempted rape?"

"According to the girl's statement, Skinner never overtly touched her in a way that can be construed as sexual. But she was drugged. If the DA's got the right person on the job, he or she is going to argue a case. But don't forget, Skinner's old man has enough lawyers to form his own law firm."

Christ. "So that's it?" she said. "Kieran Skinner might get one lousy year?"

Owens put his pencil down, leaned forward. "Skinner might not get *anything.* He might walk—if he's even charged. This is the way the system works. But I put my money on three to six years. *If* he's convicted. And if he gets six, he'll serve three."

A flare of anger shot up her tired neck. "Three years." She shook her head.

Owens sat back. "Once the DA reviews everything, there could well be more charges. Let's hope. But I've learned not to overpromise, since it's really the DA's decision what Skinner's ultimately charged with, although I make recommendations. Which I will."

"Why can't Skinner be charged with kidnapping?"

Owens grimaced. He consulted his notes, as if to remind himself of the girl's name. "Robyn Stiles wasn't moved enough of a physical distance to support a kidnap charge. She's also fourteen, and kidnap laws gets iffy at that age." Owens collected the yellow-lined sheets Colleen had written out and tamped them down, bound them together with a paper clip. "Good news: this is serious enough to get to the top of the DA's list. But it's still up to him what charges he thinks will make a solid case." He gave an uncertain look before he continued. "Just between you and me, Patrick Skinner's attorney already has a call in to my chief, making noises about unlawful arrest. They're going to put up a fight, I suspect, to try to get the charge knocked down to a misdemeanor. I've been in this game for a while."

Owens seemed to know what he was doing. But *misdemeanor*?

He must have caught the look on her face. "I don't think it will fly. But they'll try, hoping to get the kid bail at least. Assemblyman Skinner wields a fair amount of influence."

Wasn't that the truth? He'd managed to suppress Margaret Copeland's murder investigation. "I can't believe a judge would let a person like Kieran Skinner out on bail."

"You haven't seen anything. This is the People's Republic of San Francisco."

Now, she thought, the *big* question. "What about the cold case on Margaret Copeland's murder?"

"I'm certainly going to recommend the case be reopened. I'll push the chief, too."

"What if Kieran confesses?"

"Well, that's the holy grail, isn't it? But he hasn't. And I'm not counting on it. He's kept quiet for years—if he did it. All has to be supported. Proved."

And Kieran Skinner—and his father—had spent eleven years dodging the truth. It wouldn't come easy.

She cleared her painful throat gently before she looked Owens in the eye.

"What about the murder of Jim Davis? And Frank Madrid's role?"

"You mean *possible* role?" She saw the beginnings of resignation in Owens' frown. "My recommendation is going to be that Madrid is questioned in relation to the Jim Davis homicide." He picked up the pencil, tapped it. "But the assault and battery first. So we can hold Skinner while the DA reviews the rest of the evidence and we have time to take statements from Davis's widow and son. And anyone else involved. You said there's a woman at the beach?"

"I don't know her name." Wild Woman would make a lousy witness to begin with. "Why wouldn't the assault and battery stick? If the DA approves it? Which you seem to think he will."

Owens gave a smirk. "Felicia Stiles."

Colleen had been impressed with Robyn's mother at first, a tall, slender woman in wool slacks and turtleneck, with strawberry blond hair, tousled from rushing down to the site where the attack had taken place. She was a single parent who, although obviously horrified at what had almost happened to her daughter, had expressed gratitude to Colleen.

Owens let out a breath. "It's never guaranteed that a parent is going to go the distance. Watching her daughter up on the stand against a psycho like Skinner? She might decide she doesn't want her kid exposed to any more of that. I've seen it happen. More than once."

Colleen sat back in her chair. "I can't believe this."

"We've got a good shot," he said. "The kid's old enough to take it, and her mother will want justice. The DA's going to want to make something out of all this, too. You've built one hell of a case."

Except for her illegally obtained evidence: the fragment of Skinner's glasses. And the fact that she was on parole, didn't have an investigator's license yet. Oh, and the illegally obtained gun.

"You may not be assigned to any of these cases, if they *do* take, though," she said. "Right?"

"Maybe one or two," he said. "But I'll stay on it, regardless."

She had to accept that the case was no longer hers. She bent down, got her shoulder bag, retrieved her file folder of reports, notes, as well as the plastic case with the fragment. She set the file folder on the table. She set the plastic pill case containing the fragment on top of the file folder, thinking of where it had been, where it was going, what it had been through.

How it had gotten Colleen this far.

"I'm trusting you with all of this," she said. "But you have to keep me in the loop."

"I will. I'll make you a copy of all the documents."

Good enough. Colleen stood up.

Owens set his pencil down, stood up, pushing his chair back with a squeak. "Don't leave town without letting us know where you'll be."

Did that mean charges might be filed against her? She had done things that put her parole in jeopardy.

"Of course not," she said.

He looked her in the eye. "Stay away from Felicia and Robyn Stiles. It won't help if you are seen trying to influence a potential case. Same with Mary and Steve Davis." He raised his eyebrows. "We'll get statements in due course. In the meantime, stay clear."

It was as if he had read her mind. "I'd like to offer my sympathies to Mary Davis," she said.

"No." He shook his head. "This is *our* job now."

She took a deep breath through her nose. "Got it."

He put his hand out. "We'll be in touch."

She leaned forward, shook hands. "Thanks."

"You did a good job."

Did she? In her heart, she had contributed to the death of Jim Davis. All in the name of solving a murder that looked like it could go unpunished.

But at least they had Kieran. For now.

Moran was waiting for Colleen downstairs, past the metal detector, leaning with his back against the wall, hands in the pockets of a zipped-up windbreaker. She smiled and went over. He looked tired, eyes half-lidded behind his thick, dark-framed glasses. He'd come up to the city as soon as Colleen called him and had backed her up, bringing her file and making a statement of his own and answering questions.

She came up to him. "You didn't have to wait for me."

"You don't get to have all the fun, Hayes." He gave a drained smile, pushed his glasses up his nose. "Besides, you've still got my car."

"I'm afraid I left your lovely little hairdryer in front of the Conservatory of Flowers when I was chasing Kieran Skinner."

"No problem." He held up the keys to the Torino. "You can give me a ride there to pick it up."

It felt good to get out in the fresh air, walk in the wet fog to her parked car. She opened up the passenger door for Moran, moved her seat back, fired up the Torino, and set off. The engine rumbled as they crossed Market, late at night, not many people around. It was calming.

"How did it go with Owens?" Moran asked.

"It's like you said." The Torino climbed up the Hayes Street Hill with little effort. "Here I was thinking I was done—but I'm just getting started."

"What about Frank Madrid?"

She filled him in, adding, when she was done, "Detective Owens says he'll recommend that the DA's office investigate charges relating to the murder of Jim Davis."

Moran exhaled. "Wonder how many friends Frank's got."

She crested the hill, heading down toward the Panhandle. "A few." She was thinking of the men who tried to burn down H&M, whoever followed her from Half Moon Bay that night, the cop who harassed Steve Davis near the Mabuhay. "But I got the feeling Owens will do as he says."

Moran turned to look at Colleen as she turned on Divisadero at the bottom of the hill. "Me, too."

"That's why I gave him the evidence file."

Moran nodded. "That was the way to go—but that doesn't mean Frank and his buddies aren't going to be easy to nail. You'll need to accept that, Hayes."

"I'm working on it," she said.

Several young men in leather, two with military-style hats, staggered down Divisadero, arm in arm, laughing and singing. "Police work," Moran said. "I've run into crooked cops on my own turf, as you know, but at the end of the day you have to trust them. *Us.*"

She looked at Moran as she turned right, along the Panhandle now. Near where Margaret Copeland had once lived. There was a time she didn't trust Moran herself. Now he was the first person she called when she needed help.

"I'm just going to tell myself it feels better to hand everything over to someone else," she said. "Until it actually does."

"Fake it till you make it," Moran said, putting his hands in the pockets of his windbreaker. "That's what they keep telling us in AA."

"I forgot you had a drinking problem."

"I used to. Now I have a sobriety problem."

She started to laugh but it hurt her throat.

"The process of letting go," she said.

"You getting all new-age on me, Hayes?"

"I'm just a modern gal," she said, "living in the modern world."

He looked out the window. "You say *modern* like it's a good thing."

"I don't know what it is."

They entered Golden Gate Park. A couple minutes' walk from where she'd subdued Kieran Skinner less than eight hours ago. The Pinto was parked on JFK, facing traffic, next to the Conservatory of Flowers, whose white-framed glass panes glowed in the mist drifting through the park at night.

They got out. "My advice to you is to get something with horse-power," she said, handing him his keys.

"With gas at sixty-two cents a gallon?" He took the keys. "I'm living on a fixed income."

"I thought you ex-cops had all sorts of bribe money stashed."

"You're not going back to that warehouse, are you?"

She shook her head. "I'm staying at my charming little welfare hotel tonight."

"You can't be too careful."

"I'll wait until the cat's completely out of the bag before I go back to H&M," she said. "I don't want to push my luck."

"Not with luck like yours." Moran pushed his glasses up his nose one more time. "In case of emergency," he said. "I put something in the trunk. Under the spare. You don't know where it came from."

"Something that goes *bang*?"

Moran put his hands over his ears.

He had slipped her a drop gun. Just in case.

"Not that I'll need it." She hoped she wouldn't. But Moran obviously wasn't so sure.

"Keep it where your parole officer won't find it. And keep me posted on Skinner and the rest of it."

"Try and stop me," she said. "I couldn't have done it without you."

"I'm just an old man who hates retirement, living vicariously through your work. *Good* work, by the way."

She cracked a smile. "Give me a hug, old man."

They came together and hugged, the first time they'd ever had any physical contact, and it felt good. She'd never really had a father, and Moran was a pretty decent substitute for one.

She waved as he puttered off out of the park, engine pinging, headed toward the freeway to Santa Cruz.

And then she did something an irrational person might do. She walked back over to the playground, dead this time of night, only an old bum with a blanket over his shoulders wandering around the darkened merry-go-round. And she followed the path to the bushes where Kieran Skinner had tried to abduct Robyn Stiles that afternoon.

She stood there and relived that fight. She thought about Jim Davis. She thought about Margaret Copeland.

And she told herself she'd done the right thing.

CHAPTER SIXTY-SIX

Even though it was past midnight—or perhaps because it was—the Thunderbird Hotel was buzzing with human activity. Shouts and intoxicated laughter reverberated down the stairs. The acrid tang of marijuana hung in the air. Down the darkened hall from the pay phone where Colleen stood on the ground floor, a man and woman were in the throes of frenzied sex. The man's panting hinted at desperation while the woman's responses sounded suspiciously mechanical.

Colleen slipped a dime into the phone slot and dialed the Copelands in Half Moon Bay.

Harold the butler answered on the second ring, surprising her just a little.

"I apologize for calling so late, Harold," Colleen said, "but it sounds as if you were up anyway."

"We are, indeed, Ms. Hayes," he said somberly.

"How is Mr. Copeland?"

"I'll let Miss Copeland explain, Ms. Hayes. Let me go get her." Harold set the phone down.

Colleen prayed that Edward Copeland was still alive. He needed to hear the news before he passed on.

Down the hall from Colleen, the woman was giving an Academy-Award-worthy performance. The man sounded as if he might be passing a kidney stone.

A moment later, Alex picked up the phone. "Now *there's* the person I wanted to hear from," she said, giving Colleen a warm feeling inside.

"Sorry to call so late."

"It's not as if I were sleeping," she said. "And even then, it wouldn't matter. It doesn't sound like you're getting much sleep where you are either, Colleen. Did you take a side job in a whorehouse?"

"I'm staying at the Thunderbird. Ambience on wheels."

"We're going to have to upgrade your living situation."

"All in good time." Colleen took a breath. "And your father . . .?"

She heard the strike of a match on the other end of the phone as Alex lit up a cigarette. Alex rarely smoked. "Enjoying his morphine drip. No, not really. The doctor left not long ago. He says 'any day now.'" Colleen could hear the crack in Alex's voice as she uttered the last phrase.

"I can come down there," Colleen said. "I have news."

Alex puffed. "Good news?"

"I'm not sure I ever have any of that," Colleen said. "But closure— maybe that's what I can offer. I think so. I hope so, anyway."

"Now you have my full and undivided attention."

"I can come down, Alex," Colleen said again. And she meant it. She wanted to give her news in person, offer what support she could. And see Alex.

"I don't think I can wait for you to drive all the way down here," Alex said. "Even with your lead foot. What is it? *Tell me.*"

"Are you sitting down?"

"I am now."

"This is what I have," Colleen said, pulling her Virginia Slims from the pocket of her leather jacket.

When she was done explaining the day's events, and the revelation of who had most likely murdered Margaret Copeland, Alex was silent. The phone line crackled.

Then she heard Alex cry. Soft, gentle sobs. Colleen's heart went out to her.

"I'm so sorry, Alex," Colleen said quietly, her unlit cigarette and a book of matches sitting on top of the pay phone in the hallway where she stood in near darkness. She felt so far away. "I'm really so sorry."

"Don't be, Colleen," Alex said, sniffling. "It's a relief to know. It is."

Colleen gulped back uncertainty. "Even though the murder charge isn't guaranteed?"

"You got him, Coll," Alex said. "You got the sick bastard who killed my sister. Whatever happens, *you got him*. And if I have to spend every last dime my father's going to leave me, I'm going to take Kieran Skinner and his father down."

"Not a bad plan. I'll help you any way I can."

"I'd like that," Alex said, brightening. "I can't wait to tell Father your news. I'm going to do that now. Right now. While I still have time. Dad will be so grateful—as am I."

Dad. It was the first time she'd ever heard Alex use that term for her father.

"Please give him my best," Colleen said. "And you. I'm thinking of you."

"Likewise," Alex said quietly. "Talk to you soon."

Colleen hung up as the music blared from upstairs. "Free Bird," at full volume, with its ten-hour guitar solo. She trudged up the stairs, let herself into her room reeking of Lysol, pulled open the window facing the brick light well, lit her cigarette to fight the fumes. She went into the bathroom, cockroaches scampering after she clicked on the light. She plugged her ears with tufts of toilet paper, took three aspirin, drank with a cupped hand from the faucet. Then she took a final hit on her cigarette, tossed it in the stained toilet with a sizzle, went back into her room, climbed onto the sagging bed, rolled up into a ball, and fell into an immediate, deep sleep.

CHAPTER SIXTY-SEVEN

Colleen spent the next day looking at an apartment, meeting with Christian Newell to discuss the arrest of Kieran Skinner and how she might be impacted, making sure she had an adequate defense, if need be. But all she really wanted to do was find out how SFPD's investigation was proceeding. Detective Owens didn't call. She knew better than to get involved without permission. The case wasn't hers anymore.

She stopped by H&M during the day, checking for a tail before she entered, and did her rounds. All secure.

Up in the office, she called Moran, checked in. He was gardening. As bored as she was.

Alex didn't call.

As much as Colleen wanted to, she held off calling Alex. Alex had her hands full and needed space. But that didn't mean Colleen wasn't thinking about her. More so, in fact, now that the investigation was drawing to a close.

After close to two weeks of nonstop work and threats to her well-being, she suddenly felt as if she didn't exist.

Was this the way all cases ended?

She locked up, went back to the Thunderbird Hotel.

By evening, Party Central at the Thunderbird had started up again. A television was thrown out of a window above onto the street below with a crash. A woman called someone a motherfucker; a fight broke out, stopped; tears prevailed.

Grating punk music pounded from another floor. Colleen thought of Steve Davis, wondering how he and his mother were faring. He had probably heard the news by now.

Next door, the TV came on full blast. *The Gong Show.*

Colleen didn't think she could handle another night listening to the Thunderbird fight and fornicate while rats scurried across the floor. She couldn't take the smell of the grimy bedspread she had to sleep on top of in her clothes. She certainly wasn't going to get into the bed.

She picked up a bottle of Chardonnay and drove back over to H&M with her clothes and overnight bag. To hell with parole. She was going to have a glass of wine. Or two.

She told herself she wasn't too worried about Frank Madrid. He would have heard about the investigation by now, and killing her wouldn't stop it. In fact, it might do otherwise. He would know that. He would have to leave her be. For now.

Besides, she had a black Bersa Piccola .22 short barrel pistol Moran had wrapped in a brown paper bag and stashed under her spare tire. It was a cute little gun that lay in her hand but would still stop Frank Madrid, or anyone else, for that matter.

Back up in the office at H&M, she checked the clip in the Bersa. Full of short .22 shells. She tucked the little gun under the ceiling tile above her desk and settled down with a cup of wine and a transistor radio oozing jazz. Clouds roiled in the sky across the bay as night fell.

Maybe Alex would call.

Colleen couldn't stop wondering how Mr. Copeland had taken the news. Would he be able to die now? At peace?

It began to rain again, the first rain in a day or two. She refilled her coffee cup with Chardonnay as Carlos Santana's guitar wailed from the transistor radio. "Black Magic Woman." She turned it up, puffed, leaned back in her squeaky chair, put her feet on the desk.

She'd sleep tonight, cot or not. The Thunderbird Hotel could go to hell.

Then, the raucous buzz of the gate bell shook her out of her reverie.

CHAPTER SIXTY-EIGHT

Colleen got up, hit the intercom button.

"Security."

"Hello?" a familiar young voice said.

"Steve?" she said. "Steve Davis?"

"Uh—yeah," he said with uncertainty.

Detective Owens had told her to stay away from the Davis family. But he didn't tell the Davis family to stay away from her.

"Come on up," she said, pressing the buzzer to open the gate. "Stairwell on your right. Watch it, slippery in the rain."

A minute or so later, Steve Davis was standing in her office. He wore ripped Levi's, bulky black engineers' boots, and a denim jacket wet from the rain. His short dark hair was wet, too.

He looked around. "You *live* here?"

"For the time being."

"Okay to smoke?"

She tilted her head at an ashtray containing her smoldering cigarette.

He nodded, pulled a pack of Marlboros from the top pocket of his Levi's jacket. He lit one up with a Bic lighter, head down to the flame, and stood, legs apart. She couldn't tell if he was angry with her. He was one of those guys who was always angry at something. But she understood.

Colleen went around her side of the desk and sat down. She smashed out her smoke and waved to a guest chair.

"I'll stand," he said, smoking.

She sat back, folded her hands over her stomach. "I take it you've heard the latest?"

He nodded his head to confirm, took a drag on his cigarette.

"News travels fast," she said.

"Especially when your dad was a cop."

She leaned forward. "I've been told not to talk to you, Steve. Or your mother."

He smoked. "I'm talking to *you*."

"So you are," she said, sitting back.

"Word is, you're saying Frank Madrid was involved in killing my old man."

Colleen took a deep breath. "From what I've seen, it looks that way. It needs to be investigated."

He squinted at her. "Why?"

She told him what else she knew about the case, about Wild Woman at the beach identifying a cop and a man who looked a lot like Frank Madrid bringing Jim Davis down to the beach and leaving him for dead. She told him about Frank Madrid making threats, following her, his cronies setting the fire while he waited in his truck. "This is all just between you and me, Steve. It's in my statement. I probably shouldn't tell you, but you deserve to know. I can't help but feel that I played a part in your father's murder. You don't know how that makes me feel."

"From where I stand, you didn't kill my old man. Frank Madrid did."

She held up one finger. "I *think* he did. But that's ultimately for the courts to decide. If charges are ever made."

Steve shook his head. "I've seen how *that* shit works. It doesn't always pan out when cops are involved. Look at that murder you're trying to solve. All it got was my old man killed."

"I hear you, Steve. But you've got to let the system do its job before you do anything yourself." She hoped she hadn't made a mistake in telling him. She steepled her fingers. "Do you hear what I'm saying?"

"I hear you all right." He took an angry puff of his cigarette. It didn't sound as if he was necessarily going to listen.

"I know how you feel," she said. "Yeah, I hate it when someone says that to me, but in your case, Steve, I do. I felt pretty strongly about someone who did something terrible to someone I love once. I took matters into my own hands. And I spent close to ten years in prison because of it."

Steve's eyes opened in surprise. The half-smoked cigarette hung forgotten from the corner of his mouth.

"No shit?"

"No shit."

"What happened?"

She cleared her throat, looked him in the eye. "I killed my husband. For molesting my eight-year-old daughter. July 13, 1967. Stabbed him in the neck with a screwdriver."

Steve seemed to remember his cigarette, pulled it from his mouth. "No one can blame you for that."

"Well, the jury sure did. And I blame myself. Every day. Several times every day. My daughter's nineteen now. Won't even talk to me. I spent my best years in prison. Now, here I am, trying to patch things up. It'll take my whole life just to get back up to zero. If I'm lucky."

Steve looked at her.

"So I understand how you feel," she said. "Don't do anything stupid. I spoke with Detective Owens yesterday. You know him?"

Steve smoked. "Heard of him."

"He seems okay. Never thought I'd say that about a cop. But he says he's going to take this thing to completion. I believe he will. He will try, anyway. We need to take him at his word. Give him a shot."

Steve took another puff, exhaled smoke across the office, shook his head.

She threw her hands up halfway. "It's the way it's supposed to work. It's what your father would've wanted. He was a good cop, who got pushed aside by a couple of bad ones."

"My old man got fucked by the system he worked for. Pure and simple. And then he got killed."

"Yes, he did," she said. "But letting SFPD handle it is the way to do it. Trust me."

Their eyes connected.

"Don't make the mistake I made, Steve." She stared him in the eye. "Let's see what happens. And if you think you're going to do something, you talk to me first." She opened the drawer, got one of her business cards out of the box, threw it on the desk. "In case you don't have one."

He took one final suck on his cigarette, walked over to the desk, crushed his smoke out in the ashtray. It sat there, twisted, smoldering. He picked up the business card, tapped it on his free hand.

"How's your mother doing?" Colleen asked.

He stood there for a moment, shook his head, and she saw his dark brown eyes glisten over.

"She's . . . ah . . . she's . . . not doing so good," he said, ". . . with the news about Frank."

"Another reason not to do anything rash. She needs you."

Steve laughed a bitter little laugh. "Lucky her, huh? I'm all she's got. What a deal." He shook his head. "She got screwed, too."

"Don't sell yourself short, Steve. Thanks to you, I got that police report. The one your father was going to give me. That was the linchpin. Your father would've been proud of you."

He nodded and she could tell he was starting to choke up.

"If you think it won't upset her," Colleen said, "please give your mother my deepest sympathies. And when this is all finally over, I'd like to write her a letter. Would that be okay with you?"

He thought about it, looked up at her. "Yeah."

Colleen stood up. "You should probably get home to your mother." She was going to come around and give him a reassuring pat on the shoulder but she could tell he wasn't the touchy-feely type.

"Yeah," he said. "I should go."

He turned then, walked through the office to the door, opened it. The rain was falling steadily outside.

"Thanks," he said, his back to Colleen.

"No, Steve," Colleen said, "thank you."

He went out the door, stopped for a moment before he pulled it shut behind him, and then she heard his heavy boots, clanging down the stairs.

Colleen knew what it was like to be in Steve's shoes. And she had a pretty good idea what he was still thinking, despite her little speech. It was hard to listen to reason when hatred had tightened around your heart. She knew. She knew all about it.

She couldn't let him make the mistake she had made.

CHAPTER SIXTY-NINE

After mulling things over, Colleen climbed up on the desk, got the Bersa .22 Moran had slipped her, got back down, pulled on her bomber jacket. Downstairs she stashed the gun in a sock under the dash in the Torino and drove over to Paris Street, past the Davis household. No lights on. No one home.

Down on Mission, she parked across from Dizzy's. Ten p.m., it'd be a good place to start looking for Frank Madrid. Detective Owens hadn't told her to stay away from him.

She wanted to give Frank a piece of her mind.

She also wanted to warn him to watch his back.

More importantly, she needed to make sure Steve Davis didn't do anything reckless. He hadn't left her with a warm, fuzzy feeling.

Dizzy's boomed with chatter and music as she walked across Mission in the light rain. Pushing open the double doors, she found a good dozen people keeping the bar in business. Most of them looked like off-duty cops, ex-cops. "The Ballad of the Green Berets" was playing on the jukebox. But no Frank Madrid. No Steve Davis. Brenda, the bartender, of the tight gray perm, was pouring a shot for some old geezer slamming a dice cup on the bar. She did a double take when she saw Colleen.

"Didn't think we'd see you in here again," she said.

"I won't stay," Colleen said.

Other faces around the bar turned to look at Colleen. She heard whispers.

"What'll it be?" Brenda asked Colleen, pudgy hands on the bar.

That took Colleen by surprise. "Why not? Boilermaker." She remembered buying one for Jim Davis the day she met him in here. It seemed an appropriate drink.

Brenda drew a draft beer, set it in front of Colleen on a Coors coaster, got a chunky short glass out from under the bar, set it next to the beer. She filled the shot glass up to the brim with Wild Turkey. Top shelf.

Colleen sat down on a barstool, drank off a third of the bourbon. She smacked her lips, sipped some beer. It was cold and just right for following the sweet Wild Turkey afterburn.

The other people around the bar were watching her.

"How you doin'?" one old guy in a Giants ball cap said to her, friendly.

"Fine, thanks," she said, sipping bourbon and beer, surprised at the reception.

"You're Colleen Hayes," a young guy said. She recognized him, with his trim build and blond crew cut. He was the cop who intervened the night she came in to talk to Frank Madrid, the day Jim Davis was found dead. He had tried to smooth things over and asked her to leave.

"Right," she said. "You're Rick."

He lifted his draft beer and toasted her.

She returned the gesture.

Brenda was wiping down the bar with a wet rag. "What brings you to our neck of the woods?"

"Looking for Steve Davis," she said.

Brenda shook her head. "Steve doesn't drink here," she said. "The jukebox doesn't make his ears bleed."

"In that case I'm looking for Frank Madrid," Colleen said, drinking.

The bar fell silent. Brenda stopped wiping. "The Ballad of the Green Berets" hit its final note.

"Frank won't be coming in here anymore," Brenda said, wiping the bar again.

"Not if he knows what's good for him," someone else said.

Word traveled fast. Frank was *persona non grata* at Dizzy's.

"Can somebody tell me where I might find him?" Colleen asked.

"Try the Avenue Bar on Ocean," someone said.

"He lives at 1694 43rd Avenue," someone else said. "Out by the beach."

"If you find Frank," someone else said, "tell him to go fuck himself."

"Straight up," someone else said.

"If you *do* find him," Rick said to Colleen, raising his eyebrows, "be careful, huh?"

Colleen nodded. "I appreciate it."

She downed the rest of her shot, drank most of her beer. On top of the wine, a solid buzz followed. Dutch courage was just fine for where she was headed next.

She stood up, got her money out, peeled off a five, threw it on the bar.

"No," Brenda said, picking it up, handing it back. "On the house. You took care of Jim."

CHAPTER SEVENTY

It was drizzling as Colleen drove past City College, and down Ocean Avenue, a street lined with gas stations, mom-and-pop stores with bars on the windows, auto repair shops, and budget restaurants with handwritten signs displaying prices.

Past the McDonald's she saw a blue Chevy C10 parked at a slant in front of the Avenue Bar, a plain tavern across from a movie theater turned Pentecostal church. Frank Madrid's new watering hole. Colleen looked for a discreet place to park.

She heard Steve Davis's car before she saw it, punk music throbbing out of the open window of his matte black Mustang. Steve didn't see her as she drove past. He was too busy tipping a pint bottle to his mouth and watching Frank's truck across the street. She knew exactly how he felt.

But she needed to end it once and for all.

At the next stop sign she turned right, circled the block, got back on Ocean where she parked with a view of Frank Madrid's truck across the street in front of the bar. A few cars down on her side of the street, she saw Steve's blue-denimed elbow sticking out of his window.

She shut the engine off.

"I Wanna Be Sedated" boomed from the Mustang. It seemed to be in response to the live band playing country and western in The Avenue.

Steve was staking out Frank Madrid. Getting his courage up.

Colleen reached under the dash, got her Bersa out of the sock hanging under the dash. After checking the clip, she tucked the gun between the passenger seat and console, the handle poking up for quick access.

She rolled down the window, lit a Virginia Slim, let the wet air cool her off. It was late enough on a weeknight that there wasn't much in the way of traffic.

As she smoked, Colleen's heart thumped steadily. She had thought this case was over with, as far as she was concerned, anyway.

She waited.

About eleven thirty-five, the doors to The Avenue opened and out stumbled Frank Madrid, wearing a 49ers jacket over the same floral Hawaiian shirt she had seen him in the first time she had met him. The same shirt he had killed Jim Davis in, she thought, recalling her muted conversation with the wild woman at the beach, who had seen Frank and a cop lead Jim Davis up to the gun embankment before Jim was found dead.

Frank had a hard, grizzled look to his face tonight, pissed-off and unshaven. Life wasn't being good to him. Well, it was going to get worse, if Colleen had anything to say about it. But she wasn't going to let Steve shoot him in cold blood.

The music from Steve's car stopped. He was getting ready to make a move on Frank.

Colleen tucked her half-smoked Slim in the corner of her mouth, pulled the Bersa from its resting place between console and seat, flipped off the safety, readied her left hand on the door handle.

Frank got to the door of his truck, stood there, back to Colleen, swaying in the sprinkle of rain as he fumbled with his keys. The band in The Avenue had just started in on "Okie from Muskogee."

The door to Steve's Mustang creaked open. Colleen saw Steve climb out, saw the short barrel of a pistol appear in his right hand briefly as he crossed the street, heading toward Frank. He'd left his car door open. Light spilled from his car across the wet asphalt.

Colleen tossed her cigarette, got out of the Torino, her heartbeats pulsing between her ears.

"Hey, asshole," Steve said as he crossed Ocean, heading for Frank. Frank looked over.

"Steve?" Frank swayed. "What the fuck are you doing here?"

Colleen headed over, too, the Bersa ready.

"Shut up, Frank," Steve said as he closed in on him. "Shut the fuck up, for once in your life."

He raised the pistol.

As did Colleen, walking up the middle of Ocean.

"Now, wait just a minute, Stevie," Frank said, his voice wobbly. "You got this all wrong."

"No, I don't, Frank. You and Henry killed my dad and you're both gonna die. You first."

Frank's hands went up, shaking as Steve raised the gun. "Stevie . . . *please!*"

"Steve!" Colleen said evenly, her voice carrying up Ocean as she approached, the gun raised on Steve, thirty feet away. "Stop it. Right there. Right now."

Steve turned, gun still on Frank. He was half-lit, too, but his buzz was founded on adrenaline and hate, making him tense and brittle. It took him a second to register who had pulled a gun on him.

"This isn't the way it's going down, Steve," Colleen said, drawing closer, keeping one eye on Frank, who had his hands halfway up. "We've had this conversation."

Steve's face became a kaleidoscope of confusion, frustration, and anger. "This is none of your damn business anymore. Butt out."

"I'm making it my business, Steve," she said. She held the gun steady, in both hands now, stood with the legs apart.

They stared at each other for a long moment while "Okie from Muskogee" played.

"I know how you feel," Colleen said. "But I'm not going to let you ruin your life, and your mother's, over this louse. He's not worth it. So just lower the gun. Now. Just do it."

Steve took a deep breath, lowered the gun to his side.

"On the ground," she said, gun still on him. "You're not taking it with you."

"Are you serious?"

"The courts are going to take care of Frank Madrid."

Frank, for his part, stood by, shaking.

"I can't fucking believe this," Steve said, stooping to lay the gun on the ground.

Gun still on Steve, Colleen said: "Go home, Steve. Go home. Your mother needs you."

Steve stood there for a minute, exasperation and fury crossing his face until he finally relented. He stormed back across Ocean, got into his car, slammed the door, started the Mustang up with a growl, squealed out on Ocean, the stereo blasting the Ramones.

Frank Madrid watched Colleen with a wary eye.

"Thanks," he said.

"Don't thank me," she said as she walked toward Steve's gun, keeping her Bersa on Frank. "Don't even talk. Turn around, put your hands on the roof of the truck. Where I can see 'em."

Frank did.

"Now what?" he said in a jittery voice.

"Don't move." Colleen picked up Steve's gun, a beat-up .38, and pocketed it. She came up behind Frank, stuck the Bersa in his back. He flinched. It felt good to her, that animal response.

She patted him down for a gun. Clean.

A car drove by on Ocean, the driver eyeing her with an open mouth. But in this neighborhood, he kept right on going.

"I've got nothing else to say to you, Frank," she said, "except that I'm going to make sure you pay for killing Jim Davis. For covering up for Patrick Skinner. All of it. And if you come near me again, or the Davis family, I'll take care of you myself."

She jammed the gun in his back.

"Okay," Frank gasped. "Okay."

"Now go," she said. "I'm watching you leave. I'll have this gun on you the whole time."

Frank got into his truck, started it up, backed out, crunched into gear before he sailed up Ocean, his tailpipe belching exhaust.

"Okie from Muskogee" came to an end. A few shouts and cheers followed.

Colleen tossed Steve's gun in the trash, walked to her car, put the Bersa back in its sock under the dash, got in her car, drove off.

And realized how close she had been to letting Steve pull the trigger.

CHAPTER SEVENTY-ONE

Colleen hardly slept, despite being exhausted, following the confrontation with Steve Davis and Frank Madrid. She got up in darkness, pulled on jeans and sweatshirt, while rain pelted the office windows. She stood before the windows, drinking black coffee, watching dark clouds unfurl over the lights of the Bay Bridge, a picture smeared by water running down the glass. She prayed her intervention with Steve would serve as a permanent deterrent. But she also understood how deep anger could run and what Steve was going through. She had been in a similar spot once in her life, when she learned the truth about her husband. And she had paid dearly for it.

After coffee, she called her answering service. There was a message from last night. To Colleen's surprise an acquaintance of Moran's had left a brief note on Lesley Johns—Margaret Copeland's old roommate—or whatever she was—whose name was on the lease of the Frederick Street house where Margaret was crashing at the time of her murder.

They had managed to track down Lesley Johns.

Just a name, phone number, and an address in Lake Tahoe. The address itself was in Nevada, Lake Tahoe being split across two states.

Colleen checked the time again. She was itching to call. But it was too early.

At her desk she worked on her notes until daylight began to toss gray shadows across the clouds. Officially morning.

She called.

The phone rang several times, echoing long-distance. Finally, someone answered.

"Who *is* this?" a woman said, full of sleep. Not happy with being woken up.

"Sorry if I woke you. My name is Colleen Hayes, and I'm hoping to speak to Lesley Johns."

There was a pause while the line crackled. Then, whoever was on the other end hung up.

Off to a good start.

Colleen pulled on her poncho, grabbed her flashlight, length of pipe, and did an early patrol of the plant, wondering what time Lesley Johns went to work, if she did go to work, and how she might miss her if she did go to work, or whatever she did. She didn't know anything about the woman, just that she wanted to speak to her, wrap up any loose threads on Margaret. She knew almost nothing about her, really.

Twenty minutes later, back in the office, Colleen called again.

"How did you get this number?" the woman said.

"Through an acquaintance. Am I speaking to Lesley Johns?"

"What *acquaintance*?"

Colleen didn't want to mention the police and possibly scare the woman off. She explained she was working for the Copelands and was clearing up loose items on their daughter Margaret and had one or two questions. "I'm not looking to cause any problems, just—"

The phone clicked off.

Son of a bitch!

Colleen called Directory Assistance and said she was verifying an address for Lesley Johns and gave the operator the phone number.

"That is an unlisted number," the operator said.

Colleen called Moran, got past Daphne, who snapped a quick "just a moment!" before she stormed off to find Moran. Thankfully, he was up.

"Checking up on my gardening, Hayes? I haven't started yet. I'm still having breakfast."

"Ha. No, just trying to fathom why Lesley Johns keeps hanging up on me."

"No idea. I'm surprised anything came of that request, to be honest. She must have a record if we found her."

"Can you tell me who found out?"

"A friend with access to FBI CCH. I'd rather not say who."

"CCH?"

"Computerized Criminal History. These systems are being used more and more with the advent of computers."

"Any idea what Lesley Johns might have done?"

"You know more about her than I do at this point."

"Maybe she changed her name and doesn't want anything to do with Lesley Johns anymore." That would explain why she'd hung up on her.

"That would be my guess."

Or maybe she didn't want to have anything to do with Margaret Copeland anymore. She had told her she was helping the Copelands. Too bad. Had Colleen known, she might have tried a different, more devious ploy. "Any idea whether the address itself is good?"

"You're not thinking of going up there, are you, Hayes?"

"Why not? I don't have any gardening to keep me occupied."

"The Copeland case is closed, as far as you're concerned."

"Aren't you dying to know what Lesley Johns might know about Margaret Copeland?"

"Of course. But didn't Detective Owens tell you to desist?"

"I figure if anything comes of this, I can always hand it over."

"So you're doing Owens a favor?" Moran snorted. "Not knowing all the details of a case and living with it is part of the life we lead, Hayes. Get used to it."

We. Moran said *we.* She was flattered he considered her a bona fide investigator, like him. That actually made her feel more encouraged.

"Enjoy your gardening," she said.

Twenty minutes later, she was on the Bay Bridge, foot down, gunning the Torino toward Lake Tahoe in the rain. The case might be over as far as Kieran Skinner was concerned, but there were things that didn't make sense. Had there been other incidents? Had Kieran Skinner's soft incarceration by his father in a mental facility put a halt to his behavior?

By the time she reached Donner Pass, large flakes of snow were falling. The Sierras had turned white and Highway 80, already slushy, became slippery as she pulled off on Highway 89 toward Lake Tahoe. Without chains or snow tires she dropped her speed to well below the limit. Even so, she was driving along the north shore of the lake before noon.

She saw another world, one with a huge scenic lake as a backdrop, despite the gray clouds, rimmed by picturesque snowcapped mountains. The houses along the shore were the kind of houses that belonged to people who had made it: large picture windows, decks looking out onto views of the lake, all surrounded by tall pines.

She had spent most of the drive wondering what kind of woman Lesley Johns was and how life had treated her for the past eleven years. Had she left her hippie life behind and turned the page? She must have done well to be living up here. That perspective changed when Colleen turned off onto a side road past the Cal Neva Casino nestled among the trees flanking the lake.

She found the road Lesley Johns lived on up behind the main road, well away from the lake. Up here the houses were smaller, faded, with old cars and clutter in the front yards. Then older cabins prevailed, built before Lake Tahoe became a destination for prosperous Bay Area skiers, with beater cars and plenty of junk piled up. Trees were thicker, overgrown, and the roads potholed and unplowed. The odd trailer began to appear, interspersed with the cabins.

At the address she'd been given, Colleen found a small sagging wood shingle cabin with a tarp covering a section of roof and what was left of a gas grill on the porch. A rusted-out beige Buick sedan in front of the house collecting snow gave her hope that someone was home. A telltale wisp of smoke curling up from a chimney added to that optimism.

Colleen shut off the engine, got out. The cold bit at her fingertips as she shut the car door. She was out of her element. Her cowboy boots crunched snow as she headed up to a collapsing porch where a newspaper lay in a plastic bag on a rubber welcome mat.

She cocked her head, heard the murmur of a television set, but nothing more.

She stood back, rang the bell, waited.

A moment later, the door opened.

Colleen looked down to see a boy with bright blue eyes and a thatch of blond hair, three or so, dressed in pajamas even though it was midday. He looked up at her warily, holding onto the doorknob.

"Hi there," Colleen said. "Is your mother home?"

He nodded, a serious look on his face, and stood back, holding the door. A wave of heat floated out.

Colleen peered into the dark, chaotic house. Mismatched, thrift store furniture. A damp smell assailed her nose. The back of a reclining chair blocked her view. A glass about one-third full of watery orange liquid sat on the blue carpet floor beside it, next to a pair of black high heels, one on its side. Colleen suspected the boy's mother was asleep in the chair.

"Can you go get your mother, please?" Colleen asked.

He pointed to the chair.

"I know, sweetheart, but can you just go get her?"

He did, approaching the chair guardedly. "Mom?"

"What?" she grunted, obviously waking up. She was the same woman Colleen had spoken to on the phone, with that roughness to her voice.

"Door," he said, pointing at Colleen now.

"Huh?" She climbed out of the chair with a creak and Colleen got her first glimpse of a woman about thirty, fair skinned and freckled, and blond, her hair fortified by a drugstore and piled high in an updo that was coming loose. She wore a cocktail waitress uniform from one of the casinos, a black thing that was little more than a leotard with hardened cups to accentuate cleavage and show plenty of skin. The vestiges of last night's mascara smeared her eyes. Black nylons encased her solid legs, the kind that would still turn heads despite the fact that she was a good twenty pounds overweight. The Cal Neva name tag over her heart read "HI, I'm DENICE, from PHOENIX." She still had her looks, but they weren't going to last another ten years if she didn't drop the weight. Eleven years ago, she was no doubt a stunner.

She squinted at Colleen standing in the open doorway.

"Who're you?"

"Colleen—Colleen Hayes. We talked on the phone, earlier this morning. Sorry I woke you up." Colleen realized the woman had probably come in from a night shift. "Again."

"I thought I made it pretty clear I didn't want to talk."

"I know and I'm sorry. But it's that important."

"How did you get this address?"

"It came with the phone number. Through an acquaintance."

The woman marched up, stood with her hands on her hips. "You can just leave." She raised her eyebrows. "I'm not in the mood."

"I don't blame you. Actually, a contact in the police department found you but I'm not looking to cause any trouble. I'm a private investigator. I just have a few questions."

She shook her head.

"What if I said there's reward money for any new info on Margaret Copeland?"

The woman pursed her lips, thought about it. "How much?"

Colleen pulled her wad of cash out of her pocket. She needed to buy gas and get back to SF, and she needed a little cash to hold her. She put that aside. "Four hundred." That was two weeks' money. Probably a lot more up here. It was all she had left. She split it into two, held out one bundle. "Half now. The rest when you tell me what you know."

The woman eyed the money. "What if what I have to say is worth more?"

Colleen shrugged. "You tell me how much you want, I go back to my client, and ask. It might not happen. And this is coming out of my own pocket, which makes it just between you and me. If you want more, you need to understand that you also risk losing your privacy." Colleen raised her eyebrows. She didn't want to play hardball but it came with the job. "Nothing you tell me now comes back to you. You don't testify in court—nothing. When we're done, I forget all about you."

The woman seemed to consider her options. "Deal." She stepped forward, took the cash, counted it, folded it.

"All your heat is escaping," Colleen said.

The woman huffed, brushed past Colleen, slammed the door. It dragged on the rug when she did that. She stood back, money in hand, resumed her stance.

"Mom?" the boy said softly. "What's wrong?"

"Nothing, Andrew. Go get into my bed. I'll be in later."

He came over, looked up at her, unsure.

She looked down at him. "Nothing's wrong, honey. I just need to talk to this lady. Go get in bed. I'll be in in a little while. We'll tell a story."

"Okay," he said quietly, turned, padded off into the only hallway. A door shut.

The woman focused on Colleen with a grimace. "You've got twenty minutes. I pulled a double shift last night and I've got another one coming up in less than eight hours."

"I won't keep you any longer than I have to."

"Make coffee," the woman said, nodding brusquely at the kitchenette. "I'm going to check in on my son and get out of this clown outfit."

Colleen hadn't slept all night and had just driven two hundred miles. Coffee sounded great. She fixed a pot while the woman went to the bedroom. There were no signs of a male presence in the small house, no photos, no shoes by the door, no beers in the fridge. Colleen felt for the woman, and the boy. She was obviously a single mom, getting by.

A few minutes later, the two women were sitting on stools at the Formica counter, the woman in a fluffy bathrobe and slippers. The scent of faded perfume enveloped her.

They drank black coffee.

"As I said on the phone this morning," Colleen said, "I'm helping the Copelands wrap up any loose threads on their daughter Margaret. If you are who I think you are, you knew Margaret, for a short time anyway—back in the Haight. She was murdered during the Summer of Love. Her last residence was 413 Frederick—a place leased to Lesley Johns." Colleen raised her eyebrows, looking for a flicker of recognition in the woman's brown eyes. She found it. "But you know all this. You're Lesley Johns—aren't you?"

The woman drank coffee. "Not anymore."

"Who you are now is your business. But Margaret's father is dying. He never got over losing Margaret. Neither did her sister. How could they? Margaret was brutally murdered. She was trying to go home. Ironic, isn't it? If she hadn't gotten into the killer's car that night, she might have made it."

The woman blinked away that thought. Her eyes turned glassy. "Poor Margaret."

"Her killer was arrested a couple days ago, for trying to do the very same thing he did to Margaret to a fourteen-year-old girl. Thankfully, he didn't get away with killing her. But he may get away with killing Margaret. He's got a powerful father. If you know anything, you can't let that happen. Margaret deserves justice. And her killer deserves to be locked up for good, so he can never kill again. He's sick. Beyond sick."

Lesley's face fell. "They found him?"

Colleen nodded. "A couple of days ago. In Golden Gate Park."

"The same place," she said, shaking her head.

Colleen returned a single nod. "The same place."

Lesley took a deep breath. "After Margaret . . . after Margaret was murdered, I got scared."

"I would have been scared, too."

"We all were. I ditched the Frederick Street flat a few days later—after the cops came door to door, asking questions about Margaret. We had dope all over the place, and I didn't need to be busted for drugs and whatever they might have come up with on Margaret. My old man would have killed me. I left home that summer to get away from him and his fists. Who knows what the cops would have pinned on me? I owed four months' rent anyway. It was only a matter of time before I split. The party was over in the Haight anyhow. Margaret just made it official."

"Those were crazy times."

"No kidding," she said.

"Is that why you changed your name?"

"Let's just say I had a misspent youth—one I'm still paying for. After Margaret and leaving Frederick, I needed to hide from my old man. I knew the landlord or the cops would contact him, and he'd come looking for me. Then I met the wrong guy and got into the kind of trouble I had to get away from for good. He's in prison, but someday he'll be out." She frowned.

"Got it." Colleen nodded. "What do you remember about Margaret?"

Lesley took a sip of coffee. "I didn't know Margaret for long, but we had a few heart-to-hearts—while everybody else was stoned out. She wasn't really a stoner. Neither was I. Not really. We connected."

"Did she say why she wanted to go home?"

"She had a little sister she was worried about."

"Alex," Colleen said. "She's in her twenties now. She was fifteen at the time."

"Yes," Lesley said. "Alex." She raised her eyebrows. "But she also had someone else."

That got Colleen's interest. She drank coffee, staying casual. "Boyfriend?"

"Little more than a boyfriend." She brushed a strand of hair out of her face. "A *married* boyfriend. Older. He told Margaret he was going to leave his wife for her."

"That's original."

"Margaret believed it. But when his wife found out about the two of them, she went and committed suicide."

Colleen startled. "When?"

"Right before Margaret... you know... was murdered." She drank out of her cup. "After that, he backed out. Told Margaret they had to cool things down, so he could take care of his son. It wouldn't look right, he said, to get married to someone else, especially someone so young, right after his wife committed suicide. He was a local politician. District supervisor or something. He was pretty active in the Haight, set up an outreach program for runaway kids." She gave a wry smile. "Turns out he was using it to fill his little black book, too. I know. I went to him for help. He put his hand on my thigh and said he could definitely help me out. So much for that. But Margaret was so smitten she volunteered to help with the program. Whatever it was, he didn't need the publicity after his wife died. I figured he was shining Margaret on, but I wasn't about to burst her bubble."

Colleen's nerve endings tingled. She put her cup down on the counter, sat up. "Remember the guy's name?"

Lesley shook her head.

"It wasn't Patrick Skinner by any chance, was it?"

Leslie looked up, and her mouth fell open. "You know, now that you say his name, it was. Pat. Supervisor Skinner. Good-looking older guy, loads of confidence. Built like an ex-football player. Head full of red hair, just starting to go gray at the temples. Stylish dresser. Looked the part. Especially with his do-gooder routine. A real square but one the girls noticed. Margaret sure did."

A hundred sirens went off between Colleen's ears. "Any idea how his wife committed suicide?"

"Dosed herself with chloroform and pulled a dry-cleaning bag over her head. Jesus." Lesley shook. "I hope it was peaceful for her, at least."

A jolt of realization shook Colleen. She recalled the lack of photos of Mrs. Skinner during her visit to the Skinner residence. No mention of a wife. No female in the house, apart from the maid. "Do you recall Margaret ever saying anything about his son?"

Lesley grimaced. "Margaret didn't even know he had a son until his wife offed herself. Seems Pat was keeping it a secret from her. Some teenage screw-up. Margaret was pretty upset about it. He said the kid had problems, was maladjusted. Margaret shed a few tears when she found out about that. Me, I learned my lesson about married men the summer before. Margaret, though, she learned the hard way."

That was the understatement of the century. "Did you ever learn the son's name?"

Lesley shook her head again. "I wonder if he even existed."

Wouldn't it have been nice if he hadn't? Colleen picked up her coffee, sipped. But now, Kieran's motivation, as twisted as it was, fell into place. His mother had killed herself over his father's affair with Margaret, and Kieran paid him back—in spades. By killing Margaret in the very same way his mother had committed suicide. Twisted the knife.

It made sick, ugly sense.

It would also ruin Pat Skinner's political career—unless he buried it.

She wondered what that meant about Robyn Stiles. Was there a link there, too? If so, how? She was fourteen, out of Patrick Skinner's range. She hoped so, anyway. It unnerved her.

Colleen set her cup of coffee down. She would have to verify all the details, but she sensed most of them would fit. Lesley Johns' words had the ring of truth.

"This has been a huge help," she said, getting out the remaining two hundred dollars, placing the wad on the counter. "A huge help."

* * *

The rain had let up by the time Colleen got back to San Francisco early evening. Four hundred miles of driving that day, much of it in snow, the rest at high speed, after a sleepless night, had drained her. But she wanted to get to the public library on Van Ness before they closed.

The librarian frowned at her when she entered the reference section and started going through microfiche files so late. In the reference section she verified the key points Lesley Johns had made. Lesley had been telling the truth, but Colleen had already sensed that. She was just making sure.

In the lobby, she called SFPD. Detective Owens.

"Glad I caught you," she said.

"I'm just on my way home." It was after eight p.m.

"This is important."

Owens took a breath. "Important, how?"

"The Margaret Copeland case."

"Which you're supposed to be staying out of."

"And you said you were going to keep me updated in exchange for the evidence I gave you."

"I will," he said, "when there's a significant development. But that's the weakest case. We've got Kieran on Robyn Styles. But Margaret Copeland . . ." She heard Owens sigh. "It's an eleven-year-old cold case."

"And Robyn Styles might get him three years, of which he'll serve one."

There was another pause. Colleen heard chatter in the background, someone saying goodnight.

"You got it," Owens said. "Take what you can get."

"It's not enough. Not after what he did."

"I agree. I'm doing what I can. But I need a motive. It could have been anyone, at this point. Why the hell did he do it? Kill Margaret Copeland?"

"Beyond the fact that he's insane?" she said. "I might have something—but you didn't hear it from me. This is strictly a rumor. For you to act upon. And not mention my name."

"Now you've got my attention."

"In 1967, Patrick Skinner was supervisor for District 6—the Haight-Ashbury."

"Okay."

"After the neighborhood was overrun with 50,000 kids from all over the U.S., he started YouthReach, a program for runaways, to help them access services and counseling, get back home."

"Sounds like he was being proactive. No wonder he's done so well for himself."

"In this case he did pretty well with Margaret Copeland."

There was a pause. "Say what?"

"She volunteered with YouthReach. They became close. Care to guess how close?"

"How old was Margaret at the time?"

"Eighteen. Old enough. But that didn't stop Lily Skinner, Skinner's wife, from committing suicide. With chloroform and a plastic bag over her head."

There was a long pause while the line crackled.

"The same way Margaret died."

"Kieran was paying his father back. Big-time. And still is, most likely."

"Explain that."

"Felicia Styles."

"Robyn's mother."

"She works for the California State Assembly. She's new. Guess whose staff she's on."

"Assemblyman Patrick Skinner's."

"Bingo."

"And they are . . . an item?"

"She's divorced. From her college yearbook photo, she's no blushing flower. She was on the track team. Which means Kieran might have thought twice about taking her down. She would be a handful."

"But her younger daughter . . ."

"Would be a lot easier target. And would do just as much damage. More, possibly."

"But Lily Skinner killed herself over a decade ago."

"That probably doesn't matter to Kieran—not if he still blames his father for his mother's suicide."

Now there was a long pause.

"It's definitely worth looking at," Detective Owens said. "Thanks."

"Just keep my name out of it, please."

"Will do."

Lesley Johns didn't need to be involved. Colleen knew she'd be going back on her promise to let Jonathan Marsh, Lesley's old landlord, know her whereabouts but Lesley had earned her privacy. Her new life.

Back at H&M for a long hot shower, followed by an illicit glass of white wine, Colleen sat back in her desk chair, wrapped in her bathrobe, the space heater humming away.

She would sleep tonight.

She hoped Lesley would, too, when she got off work.

CHAPTER SEVENTY-TWO

The flag at Golden Gate National Cemetery flew at half-mast, snapping in the slanted rain that morning. At Mr. Copeland's request, the service was a small one, with a handful of people in attendance.

Colleen stood on the side of the hill by section L7, where the veterans had dug a small square hole at the end of a long line of grave markers, to hold Mr. Copeland's cremated remains. As she gazed across the curve of the hillside, her eyes were met with thousands of such markers. Tens of thousands more lay beyond.

Alex Copeland, in a suitably stylish black ensemble, replete with designer hat, a black feather poking out of it, and black lace veil, read from a sheet of paper in her hands. The paper was getting wet, as were her hat and outfit, but it was obvious she didn't care.

Alex's black-nailed hands shook as she read.

"Thirty-five years ago, Edward Copeland fought for his country as a young man. Although he came from a position of wealth and prestige, he joined the infantry and went to Europe as a foot soldier to serve alongside his comrades. He always told my sister and me, when we were growing up, that everything we had depended on our country, and the people who built it, and that it could all disappear in the blink of an eye if we didn't care for it. He maintained that none of our possessions were important."

Alex let her hands go slack by her side as she looked up at the group of people.

"Eleven years ago, my father lost his beloved daughter Margaret. And I, my sister. Shortly afterwards, we lost our mother. It was so important for my father to resolve the lingering tragedy of Margaret before he left us. When his health took a serious downturn last week, he changed his mind on wanting to solve the mystery of my sister's death—and I know he did it for me, because he didn't want me to have to deal with it since his days were numbered.

"But once again I went against my father's wishes." Alex gave a shaky smile. "And for once I don't regret it, because thanks to someone's deep conviction..." Alex looked directly at Colleen now, which sent a warm glow through her. "Thanks to *you*, my father was able to put Margaret's awful demise in its place, once and for all. And I as well. I was able to share the information on Margaret's killer with my father on his deathbed. And the certainty that there will be some form of justice."

Alex cleared her throat, clearly struggling with her emotions. She crouched by the gravesite then, where she picked up a simple blue plastic box containing her father's ashes. She reached down into the grave and put it in its place. Then she stood up.

"My father slept well that night after I gave him the news about Margaret's killer, the first night he slept calmly in many nights. And he didn't wake up. He didn't need to. He was finally at peace. As am I."

CHAPTER SEVENTY-THREE

They drank black champagne at the memorial. Harold and the hired staff made the rounds in the palatial living room, each with a bottle of Dom Perignon in one hand and a quart of 1929 Charrington Oatmeal Stout in the other, filling up glasses. A string quartet attired in black played "Clair de Lune." There were many more people in attendance than at the funeral and the event hummed with hushed conversation.

"Thank you, Harold," Colleen said, sipping the chilled black mixture.

"No, Ms. Hayes," Harold said. "Thank *you*." He bowed before moving on to the next guest.

Colleen wore a simple black dress with shoes and nylons to match. She turned to Alex, standing next to her, sipping her fortified champagne. "It's not bad."

"It's called Black Velvet." Alex smiled, radiant without her black hat and veil. Her hair had been curled and shone with product. "They drank it in 1861, to mourn Prince Albert's passing, at his club in London. Father would have approved."

"To your father," Colleen said, holding out her glass.

They clinked glasses. They sipped Black Velvet.

"I hope you got the check," Alex said. "Christian had it sent over today, special messenger."

"It's far too generous," Colleen said.

"Those were the terms Father agreed to."

"And a bit more." Colleen drank more champagne. "All for a little over a week's work."

"But what a week," Alex said, sipping, fluffing her hair.

"That's the understatement of the year."

"What next, Colleen?" Alex said.

"You mean, after I set myself up in some new digs—with a view of the Golden Gate Bridge perhaps? I can certainly afford to now." Colleen frowned. "I still have my parole. That doesn't go away. I have an appointment with my new parole officer first thing tomorrow. And there are the pending cases regarding your sister. Although there's not much I can do." Things were out of her hands. But not her mind. "I think I'm going to take some time off, head up the coast."

"To see your daughter," Alex said. "Pamela."

Colleen showed crossed fingers and drank. Maybe. Just maybe they would finally reconnect.

"I hope it works out this time," Alex said quietly.

"Me, too," Colleen whispered. "And you?"

"Antonia asked me to go to Buenos Aires with her."

"Oh," Colleen said, a tidal wave of disappointment washing through her, practically knocking her off balance. "The redhead," she croaked.

"A sculptor Antonia works with has a studio down there."

"I didn't know Antonia sculpted." Colleen had to fight to get the words out. Why had she been harboring the foolish thought that she and Alex could be anything but client and employee? She had put her off, for the sake of the case, and would now pay the price.

"She does a lot of things," Alex said.

Colleen could imagine. She just didn't want to.

"Well," Colleen said, taking a bigger drink of champagne than intended, trying to recover her composure. "It all sounds very exotic."

"Hello, ladies."

They turned to see Christian Newell, looking dapper in a dark black two-button suit with narrow lapels and a slim black tie. His short dark hair was immaculate and his pale skin flawless. Colleen couldn't help but think of a Ken doll, the funeral version. She just hoped Christian would represent her as well as he took care of himself if push came to shove in court.

"Again, Alex," he said, "my deepest sympathies."

"Thank you, Christian."

He turned to include Colleen in the conversation. "I'm sorry to interrupt, but I think I have an encouraging update in the middle of this."

Alex drank. "I'm always a fan of good news."

"This is all between us for the moment, but the DA has reopened the murder case on your sister. Charges will be filed against Kieran Skinner in the morning, and he will be brought back into custody."

"That's encouraging," Colleen said.

"It seems that Patrick Skinner played a more significant role in covering up Margaret's murder than previously thought and had firsthand knowledge of the murder. There's new evidence that suggested he knows much more than he's admitting. Another wrinkle is that he was having an affair with Robyn Stiles' mother."

"Incredible," Alex said.

Colleen noticed Christian didn't come right out and say that Patrick Skinner and Margaret had had an affair, which led to his wife's suicide, and, as a result, Kieran's revenge killing. Maybe he didn't know. Colleen, for all her desire to be transparent, had not passed that particular information along to the Copelands either. Alex would no doubt find out as the case progressed, but now wasn't the time.

Colleen felt a blast of victory surge through her, although there was still a long way to go.

"*Woo-hoo!*" Alex whispered, clicking glasses with Christian and Colleen.

"I need to remind you this could take years," Christian said, holding his untouched champagne like a prop. "Assemblyman Skinner's legal war chest is overflowing, and his legal team are no doubt chomping at the bit."

"But this kills his Senate run," Alex said. "It's the beginning of the end. We got him."

"One step at a time," Christian said. "But, yes. It's certainly a win."

"If he thinks I'm not going to keep after him," Alex said, "he's a fool."

"Will Kieran get bail, Christian?" Colleen asked. He'd been bailed out for the lesser charges against Robyn Stiles.

Christian frowned, gave a shrug. "Murder One? I sincerely doubt it. I hope not."

"If he does, Colleen here will take care of him." Alex gave a sly grin over the top of her glass.

"Not even close to funny," Colleen said.

"Who's joking?" Alex said, winking.

Colleen shook her head. She was going to miss Alex. She couldn't shake the thought that Alex was going to another continent. Leaving. She forced a smile on her face. "I'm glad we're being so demure and respectful at your father's memorial, Alex."

Alex drank. "He would have been the first to toast Christian's update."

"Any word on Frank Madrid?" Colleen asked.

Christian grimaced. "I hear he was questioned yesterday by SFPD Detective . . . Olson, is it?"

"Owens," Colleen said, drinking. A start, anyway. Owens was following through.

Christian, somewhat red-faced now, bowed and excused himself.

"What's the matter, Coll?" Alex said.

Their eyes met. Was Alex really that obtuse? No, it was Colleen's fault. For throwing cold water on every attempt Alex had made to get close to her.

Colleen cleared her throat. "I've got something for you. Hold this. Don't go anywhere. I'll be right back."

She left Alex with two glasses as she went into the hallway where she found her handbag. She retrieved the letter in the pink envelope Margaret Copeland had written to her little sister eleven years before.

Alex eyed the envelope in Colleen's hand when she returned.

"I got you a refill," she said, handing Colleen a full glass of Black Velvet. "You look like you needed it. Like your dog had died. Did you get some bad news?"

Their eyes met for a long moment.

"Maybe," Colleen said. She took the black champagne and handed the envelope to Alex. "This was in Margaret's ex-landlord's effects. I thought you might like to have it."

When Alex saw her name written on the unposted letter, she immediately handed Colleen her own glass. She opened the letter, read it, her eyes growing soft and moist as she brushed a curl of blond hair out of her eyes.

"She always called me 'Bobo.'"

"I hope you don't mind that I read it," Colleen said. "I was looking for evidence."

Alex looked up at Colleen. "I don't mind at all that you read it, Colleen. I'm glad you did."

"You're the reason she was planning to come home."

"She almost made it."

"Almost," Colleen said softly.

"But this . . ." Alex slipped the letter back in its envelope. "This brings me some peace."

"Yes," Colleen said. She finished her drink, looked at her watch. "Well, I better go. And you better send me a postcard from Buenos Aires."

Alex put her hand on Colleen's arm, soft, warm, as she looked her in the eye. She dropped her voice.

"I don't have to go, Colleen."

Colleen drew a breath as their eyes locked.

"No?" she said.

"All you have to do is ask me to stay."

"It wouldn't be fair to you, Alex."

"Why—because of that Latin heartthrob?"

Colleen felt as if she had been smacked. "Good God—did I really tell you about him?"

"That night we got so wasted at Peg's Place. Something about a shower."

Colleen felt her face flush. "Okay, now I am suitably embarrassed."

Alex sipped. "I was just pleased you were thinking about yourself for once."

That morning, Colleen had found a battered postcard in her mailbox, from El Salvador. Ramon had made it home and was thinking about her. He hoped she was doing well, catching her villains.

"It's for the best," she said.

"I think it's for the best, too." Alex came up close and Colleen could smell her sweet breath as she spoke. "I think he should stay right the hell where he is and leave us alone."

Colleen smiled, the first real smile in a long time. "Do you now?"

"Yep." Alex downed her champagne. She hooked her arm in Colleen's. "Have you had enough of this deadly wake yet?"

Colleen smiled at Alex's choice of words. "You're actually going to bail out of your own father's wake?"

"I did my bit. And the old goat knows it."

"Yes," Colleen said, "I think he does."

"Well?" Alex said, grinning. "How about it, sport?"

Colleen narrowed his eyes. "What exactly did you have in mind?"

Alex shrugged, crossed her legs as she stood next to Colleen. "I was thinking we could just hop in the car and head up the coast. See if your Pamela is around. After that, if we're still talking to each other, we could get back in the car and kind of see which way it goes." Her eyes crinkled as she gave a wry smirk. "What do you think?"

Colleen thought about that for the briefest moment.

Her face broke out into an uncontrollable smile. "Alex, I think that might just be one of your better ideas."

EPILOGUE

"Goin' out," Frank Madrid said, slamming the front door behind him. He skipped down the steps to his truck. It was raining again.

Pat Skinner had been ignoring his calls. The man was going to try and pin it on Frank. Frank was going over there, right now, demand Skinner help him out.

Frank's C10 was backed up into the narrow driveway of his junior five. He got his keys out, slid one into the door of the truck.

"Hey, Frank," a woman's voice said behind him.

He turned. It was Mary. Mary Davis. Wearing Jim's old blue windbreaker, loose jeans, and a pair of sneakers. Slumming it. It was raining, and she had a Giants ball cap pulled down low, her red hair tucked up under it. She wore a pair of aviator sunglasses even though it was night. Her right arm was down by her side, tucked behind her back, hiding something.

"Hey, Mary." He reached inside his jacket for his gun. He had started carrying one. "What's up?"

* * *

"This." Mary came up fast with a forty-five automatic.

Shot him twice in the face, his hand still in his jacket.

When Frank was on the ground, blood running to the curb in the rain, she shot him again.

"*That's* what's up, Frank," she said. "That's what's up."

Frank's keys were hanging in the door of his truck. She turned, shoving the hot gun down the back of her waistband, and strode across the intersection at a diagonal, head down, toward the beach. Her car was parked in the darkness of the Great Highway, a few blocks away. As she crossed the next block, she checked around, saw no one. She pulled the warm gun, an old drop gun of Jim's no one would ever be able to trace, let it slide through a sewer grate with a clank and a splash as she crossed the street. At 45th she removed her sunglasses, ball cap, and gloves, tossed them in an open dumpster as she passed, shaking her curly red hair loose. It was raining. It was raining and it was dark. Nobody saw her shoot Frank. And if they did, she didn't care.

She didn't care.